ALD

Y

SINGLE TO BRIGHTON

Lilian Forshaw vividly recreates the bustle of life in turn-of-the-century Brighton – with its busy streets and colourful kitchens – from tales her Grandmother Clara told her. Nineteen-year-old Clara buys a single train ticket to Brighton and sets off to start a new life in the fashionable seaside town. Determined to keep the child she is carrying, regardless of the condemnation of others, Clara courageously builds a life for herself as a pioneer single mother.

SINGLE TO BRIGHTON

SINGLE TO BRIGHTON

by

Lilian Forshaw

Magna Large Print Books
Long Preston, North Yorkshire,
BD23 4ND, England.

British Library Cataloguing in Publication Data.

Forshaw, Lilian
    Single to Brighton.

    A catalogue record of this book is
    available from the British Library

    ISBN   978-0-7505-3870-1

First published in Great Britain in 2012 by The Book Guild Ltd.

Copyright © Lilian Forshaw 2012

Cover illustration by arrangement with Book Guild Publishing

The right of Lilian Forshaw to be identified as the author of this work
has been asserted by her in accordance with the Copyright, Designs
and Patents Act, 1988

Published in Large Print 2014 by arrangement with
Book Guild Publishing

Magna Large Print is an imprint of Library Magna Books Ltd.

Printed and bound in Great Britain by
T.J. (International) Ltd., Cornwall, PL28 8RW

For Paul, Galia, Chris and Gem, and for my grandchildren's children.

'You travel through life with your thoughts as navigator'

Mark Twain

Author's Notes

While the stories told to me by my Grand-mother, Mother and wider family, recorded here in this book are true, some of the names and places have been changed to preserve anonymity.

My special thanks to Ollie Wardle who typed up my handwritten manuscript. Ollie, you're a star.

Preface

'Do people give you all that money for humbugs?' At four years old my eyes came just level
with the top of the kitchen table.

Uncle Arthur gave me a quizzical glance and
went on methodically counting the week's takings
from his newsagent's shop – copper pennies, half-
pennies and silver coins, separating them into
tobacco tins; brown ten shilling notes and blue
pound notes into one old shallow cigar box. Slap-
ping its lid closed he finally turned his attention to
me, smiling, and asked, 'What humbugs?'

'In your newspapers,' I insisted. How could an
adult be so dense? Before he had time to answer,
Aunt Hetty flicked her drying-up cloth at him
saying, 'I told you but none of you will believe
me. Gran's been telling this child stories ever
since the day she was born.' He laughed at that.
'There you go again, but it's true – her mother
will bear me out.'

'What's this about humbugs then?'

'Granny says it's all humbugs in your newspapers.'

'There you are, what did I say?' chortled auntie.

Family legend has it that Granma Clara Ann
started telling me her stories of family life the
moment I was put in her arms an hour after I was

born. True or not, after more than sixty years her stories still simmered in my head, until one day when a delivery man was standing just inside the back door here at Deerfold Cottage. Looking across the kitchen at our dresser he remarked, 'Cor blimey, I've never seen so much willow pattern china all together in one place ever before. Is it old?'

'Yes, most of it's been passed down from family and friends.'

'Mm, I bet that old china could tell some tales then? Ah, thank you sir,' he said, turning as my husband Paul handed back his signed clipboard. 'Cheery bye.'

Of course! Why ever hadn't I thought of it before? That one chance remark sparked off the idea of bringing Granma's stories into a book – and to think it's been staring me in the face all these years. On my dresser are pieces of china, each relating to characters in the stories. So thank you Mr Delivery Man, our short conversation gave me the theme for this book.

Granma, born in 1868, eldest of thirteen siblings, told about her life and loves, travelling alongside five generations of family and friends. And the Willows? Two of them who were beside her during her last hours sit here on my dresser today.

Lilian Forshaw
Deerfold Cottage, East Sussex, 2012

Book One: 1887–1919

Prologue

Let me put you in the picture. I never intended to buy willow pattern china or to start a collection – their purchase was, at the time, out of necessity. On the morning Paul and I got married in 1963 I realised we had no dinner plates. Nipping round to our local second-hand shop I found what just happened to be six willow pattern dinner plates for six shillings (30p). I didn't know how valuable they were until years later when we were down to the last one fully intact. The other five had not survived our robust family life. The remaining member of that set of six sits in full glory on the dresser here forty-nine years later. Now we have well over five hundred pieces. No, I'm still not a collector. I buy Willows because I like them or because I don't like to leave them sitting in a junk shop lonely and unloved. Together with those pieces handed down by relatives, which come with their stories, we give them a family home. Some pieces go back a long way into generations of our family; travelling with them through their lives they must have witnessed many unfolding human stories. They are the Willows!

As I sat at the kitchen table looking over to my dresser I thought yes, that delivery man was right, the Willows must have a lot of tales to tell. No sooner had the thought passed through my mind than my eye settled to the smallest item,

17

the one Gran gave me for my tenth birthday.

On that day in January 1951 Mum and I were visiting Granma at the old people's home where she had recently taken up residence, a mile or so away from where we lived in Brighton, East Sussex.

'Ah! my sweeting, happy birthday, come and cuddle with me.' I climbed up beside her in a big old winged chair. 'I've got something here for you.' From her cardigan pocket Gran brought out a small bundle. 'Will you look after this for me?' she asked. Within a very thin lace-edged cotton handkerchief I found a little blue and white willow patterned china plate. Turning it about I saw it wasn't a plate at all. It had two little lips on its back and a wedge that made it stand up on its rim. I must have looked puzzled because Gran was already explaining.

'Now this little plate used to stand along with lots of others like it, on the dining table in front of each place where somebody was going to sit. And do you see the blank strip across the front? Well, that's where the guest's name would be written and a menu slipped into those notches on the back, then the hostess set it on the table in front of where she wanted her guest to be.'

'There's a name on it already Gran,' I told her.

'Bless my soul, your young eyes are sharp Missy. What does it say?'

I did have to look harder to read it. 'It says "Clara Ann", but that's your name Granny.' I looked up because she didn't answer straight away. Her eyes were closed, her head resting back against the cushions.

18

'Still there after all these years. Well!' She sighed. Then she whispered something I didn't understand at all. 'Mispah?'

I looked to my mother and saw a kind smile with a little wink at me. Always wanting to know the ins and outs of a story I asked, 'What's Mispah, Granny?'

Her reply came slowly.

'Mispah is its name.'

'But what does it mean Granny?'

'It means – oh well, Mummy will tell you that when you're older, sweetheart. I want you to have Mispah to look after and maybe pass it on to your daughter onc day. Yes, I would like that dear.'

'Are these little plates called Mispah, Granny?'

'No dear, that's what I named this one a long time ago.'

'I haven't seen it before. Where have you been keeping it? Have you had it a long time then?'

'Ooh er – lots of questions!' Mum came to Gran's rescue. But then Gran put a voice to her memories.

'This little dish came to my aid at a time of great shock and sadness. I was a very young girl at the time. It was in my hands for just a few minutes, before it went on its travels across the world.' I thought Gran seemed to sleep – but no – she carried on talking and her eyes stayed closed. 'It came back into my life just before the First World War and it's been with me ever since and now it's yours to watch over you,' she whispered in my ear.

'Granny's tired now, and we must get back home to get Dad's dinner.'

It was time to leave so I gave Gran a kiss,

scrambled out of her chair and tucked Mispah inside the palm of my woolly glove. While Mum said her goodbyes to her mother I did a little circuit of the room just like all inquisitive small children do. Most of the residents were napping but one old gentleman not far away raised his hand and beckoned me over to him. I thought he wanted me to pick up the newspaper on the floor beside his chair. No, he asked me how my grand-mother was today. I told him she was well thank you.

'I see she gave you a present.'

'Yes, it's my birthday.'

'Take good care of it won't you?'

'Oh yes, she said it would watch over me.'

'And so it will – so it will,' he replied.

A voice called softly across the room, 'Ready to go?' So I waved to the gentleman as I skipped off to Mum, gave Gran a quick peck on the cheek as we tucked ourselves tightly back into our outside clothes. After all, it was January.

'Bye Gran.' I thought she was asleep.

'Bye bye Lily luv,' she whispered.

At the time it never occurred to me that the old gentleman who spoke to me had any significance.

As we walked home Mum, known in the family as Dolly, told me, 'When I was your age Gran's hair was golden auburn, not the perfect white you see today and her eyes were turquoise blue. Dear Mum,' Dolly sighed, 'her skin bloomed, my father used to say she was blushed by the winds that cross the Pevensey Levels where she grew up.'

Over the years I did learn what that half-hinted

tale of the little willow pattern plate was all about. The very words, 'I bet that old china could tell some tales,' brought Mispah and Granma's story flooding back into my mind.

So I'll start Clara Ann's story where my first piece of willow pattern china enters Clara Ann's life, and the Willows sitting on my dresser will tell you their side of events too. Oh and by the way, before we start our journey you should know that the Willows all have names. They will introduce themselves as we go along.

It's March 1887 and our first travelling companion is, as you know, called Mispah.

1

Clara

Outside the light was fading, winter still hanging on, dull and cold. Inside the kitchen was warm, cosy and unusually quiet, only the family in to dinner tonight, no guests were expected. When there were, the oil lamps blazed full bright, everybody on their toes nimbly moving from place to place around the room. This evening the wicks had been turned down low, even the range gave just a little glow being closed in readiness for the game pie, onto which Mrs Charlish the cook was putting the finishing touches, a special, because it would be the last of the season.

Nineteen-year-old Clara Ann came through

from the dining room where she had been setting the table for Mr and Mrs Franklin Anderson, their son Frank and daughter Josephine. Four courses on starched white napery, silver cutlery and cut glass tumblers for water only. The Mistress was frugal when the family were alone. Not even fresh flowers would grace the table this night. It was Clara Ann's duty to fetch flowers through from the withdrawing room on these occasions. She would do that later while the family were upstairs changing for dinner. Meanwhile she started clearing the cook's table.

'There's a dearie,' said Mrs Charlish. 'It's not your job. But thank you.' She patted Clara on her arm as she went across to the range, checked the colour of the fire, then on into the scullery where two young maids were preparing staff supper.

The door into the family quarters flung back against the dresser with a clatter, ripping a cold slice through the warm air and sending a harsh perfume clashing into rich cooking aromas. The plates she was clearing dropped from Clara Ann's hands and slithered across the table as she turned to see that a pair of searing, hating eyes had found and fixed on her.

'Get out of my house!' Soaring high-pitched and breaking from screech to squeak to, 'go, get your coat and leave!' The outburst sent spit spattering into Clara's face, causing her to take a jerk back. And louder still, 'Now!' The face was reddening and sweating, Mrs Rachel Anderson was that close.

Cook stepped back in from the scullery, horrified to see the Mistress violating her domain. The nearest she usually got to the kitchen was the pantry once each morning when she came to give her orders for the day. Mrs Charlish was affronted and fuming. This was an intrusion. And what a state the woman was in! What was she so irate about indeed?

To stop the shock shaking through her whole body Clara Ann clutched the edge of the table. Unable to help it, she stared at the sight and sound of this demon pouncing on her so violently.

'Go!' it shouted again. No lady now. No hostess showing off to all the neighbours. Skirts flaring as she turned away, the demon harridan flung back more words over her shoulder. 'And you'll get no "Character" from this house.' Behind the departing figure the door reconnected with its frame with a mighty thwack. Silence returned.

'Oh my word,' came Cook's breathy shock. Although Mrs Charlish was worried at the way Clara had been so ferociously set upon, she recalled there had been high words overheard between the Master and Mistress coming from the Mistress's parlour that afternoon. That was just after their son had left the house, followed by unexpected and brisk comings and goings among the stable lads. One of the two young maids nudged Cook, 'Look at Clara.'

Still gripping the lip of the table and now white knuckled, Clara was fighting hard to control her emotions. Leaning forward, breathing deep, struggling to stop the tears, she was swallowing intermittently to avoid being violently sick.

Clack went the latch on the back lobby door. All

four women were startled afresh. A loud whisper, urgent for attention, called, 'Clara!' A sigh of relief, it was only Thomas the coachman. 'You'd better make haste. I'm taking him to Newhaven right away. And there's more baggage on than he'll need for France.' Heaving on an old triple-caped coat, Thomas carried on in a hushed voice, 'They're in a blinding hurry to get him off.' Grabbing up the basket handed to him by one of the maids he turned on his heel and was gone.

Those few telling words hit Clara in her heart like a frozen fist. Oh no, she inwardly gulped, I've not even had chance to tell him. She dare not cry; she had to think straight.

'Oh my dear, what is it?' Mrs Charlish could see the news had stunned Clara. She had noticed, well she supposed they all had over the months, that Frank and Clara passed more than just friendly words between them. She knew it could lead to no good, but it wasn't for her to say.

Clara's head cleared. She could not let him go without a word, a touch. Taking a deep breath she walked firmly across the kitchen, the maids and Cook looking on wordless, into the dining room and over to the sideboard. Pulling out one of the shallow cutlery drawers she picked up a small blue and white willow patterned china plate with a wedge-shaped protrusion on its back. Taking a pencil from its slot alongside twenty-three more place settings she wrote her own name, CLARA ANN, boldly on the unglazed strip across the plate's face, knowing this act in itself to be defiance. Her name would never appear at a place on Mrs Rachel Anderson's dinner table. Silently

24

sliding the drawer closed she left the room and waited behind the heavy curtain that covered the service door to the kitchen. In the entrance hall Mrs Anderson was calling up the stairs, 'Frank, where are you? We're waiting.'

Clara knew Frank would always use the back staircase in the hope of a moment with her. Thank goodness he did so this time. Heavy footfalls came rapidly, slowed softly to the last stair and stopped. His fingers lifted the side of the curtain and a sigh breathed out as he saw she was there. They slipped into each other's arms and Frank kissed her forehead. Clara's arms tightened around his shoulders more ardently than was usual inside the house, prompting his reassuring words, 'I'll be back before you know I've gone dearest. It is only a trip across the Channel to check on Father's interests.'

'Frank, Thomas has to get the horses on the road before dark,' the voice came again. 'You'll miss the packet.' Then louder. 'Make haste!'

Frank encircled Clara Ann inside his warm travelling coat, laughing with good humour, kissing her face, kissing away the tears now beginning to flow.

'What's this?' He leaned back to see the small parcel Clara slid into his waistcoat pocket. It was wrapped in one of the fine lawn handkerchiefs he had given her for her birthday that year. 'Clara, what is this?'

Placing her hand across the pocket to prevent him from taking the parcel out, she replied, 'Call it Mispah.' Then taking his elbow she gently steered him towards the hallway and front door.

Catching sight of him coming from the lower

passageway Mrs Anderson stiffened, angrily moving to look behind her son. But Clara Ann had swiftly stepped away into the shadows, answering Frank's last quizzical look with, 'it's part of me, we three.' Her final words were lost in the sound of his boots on the flagstones going away down the hall.

Taking her coat from the closet Clara Ann, followed closely by Cook, went quickly out into the stable yard.

'Young Jack says he's been instructed to take your box on the cart next time he goes to market by way of The Lamb,' Mrs Charlish said, embracing Clara Ann in the fondest way. 'Oh my dearest gal, we were getting on so well you an' me. I couldn't have had a better helper. You're going to make a wonderful cook. I shall miss you so much Dearie.' By then tears were welling in her own eyes. 'Better go, she's on the rampage. Let me deal with her.' Their employer's determined steps could be heard. The woman was not about to give up. 'Here, take this. Now, go, get away,' a book was pressed under Clara's elbow, 'with all my love dear-heart.'

Outside the air was sharp cold. Quickly passing through the side gate into the lane Clara leaned back heavily against the wall. Her head ached painfully. The turmoil of events over the last hour had been a great shock, with emotions suppressed, reactions stimulated by love, fear and heart-stopping loss. She needed desperately to take breath and regain herself. Rest her burning eyes.

In that peaceful moment she caught the sound of horses' hooves coming from across the marsh on the still evening air. She could tell it was his

26

coach, pulling heavily up onto the metalled road to the mill and away, westward. The sound got fainter and fainter until it was no more. Shuddering with a sudden chill she noticed she was still wearing her soft house shoes. It couldn't be helped. Wrapping her shawl closer round her grey wool winter coat she felt the book slip from under her arm. Lovely Mrs Charlish, she's given me her own recipe book! Pressing her lips to the cover Clara put the book in her coat pocket and began her own journey in the opposite direction towards the already darkening sky. The sandy road to her grandparents' inn wound among the fields and ditches of reedy marshland. It was a long walk.

Time now to cry, time to let her tears flow for the heartbreak of loss. Let her mind go free.

Clara started running, stumbling, bawling to the sky, hitting away the tears. Loss of his thrilling love poured through her mind. Loss of a job she enjoyed, learning new things every day. It was all a mess. Finally, chest heaving, she stopped. Snivelling like a kid she reached inside her coat to find the matching grey wool bonnet her grandmother had made for cold marsh weather. A distant voice in her ear said, 'Keep feet and head warm and dry. Stay well.' Clara tied the ribbons tight under her chin to calm herself. Soon enough there'd be family reactions to consider.

Mispah

I could feel Frank's heart beating fast against me.

Urging him to go, Clara Ann released his arm. He turned, hesitated, and strode away along the hall, his boots on hard flagstones sending sharp vibrations through his body. Buttoning his coat he leaned forward to give his mother a farewell peck on the cheek. She made it obvious she did not expect anything more, her face was too stern. Rachel was still simmering in her annoyance and disappointment in her son.

With a nod of thanks to his father's man, Frank took the proffered hat and gloves and left the house. At the bottom of the steps he stopped. Father and son faced each other and shook hands.

'I'll do my best Father.'

'I know you will,' came the stark reply. Franklin had an unusual, almost guilty look in his eyes, but kept a firm stance as he handed his son a substantial package. Frank placed it in his inner coat pocket. The contents would prove, later of course, that he wasn't being at all straightforward with his son. 'Good luck my boy.' A flickering change of attitude sounded. He could see Frank had noticed his expression with a little apprehension. He did not want to alienate his only son. But no matter, at that moment it was the way it had to be. Franklin clapped the boy on his back to control his own feelings. 'Off you go then, safe journey.'

Although somewhat surprised at the bulging pile of luggage under the cover on the back of the family's coach, Frank made no comment. Thomas whipped up the horses the instant the coach door clicked closed. Inside the air was warm; on the floor, along the base of the seat, a long shallow copper pan was filled with hot water. Beside him and on the seat opposite two more smaller copper pans set upon paraffin heaters put out further heat. Above each seat hung four lanterns shedding a lemon-yellow glare through three sides of bevelled glass apertures, producing their sleepy fumes. Loosening his coat and scarf Frank eased the window in the door down a fraction, re-linking the leather strap onto a lower brass notch. At a hefty cost the household still ran its own coach and pair. Mr Anderson had never denied his wife's any whim.

Climbing the hill and onto the now metalled road towards Stone Cross Mill we headed west into the last hazy light of day. Frank had not needed to use the family coach – he could have travelled by train but his parents had their reasons. Haste and secrecy, I am in no doubt.

Leaning back into the blue-velvet cushioned seat Frank was made aware of the small parcel pressing his heart-side in his waistcoat pocket. Gently smiling at this, the gift from Clara Ann, he unwound the handkerchief to find me. Looking him in the eyes I saw him reading the words pencilled across my guest strip, CLARA ANN. Frank's expression revealed that the memory of her words had returned. 'It's Mispah. It's part of me.' As I lay in the palm of his hand he recited the meaning of my name to himself in a low voice. 'The Lord watch between me and thee when we are absent one from another.' Slowly shaking his head he whispered, 'Oh my darling girl.' I watched him muse on his thoughts of love and his sweetheart. I felt the thrill within. Abruptly his mood changed. Anger welled in him. Placing me back in his pocket he tore open his father's bulky envelope, roughly pulling out a bundle full of coins and dumping it on the seat beside him. As he expected, the instructions were only for negotiations to secure no more than land holdings in France.

The coach was slowing at the turnpike. Thomas

could be heard telling the watchman he was carrying young Mr Anderson and all was well within.

'On yur way then Tom, journey safe ye.' Now the light had fully gone. Frank pulled up the window and returned to his thoughts. His mother's harassing calls, Clara's fading words. 'It's part of me.'

Then two words more distant, 'We three.'

'Oh, my God!' He realised with chagrin he had been a fool to tell his parents his private feelings. All the trust he had grown up with was destroyed in that enlightening moment. He had naively expected them to be pleased that he was so happy.

'Well that settles it. I must return quickly. Make a life of my own desire.'

The journey was lengthy and dangerous enough, in the dark with no second up on the box, very risky in Sussex in the 1880s, but Tom knew the roads well, he was a confident driver used to handling his horses and the heavy coach. Arriving at the port of Newhaven, Thomas drew the carriage up close to the gangplank. In the darkness Frank could see this was not the regular cross-channel packet ship.

'Your father said this ship would make better time sir. Before you go, Mr Frank, your mother asked me to give you this for the journey.' Thomas handed over a small hip flask.

'I know,' said Frank, 'just to keep out the cold.' They both laughed.

'Mothers!' replied Thomas, 'they mean well. Goodbye sir, safe journey.'

'Thank you Thomas.'

While Frank went aboard carrying his own portmanteaux, Thomas organised a trunk and further baggage to quarters, along with a package that he handed to the captain's steward. Strange that Frank hadn't taken more notice that the coach had been carrying a larger quantity of baggage than he would need for a few days in France. Apparently, Thomas also had one last mission to accomplish with the coach and horses before returning to the Manor by train.

Two days out, Frank awoke in his cabin, his mother's strategy achieved. When the Captain handed the package to his passenger he was surprised to be asked when they would be landing in France.

'This ship is bound for The Cape, sir. No further ports of call. We are fully laden. You are our only passenger.'

Finally Frank understood why there had been all the haste. Why there was so much gold in the bag his father had given him. Not only had he lost all trust in his parents, but his father's betrayal gave way to something deeper than hurt.

These latest instructions were to visit Franklin's stakeholdings in the new diamond mines. It certainly wasn't planned to be a short-term visit. He was expected to become well informed about future levels of output from a number of sites and to telegraph regular reports. These reports were to guide his father's future acquisitions. A code for this information was enclosed within the letter.

Nevertheless his father's parting expression now made sense. He would do his duty as asked. Then he'd earn his own living, go his own way.

Frantic to get some word to Clara Ann his first action was to pen a short letter. He had to be quick to have it included in the satchel post exchange with a passing England-bound ship just north of the Bay of

Biscay. I sat on the desk in front of Frank as he wrote letters, full of his love, every day he was on board ship. He told her there would be no other woman but her. I couldn't say if any of these letters were ever sent. He also wrote a long letter to the one he felt would be his only ally, his sister Josephine. In that letter he asked her to find out where Clara Ann was living.

When we arrived in Cape Town, Frank made arrangements for money to be sent to Jo, as he had asked her to open an account for Clara Ann into which he could send regular payments. I gather Jo did his bidding. With me in his waistcoat pocket he then travelled on horseback up country to the diamond mines alongside a wagon train – but sometimes he kept his distance, liking to be alone.

Clara

She was well away from the Manor now. Five miles was nothing to Clara who had walked practically everywhere she had to go in all her nineteen years. It was the disgrace she would be bringing to her grandparents at the end of this journey that Clara was not in a hurry to face. At least she was having this time to unwind, to think. The air was cool and fresh among the willows at the edges of the lane. The soft flicking leaves between her dragging fingertips made a comforting sound from childhood. A slow, regular swish and huff of the tide floated on the air across the flat mile from the seashore away to her right. Sounds carried miles on the still air. The sandy road gave off a pale grey light.

Her grandfather John Pilbeam, a tall, solid, quiet man, showed his grandchildren how to be still, listen and look. As the moon rose just above the horizon, throwing a silver reflection across to the shore, owls started hooting their calls. Answers returned from either side of their territories. It brought back a memory of the day a peddler came to the inn yard. He had a beautiful barn owl perched on his back pack. When he told them it was for sale, Clara's young brothers and sisters pulled at their grandfather's sleeves hissing whispers, 'Pleeeze Granfer– Oh pleeeze can we have her?'

Grandfather would have none of it. He didn't hold with keeping any wild creature on a leash. This peddler had not visited the area before or he would have known it was no place to offer such an item for sale. Grandfather said little. Just called his wife to come and make her purchases – haberdashery and a pack of needles. The peddler went on his way. But Grandfather didn't forget. The children were all surprised one evening later in their holidays when Granny didn't send them to bed at their usual time. When Grandfather had finished his work around the yard and seen to his customers in the bar he called Clara, then but a child, and the group of youngsters to follow him out to the barn. Sitting them round him he said, 'Now young'uns, you just keep still and watch.'

The children did as they were told with a thrill of anticipation. Granfer always showed them exciting things. They waited some while before anything happened. A sudden gust of air swept the tops of their heads. All ducked and turned to catch sight of the ghostly white wingspan swooping up through the barn door away into the inky black sky. Looking back at Grandfather they saw him holding a finger to his lips curtailing their urgent questions. Moments later the shadow swept down into view again, alighting on a nearby post, owl wings closing elegantly, gently. The huge head swivelled to face the huddled group of children, two big eyes focused directly on to them.

'Hallo my luvver.' Grandfather spoke to the owl as if he was an old pal. A purr seemed to come from deep down inside the magnificent bird. 'This is our neighbour, chilrun. You didn't know he lived here, did you?'

'Gramps, he's luvverly. Why didn't you show us before?' asked Robert, Clara's third younger brother who was then four years old. Clara and the older children knew Grandfather didn't tell them these secrets until they were each old enough to understand that wild animals and birds must not be disturbed by looking in on their lives too often.

'Now you know, Robert, you can watch for Uncle Owl when he comes home from work. But keep your distance. There, off he goes out to work. He'll be back come morning.'

'What work Granfer?'

'He keeps the mice population from getting too many or they would come into our larders and pinch our food. Your Granny don't want mice prints in her kitchen do she? Off yous all go to your beds then. Sleep well.'

Clara remembered how they all sang back, 'See you in the morning.'

Dear Grandfather, he and Gran had been more

like parents to them all. What with their mother being pregnant and nursing a young baby almost all her adult days. Twelve more babies after Clara was born. Emily passed on each weaned toddler into her eldest daughter's care, leaving herself very often pregnant again and with a babe at the breast. For the next ten years Clara's little band of followers grew. Meantime, in the later years her father's accident made it difficult for him to find work. These twists and turns in all their lives now came back thick and fast into her mind as Clara walked.

At 'Halfway Bridge' Clara sat down on the bank, listening to the trickling stream. A few crocuses thrust up gold and purple heads beside the low stone parapet. It was here that Frank had seen her one morning two years back. He'd arrived home from university just the night before and was out riding early. Clara had been allowed two days off to help out at the family inn, as her grandmother was unwell. She was making a dawn start to walk back to her duties at the Manor.

'Clara, Clara Ann,' he called.

'Good morning sir.' She bobbed him a little curtsey. Dismounting, he turned directly towards her.

'We need not use such greetings Clara, please. You know me as Frank, and none of this curt-seying. Not to me.'

'Thank you sir,' she found herself saying. Dash it, she was being a fool.

'Ah now, have you forgotten so soon? Don't thank me.'

'I think your parents wouldn't approve of their

servants addressing you thus.'

It seemed he hadn't known Clara was working at the Manor now. 'That won't stop us being friends as we've always been. Here, let's sit awhile if you have time?' Saying that, he sat down on the bank where she now sat. 'How are the boys? C'mon sit beside me. We've done it often enough.'

So she sat, and before long they were like old friends again discussing the children and the wild-life. He told her about his studies. This was a different Frank. Last time she had seen him he had the body of a lanky adolescent. Now here was something altogether different. Yes, sweaty he might be, but those muscular arms and shoulders, the collarless strong neck. And still those beautiful expressive eyes. She found it almost impossible to hold herself from – what? Catching her breath, she had never experienced such an overwhelming feeling before. Was it unseemly? This man was talking to her as an equal. Now he said how he had loved being part of the group when they were all children along with her brothers, sisters and the locals roaming the marshland together in all weathers, meeting carters and their horses on the marsh road, learning about the plants, the water-ways and the wildlife from Mr Pilbeam. 'My father has great respect for your grandfather,' he con-fided. Ah and the days they spent watching the carpenters in their workshop and sometimes help-ing out at the blacksmith's; he said he had loved every minute of those days.

If his mother had known where he was she would have disapproved, but he said his father turned a blind eye. Boys had to get out, have freedom, especially an only boy. He told Clara that being in the company of the ever-growing group of her siblings he felt part of a real family. He might have been two years her elder, but she always showed wise counsel, way beyond her years. The children came to her to right their wrongs, she made cuts and grazes better in no time and knew just the right herb for a sting or a bite and then lovingly wiped away their tears into a smiles.

This man was telling her his personal feelings. She began to feel quite uncomfortable in all this unexpected praise.

'So don't ever call me sir, you who have such greater natural powers.'

She had to stop him. 'Ah, but you are better read than I.'

They laughed a lot as they reminisced. It was a golden morning. She had to break this spell. She'd be late.

Since that day Frank had engineered his movements to find Clara almost every day. When she was at work he kept his distance. He would not cause her difficulties. She addressed him as 'sir' if they met in the house. When they met again on the marsh she told him about her aspirations. How keen she was to learn from Mrs Charlish, the Andersons' cook. Her grandmother had taught her much about game and of pastry cooking and housekeeping at the inn, but now she needed further culinary skills, patisserie and more. Knowledge would take her into great establishments. After all, Mrs Charlish was an opportunity not to be missed. Mrs Anderson had gone to some

lengths to secure her cook's services. Grandmother Pilbeam had told Clara how Mrs Charlish
had been trained in the mansions of the gentry in
London.

Clara only had one half day off each week so
the pair agreed to meet out on the marsh whenever they could, Frank riding his horse to take
them well away from the Manor. At first she was
unsure of the closeness to his body and only
reluctantly climbed up behind him.

One afternoon, it must have been about a year
after this first encounter on the bridge, Frank
cantered the horse along the tide line. Clara's hair
blew out behind her, she was laughing and singing, the wind pushing the horse to become a little
skittish. They slid off into the sand and fell giggling
in between the deep dunes. Lying there in the sun,
a breeze swaying the pale green grasses, Frank
rolled over, took her in his arms and kissed her
gently. Clara loved the sensation.

She knew she had always loved Frank. From the
first time she had seen this unsure little boy of
seven asking hesitantly if she would mind him
joining her. Then she only had the company of
her younger sister Rose and their baby brother
along with two other local children. They were
rambling along a field edge. It was a spring morning and Clara noticed the mass of tiny frogs on
the far bank of a ditch. So all five children lay on
their tummies, baby left behind them safely in a
small hollow on his shawl, gurgling with a dummy
of raisins in a rag, while they silently watched the
migrating frogs leaping up out of the water, scrab-
bling over one another on the bright green moss

and scampering off into the young shooting reeds. From then on Frank found them wherever they ranged across the marsh, at times standing high in his pony's stirrups watching for signs for any movement over the land to locate the little group. He often brought a bag of bread and cheese to go with the apples Clara always carried for her small charges. His kindness, for a boy, was always noticed. Her brothers weren't unkind, they were just boys. Frank was a gentle boy, well mannered.

'After you Clara, Rose,' he'd say. Not soppy. No, more friendly – equal.

It had been such a lovely afternoon. The ex-hilarating canter along the sand with the wind making her hair fly – and the kiss, the breath-taking kiss, lying side by side holding hands, both deep in their thoughts. When they remounted Frank lifted her up in front of him. That was the first time. Afterwards they always rode that way, his arms encircling her. Now the closeness of their two bodies gave opportunity for kissing her neck, her hair, and as their meetings progressed, her cleavage, as she nestled inside his open shirt. All the while the horse slowing, carrying them along in their mutual dream.

Squawk, squirm, familiar sounds of the fantail turning the cap on Stone Cross Mill cut through the deep glow of her memories, alerting Clara to the freshening breeze coming up off the sea. The night was giving on the cusp of a new day. Clara realised she had sat dreaming by the bridge longer than she had intended, reliving those few hours of closeness, his loving kisses. It had only been on her one half-day each week, and there were times when that was lost if Mrs Anderson decided to invite an unexpected visitor to her dining table.

At first, when they met only on her half-days, her emotions were tangled. She wanted to go shopping on her half-day. Like all her contemporaries she wanted to buy little items to trim a new hat or collar and cuffs. She wanted to meet her cousin Lilian for a girls' gossip. Lilian had a gentleman although she was always very closely chaperoned. They had a lot to talk about, although Clara never discussed her own romance.

Gradually she realised how deep her feelings had always been. There came a time when her and Frank's growing youthful excitement in their love took them to secret places. In the spring and summer months they could meet in the hours before dawn or well after dusk. She would sometimes leave the house with a coat thrown over her soft muslin summer frock. No stays. Her elders would have been scandalised. The way he swung himself up into the saddle, and with a muscled arm lifted her up in front. She lay against his bare chest – it made her wilt to recall it now, even more. Knowing the area so well they went far off any beaten track to places where deep under curtains of willows the long, fine, grey-green leaves swept featherlike across their faces. The early sun or rising moon glittering up from the water lit their pathway. Here they were able finally to know each other's body in a way they had never known before – to make love. They couldn't help themselves. Both were kind and gentle with each other for they had known one another all their young lives. It felt so natural. And it was.

Even so, now Clara could not help but think of her own mother's circumstances. Was it love? She recalled hearing her mother's cry on finding 'it's 'appened all over ag'in.' She couldn't feel that love had anything to do with it, except perhaps for the time she herself was conceived. Perhaps then it was love that produced Clara, the first one of her parents' union. Frank had said she was wise beyond her years. He didn't get that right, she thought. Still, it had happened. And now look where she was, disgraced. No. I'm not disgraced. We love each other. Whatever happens, it's real love. She stood up and walked on with a purpose.

Reaching the inn she found all in darkness. There was only the tiny wayfarer's light in the porch that was always kept alight to show any soul on the road there would be a welcome at all times. Clara decided not to disturb the house. The dogs, half sleeping guard in the back lobby, knew her, giving a little happy thump of their tails as she quietly acknowledged each animal.

Lifting the wooden latch she tiptoed across the kitchen to her grandmother's chair in its usual place by the range. Kicking off her sodden wet house shoes Clara sat down in the cosy warmth and was asleep before her head touched the old chair's high hooded back, its occupant now shielded from the first misty light already seeping through the window.

The kitchen mouser snuggled up around Clara's feet. Sleek black Molly would go on loving the young woman whatever her grandparents' reaction, when the new day finally came.

A bad day – there was no hiding it. The whole household seemed to tremble with the shock of Clara's sudden dismissal. Annie and John were extremely upset and annoyed with their grand-daughter's thoughtless, foolish behaviour. They said she'd thrown away the great opportunity to learn from one of the best cooks in the country. She had brought it all on herself. Nobody could ever expect the Andersons to tolerate their son keeping company with a servant girl.

Oh dear – John had held back his doubts. Although he'd caught sight of the pair over the past two years he hadn't wanted to worry his wife, but now realised he should have said something more direct to Clara and not relied on his stories to create a thought change. No, it hadn't worked – and as always the inevitable tattle had reached Annie's ears. She had cautioned her granddaughter discreetly, not wanting to anger John. Obviously she had not been firm enough.

The young people in the kitchen and yard blazed with annoyance at 'her highness old Ma Anderson', but they too knew Clara had been wrong allowing herself to be swept up in thrilling temptation. The girls secretly knew they could never have resisted if they had been kissed by Frank. He was so swooningly handsome, so exciting. They were giggly and rather tearful at first, then full of how sinful it all was, but so full of gossip to tell around the village, youngsters bragging about the goings on.

All the while and wide eyed, Clara's three

youngest brothers and two sisters were too young to understand fully what had happened. So excited to see their Clara in the kitchen but, oh dear, the feeling their lovely sister was in trouble made them cry and cling to her. Even the dogs were ears flat and tails drooped, staying well away from the back door. The cats slunk outside to avoid the erratic feet going in all directions.

Oh yes, the atmosphere was thick, horrible, grey-yellow that day. Although she woke from a heavy dream-dotted sleep Clara had already formulated a plan, at least for her immediate future. John and Annie were angry and exasperated, but as ever prepared to listen; after all it was Clara's life and Clara's responsibility.

She told them she would find herself another position. Yes, it would be difficult without a character reference, that was her own fault and she hated herself for her stupidity, but she had to make the best of the situation she had got herself into. However, she resolved not to reveal the full extent of that 'situation' and to live with the guilt that was hers alone. She had to spare her grandparents the further dreadful disgrace and shame it would bring them if it was known in the community.

Meanwhile as far as they were involved they agreed her plan was for the best: to go home and tell her parents about the dismissal, through associating with the Andersons' son, and to get their permission to move further afield. After all she was still under 25 and needed her parents' consent to travel away from home.

When all the talk was burnt out they let her be for the rest of that day.

The Willows

'That was the day I lost my handle,' a small querulous voice piped. It came from a slim elegant straight-sided jug high up at the end of the second shelf on Deerfold Cottage's dresser.

'Oh Florrie, no, what happened?'

'Was it because of Clara?'

'No surely not.'

'Yeah, and on that day I found myself with a new job,' came a disdainful interruption from across the kitchen. That was Big Pol, a wide-based jug, matronly in stature, made to take two pints of liquid and now hanging in a line of jugs above the marble pastry-rolling counter across the other side of the room.

Suddenly a chorus of voices rose in crescendo, all wanting to be heard at once.

'I'll tell you all about it.' Big Pol's offer was heard above the rising noise.

'Yes we want to know.'

'Be calm, all of you.' The claimants' voices died away as Mrs Potter teapot, rarely heard these days, took charge. She was a very elderly teapot, in fact the oldest teapot on the dresser and originally made by an English pottery to better any blue design coming out of China. She has seen more of our parallel lives than any other – but a few.

The dresser was a whirlpool of emotion at the shock the Willows felt to see the strained faces around the human story, with the rough times anticipated in their own lives and now stirred up by hearing about Florrie's handle loss, only to be followed so suddenly

44

by Big Pol's sharp interventions.

'It sobered us all up, especially Mrs Ann.'

'That was unkind Pol,' rebuked Mrs P.

'Well, so it did. Missus gave that silly girl the job an' she's the one that sent Florrie arse over tip an' broke 'er handle ORF!'

'Big Polly, don't be so vulgar girl!'

'She's right though,' the more ladylike Florrie rejoined.

'Maybe so Florrie, but there's no need for vulgarity. Of course Mrs Ann was upset, she's always taken great care of us Willows. We're family just as much as Clara and you know how she's loved that girl. More than any of them and shed more tears for Clara than any of us know.'

'We know.' Attention was drawn towards Ann's teacup and dish. 'You're right, of course you are,' agreed Mrs P.

'It's always the cups and saucers, especially the old style tea dishes, they feel the real emotions first-hand in our owners,' added Laura and Bea.

Poor old Willow cups and saucers, they do toil with us humans through some of the most soul-searching events in our lives.

The Lamb Inn

After all the pent-up emotion and tears before breakfast, life carried on apace for everybody else at the Lamb Inn. The rest of the morning turned out to be exceptionally busy. A nip in the air had brought more than the usual number of carters, delivery lads and travelling salesmen all calling in

45

for a warm. Ann was kept busy back and forth between kitchen and bar parlour with bowls of hearty soup or, 'A cut of your good ham Missus please,' came the requests, while others called for 'Bread and cheese and a pot of ale innkeeper, if you will.' John served more jugs of ale before midday than he had for the whole of the past week. Big Pol was kept busy up and down from the cellar, keeping customers' pots filled. Every chair around the room was taken. The floor was littered with bags, satchels and dogs – spilling out among the horses being fed and watered in the yard.

Annie's hens, always nosey and keen to poke around where pickings were scattering, strutted and jumped and squawked in startled exclamations between the horses' hooves. Even the ducks came across from the pond one behind the other to investigate the throng.

Then, as suddenly as they arrived, they were gone on their way. All was quiet once again.

Making sure the young kitchen and stable helpers, including John's potman Jim Tidy, stopped for an hour after they had all eaten, Ann could take her own rest. John, as he grew older, stayed in his high-back chair close to the inglenook taking forty winks before going back to his outside work.

Following her usual routine Ann changed out of her soiled kitchen dress and apron. She still preferred the printed fabrics of her youth; flower-sprigged cotton muslins for summer or a fine-patterned dark wool as on this cold day. All her dresses had long sleeves finished with white lace cuffs and detachable matching collar, her favourite silver brooch at the throat. Her plain cover-all kitchen cap she exchanged for one of her grand-daughter Rose's pretty lace caps, highlighting her white-flecked, chestnut-brown ringlets. All the rich, bright hair had been inherited by Rose's elder sister Clara Ann.

Countrywoman she may be, craftswoman she was, but Ann had always kept a gentle ladylike way about herself. Setting aside the button-up boots she wore for working, Ann slipped on the soft lamb-suede pumps John had the snob at Bourne Cross make for his wife. Now refreshed, Ann went to greet her friend Henrietta (Hetta) Deeplove at the house door. The two women had been friends for over sixty years. They'd played together as very little girls at the dame school they'd attended in the village where they were born. Even through the busy years bringing up their families, Ann and Hetta had tried to keep their weekly meeting.

Hetta's husband George had just built his tower mill at the Cross, the year John and Ann took over the licence at The Lamb Inn back in the late 1850s. Very few weeks had gone by over those thirty-five years without the pair meeting for tea on a Wednesday afternoon. Both were now in their sixties and grandmothers, so conversation was in-variably about family and grandchildren. They had enjoyed a special friendship, been a support to one another.

A finger to her lips brought a ready nod of understanding from Hetta. Ann picked up the tea tray and led the way up the narrow wooden

47

staircase behind the bar, tiptoeing to avoid disturbing John. Well, they thought they did. Big Pol reported that he always opened one eye and smiled a knowing little glance as the two women whispered and had their little laughs.

Setting the tray on a low table in front of the small arched fireplace, Ann and Hetta sank back into their armchairs with sighs of contentment. Ann stared into the fire, a faraway look on her face, eyes verging on sleep.

'Busy morning, Annie?' Hetta asked.

'Yes, we've all earned our keep this morning Het.'

Hetta could see her friend had more on her mind than a morning's hard work. She was used to hard work. Hetta wouldn't ask. Ann would tell her what was bothering her when she was ready.

'They're all so different. Give 'em wings and they'll fly off in all directions. No telling where.' Ann was thinking aloud.

Hetta knew Ann was referring to the grand-children. 'Well, at least we know where your Lilian's heading. Our Fred's a lovely young man.'

The two women were about to be related for the first time in the summer when Ann and John's granddaughter Lilian was to marry Fred Deeplove, Hetta and George's grandson. George was retiring now and Fred could take over the mill, so Lilian would become a miller's wife.

'Maybe Clara will find a husband soon. Let's hope so.'

'Don't think there's any chance of that yet, her mind's too full of cooking.' Not wanting to pursue the subject any further Annie poured the tea, Hetta's into the latest fine bone china cup and saucer, with the milk in first to prevent the hot tea from cracking the cup, while Annie took her tea from a dish. She called it her 'dish o' tay' and never gave it any thought to change her ways.

'You've forgotten to bring the kettle upstairs to top up the pot my love.' That was unusual for Annie to forget.

'No, not exactly. We had a slight mishap coming up the stairs just before you came. You see–' Annie didn't get time to finish what she was going to tell Hetta before there was a light tap on the door. 'Ah, there you are Jessie.'

Jessie braced herself ready to receive a dousing of ice-cold water. Eyes squeezed closed, head lightly turned to one side and holding her breath, she waited. It didn't come. Instead a gentle but firm voice asked, 'Whatever's the matter with you gal?'

Jessie peeped through her long dark lashes to see the missus, her new employer, arranging some of the flowers from the vase on the windowsill into the jug Jessie had just filled with water at the pump in the yard.

'Well?' questioned Mrs Pilbeam.

'I thought you were going to throw the water over me Missus,' Jessie answered.

'Tut! What a strange girl you are. I wouldn't do such a thing, it would give you a chill. But I am still cross that you damaged my beautiful Florrie water jug. She's been with the tea set since my grandmother gave it to me when I married Mr Pilbeam near on forty-five years ago. Still, no use crying over spilt milk. Florrie can keep me company up here in the sitting room. The flowers will hide the stub of her handle. She'll see her family the Willows when they come up here for tea in the afternoons.

'Now, take little jug down to the kitchen for some more milk Jessie, then you can bring Big Pol back up with hot water for Mrs Potter. Big Pol can replace Florrie!'

Jessie didn't move, just stood there looking puzzled.

'What is it now, gal?' asked Annie.

'Oh Annie,' her guest intervened, 'you and your willow pattern china. You must be the only family I know that has a name for every piece of willow china you own.'

'Yes, of course you're right,' Ann chuckled. 'Sorry Jessie you wouldn't know who Big Pol is. Big Pol, she's the jug that stands on the end of the bar counter. Fetch her up here with hot water for Mrs Potter.' Annie pointed to the teapot.

As Jessie, now enlightened, left the room she overheard the missus tell her friend, 'John will have to find another jug for ale on the bar counter, he won't like that. Big Pol comes from his side of the family.'

'I should have thought the brewery ought to supply a good set of jugs for the bar after all the business they get from The Lamb, Annie?'

Hetta didn't know the accident with the water jug had all been set off by the emotional upset with Clara that morning. She didn't even know Clara was upstairs in her bedroom. Everybody was on a nervous edge and Annie hadn't wanted to go over the story yet again. Not even with her closest friend.

The Willows

Later that afternoon, back down in the kitchen behind the bar, the Willows that had been on the tea tray were bombarded with questions from other members of the willow pattern family. 'What's happened? What was all the commotion about up there?' twittered the pots and plates from the dresser.

'You 'old 'ard for a bit,' said Mrs Potter teapot. 'Just you give us a breather while we get washed up an' then we'll tell you all about it.'

Robert, the major meat dish, whispered to Mrs P, 'Isn't Florrie with you? I caught sight of that new girl filling Florrie at the pump in the yard just a while ago.'

'No, our Florrie's staying upstairs with Mrs Ann, that's what the fuss was all about,' Mrs P told him. 'But I'm glad Missus didn't see Florrie taken out to the pump. She'd 'ave 'ad a fit to see her family china out in the yard.'

Mrs Potter and the rest of the tea set – Laura and her sister Bea, Ann's teacup and dish, Polly little jug, Martha sugar bowl, Victoria and Albert teacup and saucer – came over to sit on the dresser, followed lastly by Big Pol who found herself a space near the door to the bar counter. Usually Mrs P lived on the back of the range, keeping warm for tea making, but today was different; there was Florrie's accident to tell about.

'Now keep calm everybody. Florrie took a tumble down the stairs and lost her handle but otherwise she's

51

all right.'

*'Oh dear,' cried some of the younger Willows. They
had little experience of breakage and loss.*

*'Missus wants Florrie upstairs alongside her
armchair where she can be safe every day,' went on
Mrs P, 'and when she's filled with flowers the broken-
off handle will be covered by floaty leaves so Florrie
won't be embarrassed to be seen with her damage in
the best room.'*

*The older Willow family members were relieved to
hear the news. The Willows had all seen others come
and go over the years. Many a mishap befell the
family but Florrie – well Florrie was one of the
originals from Granny Hartshorn's wedding gift.
Visitors to the inn often admired the blue and white
china. Annie, usually just 'Missus' to the Willows,
looked after her china so it was not surprising she was
cross about the damage to Florrie water jug. Knowing
Missus, she wouldn't be cross for long.*

*Thoughtful kind Annie was always ready to make
good out of bad, so all was soon calm again. Anyway
that's what Jim middle meat dish thought.*

*'Oh lovely,' he called out when he saw Big Pol join
them on the dresser. 'We don't see enough of our Pretty
Pol. Welcome to the dresser.'*

*'I'm pretty too!' Polly little jug called out, while Big
Pol blushed and gave a bob of a curtsey. The others
chuckled because they knew Jim had set his cap at
Pol, ever since he'd met her in the bar at Christmas
time when he was being used to serve Mrs Pilbeam's
famous hot savoury to the regulars. It was a 'famous
savoury' because the regulars came for that every bit
as much as John's good old ale, but the savoury was
made ever more intriguing as the recipe was a family*

secret. Once they'd tasted it, everybody asked for the recipe, and that Annie never divulged. Only the Willows shared Annie's kitchen secrets.

I'll tell you the recipe, it's very simple but the simplest ones are often the tastiest. Don't you tell anybody else, it's just between ourselves.

Famous Hot Savoury served at The Lamb Inn

1/4 lb good Cheshire cheese (grated)
2 egg yolks
5 oz grated wholemeal bread
1 tablespoon mustard made with a little stout beer
1/4 lb good butter (softened to room temperature)
Salt to taste

Mix the grated cheese and breadcrumbs with the softened butter. Add the mustard and a little salt and the egg yolks. Mix well, beating until smooth. Lay the mixture neatly on slices of crispy toasted bread. It doesn't need buttering. Put in the oven or under a grill until thoroughly hot and slightly brown. Granny used a 'salamander' that was always kept ready on a pivot beside the fire to brown her savoury slices. On the days she served her savoury the face of the salamander was kept in the fire and swung out to hang across the toasts to brown the surface before serving. Strew a little cayenne pepper across each piece before serving piping hot.

The Lamb Inn

'Ah well,' Hetta sighed, 'I must be off, see if my George is home yet. I don't know what's more bother, young men dallying with silly young gals or retired vigorous sixty-seven-year-olds with time on their hands riding all over the countryside making a nuisance of themselves. Life is always changing.'

Annie kept her thoughts to herself, adding no more to the conversation.

As Hetta pulled on her bonnet she glanced out of the window. 'There's your John with my trap. Grand man you've got there Annie. We girls were all jealous when he chose you my dear. He's never changed has he? Still has the same kindly humour. Oh look at my little Dora down there. The lads have given her a lovely groomin'.' With a deep sigh Hetta became all crisp and ready to go. 'I'll be on my way then. See you next week for another dish of tea.' The two women gave each other a hug.

'Bye my love,' returned Annie. She couldn't help feeling compassion for Hetta. George hadn't always been a good husband.

The Willows

When the Harriers Meet had gathered in the yard with their terriers the previous weekend, the Willows had seen for themselves just what kind of man George Deeplove really was.

Wally watercress dish saw the start of the trouble from

his position on the windowsill. Looking out into the yard Wally described how George quite deliberately let the small glass stirrup cup, offered to him by Kathy the kitchen maid, slip through his fingers to crash into sharp splinters on the cobbles.

'Oh, poor Kath!' Wally squealed. Kathy was being called all sorts of names for dropping the glass. 'She's coming back in here,' Wally told the Willows. Kathy, a sensible girl, was running through the scullery into the kitchen towards the range for a pan and brush. She knew the glass shards needed gathering up very quickly to avoid pieces getting into the terriers' pads. As she turned back towards the yard door old George Deeplove stepped stealthily up behind her and whirled the girl round behind the door, pinning her against the wall. The Willows on the dresser and all around the kitchen were watching, hearts going out to their Kath. Cupping his great hand over her mouth to stifle the scream that was already half out, he gruffly whispered, 'I didn't mean it girl. Give us a kiss and make it up to me.'

Mrs P on the back of the range was close enough to hear George's heavy breathing and get a whiff of his bad breath. She was frightened for Kathy. Then Wally motioned from the windowsill. He could see Missus moving through the throng in the yard between the men and animals. Fortunately Annie had caught sight of George following Kathy into the kitchen so she briskly made her way through the scullery door, picking up a jug on her way. As she entered the kitchen she called out, 'Kathy, where are you?'

George angrily let the girl go free. Annie came right into the kitchen. Without looking at George she said, 'Ah there you are girl.' Handing her the jug she went on, 'Fetch some water in this jug for the young terriers, *but don't let them drink too much before they move off. Now hurry yourself, that glass needs clearing up.'*

The Willows were all of a shiver around the room wondering what would happen next. They need not have worried. For quick as you like Annie flung the door closed behind the retreating girl and swung round to face George. In that moment the tables were turned.

'Now then George Deeplove, if our families are to remain friends you are going to leave my girls alone. Never lay a finger on any of them. Family or servants, they are our responsibility, in our care.' George, red with anger and still breathless, opened his mouth to speak, but before he could curse her she silenced him once again. 'And, don't you blaspheme at me or mine.' With that she quietly turned, opened the door and went out, leaving George stunned and fuming in frustrated rage. He wasn't used to a woman speaking to him like that.

'Damn the woman!' he rasped under his breath, stumping out the way he had slipped in.

George had not seen the figure standing back in the short shadowy passage leading to the bar. John had been coming through to fetch a jug of water for the young terriers himself. He caught the sound of Kathy's gagged scream. Holding back he waited to see exactly what George had in mind before intervening, remaining still as events unfolded on the other side of the kitchen. Turning to leave, John glanced across at the Willows on the dresser. He gave a little snort and a smile as if to say, 'That's my Annie.'

The Willows family took a collective sigh of relief. A buzz of excited chatter followed, with an agreement on how proud they all were of their Missus.

'The things you see when people think there's

56

nobody watching them,' commented a young dinner plate.

'That's going to be a common experience all your life,' Mrs Potter teapot wisely told the younger Willow family members.

'It looks as if we've got a "bad lot" coming into the family. Sad, because Mrs Ann and Henrietta Deeplove have been such close friends all these years,' Martha sugar bowl said, adding, 'what about this other close friendship blossoming between two young people?'

'Come on Pol, what 'ave you 'eard?' asked the tea set all at once.

'They've been seen,' said Pol slowly.

'Come on, come on hurry, out with it,' squealed the younger Willows from the dresser.

'They've seen our Clara Ann meeting young Mr Anderson on her afternoon off.'

'Who's seen them, where?' Mrs Potter Teapot butted in very brusquely.

'One of the men in the bar's seen 'em, in Eastbourne.' Big Pol replied.

'I expect she just bumped into him when she was doing a bit of shopping,' offered Martha.

'No,' returned Big Pol, 'I overheard a fellow talking in the bar and he was saying how Mr Frank was waiting at the station and met Clara when she got off the train at Eastbourne. And, he gave her a little kiss on the cheek.'

'I won't believe you!' cried Mrs Potter. 'What would her grandparents say? Did Mr John overhear that gossip Pol?'

'He must have, Mrs P'

'Oh dear, oh dearie me, whatever will come of that daren't be thought! The Andersons won't want their *son walking out with a servant, to be sure.'*

So the Willows had got wind of that story through bar talk the previous Saturday.

Clara

Clara was grateful to be allowed the rest of the day to herself. She retired up to the little bedroom, always known as 'Clara Ann's room' just beneath the eaves where the swallows' nests clustered round the window year on year. She called it her refuge – where as a young surrogate mother she could close the door and be a child herself for a time. Behind that door this day, her first reaction was to release hurt into tears. But now she had to fight off the growing loss deep in the pit of her stomach. She had to think clearly, put all that behind her.

Clara Ann sat down to write a careful letter to her sister in Brighton. Rose had been asked to accompany the family in whose employ she was, when they moved to Brighton because their young daughter declared her fine dressmaker's needle-work 'indispensible'. Clara reasoned that if she had somewhere to stay already arranged, prefer-ably with Rose, her parents would readily agree to Clara's plan. The full extent of her situation was left to tell when she was face to face with her sister. Although she had little experience of the wider world, from what she had already seen she realised men had their way and moved on while women were expected to fit in with their needs and wishes. No, that sounded too unkind, it couldn't be Frank

– no she wouldn't believe it of him. Nevertheless she had to follow her instinct and fend for herself; she didn't want anyone else involved in her difficulties.

By late afternoon Clara's box arrived at the inn from the Andersons'. Last thing that night, while Annie was banking up the fire in the kitchen range, Clara had had the opportunity for a few moments alone with her grandmother. Annie was still sore with Clara but not so much that the pair couldn't embrace one another. They were after all two women, although at the opposite ends of their respective lives. Annie wished her dearest grand-daughter every success. To her it was the end of an era. Now the child was to take wing and fly alone. Annie took a small bag of coins from the dresser drawer and putting the bundle into Clara's hand she said that Granpa and she wanted her to have a little behind her to help her along. The thoughtful gift brought tears to Clara's eyes.

'Thanks Gran. You and Granfer have always been my rock.'

'That's the way it should be my dear love. Now you get your rest. Off, up to bed you go.'

Clara was away by 5 o'clock next morning on the carrier's cart, but not before a very loving cuddle from her grandmother. The sky was smeary grey like a wash of ink beneath silhouetted black skeletal trees that cracked in a sporadic dry breeze. It was sharp cold. The old carrier man flicked his whip above his horse's ear setting the cart trundling off along the narrow sandy lane. This was the cheapest way to travel across the marsh. Clara hadn't wanted to involve anybody else further in her affairs.

A mile into the journey the cart topped a rise where something, instinct maybe, made her look back over her shoulder towards the sea. Grandfather John was standing tall on a beacon mound near the old salt barge canal. The figure raised his arm straight up above his head, the flat of his white palm reflecting the first rays of pale morning sun cutting through a break in the clouds. It was his final salute. Clara realised how much he must have been hurting to station himself in the one position where he knew he would see the cart before the road wound off down the hill.

Clara half stood to wave her scarf high over her head as the swaying cart creaked and squeaked its way out of sight along the road eastward towards her parents' home in St Leonards.

John watched his granddaughter's waving figure disappear from view. She was gone. It had been just a few minutes' sighting, and seemingly just a few minutes since he married Annie – sweet woman and such a short time since the children came and went their own ways.

Robert, their eldest was a big strong gentle observer in the fields, long since taken by nature's own.

James, quick with numbers, got the answers before all others, away now profiting from his canny brain.

Elizabeth, a hard girl, wilful woman – he felt sorry for Horace but he had fathered a fine, steadfast, loving daughter. A first grandchild, Grace, always the special one – wasn't long before she was up and off clean across the ocean.

Charlotte, too loud for his liking, she was too self-important, no time for the frailties of others.

And Emily, over-friendly, a scatterbrain – hard worker though. Thank goodness she's a sturdy healthy woman.

He had always tried to lead his family by example in all aspects of his life. And he'd brooked no nonsense from the smuggling fraternity. His father had always cautioned, 'Never let them draw their ship on our walls. They just bring us problems.' People have eyes, ears and loose mouths, and they use them at The Lamb Inn. Nobody has secrets.

Or do they?

He'd noticed the first time when Clara Ann made excuses and cut short her visit to her grandmother. On that afternoon he'd caught sight of two figures hand in hand, standing far off up on the dunes. Not so far that he couldn't see Clara's golden hair blowing in the breeze, not so far that he didn't recognise the young man by her side; he looked too like his father Franklin at that age.

Maybe instead of using his stories to guide his flock, he should have been more direct.

Clara clearly knew her own mind, she'd taken on childcare for her mother, nurturing her brothers and sisters with kindness and an unusual sureness for one so young. He and Annie couldn't have loved her more.

The dogs had given up on him and were now lying waiting for their master's direction. The wind freshened, flicking up the silver undersides of the leaves. He had only stood deep in his thoughts but

61

a few minutes. No, the sun had moved too far. He knew no clocks.

'C'mon lads, she's gone.'

When Clara opened her box back in her parents' house she found a surprise on top of her possessions, in an envelope with her name on it. The day after Clara and his son each departed the household in their separate directions, none other than Franklin Anderson had searched out John on the marsh and gave him the envelope for Clara. It contained her full pay for the rest of the year, all nine months' worth. Her grandparents had placed it in her box on a sheet of paper folded once to lie under the envelope. On it Annie wrote to Clara how Franklin Anderson had found John himself to give him the envelope. He told John how sad he was that this had to happen. He was sorry to see the girl go. 'Wasn't that kind of him?' her grandmother noted.

The Willows

'I heard more about that later,' announced Big Pol. 'The day Clara departed, John and Ann sat in the inglenook each taking a small ale. John always liked it when Ann joined him on an evening when there were no customers. You remember how they both used to sit knitting either side of the inglenook? The grandchildren always had warm woollies when they came to the inn on cold days.'

'Yes Pol but let's get back to the story,' urged Mrs P.

'There were no customers in that night,' Big Pol

went on, 'so John dunked a red hot poker into their ale mugs. Being still almost half full I was sat down on the hearth; it was lovely to be with them in familiar comfort. Well, while Ann sipped away, John explained how Franklin had said he'd never forgotten that he long owed John a debt of gratitude. Now he felt he could repay that debt, although he was sorry that it had to be in such circumstances.'

'Gracious John, whatever's that about?' Ann asked.

'You remember what Franklin Anderson's ol' father was like? 'E 'ad a real cruel streak in him that man, nobody liked the beggar.

'I hadn't got much time for 'im meself but 'e gave employment so I 'ad ter keep my peace. Years back now 'e 'ad man traps put out on the marsh to stop poachin' on 'is land. 'E even forbade those men who set the traps ter tell others who worked for 'im where they'd set 'em. No, not even people likes o' me who had to range his pastures! Well I always kept careful watch out for signs. I know where fellas took their carts across pathways and rummaged the undergrowth. I was certain I knew where they traps were all set.'

Ann said it frightened her just to think of it.

'I weren't goin' ter let that beggar cause me physical damage. So what do you think 'appened? His own son, out with a rod early one morning, got himself clamped tight in one of them blasted contraptions! I caught sight of a reed head floating away up high above the banks. "Unusual," I thought, so I went to investigate. Soon's I neared I know'd one of them damn traps were just at that very spot. Franklin, he'd fallen down and being at an odd position were unable to raise hisself or call out. So he'd tied a reed stalk to his fishin' rod and waved the head higher than the surrounding reeds. 'E must have

63

known I'd catch sight of an oddity. We didn't say much to each other at the time, 'e were in great pain. Anyway he did tell me he didn't want his father to know. The old man would have ridiculed him. We both knew he'd use any tack to show the locals who's who hereabouts. Nar, didn't matter to 'im man traps were outlawed – he always 'ad his way. I prised open the trap and made it useless. I told young Franklin ter let the blood run clean, don't let it coddle, then got the lad back near 'is 'ome. He and I just shook hands, just like we did yesterday. I've never told a soul – 'till you now, that is.'

'Yes John I've always thought Franklin Anderson a good man.' Ann sat staring into the fire. 'Mm,' she murmured thoughtfully, 'shame that he has such an unfeeling wife.' John raised an eyebrow in question, but Ann said no more on the subject.

Laura and Bea then said they heard what Ann knew about the Andersons.

'Hetta told Ann some time ago that one of her nieces, Cissy it was, used to be lady's maid to Rachel Winterton, younger daughter of the Andersons' family solicitor when she married Franklin Anderson. Cissy said that after she married there were some mornings Mrs Anderson had a ritual of hand cleaning she'd never done before.'

'A weird thing to do,' was all her Aunt Hetta re- marked.

'Yes, made me pull these white silk gloves off her hands and go straight way to burn them in the kitchen fire. Then she'd wash her hands, all a shudder she was sometimes, washing 'til she were red raw. Cissy said there were lots of pairs of those silk gloves in the drawer by Rachel's bed. Hetta said that Cissy was very young at the time when she asked her aunt

64

*what she thought was wrong with Rachel. Anyway,
Hetta felt she didn't quite know how to answer the
girl. Hetta told Ann how in those days she had known
Rachel Anderson's closest woman friend – well, not
that she had very many woman friends because she
had such a sharp mouth on her. So this friend told
Hetta that Rachel Anderson hated having intimate
relations, let alone touch her husband, so she always
wore gloves when he came to her bed. Told him it was
to avoid getting her scented hand lotion on his skin.
Rachel said she was determined to go through with
this necessity until she produced a son. As you know
Josephine came first but as soon as Frank was born
she never allowed her husband back into her bed. So
Cissy, being a few years older by then, had the answer.
She said Mr Franklin only got into the missus'
bedroom after a roarin' row a couple of nights a year.*

'Ann and Hetta never laughed over that morsel of
gossip,' commented Laura and Bea.

2

Frank and Clara

Frank's letter made slow progress. Buckled inside
a leather satchel with messages from husbands,
lovers and servants, their carrier ship was forced to
make port on one of the Channel Islands for repairs after a storm. A fishing boat took the satchel
as far as the Scilly Isles and waited for the weather
to aid another vessel to deliver them to the Cor-

nish coast, thence up the Channel to Portsmouth where their various ways parted, limping in all directions each to their own address of destination.

Life went on.

Frank sailed on his inevitable way south, writing to Clara every day. He never knew his first letter was delayed.

Meanwhile Clara received a very prompt postcard from Brighton. 'Yes come. Love Rose x.'

There were seven children with Emily, Tom and their lodger in their two-up two-down terraced cottage in St Leonards, and Emily was pregnant yet again. Eventually Emily would have thirteen children in all. Clara knew there'd be no room for her more than an overnight shake down. She also realised that if her mother once organised a bed for her she would be expected to stay on to look after the children. Clara was therefore quick to point out to her mother that regular money sent home for the family was a better option all round.

The Willows

Uncle Bert tureen might have looked as if he was always asleep on the dresser but he was fully awake at the right moment to have his say.

'You may not know this but Old Po lived with Clara's parents in St Leonards. And as he's rarely in the kitchen to listen in on your storytelling he wouldn't know you were talking about his owners.'

66

'Who would want a gesunder in a kitchen?' called a snooty voice. It belonged to a finger bowl – well what else could a remark like that come from?

'Take no notice,' Big Pol cut in.

'Yes, Old Po, he'd know about Clara's family,' Laura agreed.

'You talkin' about me, you folks?'

'Ah! You are with us,' Uncle Bert answered. 'You were with Emily and Tom Dann an' all their kiddies when Clara lost her job at the Andersons' weren't you Po?'

'Can't really 'ear too well these days. Lost me 'earin' after years with all them boisterous children. When Clara came 'ome you say? Well she did that sometimes. Not often mind. Yes that time you're referrin' to there were a bit of an uproar. 'Er mum an' dad were tryin' ter get the youngsters off ter school, an' Tom 'e were draggin' a basket o' freshly ironed linens through the front door an' onto his cart, 'cos 'e delivered the clients' laundry back to 'em.'

'Oh dear Uncle Bert, what have you done? Now he's got started we'll never stop Ol' Po. You know what he's like.'

'Two of the little babbys were scratchin' each other an' cryin' when the carrier stops in the street an' let our Clara down with 'er box an' all. What a carry on, family 'adn't bin expectin' 'er right then so they were all surprised. Yes, I saw it all. Emily'd been standin' at the bottom of the stairs 'oldin' the door open for Tom strugglin' with the laundry basket, an' she'd put me down on the bottom stair 'cos she'd just emptied me night's contents an' washed me out.'

'Thank you Po. That's enough,' Mrs P nipped in.

'What else Po? What else did yer see? You tell 'em

67

now *they've arst!'* Uncle Bert was still awake and sticking up for Old Po.

'Now let me think. Yes. Yes, that's right. I remember I got left on the stairs all day. They forgot me.'

'What happened then?'

'Aw, silly old thing, it's not nice telling everybody a po is left on the staircase for anybody to see.'

'I 'eard that. That weren't my fault. Our Emily was so surprised ter see Clara an' anyways she always covered me 'ead with a clean white clawth. So stop yer ol' snooty nose up there on yer elevated shelf.'

'Hoh cheek!' Mrs P took that with a toss of her head, eyes firmly shut.

'Go on, go on Po,' the younger Willows urged. Old Po stood tall and turned to peer into the kitchen. He knew he had centre stage now.

'Tom, 'e shoved the box onto his cart. You know Tom had trouble doing any liftin' and haulin' cos of 'is badly injured arm dint you?'

'Yes, we did.'

'No we didn't,' called two adamant voices with French accents, extra loudly to make themselves heard.

'No of course you two wouldn't, would you?'

'No,' replied two tiles, 'we have only been in England since 1919.'

'Well, do yer want me to tell yer or not? Now yer's arst, listen. Clara's father Tom 'e came from Staffordshire.'

'Oh no,' said somebody under their breath, 'this is going to be a long one.'

'He came down ter Sussex in 1865,' went on Po. 'Somethin' ter do with poultry 'e were. Well after he got married to our Emily he used ter deliver poultry and game to all the big houses round about. Worked

68

for some 'igh class provisioner's shop in 'igh street, been with them years. One day he was doing 'is deliverin', big basket on one arm, when this woman driving a carriage 'n' pair at a 'ell of a lick got so close to him, knocked Tom right orf 'is feet. Whirled 'im right in the air, they say. Well, wot with tryin' ter quieten 'is 'orse an' get 'im back ter yard, when 'e got home that night he said 'e near on fainted. Jock the stable manager took a look at Tom's arm.

'"There's no blood," he said. "Orl right Tom, I'll tell Guvner tomorra – you get 'ome, I'll see the lads rub Bobby down and give 'im 'is feed."

'Next day Tom was so poorly he couldn't raise 'imself from 'is bed. Mrs Emily she was so worrit she sent one of the children to the yard to tell Master, "Daddy very bad." 'Er next door, the layin'in woman, came ter see Tom 'n' gave him a hot compress an' told 'im, "You ought to go down the doctor boy."

'"We 'ent got that kinda money in the 'ouse Missus."

'"Well me lad, you's not gonna work agin with an arm like that there."

'Jock called in on 'is way home from work that evenin' an' when he took another look at Tom's injury he 'ad ter sit down quick. 'Cos by then it was black 'n' blue 'n' yeller. Tom couldn't move.

'"Ol' quack needs to see that Tom." Emily was worried 'cos there'd be no money comin' in. Were a few days before Tom got to the old quack who told 'im, "Up the orspital for you man – why'd yer leave it so long?"

'"I can't afford no orspital sir," says Tom.

'"Well it's that or lose your arm man – be sensible. You'll have to sell something, find the money, ain't

69

there a benevolent society to do with your employ-ment?" There wasn't of course, but old quack he was so concerned he found the funds to send Tom up the orspital. They said he'd smashed 'is collar bone and broke top of 'is arm, but they couldn't never get it right, so he lorst 'is job an' the guvnor docked 'is wages 'cos 'e hadn't finished 'is round on the day of his accident.'

'What about the woman who knocked him down, Po?'

'Didn't know 'oo she were, just visitin' seems. Anyways, apparently she shouted at Tom ter "get outta the way man". Other people in that road didn't know 'oo she were neither. They just said better watch out for them women drivin' 'orses by 'emselves.'

There was a long pause. Seemed that Ol' Po had forgotten where he was in the story.

'Oh yes. Clara came home. Tom 'e were so pleased to see her. Loved that gal 'e did. Put is good arm round her, give 'er a big kiss on the cheek.

'"Allo my lass. What a sight for sore eyes."

'Emily, 'ands on 'ips, smilin' quizzical like, "Wot you doin' here middle o' week then Clara?" "Better get that laundry delivered Tom or we'll lose the business," she added turning to her husband.

'The children were like a bunch of rosey radishes running round in their excitement to greet Clara.'

'Listen to him – radishes indeed! What's that got to do with anything? Huh!'

'Never mind that. Go on Po.'

'Clara had brought a basket of gifts from Granny Ann so Emily was pleased and made Clara toast and tea with an egg for her breakfast.

'"Well then, c'mon gal, what's all this, 'ome in the

week? Mothers know yer know."

'That's when Clara told about her dismissal. Blunt as ever Emily straight orf arsts, "Wot yer gonna do about it then Clara?"

'I think Clara knew exactly wot 'er mother's reaction would be 'cos she ups and says, "I just want yours an' Father's permission to go to Brighton to look for another job."

''Ow yer gonna get that then? Don't 'spect that woman gave yer a character after the way she threw yer out now 'as she?"

'"No, but I'll manage."

'As they were a-talking the postman knocked on door with a card for Miss C. A. Dann.

'"That our Clara 'ome?" Postman pushed 'is 'ead round the doorway. "Hallo luv, nice to see yer dear. You look bonny 'n' well. Tell my missus I've sin yer. Bye now."

'"It's a card from Rose, I wrote askin' her to put me up for a bit while I look for a job."

'I could see Emily was relieved. There weren't much room in the 'ouse for another body. Not with mum and dad an seven littluns and a lodger they'd just taken in ter 'elp out with a bit o' extra rent.

'"Right," said Emily. "C'mon then girl you can 'elp me to finish this gofferin' for the Saxon household for t'weekend delivery an' we'll 'ave a nice dinner with the rabbit yer gran's sent with yer. Yer father can 'ear yer news t'night, train over ter Brighton goes through in mornin' time. Good ter 'ave yer company. I'm due again in another month so I need an 'and."

'"Oh Mum, I didn't know."

'"No, it dun't show much these days, this'll be thirteenth."

71

'When the children came 'ome Clara gave them each a currant bun their Granny Ann had sent in the basket from the inn. Aw they were pleased.' Old Po sat back.

'Is that it then?'

'Not quite,' replied Ol' Po. 'Her father was really upset, 'e wanted ter know all the reasoning behind 'er dismissal.

'"Damn them people! An' fancy you gettin' yerself involved with one o' them." All the evenin' 'e raged the story around like an old dog worrying a bone.

'"That's it then Tom, it'll do no good you rantin' on about the Andersons no more," Emily said, "but our Clara's off to try for a new place, best we let 'er get going in mornin', sooner she can send us a little money."

'Later she remarked to Clara, "Tell't yer didn't I, he'd rail on a time. Upset 'im it 'as. Dad 'ad such hopes for you luv."

'Clara went off early up hill to the station – never saw 'er for a long time after that.'

'An' I s'pose you're gonna tell us Emily stood on doorstep cuddlin' you in 'er arms while she waved bye bye to her daughter!'

'No – an' don't be so cheeky. Tom took Clara an' her box on his cart up to the railway station early so all the children even got up early too 'an waved to their big sister out in the street.'

Sleepy as he appeared, Uncle Bert Tureen was nevertheless watchful. He had observed that Clara Ann's father, Tom, was a disappointed man, and this is what he had overheard. Tom left his parents' home in Staffordshire and travelled south to find work. He wanted to make a success of his life. Somehow he'd always been overshadowed. He didn't have a rapport with dogs as a young child and that caused friction with his father who was the original breeder of the Staffordshire bull terrier. Tom could never please his father so he left. Walked to London then carried on until he had gone as far as he could go before he walked into the English Channel, ended up in St Leonards. Tom fell in love with a buxom country girl named Emily Pilbeam who was in service as a lady's maid. Emily made him feel 'somebody'. They quickly married, got a little cottage and both worked to make a better life. Emily knew the bar trade and although it was unusual for a married woman to go out to work, Tom agreed to let Emily bring in the money so they could save for a business of their own.

Soon, too soon, Emily became pregnant but they were both happy with their little girl and Tom even agreed to Emmie working some weekend evenings. Their prospects in life still seemed rosy for a while, then Em was pregnant again, and again, and again. Things got tight. The cottage couldn't hold them all so they moved to a two-bedroomed terrace.

Then Tom had his accident and with little, and at times no, money coming in they were forced to move again back to a one-up one-down. And still more babies came. Tom did his utmost to find work but the badly damaged arm and shoulder limited his capability badly. They weren't just poor, their little family met real poverty.

As soon as Clara Ann was earning she sent a little money home, as did Rose. But Tom decided he was a complete failure.

Clara

Clara sat in the third class compartment waiting patiently for the train to move off, the oblong cardboard ticket bearing the words 'Single to Brighton' lying in her lap. Trolleys trundled along the platform, footsteps ran, carriage doors slammed, somebody called out, 'Cheerio.'

'That's it! Why ever didn't I think of that before? The postie was saying "Cheerio" to Gran and Granfer. He wasn't saying "Cheer up", it was "Cheerio". I just didn't understand the old postie's accent.' Laughing at herself alone in the compartment she sat back with an inner satisfaction. It was only a small question from childhood answered but it had a good effect. It seemed to close a door.

As she watched a few last-minute passengers running past her window, the last door slammed and the train jerked forward into the tunnel.

Sharp sunlight hit her face, lighting up the bright green fields and the sea glittering on her left. The line would be passing hamlets, church towers, dark woods and marshland, then along the back of the Downs with their stark white chalkpits. Her hands resting in her lap and her head leaning back against the crisp white antimacassar, Clara watched the changing scene until the steady clumping rhythm of the wheels faded from her senses, allowing memories to flood their pictures into her mind's eye.

Frank's image took form, emerging from the frame: he was waiting on the platform. She had

74

taken the train to Eastbourne on her afternoon off with the intention of buying trimmings for the outfit she planned to wear at Cousin Lilian's wedding. Clara was so surprised to see Frank there and even more surprised when he, having caught sight of her as the train slowed, walked directly across to her carriage and opened the door. The porter who had stationed himself purposefully by the stopping point of a 'Ladies Only' carriage was almost knocked aside.

Frank took her hand and on helping her to step down onto the platform, to her amazement he brushed her cheek with a kiss. So shockingly fast. It had only been a few days past that they had met again early on that morning, for the first time in years. She couldn't deny her heart was bursting with joy. Oh, that feeling again! He was dressed so dashingly smart, no open-neck shirt this time but a high collar, neat narrow tie, pale-grey fitted jacket and slim dark-grey trousers. Oh dear there was that feeling, was this seemly? She had her doubts. He had none. Here was a lovely young woman in whose company he felt truly comfortable. After all they had known each other since childhood. No longer a child of course, now she'd developed this delicious dress sense.

Drawing her gloved hand through the crook of his arm he walked her slowly down the platform, taking in her auburn hair piled softly under her version of a jauntily set little 'Dolly Varden' hat that she had trimmed with a slip of sky-blue forget-me-nots. Thank goodness she had made a special effort with her dress that afternoon, she thought. He could see a pink cheek, and turquoise eyes beside him. He had noticed how well the deep pine-green velvet dress and matching hat showed off her natural colour. The high collar was trimmed with a little cream lace edge, as were the wristlets of the tight lower sleeves, the upper part being full and soft in the fashion of the day. Her bodice wasn't too revealing although it did narrow sharply into her slim waist – eighteen inches when she was nineteen years old. The skirt, fairly full, touched the last button of her side-buttoned boots, modestly covering her ankles. No words had so far been spoken between them.

'Will you walk with me along the seafront, Clara?'

She paused and smiled up at him. The sun was shining. She had the rest of the afternoon and evening away from work. 'I think I have the time sir, yes, I will.'

'Oh, thank you,' Frank replied, revealing his pleasure. Then they hesitated, both realising she had called him 'sir' and he had spoken the way he had as a small boy all those years ago when he'd asked to join their group. Laughing in mutual understanding he guided her across the station forecourt to the line of hansom cabs where a flower seller sat and requested a dainty corsage of violets, insisting on attaching it to her sleeve at the wrist.

Their walk took them along the seafront on the upper-level walkway to the pretty birdcage band-stand where they lingered to listen to the silver band. Clara remembered the band was playing 'Love's Old Sweet Song' because it was her grandparents' favourite and they too had heard it at this very place. Bringing her back from her daydreaming Frank asked what was her favourite tune. Her first thought was the one the band was playing, then she quickly realised that was a bit old before she recalled something she had heard at the little playhouse when she was last visiting her parents.

'I like the one they call "The Boy in the Gallery".' Perhaps he gave her a knowing smile before going on to tell her his own favourites – she'd never heard of a man being interested in what a young woman liked. Men, to her small knowledge, were only interested in their own likes and dislikes. Frank was different; he wanted to please her. Anyway with Clara he didn't need to protect his personal preferences from ridicule. They skirted the Wish Tower bedecked with flowers and lawns. Stopping to look at the view back along the sea-front to the pier, Frank politely asked, 'Would you care for a cup of tea, Clara?'

'That would be very welcome.' Clara wondered where they would find tea. There were hokey-pokey sellers and lemonade on the edge of the beach but she couldn't see a tea stand.

'Then we shall have some. Come along.' Across the gardens and down a short hill brought them to a row of elegant new shops in a colonnade along the back of the Grand Hotel. He stopped to look into a window showing two huge ostrich-feather-bedecked hats.

'Oh,' Clara couldn't stop herself remarking, 'I don't like those great top-heavy affairs.' As they looked at the display Frank whispered in her ear, 'Don't forget, no more sir and definitely not Mr

Frank.' Before she could respond he had turned their steps along the walkway and sedately into the entrance of the Grand Hotel. A footman doffed his hat murmuring, 'Sir, madam.' Frank took off his hat, laid his gloves inside it and handed it to the footman. Clara felt all the women promenading in the entrance would be staring at her. She hoped none of them had been guests at the Andersons' dinner table. Firmly taking hold of Clara's hand on his arm Frank guided her up the elegant staircase and into a salon facing out to the sea. Well, if they were staring she wouldn't even look at them. Looking ahead with a small confident smile she gave just a hint of a nod to the waiter who came forward bowing formally, saying, 'Good afternoon Mr Anderson. Good afternoon madam.'

'Good afternoon Joseph. We would like to take tea, perhaps over there in the corner by the window.'

'Thank you sir.'

Frank could feel Clara shake just a touch and immediately steadied her as they followed their guide through the room to a group of soft chairs round a low table. Frank drew his chair closer to Clara almost masking the room from her. Side by side they sat looking out to sea. He pointed to a sail on the horizon. Neither of them noticed that the table was now covered with a white embroidered cloth, fine china cups, saucers and tea plates, lace tea napkins, silver spoons, knives and cake forks, with a table drawn alongside carrying ornate silver teapot, hot water pot over a spirit burner and cream jug. It wasn't until two delicate three-tier stands were set on the table in front of them that the head waiter standing nearby attracted their attention.

'May I pour for you now sir?'

'Oh yes, yes thank you.'

'Milk, cream, or lemon madam?'

'Lemon please.' Clara remembered where she was. Experience now came into use. Although she had never been in the residential area of an hotel before she knew what everything was for and how to use it. She'd seen the etiquette, now was the time to become an actress – well, that did seem one way of getting through the whole experience. Lace napkin placed delicately across her fingers under her cup and saucer, Clara accepted one sugar lump offered with tongs. Sipping a little of her tea she dabbed her lips with the napkin and put the cup and saucer on the table. She indicated her preference from the selection of tiny sand-wiches on the savoury stand, again holding the plate with the lace napkin draped underneath, ready for easy transfer to her lips with the other hand. The colourful arrangement on the sweet stand was a very tasteful display of confectioner's art, with fruits and crystallised petals on neat sponge shapes topped with piped cream and chocolate shapes. She was handed her choice placed on a fresh tea plate – hardly a single mouthful to require the silver cake fork. The tiny artwork proved to be as delicious as it looked. She noticed everything, but mostly Frank's attention to her needs. They talked of the sights, the flowerbeds, and an awful lot she could not re-member.

At the station he saw her onto the train and waved from the platform. She was coming slowly out of a dream, still sitting in the warmth of her memories as she tried to recall the tiny savoury morsels and dainty pastries on those elegant tiered stands. Oh dear, she'd only had eyes for Frank, but she could remember enough to tell Mrs Charlish one or two new ideas she had not seen the cook do at the Andersons'.

Oh my goodness! Clara realised she'd forgotten to buy the trimmings she had gone out to get that afternoon. Botheration, she thought. 'Next week I promised I would visit Gran and Granfer; no shops out in the marsh. Now what shall I do?'

The train was slowing. A porter called out, 'Lewes Town'. Only a short distance now before Brighton, over the ridge of the Downs and there was the sea again.

Thoughts of Frank had passed through her mind but not about where he might be. Since she had left the inn Clara had been pushing the future out of her mind – take one day at a time, she told herself. Of course she still loved him. Oh damn it. The heartache had to be pushed aside. It was the only way she could survive. Living so close to nature she'd witnessed that life was hard. Work to eat, eat to live, or you died. She had a job to find; re-establish her reputation and bring another life into the world. No good feeling sorry for herself.

This time a porter helped her down from the carriage and carried her bags, finding a carrier's cart to take them to Rose's address in the Steine.

She had packed one small trunk with a view to staying for at least a year. After sitting for more than an hour on the train Clara decided to walk to stretch her legs. She was satisfied she had made the right decision to spend a little of her savings on a train ticket. The journey by bus would have been long with changes and waits for her trunk.

As she walked down Trafalgar Street there was a spring in her step. She felt so full of life and energy. The guilty feelings drained away, Frank was sent to the back of her mind. There was the tall white church she'd been told to look out for and there at the junction she turned right along the gardens towards the sea. It was her first time in Brighton. In the distance a vision loomed like something out of a fairy tale.

In Rose's first postcard home she had written that there was a royal building in the Steine and it had big onions on its roof. They had all thought she was joking, but nothing in Clara's imagination had conjured up what she now saw in front of her. Not only onion shapes set around with tiny windows but also sweeping upturned cones, soaring pinnacles topped with little temples and lacy-edged arches shielding tall windows. Clara thought, Oh my, if this is the first sight Brighton has to offer, what next?

Rose

Rose was younger than Clara by two years, shorter by an inch, more heavily built and had dark curly hair. The only principal characteristic

81

they shared was the same round, smiling face.

Always good with her needle, Rose was just fourteen when a local family took her on as apprentice to their two maiden-lady dressmakers. She learned quickly, making such good progress that she was put in charge of making all the youngest daughter's clothing, a girl the same age as herself. When the family decided to move to a town house in Brighton the now elderly dressmakers preferred to stay near Hastings, so the family asked Rose to go with them and gave her a workroom over the stables with her own bedroom next door.

Although Rose had responded right away to Clara's request she immediately sent off a second card telling her sister how to find the Steine Gardens. She was excited to hear from her sister Clara. She hadn't been lonely, but company, especially her own sister's, was an exciting prospect. While she was fitting her young Miss with the latest fashion in summer blouses she had been so animated about her sister's visit that the housekeeper said the family were happy for Rose to have her sister's company while she looked for a new job, so all was well.

Rose was busy with her sewing when Clara knocked on the door. 'Come up luvvie,' she called down from her workroom. 'I'll have to ask you to make us a cuppa, I'm gonna be busy here for sometime yet.'

Clara stood in the doorway to Rose's little domain. 'Oh Rose!' She laughed with delight, 'What a lovely bright room.' Rose laid down her work but before she could show her sister round

Clara exclaimed, 'Just look at that beautiful mirror!'

'Yes, Miss Thora had that put there. She said it would reflect the light from the sea back onto my work table. And look, I've got two oil lamps as well.'

'The mirror certainly does what your Miss Thora says. Crumbs Rose, they do think a lot of you. Oh! You've got a sewing machine!'

'Yes but it's taken a bit of getting used to.' Rose gave a chuckle. 'I got into some awful tangles, but I love it now. Look at this.' Putting a scrap of material on the needle plate Rose turned the handle. The little machine's arched arm curved up and down to the rhythmic sound, put-put-put-put – gentle, quiet, almost soporific. 'See, it sews a line of chain stitch.'

'I'm so thrilled for you Rose. Do write and tell Mum all about this room, she'd love to know.'

It wasn't very long before Clara picked up a needle to help out. 'Rose, whatever is this material? It's so unusual.'

'Yes, it's called rustling silk. It's for Miss Thora's dance petticoat. Gorgeous isn't it? There'll be some pieces left. I'm going to make a frill on a petti for myself.'

'Cor, Rose, mind they don't catch you wearing that.'

'Oh it's all right, Miss Thora says I can have all the oddments, an' I can cut economically so I gets some really good bits.'

It was just like old times chatting together that first evening. Clara told Rose what had happened about being dismissed – but not quite all. Two

83

pairs of hands making light work, Rose's job was soon done.

'Tell yer what,' said Rose, 'I've just to nip this dress up to Geraldine, she's Miss Thora's maid, then we'll go and find some pie 'n' mash, all right?' The little cook-shops were open until late at night on the street corners up Carlton Hill and George Street behind the Steine. From up on the hill you could look down on the Royal Pavilion. Queen Victoria didn't much like the place so few candles lit up the odd window. Rose said nothing much happened there these days. The girls wandered down to the seafront with their papers of pie 'n' peas to admire the ghostly shape of the Chain Pier, its heavy arches just visible fading out into the sea.

Clara woke early with a few butterflies for what the day would bring. She lay listening to the harsh call of seagulls where normally she'd heard the gentle cooing of pigeons around the Andersons' manor house. Then she realised Rose had already left her bed. She found her in the workroom as she expected.

'I start at first light,' Rose told her. 'You look smart Clara, good luck then. See you later.'

Clara set off into the brisk sea air. Clouds of little birds picking at flecks of yesterday's uncollected horse manure flew up as she passed. So many new sights and sounds in a town. She missed the variety of bird song, replaced by the wittering of starlings; even the smell of horse manure was sour and unwholesome. Being early there were work people about but no carriages. She was so excited by all these different sights and sounds she almost missed the employment agency for domestics that Rose had given her directions to find. Clara expected the toffee-nosed interview. Thank goodness Mrs Charlish had been as good as her word. The post had caught up with her so she had arrived at the agency holding a good professional 'Character' in her purse.

'Of course families keep their cooks for life. Usually other staff come by recommendation. I don't hold out much chance. Just wait in the next room. We'll let you know.'

Know when? Clara sat there until past midday and it was Rose's afternoon off. Determined to spend as much time as she could with Rose before a new job took over her life once again, Clara made to leave. The agent, who apparently expected her to sit and wait all day if necessary, snapped, 'Well, if you don't want the position...'

'I'll be here bright and early in the morning. You have my references. Good afternoon.'

It really was a high-handed attitude for Clara to take in the circumstances, but she wasn't going to just sit there like a silly when she could be trying for a position elsewhere.

The two young women had a gloriously happy few hours. Clara was enthralled watching the comings and goings of the aristocracy, the women's clothes and hats as they went from carriages across the pavements accompanied by handsome gentlemen. Ugh – some were so fat and ugly! The girls smiled impolitely behind their gloved hands.

Tea, followed by Variety at the Hippodrome in the evening. They laughed till they cried all the way home to bed, then could hardly sleep for whispering and giggling into the night.

True to her word, Clara attended the agency bright and early, sitting patiently again almost all the morning. She was about to leave when a young woman rushed through the waiting room and went without knocking into the main office. Clara overheard her breathless words.

'Lady Wellborough needs a cook – can you find us one? The family have visitors coming at the weekend and we are without a cook, we are desperate.' Once started the poor girl couldn't stop talking. Then she slumped into a chair unbidden, her energy drained.

'Well, er, I think you may be in luck. Mrs Dann, are you still there? You are available immediately aren't you Mrs Dann? Remember this is only a temporary position.'

Good enough for me, Clara thought. Her luck was in at last. It didn't take long to realise the household in need of a cook was Rose's employer. 'What a coincidence! After the agency's necessary formalities Clara followed the young girl back into the Steine and was shown the door to the kitchens. Telling the girl to let the housekeeper know she was on her way Clara went up to tell Rose the news, but she had already heard about Mrs Round the cook being indisposed. From her position seated at her work table Rose called out, 'Good luck Clara.'

It was rather presumptuous to dress in her cook's clothes for an interview, but the family were desperate for help. Throwing her coat over her apron and buttoning it neatly right up to the neck, she folded her kitchen cap into her pocket and presented herself at the entrance to the kitchen door.

Shown into the housekeeper's room Clara found herself facing a motherly looking woman sitting at her desk, account books open in front of her.

'Good morning. I'm Mrs Cromer. I'm so pleased to meet you Mrs Dann. I hope you will be able to help us out.' Then she stopped. 'Oh my dear, may I say you do look a little young,' looking back at Clara's 'Character'. 'I see you have good experience, and we do need help immediately. I'm told you are Rose's sister and that is certainly a recommendation. We are all so busy. I'm going to take you and introduce you to the kitchen staff. Janet, you met her at the agency. She's our under-cook. She will show you where everything is.' As she spoke a kind friendly smile filled her face in a reassuring manner. Mrs Cromer stood up, revealing a very tall woman neatly dressed in black, high collar, long sleeves with a chatelaine of keys and a variety of items hanging from her belt.

Clara placed her cap well over her hair before she entered the kitchen. The kitchen staff came forward to meet Clara, clearly showing their liking for the housekeeper. Mrs Cromer introduced Clara as Mrs Dann, then introduced each staff member by name: Janet undercook, Beth and Maud, kitchen maids, and a scullery boy, Sydney.

'I must leave you now to report to Lady Wellborough. Would you come to my room for the day's instructions as soon as I return, Mrs Dann?'

The stale smell in the kitchen assaulted Clara's

nostrils even before she entered the room. Janet gave her a welcoming smile, but the mixing bowl on the table in front of her held pastry crumb, and the fingers that had produced that crumb had filthy nails. Beth and Maud each gave a little bob. No caps on any of their heads, thought Clara.

Pulling on the white cotton gloves she always kept in her apron pocket for dirty jobs, Clara looked at each assistant in the kitchen. 'I want you to leave whatever you are doing and follow me. Janet, show us all round the kitchen and explain the facilities, where you keep what foods and what each cupboard and drawer holds. And, as we go, I want each of you to tell me your own particular jobs.'

The rather reticent little group shuffled on behind. Clara listened to their explanations and argy bargy as to who did what. A large stockpot stood on the side of the range. Lifting the lid Clara didn't have to sniff its contents to know that what it contained was off. Beth said her job was to lay out the cook's table and clear away. She pointed to the higgledy-piggledy collection of pots, pans and cutlery on the draining board. Greasy dribbles hung round the lip of a saucepan and scraps of old dried food were stuck between the prongs of a fork.

'I don't see a pot of silver sand. Where do you keep it Beth?' Beth's face was blank. Well no wonder the pans were inadequately cleaned.

'And you were about to make what?' Clara asked Janet.

'Pastry Mrs Dann.' Clara noticed that the fire

in the range was low to very dull. The dairy larder smelled rancid; none of the dishes had covers over their contents. When the door was opened to the game larder a cloud of flies rose up from their business in protest. She didn't bother to see inside the meat safe. At least a week's worth of kitchen linen lay in a heap on the stone floor in the wash house, and only a heap of spent ashes showed under the copper. Sydney called out, ''Scuse me Mrs Dann,' as he ran up the area steps.

'It's just the potato man,' said Janet with a shrug. Clara went out into the yard to see Sydney carrying a heavy jute sack down the steps. As he went towards the vegetable store Clara could see and smell that the bottom of the sack had rested in the road, bringing with it sure signs of horse urine. Looking up through the railings she could see the horse standing uphill of its cart and still energetically relieving itself in clouds of steam.

'Sydney, take that sack up to the man and ask for another one. Don't let him rest it on the road. Heave it onto your shoulder from the back of the cart.' Clara watched the whole operation. Back inside she asked, 'Do you have a bone box?'

'No Mrs Dann. The bone man comes every day.'

'Bring that enamel bowl down off the shed roof Sydney, if you please. Maud...' But Maud had disappeared.

'She's making Mrs Round's arrowroot, Mrs Dann.'

'Beth, take these bones out of the stock pot, put them in the bowl here and tip the rest of the stock pot down the outside drain.'

There was a loud sound of indrawn breath from the women, along with looks of scandalous horror on their faces. 'That's a waste,' Janet blurted out.

'Janet, please tell me who is in charge of the stockpot when Mrs Round is off duty?'

'Well. Nobody really, Mrs Dann.'

'So, when was this stock pot last brought to the boil for at least fifteen minutes?'

'Erm. Thursday, no, Wednesday I think, Mrs Dann.'

'That's five days ago. Throw it away please Beth. Now I want you to make a cup of tea then all sit down and wait until I come back. Please do not allow any tradesmen into the kitchen today. Tell them there'll be cake with their tea tomorrow.'

Having started off feeling sorry for Mrs Round, Clara began to see and hear more than enough to know the woman was not only too easy-going but also a slovenly cook. It was more than neglect; the food coming out of that kitchen was unsafe. And she dare not let herself become responsible for allowing further illness. Clara felt she couldn't just walk away from the job when she had the knowledge to do something about it. But would she get the approval she needed?

Knocking and entering on Mrs Cromer's 'Come in,' Clara was asked to take a seat but remained standing.

'I would prefer to stand for the moment Mrs Cromer, if you please. Before we go any further, I need to speak candidly.' She had the housekeeper's attention immediately.

'Not leaving us already I hope Mrs Dann?'

Smiling, Clara raised her hand to halt Mrs Cromer's concern. 'No, no,' she reassured, 'but this is very serious indeed for the whole household.

'I've taken in just how ill your cook really is. I've noted indications of illness in others, Sydney for instance. Now that I've seen the kitchen and the food I would like permission to clean the kitchen and scald out all the utensils, scrub every surface down and boil wash all the kitchen linens including staff clothes. I have had experience of this kind of illness and see how to control the situation.' Clara paused but did not stop. 'I will check the foodstuffs but I might have to throw things away,' she continued.

'May I suggest Mrs Round is kept isolated and be attended by only one person who does not enter or work in the kitchen area. I would also like to ask the scullery boy to stay away from work for a week.'

Mrs Cromer looked thoroughly shaken, and by somebody so young. After a pause she said, 'Sit down my dear, please.' She motioned Clara to an easy chair and was silent for a few moments in thought. Clara thought the housekeeper was about to give her a ticking off. Mrs Cromer's thoughts were far from it. She didn't voice those thoughts at that stage but felt this might be the very shock the kitchen needed to get matters changed.

'I agree with all you say Mrs Dann, but as your requirements are so detailed we must get Lady Wellborough's approval for what we propose.'

Clara relaxed. Hmm. What 'we' propose. So Mrs Cromer had taken her point and backed her straight away. It remained to find out how Lady Wellborough would react.

'Just one thing. What about luncheon and dinner today, especially as there's so little time to make preparations?' When Clara explained her planning the housekeeper quickly nodded her agreement, saying, 'I will leave that to you then.'

Lady Wellborough listened to her housekeeper who made the proposals as diplomatically as Clara had been forthright.

'Well, you know in the matters of the household I am guided by you Mrs Cromer.' Turning to Clara, Lady Wellborough asked, 'And where do you get this kind of knowledge Mrs Dann?'

Clara told how she had been present when her uncle, who had worked with Miss Nightingale, had brought his experience to the aid of customers and the family at her grandparents' inn.

'He was able to prevent the spread of a nasty illness by isolating the patient who eventually recovered because he had got care in time.'

As Clara was speaking, Lady Wellborough's expression changed to a smile of understanding. 'I know Miss Nightingale well and respect the experience she has passed on. Now, let us co-operate. I suggest we get a nurse in to attend Mrs Round. We can't have the children's nurse anywhere near danger for their sakes. I'll leave the hiring to you, Mrs Cromer. I suggest I send my own maid round the house to collect any domestic china and leave it all outside in the kitchen corridor. Are you able to provide us with a simple

92

luncheon today Mrs Dann?'

'Yes your Ladyship and a further hot but simple dinner this evening if that is satisfactory for you?'

Lady Wellborough smiled her approval. 'Thank you. If you need to see me again today Mrs Cromer, please do.'

On their way down the back stairs Clara commented on Lady Wellborough's quick understanding.

'She's the most co-operative employer I've ever worked for. She even likes to be involved.'

Clara did have one more item to mention. 'How many water closets are there in this house Mrs Cromer?'

'Ah yes, very sensible. Two, one upstairs for the family and one other outside in the yard for the staff.'

Clara immediately offered, 'Then I will make sure the staff area is cleaned and all the staff chamber pots and buckets. I'll leave the upstairs to you.'

The rest of the day saw the kitchen and larders in a controlled uproar. Fires in the range and under the copper were built up to almost industrial heat. Water boiled, pots, pans, bowls, all utensils were scalded out, carefully dried, and packed away in relined drawers and cupboards. Larders were emptied of all foodstuffs, fresh and dried and preserved. Much, especially the fresh food, was thrown away. Wooden and slate shelves were scrubbed. All linens, cloths and muslins were boil-washed. The outside yard was scrubbed down. Wooden tables, chopping and pastry boards were scrubbed with salt and rubbed with lemon halves then given a final flush off and left to dry.

While the staff undertook all these jobs in the order of priority Clara had instructed, she prepared a simple vegetable soup with shop-bought bread, cheese and apples for luncheon. When the large pans were once more shiny bright and the fire in the range settled to a good red glow, Clara made a large casserole of fresh meat delivered by the butcher who came twice a day, with new vegetables. Clara was reminded of Mrs Charlish saying always weigh the joints the butcher brings you and never forget to ask him for the paper of weight. Examine all meat and vegetables and if it's not good do not receive it.

Two gorgeous apple pies completed the meal. Everyone in the household shared and enjoyed the same fare that evening. Despite all the upheaval, Clara was determined to excel herself. And she did.

Lady Wellborough sent down a message to the cook. 'Thank you, Mrs Dann, we've never enjoyed ourselves so much.'

The last job of the day was to scrub the floor, which they all helped in doing – Clara included herself much to Janet, Beth and Maud's surprise. They finished their sections at the back door, washing out cloths, brushes and buckets at the outside tap. As they put their coats on, Clara locked the door saying, 'One more thing. Thank you all very much indeed ladies.' That was another surprise – 'ladies' indeed! The women had never been called ladies before.

'I will be in bright and early in the morning. I

would appreciate it if you were all here with me. I know you are tired. Goodnight.'

Dear Clara, she was so enthusiastic. All the detail she had learned from kind women she meant to pass on in the same vein.

Sitting in their beds at the end of an exhausting first day Clara and Rose sipped their cocoa.

'This is a grand treat, Clara,' Rose took a long soothing swallow. 'Good idea of yours to bring these lovely cups.'

'They were Granny's, don't you remember? She gave them to me when I left last week.'

'Yes, I do, come to think of it. Didn't she used to give them names? The Willows, I mean.'

'That's right. Sama and Joey. You've got Joey.'

'Oh Gran had such funny lovely ways. Sounds friendly though doesn't it? Just like having friends from home.'

Rose asked Clara what had got her doing all that cleaning and turning out on her first day in the job.

'Rose, I'll tell you. That kitchen wasn't just an eye-sore, it was a den of death.'

'Hold hard, Clara, that's goin' it a bit ain't it?'

'No, certainly not. It smelled mucky. Food had gone off. I know they finally let on Mrs Round had been ill longer than they said, but by the mess everywhere and the staff laxity, things had been like it a very long time. Wonder you're not all dead by now.'

'Strewth Clara, ain't yer layin' it on a bit thick?'

'Do you remember when Uncle Barney took over nursing that chap in the barn at the inn and kept everybody away?'

'No, when was that then?'

'No, you're right, you weren't there that year were you. It was one of those times when the wagoners had camped overnight in the yard. They were a lively bunch and lovely people. Well, the wagoners had left and the yard was all clear, and Gran went to let the hens out in the orchard. Tommy caught Granny's eye and whispered, "There's a man layin' in the barn an' 'e looks right ill, Granny." Gran takes a quick look in at this chap an' hightails it out front to find Granfer where he's standing talking to Uncle Barney. I overheard her tell the two men about the chap in the barn. Uncle Barney up and says, "You say this chap looks like 'e's oozing black stuff from the side of his mouth? You two stay here I'll take a look." Granfer went along but Barney made him stay by the back door well away from the barn. Granfer backed away at Uncle's direction and listened to his instructions. In the kitchen Granfer told Granny to wash her face and hands real good with lots o' soap. Now Barney says we've all to stay away an' don't let the stable boys back to the yard an' keep the animals up in the old barn. He wants boilin' water now, then he's goin' to light a fire in the yard to boil drinking water and make his own and the man's food. Granma had to boil all the drinking water for family and customers too.

'Barney stayed with the man out in the stable for two weeks together. When he was well enough to leave the barn all the locals donated clothing because Barney said he would be burning the man's clothing, and his own, as well as the sheeting and blankets Granny sent out to them. He also scalded out the cauldron and tin cups and mugs every time they were used. And when he left the barn every scrap of straw was cleared and burned on the fire in the yard. Finally Uncle Barney took a flaming wood from the fire and burned the surfaces all round where the sick man had lain. That stable looked like it was toasted black inside and out for all the time I knew it.

'Uncle Barney told us the man had arrived just as the wagoners were leaving but decided to sit down and rest because he felt so ill. He said that he'd last eaten somewhere 'up country', Uncle never discovered where. The man was lucky to survive because he had cholera, and even luckier that Uncle Barney had learned how to deal with cholera in the Crimea. He'd seen how Miss Nightingale had ordered all to be done. Lucky for us at the inn, for if Uncle Barney hadn't been present we might all have been infected. The man would certainly have died and the reputation of the inn – well we could see what had to be done was drastic but, said Uncle Barney, simple indeed. Yes, and so the man went on the carrier's cart to the railway station and boarded the train for London.

'When I mentioned Miss Nightingale had been Barney's fount of knowledge out in the Crimea, Lady Wellborough, she sat up and listened. All for it she was. And everybody enjoyed their simple fare today, didn't they?'

'Good for you Clara.'

'I couldn't just walk out an' say I wouldn't take the job on. Anyway there was my sister to think

97

of too wasn't there?'

Rose laughed. 'Thanks luv, best sister in the world.'

'The staff might not agree with you tomorrow. I'm going to have to give them some fast lessons on kitchen practice. Mrs Charlish, she always explained why she did everything. And that's what I'm gonna do, starting first thing in the morning.'

The Willows

'I'm on my own now,' a voice from the dresser commented, 'but that night Joey was still with us. It did feel like being with old friends from home. He's been broken and lost for some years now. There wasn't anybody around to put his handles and knob back on again.' Feeling sad, Sama sat in her saucer on the lowest shelf on the dresser, looking like a squat fat lady with her hands on her hips and a Tam o' Shanter lid on her head.

'Up in that tiny bedroom over the stables it was rotten cold and draughty all year. We were just the job for hot cocoa in bed 'cos of our lids.

'It was so good being involved in the next generation of the Pilbeam family.' Sama sighed with a sad smile.

Clara

'Janet, I'm putting you in charge of the stock pots. The brown stock is for meat bones only with fresh onion, carrot and celery. When it's come to the boil skim it off then slow simmer to draw off the meat juices for two hours before it's put to use. If I tell you the stock is for making a bouillon don't let it come to the boil. And never put potatoes in a stock pot and only vegetable leftovers after the first use. Remember, if we keep that stock pot the contents must be brought to the boil and roll boiled for at least fifteen minutes each day before it's used. We will never keep one mix for more than three days. The white stock pot is for poultry only and can include shallots and celery and sometimes the herbs I suggest and a little olive oil. This stock pot should be brought to the boil and simmered for one hour only. Do you know how to use a tammy and how to clear stocks Janet? Good. I shall tell you each morning what stock I will be wanting.'

When Clara asked after the leftover wine from the dining room she was met with blank looks so she dropped the subject. 'Then make sure all utensils and containers are kept well scalded. Now we do have a bone box? I want that kept scrupulously cleaned each day after the bone man has collected.' Clara listened to questions when everybody had got started on their jobs.

'Beth, this is how I want you to lay up my work table each day. You will clear for me. Everything must be as clean as a whistle and please remember never scrub the pans out and especially the frying pan, always rub them with the silver sand and rinse with hot water. You are also in charge of the dairy larder. Every dish must be covered with muslin. Make sure the floor and shelves are kept as clean as they are now.' Clara had assumed, correctly, that the young woman could read. Looking at the menu for the day Beth scurried away to collect utensils. But Clara stopped her, saying, 'No running in the kitchen dears, somebody could get hurt.

'Maud, you are in charge of the cleanliness of the meat larder, cleaning and blackleading the range and flues. You may come in later in the morning but you are responsible for the final cleaning of the day and will stay later to finish.' Clara noted the surprise on their faces. It was unheard of for servants to have 'time' for themselves; 'come in later' indeed! Normally their every waking hour belonged to their employers.

'I know what you are thinking Maud, but I want my staff to do a good job, even at the end of a long day. You can't do that if you are too tired.' Clara brought a lot of new thinking with her.

When young Sydney came back to work, Clara said, 'Sydney, I'm pleased to see you're looking better.'

'Yes, thank you Mrs Dann, Mother says to say thank you.' Clara had not turned Sydney away for a week without pay. She couldn't do anything about money but she gave the boy food to take home for his family, with the blessing of Mrs Cromer of course. It was unusual but it wasn't the lad's fault he was poor, why should he lose his job because of Mrs Round's bad management?

'Your responsibility, Sydney, is keeping the root store clean; also the fires in the copper and the range so you need to keep good stocks of kindling. Please keep me fully informed on stocks of coal.' Before she could finish, Sydney leapt to his feet making for the back door.

'Hey, where d'you think you're off to my lad?' She thought he was running away.

'Goin' ter fetch paraffin Mrs Dann, the fire's gone low.'

'No you're not. You stop doing such dangerous things. A teaspoon of sugar will get that fire restarted and you remember that. Paraffin is only for your oil lamps.'

'Thanks, Mrs Dann.' The boy smiled.

'Yeah, 'e's burnt 'is fingers a good few times 'e 'as,' commented Maud.

'An' singed 'is bloomin' eyebrows too,' murmured Janet under her breath.

'All right then, we will all remember to wash our hands thoroughly between jobs. It's Maud's job to make sure there's a bowl and soap over beside the sink. This will be your kettle kept full of hot water for hand washing and clean dry hand towels. Sydney, please see there's a pitcher of cold water kept filled ready to use. You too, Sydney, wash your hands like the ladies. No sense in any of us having dirty hands if we are trying to keep food and drink clean and wholesome.

'Maud you're in charge of laundering the kitchen linens. And of course you will carry on doing Mrs Cromer's room.' Maud gave a little bob and a nod of her head, Sydney touched his forelock, feeling part of the kitchen family again.

'Janet, today Lady Wellborough has ordered fish to be served so I will show you how to fillet fish. Beth and Maud, if you'd like to watch, because there will be useful lessons for you too. Now you get started with your sponge mixture

Janet, and make sure you whisk those egg whites till they'll bear the weight of an egg.'

And so Clara started as she meant to carry on. While the job lasted she would give time to staff training. She knew from experience that being shown what to do was better than getting into trouble for doing things wrong. Nobody in this kitchen knew she had only been employed in one other kitchen apart from all the years she had watched her grandmother. What she was putting into operation in this temporary post was all she had seen in Mrs Charlish's tutelage.

Tasting the freshly made stock, Clara's nose wrinkled before she remembered the chalk Downs she had seen from the train and Mrs Charlish saying that soups should never be made with hard water unless it's for green peas to preserve the colour.

'Oh dear, I must sound a right bossy boots. Never mind, there's a job to do here. No time for thoughts to wander.' She was thankful for that.

Clara was very proud of her staff when at the end of the first week Mrs Cromer complimented them all on their smartness. She even referred to them as 'ladies' just as Clara was doing. 'Caps on and not a hair out of place,' she had commented. That was more to avoid any chance of a loose hair falling into a preparation, Clara told them. She also showed her staff what Mrs Charlish had explained to her.

'Have your staff wear close fitting dresses,' she'd said, 'and a large apron wrapped and fastened tightly round to avoid the risk of catching in the fire.'

Later, when Clara brought the subject of left-over wine from the dining room being sent down to the kitchen for use in the sauces and stock pot, Mrs Cromer said Lady Wellborough always had the undrunk wine emptied into his Lordship's pisspot in the corner of the dining room to stop the maids from getting tight.

The Lamb Inn

'Postie! Postie! Postie!' The call slowly came closer down the lane.

'John, better get a half poured out,' Barney called from his seat in the sunshine outside the front door, 'Postie's got something for thee.' John was already out in the yard with a half pint pot as the post horse with his rider ambled into view.

'Thankee Maister,' said the postie as he took his drink. 'One for Missee Clara Ann.' It had been four weeks since Clara had left her grand-parents' inn. John looked at the package and angled it for Barney to see.

'Come from shipboard by the looks,' remarked Barney.

Bob the postie drained his pot and handed it back to John. 'Chirrup,' he said as he nudged his horse's flanks. The horse didn't move. Well, he hadn't finished his conversation. 'Bains't keep Her Majesty's post waiting Maister.' Bob was getting garrulous.

With a friendly pat Barney gave the horse a palmful of something juicy. Then the horse went on his way again at his own leisurely pace. Ah ha, old horse – he knew if Barney were nearby he would get a tasty morsel before moving on.

In the kitchen Annie glanced across at the package John placed on her table. 'What do you expect me to do with that John, the girl isn't here,' she said, carrying on with her pastry mixing. 'We don't know Rose's address do we?' Kneading the dough and thumping it flat with the rolling pin, she continued, 'I'm up to the village tomorra afore noon. I'll take it into the post place.' Then she gave her pastry dough two or three sharp pressure rolls before turning it and folding it in three layers. 'Better re-address it to St Leonard's. Emily'll know where the girl is now.'

Clara

Things didn't appear to be going so well for Mrs Round. Maud alone made up the nurse's sick room requirements, leaving the items of food and beverages for the nurse and her invalid on the table in the kitchen passage at agreed times. Clara only caught sight of the nurse once and thought the woman looked all in.

Over the past two weeks Clara's kitchen had been running smoothly and the staff couldn't have been more co-operative. In the sick room the nurse had a second nurse in to relieve her as she had spent night and day on duty without assistance for the two weeks.

Sadly, after a struggle lasting more than a month, Mrs Round passed away. The family were very sorry for her loss. Cook had been with them all their lives. Mrs Round originally joined the family as her ladyship's nursery maid when she herself was a babe. A hush descended on the household until the funeral was over – society demanded it even though Mrs Round had only been a servant.

The events of Clara Ann's last two months had been for her, at first, calamitous and heart-aching, then so positive and all-enveloping that she had lost all sense of time. The job she had to tackle in the kitchen, the organisation, had so overwhelmingly taken her attention that Clara had given little thought to Frank, or what was happening in her own body, let alone how the poor woman was faring whose shoes she had stepped into.

For Clara two lifetimes had gone by. Without drawing breath it seemed she was being asked to join the household as their resident cook. Clara accepted. Mrs Cromer treated Clara as a friend and although the dreadful state of the kitchen was never mentioned directly, Mrs Cromer did confess that she had never been allowed to set foot over Mrs Round's kitchen doorsill. Although it had at times been obvious that they had all suffered from the laxity therein, Lady Well-borough would not hear anything against Mrs Round.

The position was now Clara's own and the rou-tine picked up again after a sombre day, relentless in its constant need. This family followed the fash-ion of their day in being lazy risers and late eaters. However, thankfully they didn't go in for starting dinner as late as ten in the evening, as Queen

Victoria often did. Their last dinner at night was set for eight p.m. It still meant the kitchen started at five in the morning but never finished until midnight, or later when there were guests staying in the house.

So far, hopeful energy had been her fuel. Now the adrenalin was in full surge. Clara's love of cooking had been ignited by Granma Annie. Mrs Charlish had given her vision. Both had furnished her a wide knowledge of foods that blend and recipes that work. Here was her opportunity to let her imagination play its part. For she recognised that the family, much as they had enjoyed their rustic bread and cheese interlude, expected the daily sophistication as befitted their station, the more so when guests were present. Clara wondered whether there might even be a chance for her to serve Lady Wellborough's guests some of the ices Mrs Charlish had taught her. She'd have to investigate the equipment available to her.

Mrs Charlish had told her about her early days in London and how she'd had the privilege of attending Agnes Marshall's cooking school to learn about making ice desserts. Clara would relish the opportunity to make ices in her own kitchen.

Clara had almost forgotten the new life growing within her. Only in the privacy of her own bed under the blankets did she allow herself to think of Frank, to wonder where he was.

The kitchen had been in her sole charge for a week. Preparations were going well in expectation of guests arriving to stay with the family for a week of theatre visits and balls. Brighton was in full festive mode. Clara was glad to retire to the bedroom she shared with her sister; it was past midnight but Rose was still at work in her sewing room. For the past fortnight Rose had been burning the candle at both ends to complete the new set of dresses Miss Thora would be wearing at the various functions. Both girls were fully occupied with their work so Clara didn't bother her sister as she went to their bedroom. In fact she was pleased to have a few moments entirely to herself. All day she had been feeling a tightness within.

Granma Annie had advised her never to go to bed at night without first washing her feet.

'When you're on your feet all day long girl, you need to keep your feet as healthy and well as you can,' she had told Clara. It was as Clara bent to soap her feet in the bowl of warm water on the floor that she was brought up straight with a jab in her abdomen that took her breath way. Aah! She had to lean back on the chair to compose herself. With a sudden shock she was brought down to earth, realising she could no longer squash her midriff into a tight band. It must now be five months and a little flutter of movement reminded her that time was against her. No more hiding the facts.

She had sailed through so far on healthy youth. Get these next few days over, then I must take my body seriously, Clara decided.

Emily

Opening the front door at Number Five, the post

boy called out, 'Letter for yer, missus.' Emily came through from the scullery wiping her hands on her apron. 'Seen too much of you lately Alf,' she chortled.

'Yeh, you're right there Em, two letters in few weeks, folks'll start talkin'.'

'What yer got then Alf?'

'Looks like another for your Clara, overseas this one.' Alf's eyebrows rose in hopes of further information. Gossip was the price for many a cup of tea, but Emily was tight-lipped. She could see who the letter was from even though it bore no sender's written details.

'Ooh 'er,' she started, all innocent. 'What do I do with it? She's gone to 'er sister's in Brighton.'

Emily hadn't a penny in the house, but the most important thing was that she was facing a dangerous situation. She knew if Tom saw who the letter was from, he'd tear it up, and they would never hear the end of his ranting. And after all, it was her daughter's life. Better get it away from this house before her father got back.

'Can yer take it back Alf, if I give yer the right address? Please?'

Ah, the post boy knew here were some gossip, not much, but it says something's up. 'Well Em, I shouldn't but 'ere, I've got a pencil.' Licking the tip of his indelible pencil he waited, poised. 'Tell us Rose's address then.' Emily looked up into her head and slowly spoke what she remembered Rose had written some time past, and hoped she'd got it right.

'Our office in Brighton'll know the Well-borough household and they'll see Rose gets this.

Hope all goes well m'dear.'

'You're a brick Alf. Thanks.' She nearly said, 'That's a lot off my mind,' but decided against just in time.

The Willows

We never went down to the kitchen at the Wellborough house. Clara kept Joey and me up in Rose's little domain. Rose was so happy that Clara had got the job permanently.

'Mum and Dad'll be so thrilled to hear you've got yourself settled so quick, won't they Clara?'

Although she looked tired after that first month, you could see Clara was enjoying the job and she looked really blooming. Joey and I remarked so to each other.

Clara was rather quiet for a bit then she said, 'I'm pregnant, Rose.'

Well, Rose was so surprised she nearly dropped Joey an' all 'er cocoa over the bedclothes. 'Oh, my gawd Clara, what we gonna do?' Thankfully she put Joey down on her bedside chair.

'What do you mean, "we"? I mustn't involve you love.'

'What yer mean? I am involved. You're sleepin' in my bedroom gel!'

'You know what I mean.'

'Now 'old on we've got ter think this through. You've 'ad those gloves on all these days. Nobody's much seen your 'ands 'ave they?'

'No I suppose not. Why?'

'"Why", she says! Why d'yer think yer dulap dollop? Wake up gal. Nobody would have accepted an un-

109

married pregnant woman into their household. I've got a gold band ring. It's in my sewing box. I keep my own little store for sewing up here. Ah, here it is. Try it on. Go on. They already call you Mrs Dann, an' if anybody says that they saw you without it, say you take it off when yer makin' certain things.'

'Phew, you sweep me off my feet Rose.'

'Well somebody's got ter think this thing through. Yer wern't thinkin' straight when yer got it did yer? Oh I'm sorry, it was Frank wasn't it?'

'Of course Rose – now who's being a big dollop?'

Oh dear, did those two laugh. Out of nervous energy I think. But Joey and I thought there'd be ructions sooner or later.

'Oh that reminds me, your news nearly made me forget, there's a letter from somewhere overseas for you,' said Rose.

'It's from Frank.'

Rose picked Joey back up, as if hiding behind her cup of cocoa while Clara read her letter.

3

Frank's Letter

My Darling Heart

I am in total despair knowing I am responsible for bringing you such deep hurt. How can I apologise enough. Please my Clara. Please forgive me.

I am aboard ship bound for Cape Town, South

Africa and unlikely to return soon. May I hope that you will, in due time, consent to join me and become my wife? I know there are barriers to this wish I have, but please, if you can forgive me, at least please give me hope.

I will send money for your confinement. I am with you in my heart if not my bodily presence.

This has to be short note as time is at the behest of catching the post transfer to a passing homebound ship here in Biscay Bay. Mispah will live close to my heart until we are together again. I am forever yours.

My deepest love,
Frank

PS: At night I look at the stars that I know you can see, for soon I will be seeing a different sky.

Clara

'Having a baby? Well I've never heard of such a thing.' Mrs Cromer was informing her ladyship of Clara's pregnancy.

'Get rid of the woman. We can't have servants having babies. Well don't just stand there Mrs Cromer, whatever's come over you. Find another cook, an older woman this time or a man maybe. Yes, get a man.'

That was it then, nothing more to be said. Just a few short weeks in a job she loved. Clara knew it must come to an end as soon as her pregnancy was known. Although she had allowed herself

111

just a teeny bit of hope that she would be asked back. Poor Rose. Clara was very concerned that her sister might lose her job because of her own situation. Rose had been right to use the ring. They both knew it was a lie but with a letter arriving from overseas they had a back-up to their story. The two girls decided the best thing was for Clara to leave immediately and let her sister know as soon as she had found a room.

Clara was already well liked by all the kitchen staff. Janet particularly had learned such a lot from Clara in the short time she had been in the job. Hearing the gossip and knowing her ladyship's reaction, Janet Brownlow sought her mother's help, so Clara didn't have to walk the streets that day as she had expected to. Janet's parents kindly offered the use of their son Jake's bed for a few nights. Janet's father was a fisherman. He and her 18-year-old brother Jake were crew members on an old hog boat. Neither would be at home night times that week, so Clara had her box taken along to South Street where the Brownlows lived in the cottage built by Fred Brownlow's great, great grandfather in 1700.

The day after Clara told Rose of her condition was the first day she noticed how unusually tired she felt. Nevertheless she spent the long day walking the cobbled streets, lanes and twittens looking for a room. Every surface in those narrow alleys glittered with fish scales stuck to the walls and underfoot. Everything felt sticky. But the people, they were good people. It wasn't difficult to find a room. Everybody was in need of extra income. Nobody minded shoving over to share the foot of their bed, that was easy to find. But Clara had to find a room of her own. That proved far more difficult. She enquired in the little cook shops and stopped to ask groups of women talking on street corners.

Mrs Brownlow kindly included Clara in their family meal which they ate middle morning after the two men came back from their night's fishing having sold their catch on the beach. Fish was their daily fare, plenty of it, fried in a pan over an open fire. The Brownlows didn't possess an oven of any kind. Whatever it was, Clara was glad of the meal and fish was good for a growing baby, she thought.

For the rest of the day Jake took to his bed. No bedding was changed. They didn't have sheets, the family couldn't afford them. Clara had taken her own pillowslip which she was careful that Mrs Brownlow did not see. She didn't want the woman to feel belittled, because she had been so kind to Clara. For long hours each day well into the evenings Clara had no resting place – nowhere to lay her head, just when an expectant mum needed the odd rest.

At least it was good weather. It hadn't rained all that week while she walked through the courts and alleyways in Brighton, beyond South Street from West Street to East Street and North Street, then east up into Kemp Town behind the big houses along the seafront, in and out of this mews and that coach yard. It seemed every room was full of human occupation; single men lodging with families was a norm and quite acceptable but not single unrelated young women. The townspeople were so different from the country dwellers, bluff and hearty but deeply suspicious. Of course working the long hours in the Wellborough kitchen she'd had no time to get to know anybody or even the town outside that kitchen. On she went through all the narrow streets around the railway station. Peel Street, York Hill across into Hove and the roads along the back of the Western Road into Church Street even as far as Hove Street, then back among the stable yards behind Brunswick and the meat market towards West Street again.

Sitting down on the edge of one of the graves in St Nicholas' churchyard late one afternoon she looked down at her shoes, thinking how they wouldn't be taking her very much further. She suddenly felt she was being watched. A little old lady obviously with poor eyesight was peering at her. Clara jumped in surprise.

'Whoops. Oh dear, did I give you a start? Don't mind me,' came a tiny, high, piping voice. Clara had been so far away in thought she was startled, but such a sweet little old thing stood in front of her – a rosy weatherbeaten face, fine white hair with a wee curl on top and a pair of men's old work boots on her feet. No laces. She had some washing hanging over her arm and was gesturing towards her back garden gate in a low flint wall. Clara hadn't realised how close she was to the backs of a row of cottages.

'You look all in luvvie, could you do with a cuppa tay dear?' Her words were so like Granma Annie's, Clara nearly cried.

'Thank you, I would.'

'Come down then dearie.' It was quite a steep

bank down to the back gate so the lady said, 'Go round the path and down to the front, number two in the row.'

In the low-ceilinged back kitchen an ancient white-haired man sat in a battered armchair smoking a churchwarden, a high-crown bowler hat on the table beside his elbow.

'Tek no notice of my 'usband luv, 'e can't 'ear yer or see yer. Sit ye down 'ere, I'll move me sewing basket. Go on, get off Tab, young lady needs your chair, move yersel.'

'Oh shame, don't disturb her.' Clara stroked the big tabby cat, which mewed its displeasure and slunk slowly out into the yard.

'Now don't you go layin' in my washin' basket, get on with yer!' The cat received a friendly pat on the back as it jumped up on the wall. Sitting in the sun it stared back down into the yard with a 'don't care' look.

Clara sat down on the cat-warmed floral cushion. She thought she had never enjoyed a cup of tea so much as she did that afternoon. As the two women talked, Mrs Luckins kindly folded her husband's hand into the handle of his tea mug, giving him a loving pat on the cheek, a bit like she'd patted the cat really, but this time she was thanked with a sightless smile.

Mr Luckins had been a fisherman all his life. The fishing families were a great big clan, she told Clara. All knew each other. They knew the Brownlows well – all related in some way or another. Yes, she and Mr Luckins had two boys. Neither had wanted to be fishermen. Their eldest, Ben, had joined the Sussex Regiment; they hadn't seen him for some years. Didn't know where he was now. Their younger son he was married, she told Clara, lived over Newhaven. He was a ferryman. They had a daughter too. She was in service and worked for Thomas Stanford at his manor on the road to 'Lunnon'.

When Rose and Clara had had their discussion about her condition and Rose had produced the ring, Clara had told Rose that the one thing she was absolutely determined not to do was allow her child to be labelled a bastard. Even if it took some lies and deceit on her part she was determined. Rose had agreed.

So kind Mrs Luckins, like the Brownlows, heard that Clara's husband Frank had unexpectedly been sent to South Africa on business and she had decided to move to Brighton where she found work as a cook before she realised she was pregnant and – as they all would expect – got flung out. That's what employers were like. No one in the aristocracy wanted to get tangled up with servants' lives.

Clara told Mrs Luckins about the Brownlows' kindness and how she had been searching for a room to herself – somewhere where she could have her baby. Mrs Luckins listened as she slowly went about her ironing. While she had been telling Clara about her family, the irons had overheated on the back of the range. As she waited a few moments to test the temperature with her spit before rubbing her block of beeswax onto the flat iron, the atmosphere in the kitchen was filled with steam and the smell of honey. A cool breeze wafted through the white lacy half-curtain at the kitchen window. Old Mrs Luckins carried on her ironing, watching Clara as her voice gradually slowed and the young woman leaned back into sleep. Smiling to herself Mrs Luckins quietly finished her ironing and took the cups out into the scullery to wash up.

As she drifted off, Clara noticed the table leg beside her chair was almost worn through to a stick that would barely light a fire. Although this was an odd sight she had sunk too deep in a haze to question why. It was the last thing she saw as she fell asleep. When her eyes opened again she saw Mrs Luckins sitting opposite her husband on the other side of the range mending a sock on a darning mushroom.

'Oh I do apologise Mrs Luckins, so rude of me.'

'You look a lot better for your little snooze dear, I'm so pleased.'

'My goodness the light's fading into evening. I'd better be going. I don't want to walk down through the town when it's dark.'

'Yes lovely, you go. Will you drop in tomorrow? I've got something you might like. Will you do that?'

Clara did go back the next morning. On her way she picked a little bunch of tiny flowers growing wild on the bank against the flint wall surrounding St Nicholas' church.

Mrs Luckins had a surprise for Clara. 'Dad an' I sleep downstairs in the front parlour. 'E can't get upstairs any more see. The two upstairs rooms don't get used. We've had a little chat an' we're both agreed that if they would suit you, why, you can 'ave 'em.'

Clara was astonished and elated all at once at the generous offer. The first thing that came into her head was quite unexpected. Ordinary people can be extraordinarily kind. Grandfather had told her that.

'Oh could I Mrs Luckins? That would be such a help.' And she flung her arms round the old lady, not thinking what a tiny birdlike creature she actually was and nearly knocking her over in her enthusiasm.

'Well you 'aven't sin them rooms yet, go up an 'ave a look, see if they'd suit.'

'I know they will. Oh thank you so much.'

Mr Luckins could feel the atmosphere, his smile showed it. But then he too had a surprise when he felt a warm kiss planted on his cheek.

'I'll 'ave another one of those Missy please,' the old man said with a grin.

'Oh cheeky ol' devil,' chirruped Mrs Luckins.

'My Rose will be so relieved. I must go and tell her the news.'

Clara had been very cautious with the little money she had earned and what her grandparents had given her. She calculated that she could pay for a room and, with care, see herself through until after the birth. Meanwhile she had a few weeks to work, but what could she do? Who would give her a job? During the week of searching for a room she'd had little time for thought about jobs.

As she left the Luckins' cottage in Regent Row to go down to the Steine to tell her sister the good news she passed a tea shop, which earlier in the week had attracted her with the sweet smells

118

coming from its kitchens at the back. It wasn't a premises Clara could approach through the front door, although she did go out of her way to take a look and was glad she did. The tea shop was closed but a notice on the window said they were in need of a patisserie cook.

Well, there it was then. But she wasn't a pâtissière. 'Who says?' she thought. She'd got Mrs Charlish's 'Character'. On her way back from telling Rose she'd fetch her bags with her Character and try her luck.

After giving Clara a great hug, Rose handed her a sealed envelope.

'What's this Rose?'

'Mrs Cromer brought it over this morning. Seems Lady Wellborough felt she couldn't let you go without showing her thanks for all the work you did when Mrs Round was so ill.'

'Did she say what was in it?'

'Your "Character" luv. That's what's in it.'

'Well, I've already been paid up. Shall I open it or has it got to be left unopened for the next employer?'

'I think you can trust Mrs Cromer that it will be complimentary luv.'

'Only I've got something in mind. Thanks, hope this luck keeps going. Cross yer fingers for me gal. I'll try to drop in later.'

'Bye luvvie, I'll do cross stitch all over everything till yer come back!'

With little time and tight funds, on her way back up to the Luckins' Clara bought eight ounces of flour, a screw each of bicarb and cream of tartar, two ounces of butter and an egg at the dairy where they gave her a gill of sour milk. Then she headed off, hoping that Mrs Luckins had got the fire in the range lit that morning. As she passed by she saw the notice was still in the tea shop window and smoke was coming from the chimney of number two.

Clara told Mrs Luckins what she'd seen and asked permission to bake some scones all in one breath. Mrs Luckins began to laugh till tears ran down her cheeks.

'My luvverly girl, it's so nice to have life around the house again. You use what you want. I'll get that fire a goin' well. You'll need a quick fire for scones.' She even sounded like her own Mrs Charlish. 'Won't you want a bit of fruit in those, love, and some sugar?'

'Oh, no!' With all her planning, and the chaps in the dairy joshing her they wanted a scone for their tea, Clara had forgotten the fruit and sugar.

'Don't you worry, Bibby next door owes me a cup a sugar an' I'll see if she's got some dried fruit left over from Christmas. She's a bit of a cake maker 'erself, loves doin' cakes for when 'er grandchildren come in.'

So, before the scones were even baked, women along the row were craning their necks out of their front doors and tweaking back the nets in anticipation of the outcome.

With the scones set out prettily on a lace plate cover and with a crisp white cloth overall supplied by Mrs Luckins, Clara, neat and tidy in hat and gloves and well-polished shoes, walked carefully round to the back door of the tea shop kitchen. Voices in the kitchen were a little raised.

'I shall have to give you a test Mrs Bradstock.'

'Can't you take my word from my "Characters" Madam?'

'No, I want to see your baking. Come back in the morning will you?'

'Oh well,' and a large lady in widow's weeds, small black veil and all-enveloping shawl swept past Clara without noticing she was there. Giving the owner a few moments to settle from the previous interview, Clara tapped on the back door.

The tea shop was still closed. At the kitchen table Clara stood while two ladies dressed all in black with high collars ruffle-edged with white lace, cut the scones, buttered one, added cream to another and strawberry jam with the butter and cream to yet another. They began to nibble. Clara might as well not have been there. Tea was made. They began to drink. Silence reigned except for the sound of munching. Delicate lace-edged hankies touched lips. Still nothing was said.

A soft padding sound descended the narrow boxed-in staircase between the shop and the kitchen. The door at the foot of the stairs opened to reveal a cat's face; the animal walked across to the table, its tail pointing straight up like a ship's mast. One of the ladies crumbled a piece of scone onto a tea plate, added cream and put it down on the floor in front of the cat. The cat ate – ate it all.

'I think you have the job Mrs Dann, but how long would we have your services for?'

'I live very close by, madam. I will be indisposed for a short while in about six weeks' time.'

'Our lady guests are very particular. They like rich cakes, beautifully decorated cakes. We can't

121

open unless we have cakes fresh every day.'

'Lally, we need to open again tomorrow. Mrs Dann will do very well and especially if Lady Wellborough thinks so highly of this young woman. Besides a cook from Lady Wellborough's establishment will be an asset to our tea room. Lally, are you listening to me?'

'Yes, Toddy is in agreement.'

'Oh thank goodness for that. Toddy agrees.'

'Can you start right away Mrs Dann? Oh yes, payment – yes. I wonder, what does Toddy have to say about wages?'

'If I may just go back and change, I'll start straight away.'

By the time Clara got back to Regent Row there was a crowd of women standing together near the open door of number two. Her smile told them all they needed to know. Delighted just to be involved by neighbourliness, they waved as they walked back to their doors, calling, 'Good luck girl, good luck luvvy.'

Clara had not even had time to move in. Mrs Luckins had found some old stone hot water bottles, and a brick that she had put by the range, so before Clara went off back to the kitchen Mrs Luckins had filled the hot water bottles for Clara to take upstairs and leave in her bed under the blankets with her own sheets and pillow cases, ready to make the bed when she got back. She couldn't expect the old lady to climb the stairs.

The Misses Crimmins, Lally and Maud, had got the fires in their big double-oven range going well by the time Clara arrived. Their store cupboards were full so Clara baked for the next six hours. The two sisters were so thrilled they even opened for afternoon teas.

'Leave that apron and cap here Mrs Dann, we'll have them washed and ready for you in the morning. Toddy is very pleased with your day's work.'

'Goodnight,' they chorused together. Oh dear what a carry on. So lighthearted and friendly.

When Clara got back, it was but a few hundred yards up the hill to Regent Row, she couldn't believe her eyes. The neighbours had taken the box that Jake Brownlow had delivered, upstairs and the women had made her bed. Clara felt overwhelmed. What was it she had thought earlier that week? Town people were all bluff and suspicious. Get to know them and you find something special.

By the time Grandfather Luckins had done his shuffle along to the Lathe Cleavers Arms that evening and sung a few songs with his old friends, the Wheelers and their concertina, he had also lined up a laying-in woman ready for Clara's confinement.

Now, to pay her way, she aimed to work for as long as she was able. For the next six weeks if at all possible.

4

Clara

Wrapped in a voluminous dark-coloured overall and apron, Mrs Turk was in charge. 'Now breathe shallow, like me. Listen dearie, shallow, shallow, good, lay back.'

Clara felt she had been in the little front bedroom in the Luckins' cottage forever, although she had only taken her last batch of cakes from the oven at the tea shop less than three hours since. That was all behind her now. She was hot with a different purpose, made the more so by the fire built up to keep the collection of steaming kettles in readiness.

'Push – now push, push, push. That's enough.' Mrs Turk pressed the flat of her hand on Clara's thigh to remind her patient this meant gentle breathing. The old midwife had a little cone of cardboard that she placed on Clara's stomach then put her ear to the point end. Mrs Turk had strangely large ears.

'Still strong but he's a lazy little bundle this one. Slow down for a moment more dearie.'

'My mother always pulled against a towel rolled up like a rope round the end of the iron bedstead, Mrs Turk.'

'Well there's gonna be none o' that for my mothers, missus; puts too much strain on your

124

muscles. And it causes more pain. Right, slowly now. Here we go. Slowly does it, breathe shallow, breathe shallow. That's it. Now push push push. Lovely, here we are, gently now.'

A great wail announced the baby's arrival.

'You've got a boy Mrs Dann. My, he's a lovely one, not too big.'

Clara cradled the little one in her arms for a few moments before Mrs Turk ordered her to give another push. 'There we are. Now let's just put him to your breast and we can clean you up.'

'So soon?' Clara asked.

'Yes, the little chap will stimulate your system to clear away all that ol' unwanted tissue. That helps me clean you up thoroughly well. What you gonna call 'im then luv?'

'Frankie.' Clara was quite clear. 'After his father.'

'That's lovely.' Mrs Turk bustled about the room. 'We'll give baby a lovely wash later. Still I 'spect you've 'ad plenty of experience 'elpin' your ma with all those brothers an' sisters you've got?'

'Yes, this'll be the thirteenth baby bottom I've washed.'

'I'm sure I've washed 'alf the bottoms livin' in Brighton dear.' Mrs Turk winked. 'Now before I fetches yer up a cup o' tea gal let's get yer into good clean sheets and pad yer up nice 'n' comfy.' Mrs Turk chatted away to Clara as she tidied the bed and the room, whisking away all the soiled paraphernalia and shoving it into a laundry bag. Taking off her wrap-around apron she said, 'We'll get this ol' mucky overall off, don't want ter frighten the men with the sight o' blood do we. No, I won't have no man in my childbirth room.

Mothers get to scratchin' and bitin' in their birth pangs when men's around. Although I dare say their men deserves it,' she said over her shoulder as she opened the window to let the cool air flow in.

On the wind, women's voices called up from out in the street, 'What she got Mrs T?'

'Aw luvver duck! 'Tis always the same along the row. Shall I tell 'em dear?'

'Yes, why not, they've all been such nice neighbours.'

'It's a boy!'

There was a chorus from out in the row, 'Good luck Clara. Good luck girl.'

Mrs Luckins sent up a cup of tea and called up the stairs, 'Give 'im a kiss for us, sweetheart.'

Rose couldn't get away until the evening but came rushing into the bedroom, all shrills and laughter and flowers. 'You won't believe this Clara, Miss Thora gave me these to bring yer and said Lady W wishes yer luck. I'll have ter go and tell 'em all. Oh isn't 'e luvly Clara, are yer calling 'im Frank?' she whispered.

'I thought Frankie.'

'That's nice. Have yer written to 'im yet Clara?'

'No Rose.'

'Well? Are yer going to then?'

'I thought I'd leave it 'til after, I'll do it while I'm up here on my own. Give me time to think it through.'

'Do yer think yer might go out to 'im then?'

Clara had already had four letters from Frank. Gran and Grandfather Pilbeam had sent them on to Rose's address in Brighton. Frank had been sensitive enough to write to 'Mrs C. A. Dann' and in each letter had urged her to follow him out to the Cape.

'No Rose. I don't want that life. He said he'd be moving around the country for some years yet. I don't want that.'

Each seemed lost in their thoughts for a while until Clara spoke. 'You know what Rose? When this little one was put into my arms I saw Frank. So peaceful, his little face just looked, well, satisfied. I just lay there looking at him, just looking. He opened his big beautiful eyes for a moment and looked at me, don't suppose he focused. Well, I was so surprised, don't know why, I felt Frank was there in the room with me. I had him in my arms. I didn't need to travel half way round the world. There he was.

'All the while Mrs Turk had been chatting away. Tidying this and cleaning that. I would have been the same if it were my kitchen. Keep everything clean and tidy as you work sort of thing. We got on like a house on fire. She was lovely. I was lucky to have found Mrs Turk.'

Clara recovered in a much shorter time than current fashion recommended. She was up and around the room on the second day. The older neighbours calling in were shocked to see her out of bed and downstairs with the baby to show the Luckins. Clara had seen her own mother up and about the very next day after each birth. She'd had to get a move on. Granny Ann wasn't always available to help out at St Leonards.

The younger women in the row told Clara that

Old Mrs Turk had never lost a mother. Scrupulously clean woman, hands and nails. They said she never attended any other ailment or performed a laying out. That's what Clara had heard when she had first been introduced to Mrs Turk and she was relieved because it was something her own grandmother had told the family. 'Keep ole quack away from childbed if you can, he could have just been to a death bed. Two don't mix.'

Frankie was a healthy sturdy baby. Rose was so excited that she immediately wrote a note home to her mother using a sealed envelope. Usually everybody sent cards. Nobody in the family other than Rose had known the truth, not even their mother. But when Emily read Rose's letter she was not surprised at its news.

Rose gave a gentle tap on the bedroom door so as not to wake Clara or baby Frankie from their afternoon nap.

'Come in love, it's all right, just giving him a feed.'

'I've brought a visitor for you Clara.'

Clara looked a bit worried, mouthing to her sister 'Who is it?' The door pushed open wider revealing Emily. 'Oh Mum! Rose you never?'

'Come on now love. You couldn't keep yer Ma completely outta yer life forever.' Emily enveloped Clara and the baby.

'Oh my lovely girl, 'ow are yer?' Both had tears of sadness and joy.

'I'm really well Mum.'

Rose came and sat on the end of the bed holding Emily's youngest.

128

'Where's all the littluns?' asked Clara, peering round behind her mother.

'Oh, I 'avent got them all 'ere. Dor's got 'em for the day. Gawd luv 'er, she's a good'n is our Dor. Let's 'ave a cuddle of 'im then sweetheart; he's a lovely baby, my first grandchild!'

As Emily nestled him into her neck he wriggled his head and started sucking at her chin. 'Look at that, he can smell my baby's milk on me! 'E's a strong little chap.' Looking into his face Emily smiled at Clara and said, 'An' 'e's the spit of 'is Dad.'

'Ma – shush.'

'S'all right Clara, Mum knows.'

'Course I do. 'Ad me doubts when you went orf so quick. An' no, I 'aven't told yer Gran and Granfer, it would 'urt them, and after all, yer Gran 'as spoke up for us against Lizzie and Lottie. We'll keep that to ourselves for the time being. But I don't know how long I can keep it from yer father, Clara. So are yer goin' out there to 'im then?'

'No Mum. I'm not.'

'How yer gonna get the birth certificate then?'

Rose cut in directly. 'We've got that all sorted out Mum. Don't you worry about that.'

'Yer do know it's got ter be the father who registers the birth don't cher? If you go on yer own you'll get 'im labelled Bastard.'

'That's what I'm determined to avoid Mum.'

'I know, Rose told me.'

'And it's all sorted out Ma.' Rose said again.

'What do you intend to do for a livin' then gal?'

'I'm going back to the teashop down the road, that little job'll just see us through. An' I can keep these two rooms on while I'm there.'

'An' 'ow yer gonna do that with the youngun in yer arms?'

'Oh, Mum, 'ave you ever seen an Indian woman with that, what's it called Clara?'

'Papoose.'

'That's it, papoose, on her back? There's Clara walkin' round with baby in a sling on her back.'

'What d'yer mean, you've already been up 'n' out gal?'

'Yes of course I have.'

'But you've only given birth three days ago.'

'Mum, it's the best way to keep the body going, and anyway, haven't I seen you up straight after you've given birth?'

'Yes, but that's different. I've 'ad a 'usband around the house, an' I aren't goin' out before ten days.'

'Well I've got to get back to baking cakes and I must have him on my back out of harm's way. We'll be all right you'll see.'

Emily gave Clara a wry smile. She'd no doubt her daughter's strong will would see her through.

Mother and daughters stayed together for the rest of the afternoon. They hadn't spent time together like that since the girls were children.

'You were lucky to find this place Clara. Mr and Mrs Luckins really are a dear old couple an' they think the world of you love.'

'They are all such friendly people along the row, all looking out for each other,' Clara told her mother.

Emily walked through into the back room and half turned saying, 'I can see why you've got your

130

bed in the front; anybody walking across the old church yard can look straight in this back window.'

'Yes, and it does have a fireplace above the Luckins' kitchen range so I can get a nice fire going to keep a kettle on the boil and do a bit of dinner.'

'Just right for her isn't it Ma?' Rose said. 'So you won't need to worry about her.'

'Gran says she's put aside a few items for you Clara. I'll tell her she can put them on the carrier to bring over to Brighton.'

'She's having a clear out then Mum?'

'Maybe.' That was a short answer for Emily and it made Clara look up.

'Everything all right at the Lamb, Mum?'

'Hmm. Probably Lottie's getting them to clear the place up a bit. Now you and Rose have got work over here they don't expect to see so much of our children visiting every holiday.'

'Aunt Lizzie's bin tellin' Gran and Granfer that for years,' commented Rose, then she offered, 'Better 'ave ter start sending the kiddies over to us for their holidays.'

'Oh yes, you'd love that I'm sure,' Emily laughed.

'No, seriously I mean it Ma. I was keepin' this ter tell you Clara. Tony an' I've bin thinking of getting married.'

'Oh Rose, you—'

'No, I know I haven't said anything before, not after you got so roughly pushed out by Lady W. We thought if that's the way they treat servants they'd be bound to want us out if we said we were

131

gettin' married. So Tony, he's found a lovely place up St James Street above Dorset Gardens. Nice gardens out front. We can 'ave some vegetables.'

'What does Dad say then Mum?' Clara asked.

'Oh 'e says they're all going an' leavin' us soon. Tell Rose she might as well take 'er chance for happiness as it's turned up.'

'Oh, good. I'm so pleased for you Rose. An' Tony seems a nice chap, but you know I hardly remember him.'

'I'm not surprised gal. You did nothing but work in that kitchen at Lady W's and then slept like a log on that little truckle bed in my bedroom. Don't remember 'ardly seein' yer meself.'

'Only when we sat in bed chattin' and only if I could keep my eyes open,' Clara said.

'So you see Mum, Jack and Tom could bring Fanny, Harry an' Nancy.'

'They're big lads now Rose. I don't know if they'd want to be saddled with three little ones.'

'Oh Ma, didn't Rose and I look after them? Heavens, when I think of all the miles I've walked with those boys. You just tell them they've got to give a little. You know, I'm sure Jack will. He's a thoughtful lad.'

'Yes, you're right there, an' 'es bin like 'is Dad's extra arm. Aw I shouldn't say that. No, but it's time, he's bin a helpful boy, always noticed how to chip in and take a hold of something when 'e sees his dad can't manage.'

'I expect he just gets it right afore Dad notices – then it doesn't really look as he's havin' ter do it for 'is dad.'

'Oh dear, your dad 'as always been so

132

independent and over sensitive. He makes it so difficult for folks who try to lend 'im an' 'and. Well I best be getting off up the station now gals, or I could call you my "gorrals", like yer Gran calls 'er chickens.'

They all laughed at the memory of dear Granma Ann calling her hens and cockerel in from the orchard.

'I'll just 'ave a little chat with Mr and Mrs Luckins on my way out. You a-comin' up the station with me Rose?'

'Yes, I'll follow yer down Ma.'

'Bye then my lovely girl. Look after that babe o' yours.'

'Bye Mum, and thanks for coming.'

Emily went carefully down the narrow flight of wooden stairs. She was a fairly weighty woman after all her pregnancies.

'So what's all this about "we've got it all sorted out" Rose? The birth certificate I mean.'

'Oh that. Tony an' I'll do it for yer. Don't worry.'

'You be careful you two.'

'It's all right. I'll walk up ter station with Ma. When I get back we'll have a cuppa an' I'll tell you more. Bye now.'

'I don't know how to thank you for all you've done for me, Rose luv.'

'Don't 'ave ter dear – you've looked after me when I was a little 'un. Yer know, Ma is really worried about you Clara, don' cher really want to get married? Ma said it would be sensible to take up Frank's offer.'

'Of course I'm worried about the future.'

'Was it just a passing pash for him then?'

'No Rose, I really do love him but I don't ache for him anymore. I don't want that life, moving from place to place, no sooner settling than up sticks and moving on again among mining men and dust. No thank you.'

Mispah

Clara was right. He'd really got into the life. First time he'd enjoyed being among working men, tough men, hard as nails. It hadn't taken long before he became one of them, just revelled in the real and urgent thrill of riding miles across wide open country, experiencing the vast great plains of swaying grasses topping a mountain plateau and sitting motionless in the saddle, gazing at the land for miles into the heat-seared horizon. Everything was so enormous. England became like a miniature landscape in his memory.

As soon as he got to the Cape, Frank telegraphed to his father. By letter they had agreed a code of communication and this he used all the years thereafter. It was the only way father and son made contact. Frank wrote a short note to his mother each Christmas, never more. He did keep in regular touch with his sister Josephine by letter. Jo was married to a Mr John Compton a year after Frank left England.

I think Frank's severance from his parents and journey to the Cape released him completely. He didn't forget Clara, but he soon became one of the blokes, plunging himself into the mining life and business. Rugby football became one of his great enjoyments; all rough dust, red sand in every orifice, rushing, rolling, grabbing and smashing shoulder into shoulder. Their game was hard and fast, sometimes winning, always aiming to win, at times losing. Frank merged fully into his new existence. He met and became friends with Cecil Rhodes, good friends. He was Rhodes' aide in setting up many of the rugby events and organised visiting teams out from Britain. No, as far as I could see, Frank didn't ache deeply for Clara either at that time. There were few women there. All the clubs were for men, nothing feminine around their lives.

Men love their mothers but they don't want them around their male lives. If he'd had a wife and child along with him it would have been like a wedge between his mining work and the rough relaxing hours playing rugby, sparring and heavy drinking nights, shouting with laughter. Clara was right, that life wasn't for her.

Frank still wrote regularly; after all, it filled those little gaps when contemplation had its moments. Writing to Clara was like talking to her of his love, and as he wrote he could imagine them together caressing each other and making love. In his imagination they always remained the same age. That seemed enough. He didn't want any other woman.

In his first letter after we landed in Cape Town, he described the shallow sweep of the bay and the many dolphins escorting his ship into harbour. Frank wished Clara had been there to share with him the sight of the breakers along the shore and the sparkling white buildings at the base of Table Mountain. They call it the Cape of Good Hope, he told her, and it feels just like it.

Frank couldn't stay in Cape Town too long, he had to get moving, but he did write about the variety of people of many colours and languages, the sailors and the bars, with the movements of people on their way elsewhere by horse and the long spans of oxen pulling wagonloads of goods up country. He wrote about his life, the dry dusty workings, the mining and the diamonds in the rough. He didn't want to bore her, so described the huge open spaces and environment filled with luscious plants, their shapes and rich colours – like the wide expanse of shimmering bright orange he thought was a great golden lake but discovered was a vast sweep of marigolds flashed with tall white-throated lilies. 'I wish you could see it all with me Clara.' In those early letters he recorded the hundreds of miles he travelled, seeing wild animals in herds of many thousands.

He knew her well enough to know she would be interested in the sights of the country. He described the huge sweeping weather patterns, the shining hot times, the violent dry storms loud and echoing among the mountains or the view of storms moving far away across the plains. He gave her a word picture of the ox-wagon trains and the dogged determination of the traders travelling for miles in their covered wagons to the most remote places. Frank got to know and understand the tribal sensitivities of the folk who lived nomadic lives, taking their daily sustenance from the land. He told her what the southern night sky was like. And, of course, he sent money when he could.

Frank looked forward to her letters, sometimes hoping almost ravenously for the landmarks she described in Frankie's progress. He was proud he had fathered a son. I went with him everywhere in the watch pocket of his waistcoat. He never carried a watch. He had the sun and the stars. That was enough for him in those days.

Clara

As Clara read Frank's letters she could see him riding high on a great bay horse, booted to the knee, strong jodhpur breeches, light, loose, open-neck shirt, sleeves rolled back and a wide-brimmed bush hat shading his eyes.

In one letter he told her he'd grown a beard and it had become very ginger. In another letter he described how his horse gave early warning of the presence of lion and how he watched, still, unmoving for a long period – the wind on him so the lion didn't pick up his presence. He did tell her he carried a rifle just to reassure her of his safety, but as he said, it was the very last action he wanted to take.

Clara left most of the money Frank sent in a bank account for their son. Frank had anticipated this and in one of his letters asked her to promise she would never allow real difficulties to overcome her and the boy when the money was in the account for them both.

When Frankie was eight days old, Clara tied him onto her back in the neat sling she had made, and went back to work for the Misses Crimmins at the Blue Rooms tea shop six days a week, starting at eight thirty in the morning until six in the evening.

The kitchen was very compact and had to provide for the comings and goings of tea making and its crockery used by the tea maker Miss Lally Crimmins who was silently assisted by Toddy from the bottom stair. She told him all the time what she was doing, but he never answered. Clara's preparation table took centre position and beneath it were racks and shelves holding cooling trays, tins and pans. A large cooking range took up one wall with shelves above for drying pots and pans, while out back a cool larder housed the perishable items like eggs, milk, cream and cheese. Next door was a scullery with a stone sink where the china and cooking pans were washed. Opposite that, away from the heat of the range and damp of the scullery, was the door to a deep dry stores cupboard where flour, sugars and dried fruits that were turned daily into fruit cakes were stored on the shelves in tin boxes ready for those Christmas orders. Lastly the dresser cupboards in the kitchen and the shelves above held all the serving china. Everything was well ordered.

The tea shop opened six days a week from ten until five thirty, catering for a select group of lady clients who liked to meet their friends while out shopping – a place where women could converse without the restrictions of men's presence.

A small bell on a high curved spring above the door tinkled most prettily as customers entered, causing the waitress to stop whatever she was doing. Turning towards each customer she'd give a little smile, a curtsey, and carry on serving. Miss Maud Crimmins would then come forward to guide the customer across to a selected table, making sure of their comfort and leaving them to choose and decide their requirements. Customers' umbrellas or sunshades would be stowed near the table. Gloves might be drawn off, buttons delicately unhooked first of course, each glove smoothed and laid in or on the customer's reticule. Hats were never removed. As more ladies arrived, those already in occupation of their seats looked up to see who was being heralded by the ting-tinkling bell. Each lady would smile and give a slight nod but only if they approved of the newcomer. The whole room began to appear like a beautiful garden full of flowers nodding in a breeze. In those years the fashion for large hats covered in flowers, fruits and often birds or their feathers made the places where women gathered, look so gay.

The Blue Rooms tea shop was at the Clock Tower, the centre of a growing spread of fashionable shops. Facing directly onto the shopping thoroughfare the window comprised three full-length panes of glass with a fourth of curved glass leading round into the entrance, a half-glazed door. The head of each glass pane, including the door, had an elegant carved wooden arch. The woodwork frontage was painted in blue because the shop was called the Blue Rooms.

Behind the window there was a space a few feet from the pavement containing a display of a fine china to serve two, accompanied by two lace napkins, silver teaspoons, tea knives and cake forks all arranged on a tray covered with a tray cloth. Beside this place setting stood a three-tiered cake stand showing a selection of savoury and sweet dainties all made of sensitively painted plaster. Opposite the cake stand, clipped into a silver holder, stood a neat hand-written bill of fare. The appearance was of a calm, select salon.

On very sunny days a parchment-coloured scallop-edged sunshade would be drawn out from above the shop window. It had a blue teapot printed on its centre. On hot days a blind of similar-coloured canvas was hooked up on the front half covering the window to keep the heat off the tables near the window. Behind the window display at about shoulder height on a brass rail hung lace curtains with an extra lacy frill at the hem. These shielded the tea takers from the gaze of passing eyes.

Inside the shop the wood-panelled walls were painted in a slightly hazy greenish blue with a decoration of twining flowers and hanging wisteria blossoms in arches and swags. Hand painted by Miss Lally Crimmins, this decor looked as fresh as when she finished what she described as the love of her life, back in the days of her youth.

Many small round tables for two or four, surrounded by neatly cushioned chairs, stood ready for service covered with sparkling white lace-edged cloths. At its centre each table had a replica of the hand-written bill of fare from the window, all scribed by Miss Lally. Along the back wall the counter displayed an array of high glass domes covering a wide variety of Clara's cakes and pastries.

There was no vulgar, shiny, ringing cash register, instead a heavy wooden block with circular bowls hollowed out for coins resided, out of sight, behind the counter where the Misses Crimmins gave change against the notes of reckoning brought from the customers' tables by the waitress.

Monday and Saturday were rich fruitcake days.

Tuesdays and Wednesdays offered fresh cream cakes, choux buns and fruit pastries. Friday had everything plus Battenbergs and meringues, custard tarts, chocolate cake and lemon cake. The fruitcakes containing alcohol were made most days for store and sold at Christmas. Scones and rock buns were available every day. The savouries were mostly made for luncheon and described on the bill of fare as 'triangles of toasted cheese' or a 'fluffy little concoction of egg-soaked toast fried in a knob of butter', and a third 'rosettes of devilled kidneys on toast'.

The elderly Misses Crimmins' parents had originally opened the tea rooms for men preferring a hot drink and to read the papers, but when more high-class ladies' shops opened, the clientele dictated a change of decor and that's when Lally Crimmins painted the walls. It was Lally who owned Toddy the cat who was in charge of mousing.

Miss Maud Crimmins was out front serving the cakes and taking the receipts, helped by one waitress, a slim, sprightly, white-haired lady with a jolly smiling face who made all their ladies feel welcome and at home. She was Edna who had been Maud's best friend for many years. Finally Lally and Maud's cousin Hilda, a lady with one leg shorter than the other, washed up in the scullery and generally helped Clara with preparation and clearing.

They were a happy group of five women. Four older unmarried ladies, three wearing black dresses, white pinnies and frilly white cotton caps, except Hilda who wore a heavy sacking apron, and

141

one young mother dressed in a pale blue overall, white cap and apron with an extra – a baby on her back. With the advent of baby Frankie a certain Mr Toddy rather had his nose put out of joint at times.

Clara enjoyed the bustle and warmth of the tea rooms and kitchen. The three ladies enjoyed their cuddles with baby Frankie, well, it gave the little chap a rest from being on his mummy's back. One lady never offered to hold him, for she had lost her only chance of a family when her baby died in a difficult birth and she couldn't bear to repeat what it felt like all those years ago, to have wanted to love but lost. Instead she gave her bright chirpy words to her regulars at their tables, making all her days happy to see others enjoying their lives.

To Clara it was bad enough to lose a lover, but to lose a baby as well would have been bereavement to break your heart. Clara took silent counsel from another's extreme experience. It made a meaningful impression on her at that juncture in her life. There wasn't much time for thoughts of affairs of the heart. Quietness and correctness in front of the customers, perfect service at all times, was their aim while in the kitchen and scullery, although the quiet banter and laughs from all five women would have astonished the tea-drinking, cake-tasting ladies out front.

It was Maud who kept the ship tight and sailing smooth. Maud checked in and paid for the comestibles and stores. Maud made sure the premises and everything therein was kept pristine. Everybody did their part but Maud gave the final nod of approval. That also included the clients' behaviour. If a lady proved not to be a lady and laughed far too loudly she'd soon get a withering look from behind the counter. And Maud was known to throw people out if she felt the misdemeanour called for such a drastic step. She didn't actually physically throw anybody out, or even ask a lady to go. She simply wouldn't serve them. On one occasion a lady made an adverse comment for all to hear, about how much she disliked one of Clara's cakes. Maud immediately walked across and without a word or a look cleared away the woman's tea plate, cutlery, cup and saucer and tea napkin, then went back to the table with the crumb brush and tray, swept the table clean in front of the particular woman at that table, then stood up straight looking with a very stern look into the ex-customer's face, before she strode positively back to her position behind the counter. The customer very quickly withered out of the tea shop probably never to return. Maud's manner never seemed to put anybody off. They just had to know their manners.

Clara earned six shillings a week. She paid the Luckins one shilling and sixpence for the two rooms and managed everything else on the remaining four shillings and sixpence. She felt she was doing well – after all, every Sunday was her very own, all day. Everyday Clara went to bake cakes was a joy. Frankie proved to be an easy baby who grew well and thrived in the kitchen's warmth.

The Willows

All that could be heard in the room was a harsh tinny noise coming from the disc musical box. The only physical presence Tony had left. Clara and Rose sat staring glumly into us cups on the kitchen table on an even duller Sunday morning.

Granma Ann had packed us Willows carefully and now here we were me and Laura, Mrs P, Little Polly and Hetta's china cup and saucer, Victoria and Albert on the breakfast table in Rose's cottage just off St James Street. Thank goodness the sound of the music coming from those great brass discs stopped. What a raucous noise that round thing made. I don't know what Mrs Ann would have thought of it.

'I expect she would say it was like all the animals in the yard shoutin' at once,' Laura said.

'Queen Victoria would have one I'm sure of it, don't you think so Albert?' Victoria teacup asked Albert saucer.

'Yes, yes my dear, of course she would. But we all lived a rural life at the Lamb so it's not surprising we find Brighton and all these people huggermugger in these rows of cottages, well, all so noisy.'

'Oh Albert,' simpered Victoria. 'You see things so clearly my love.'

'You're right he does Vicky,' added Bea. 'So do Laura and I. Haven't you noticed how very different are the lives of the two women sitting here at the table with us now?'

'From a well-ordered, regular, united couple came three very different women,' Albert went on. 'Elizabeth, tight-lipped seemingly guilt-ridden; Charlotte, full of herself, and her pride and both condemning of their

sister Emily just because they say she's had too many children. And Emily such a loving happy-go-lucky girl has all those children with a man who is so disappointed with his life and everything he's tried to do.'

'But don't condemn their children,' Bea returned, 'they're such lovely, lively youngsters and so enjoyed being with John and Ann at the Lamb.'

'You're right there,' laughed Vicky. 'I was frightened I'd be dropped many a time from those little hands wanting to wash up Granma's lovely china. You know, Gracie was the one who calmed them around that stone sink at washing up time.'

'Sad she's not with the family any longer,' commented Bea.

'Well she had to get away from Elizabeth's hard hand,' said Albert.

'And she followed her heart though didn't she – at least she didn't run off with just anybody to get away.'

'I think that's what Rose did though,' observed Mrs P.

'Tony was never satisfied.' Rose sighed, tipping Victoria upside down onto Albert to let the dregs drain out.

'Lady W making that rumpus about him takin' on the rent of this cottage. I think that's what unsettled him, Rose.'

'You may be right luv.'

'Yes, it wasn't your fault. He was so pleased you wanted to make a life with him and have your own place. You helped him take that leap out of service and get the personal freedom he's always been talking about.'

'Yes but now he's taken it a bit far, forsaking me

and baby.'

'Didn't he say he'd let you know when he got a job, and he'd be back on Sundays?'

'Well, maybe. I certainly hope so, I've the rent to pay or I'll be out on me ear.'

Before baby Frankie was a year old Rose and Tony got married and by the time he was two years old he had a cousin, Leslie. Together Rose and Tony weathered the storm Lady W made about her coachman moving out of his room with the stable lads and, even worse, taking her dressmaker Rose from the lovely bedroom the family had provided her with over the stables, and so close to her workroom too. But Tony never settled and now he had gone.

Rose turned up her cup and gazed at the formation of tea leaves. 'Can't see any mistress here,' she observed.

'Let me look.' Clara took the cup. 'Goodness, what a mess. No. Can't see what's coming out of that lot. You can't have used the tea strainer.'

'I did,' Rose retorted. 'Oh, there goes Les needin' 'is feed.'

'Go on you fetch him and I'll wash up.'

'Put another one of those discs on, Clara. We might as well 'ave a tune, make the best out of all that money it cost. It's the only thing 'e's left behind.' Rose returned to the kitchen with four-month-old Leslie and sat back in her chair, putting the baby to her breast.

'How many of these discs are there here Rose?'

'Aw don't ask, forty-five I think 'e said. All our bloomin' money I can tell yer that.'

'Well, then he won't want to go off and leave

146

that as well as a lovely baby boy and his lovelier mum will he?' Rose didn't answer.

The two young women spent the rest of their Sunday out along the seafront walking with their babies in their second-hand perambulators, Rose all the while trying to laugh off her worries. This time it was Clara who was the anchor.

'Well I must get back now and get me undies ironed ready for the week.'

'The Misses still do yer overalls and aprons then Clara?'

'Yes they're loves, won't hear of me using my only day off doing washing and ironing when I've got the baby to take out.'

'You were lucky to find that place. And you've been good for them too. That tea room's got the best reputation in town, so I've heard. Not surprising if this cake's anything to go by luv.'

Before Clara left they shared a piece of fruit cake Lally had given Clara to take home when they closed up on Saturday evening.

'You see what I mean?' Mrs Potter said. 'Tony's an unreliable specimen of a man. Sad because our Rose is such a dependable little seamstress.'

'Lucky for her, Lady W relented and let her live out and come into the workroom each day,' Albert added.

'She'd have no home without her earnings if she'd not got that job now he's hopped it,' said little Polly milk jug.

'Hopped it? What a way to talk Polly!' derided Vicky.

Laura spoke for them all saying, 'Whether you like the words or not, Tony's fecklessness with money made

147

life very hard and I'm sure you could see Rose's practical upbringing wouldn't tolerate that for long.'

'And who says he'll come back?' added Albert.

'Every generation of humans has to work through their difficulties,' Mrs P announced.

'Yes, they are always based on the mix of characters, and as we older Willows have observed that never changes, whatever the turns of history,' Uncle Bert said.

'You could say that we pieces of china have changed over the years with the social needs of our humans. No need for a gesunder or even teapots,' laughed Ol' Po.

Clara

The tea leaves had indicated nothing, but everything. Only a few days later both Rose's and Clara's lives were in complete turmoil.

The event that started the chain was the sudden death of Maud Crimmins. It didn't at first herald complete disaster because, although Lally went to pieces, Edna and Hilda shored things up and got Lally to see she could carry on with everyone of them pulling together. Then the council got involved saying, in the light of Miss Maud's demise, they were taking the opportunity to make their future plans known to Miss Lally. The Blue Rooms tea shop would be part of the whole area of buildings, cottages and shop fronts at the end of Western Road to be demolished as part of a new shopping street, so this would be a good time for the council to buy the short remaining lease from 'Miss Cummins'. They couldn't even spell her name correctly!

Miss Lally had little behind her financially. It had been a rare thing that a lease went from father to daughter, let alone span the life of two daughters. Acting on sensible advice Lally Crimmins saw it would be in her best interests to sell what little she had and move on. It wasn't until all this happened that Clara discovered Miss Lally's age. She was sixty-nine, and Maude had been seventy-two. They'd seemed so full of life and energy.

Edna had enlightened her. 'Ah well,' she said, 'this past two years with you and the baby here has given them new sparkle.' Edna had always kept on her rooms along in Upper North Street and invited Lally to move in with her. Hilda was out of a job although not completely destitute. Unbeknown to any of them, even her cousin Lally because they'd never asked, Hilda was married to a much younger man and they lived in a house he owned.

Maud and Lally had given their cousin a job washing up as an act of benevolence to help their poor uneven-legged relative. They hadn't been unkind not to ask, Hilda just hadn't told them. It was convenient for Hilda to go out and bring in a bit extra. Her husband worked in the flies at the Oxford Playhouse in New Road and his job could be erratic. But the pair never minded, never changed because they had the house next door to the Playhouse. It had been left to him by his actor parents. He and Hilda had no children to worry about so the closure of the tea rooms would hardly change their lives.

So that was it then. Lally decided to close the

tea shop at the end of the month – in three weeks.

On the Tuesday evening Clara came running in, straight from work after the tea room closed, little Frankie under her arm, calling to Rose, 'Rose I'm going to be out of a job again.' Clara must have run all the way down North Street across Castle Square and up St James' she was so out of breath. 'What am I going to do? I won't be able to pay the rent if I can't find a job pretty quickly.'

'Won't Miss Crimmins give you a recommendation? After all, they do know your cooking?'

'I'm sure I'll be given time to go looking for something else,' Clara said when she and Rose had talked things over and both were more calm and able to see a little ahead for planning.

Clara asked Rose, 'Have you heard from Tony at all?'

'No. Don't really expect to yet anyway.' Rose seemed to want to push the subject aside. 'What's happening to you is more important. Now let's see how things go. I'll see if I can organise my sewing so that I can bring some work home for when you have to go to, say, an interview then I can have Frankie here with me an' Leslie.'

'Oh that would be a help Rose. Trust you to keep a cool head.'

'Yes, but luv you know I'd help you out.'

'Yes I know Rose. But thanks, you've taken a big worry off my mind.'

Nevertheless Clara had a few tears when she was tucked up in her bed that night. The fact she would never have seen the sudden closure of the tea rooms coming, was what gave her the big shock. Worse came just two days later.

Dear old Mrs Luckins passed away in her sleep. Clara knew nothing of it until she got back home that evening and saw the curtains in her front room closed. Strange, she thought, I didn't leave the bedroom curtains closed. Then she noticed the downstairs curtains were closed and all the other cottages in the row had their curtains drawn. She wondered who could have died. Going straight through to the back kitchen it was unusual to see the door closed, so she knocked before going in.

Mr Luckins was sitting in his usual chair by the range but two other people she didn't recognise were there, and another she did recognise.

'This is Clara.' Mr Luckins had smelled the sweet smell Clara brought home on her clothes. The lady Clara recognised was known as the layin' out woman thereabouts. She got up and guided Clara to the chair she had vacated.

'Sit down luv. Dear Mrs Luckins has passed away. This is her son Jack and his wife Dorothy.' They both looked grim and only nodded towards her.

Clara sat down heavily, overcome, unable to speak. She felt tired out.

'Hope yer don't mind me going in an' drawin' your curtains dear. Mr Luckins told me I might.'

'No, no.' Clara hardly heard her.

Jack Luckins spoke up. 'Father's been telling us what a help you've been here Mrs Dann.'

'I want to stay here boy. I ain't got much longer meself an' I don't want being turned outta my bed, not at my age.'

151

'Well we'll 'ave to see Dad. Dot an' me, we can't com an' live over in Brighton. We'll 'ave to see.'

'I don't mind looking after your father,' Clara offered, 'if that would help.'

Mr Luckins heard that. 'You are a luv, that would be just right Jack. That's what I'd like.' Clara didn't show her surprise that Mr Luckins had heard what she said. His son didn't notice.

Mr Luckins slept sitting up in his chair by the kitchen range that night as Mrs Luckins' body lay in its coffin along the end of their bed. Clara got him his breakfast and left other items on the table beside him, telling him what she had left and where it was. Then as she went out of the door, Frankie hoisted up on her back, Mr Luckins thanked her. Cheeky old soul, thought Clara as she walked down the road to work. He's been able to hear us all the time.

Clara hadn't the time to walk up to Rose's place again that week so she dropped a postcard in the post box near the tea room – just telling Rose the situation.

By now the tea room regulars had heard about the closure date and were not only filling every table all day long but asking if there would be any possibility of ordering fruit cakes to keep for Christmas before the business closed. That heralded more work for Clara.

Arriving back in Regent Row that evening she found a card from Jack Luckins in Newhaven telling her the decision had been made. His brother wanted to stop paying the rent on the cottage. Of course Clara hadn't known Mr and

Mrs Luckins' eldest son had been paying the rent on his parents' cottage, mainly because it gave him a home to come home to between tours with his regiment. Now their father would have to go into the workhouse, as Jack and his wife had no room for the old man at their home. 'That means we have to ask you to move out by Saturday evening after the funeral,' he wrote.

In the last delivery at ten o'clock that night Clara received a card from Rose sending her condolences.

Mr Luckins was very pleased with his bowl of stew that evening. Clara stayed downstairs to eat her meal alongside him at the kitchen table. He told her, 'I could 'ardly contain meself sittin' 'ere beside the fire with that stew pot you put on simmerin' away all day.'

It was obvious the poor old man had no idea what was in store for him at the end of the week. Or, for that matter she wondered, what had been planned for the three old cats that all their lives had daily sharpened their claws on the table leg.

That's it, thought Clara, angered at the son's coldheartedness. I'll do my best to make him comfortable for his wife's sake. Nice meals each day. See if I can't bring him home a cake or two as well.

The next-door neighbour popped in to make sure Mr Luckins was going on all right and see if he needed any help during the morning. He kept to his regular routine, taking his short trot along to the Lathe Cleavers Arms at lunchtime for his 'half' and back to have a snooze in his chair in the afternoon.

The old gentleman was active enough to tend the fire and keep it in good fettle for his evening stew pot. No, he wasn't an invalid by any means. Mrs Luckins' constant words had been, 'No you stay put old luv, I can do it, I'll go an' fetch that.' Seemed like she'd run herself into the ground, as so many women do. So, as tradition takes a long time to change and die, while Clara cleared the dishes and washed up then prepared food for the next day, she also got her writing things out to scribble off a letter telling Rose the latest news; this would go in the first post at six the next morning. Mr Luckins spent the rest of his evening sitting beside his wife's coffin having a chat with her before bedtime.

Clara tended to Frankie, settling him down for the night. None of this was unusual for her. She had spent her life tending to the needs of the young ones in her family. The only difference now was the age of the one receiving her care.

They say bad news comes in threes; well, that week it came in fours. The day after Clara got her marching orders from the Luckins' cottage Rose heard that Lord and Lady W had decided to leave the Brighton house and return to London. Lady W would not need Rose's services anymore. This time it was Rose who nipped to the post box sending her news to Clara, and it was only Wednesday.

On Saturday night Clara moved in with Rose. Jake Brownlow trundled everything across town on his cart. Dear Jake, he was a pal. In two years Clara had acquired her own feather mattress and linens, also a tin trunk to store her crocks and saucepans. Balancing a case with her and Frankie's clothes on the end of his perambulator, she set off beside Jake and his hand cart down North Street and up St James Street. But not before giving Mr Luckins a kiss on his cheek and a promise to look in on him when she could.

Rose said she didn't know how long their arrangement would last because the rent book was in Tony's name, but she'd told the agent he was working away and sending the rent home and that he would be back every other weekend. So far he'd sent no money. Clara solved the next two weeks' rent money while she was still working at the tea shop because she didn't have to pay rent at Regent Row.

Rose's cottage was along a narrow brick path between two streets of houses. There was an enclosed front garden where their boys could play safely. Frankie was two years old and Leslie nearly a year but they'd be safe enough on a blanket on the grass. The front door opened straight into a room that was mostly kitchen with a wooden staircase to one side and a scullery at back. Behind the scullery a very small yard had a lavvy they shared with next door. Upstairs were two rooms. The front took a double bed while the little back room over the scullery would hold two tiny beds or, as it had to, gave floor space to Clara's feather mattress and a drawer from a big old chest of drawers for Frankie to sleep in because it kept out all the draughts. Rose's cottage had a bright happy feel about it.

Rose gathered a few bits and pieces of sewing

155

and visited all the ladies dress shops she felt were 'quality', offering her services to carry out alterations. But like Tony, when he had tried for a position in a gentleman's outfitters in North Street, they had wanted staff to live in.

Rose left her contact information but she didn't leave all her eggs awaiting one basket. She got herself an evening job behind the bar in a pub a few streets away in Liverpool Street. Bit rough with all the brewery workers and the railway men from the Kemp Town shunting yard but if she and Clara were to pay their way, needs must.

When Clara got back after the tea room closed, Rose left Leslie and went uphill and across through the streets to her bar job.

In the three weeks before the tea shop closed Clara made more fruit cake than she did in the rest of her life – or had done before. When ladies heard others were placing orders for collection by closure day the number of orders grew and that's where Edna had to step into Maud's shoes, because Lally would have said yes to every order that came. Edna told her there had to be a stopping point. Extra fruit and flour would need calculating so that there was none left over, but more importantly, there had to be time to make their daily cakes, besides making the lunch-time specials. Add to that, a huge quantity of fruit cake mixture needed preparing, let alone the time and space to bake everything. All that would need more fuel.

'Oh Lally, you would never have made a business woman. Maud would have charged a premium on these closing down orders but now we've taken orders we can't suddenly ask for more money for each one.'

Lally wasn't downcast at her silly mistakes, all she could say was how much she was looking forward to the spare time she would have to take Toddy and show him the sights of Brighton.

This time Clara had no time to visit any agency and sit waiting in their waiting room in case a call for a cook came in. She just left her name on their books, told them where she was to be found and went back to her baking. Frankie carried on being the light of three elderly ladies' lives. Even Edna acknowledged she'd miss little Frankie.

Nothing came from the agency for Clara until the day before the Blue Rooms tea shop closed. A lady customer came up to the counter asking if their cake maker needed a position. Lally said she certainly did and would herself be giving Clara a Character. A visiting card was left for Clara to call in at the lady's home in Lewes Crescent the Monday following the tea shop's closure.

Clara worked all night on the Friday before the last day. Little Frankie slept upstairs in Miss Lally's bed. The huge crescendo of work, customers finalising all the cake orders and clearing up, stopped at six thirty in the evening. Clara received her wages with a little extra for the longer hours, and one of the fruit cakes. Lally wouldn't hear of her spending her Sunday off coming back to help with their packing up.

'You give your time to your baby dear,' she said. 'If you come back here on a Sunday all we'll do is spend time playing with the little chap. No, you go home and rest. You deserve the time to your-self.'

The late offer of a job was all too good to be true. Clara attended the address on the card early on the Monday morning. Rose had kept Frankie while Clara was at her interview, but the woman expected her to get straight down to work. When she heard Clara had a small baby who would have to be with her daily, the prospective employer was very angry. Lally had told her there was a baby that came with the cake baker but the woman had dismissed such silly thoughts.

'I'll have no brat in my kitchen. You can leave it up in your room.'

'But I'm not able to live in missus.'

'Then get out of my house.'

Clara held her hand out for the return of her Character. 'Just get out,' barked the woman.

'Not without my Character missus,' replied Clara, leaving her hand extended to receive the letter and envelope written by Lally Crimmins.

'How dare you be so barefaced speaking to me in that way.'

'Madam, if you keep my Character that would be stealing my property.'

Speechless with shock the woman threw both paper and envelope in Clara's face. Clara turned and left in silence, shaking at her own boldness. Servants never spoke to employers in such a man-ner. People had been sent to prison for answering back. But in this case Clara wasn't actually an employee. And the woman should have known cooks could be a law unto themselves. Frankie had to come first. Rose needed her to care for Leslie when she went to work and they needed each other to pay the rent and find enough money for food.

So far the rent book was safe for the next few months. Nothing had been heard from Tony. Rose didn't know where he was and Clara's earnings would just cover the rent for another six weeks. With Rose's one shilling and sixpence a week wages from the hours at the pub, they could feed themselves and buy the milk for the babies because neither girl any longer had enough of their own milk. Talking over their situation, Rose said unless she could find sewing and alterations work she would try for longer hours in the bar while Clara looked after the babies.

Twice a week Clara walked the perambulator with Frankie and Leslie up Elm Grove to the top where she knew she would find Mr Luckins looking over the high wall surrounding the workhouse. The elderly men sitting on the top of the wall or hanging over with their arms out asking for baccy had a rope or two with old shopping bags or sacks knotted to the ends.

When she asked for Mr Luckins she would either hear him call back to her or somebody would make space for him to stand on something so that Clara could see him. She took him a pennyworth of tobacco, which somebody would pull up in one of their bags on a rope. She could well see Mr Luckins was not happy at all, but at least she was doing a little something to ease his lonely state.

'I don't know how we can feed the children when

the boys bring them over for the summer holidays. One of us has to be here with the young 'uns.'

Clara said she'd got an idea. She would go out early next morning and see what she could find.

'What's that about then Clara?'

'Let's wait and see,' Clara said, giving a wink and holding her palms together as in prayer.

Very early next morning Clara left Frankie with Rose and set out to find the bone-collecting man on his rounds. When she asked him if there was a leftovers food collector in the town, he looked a bit taken aback at first because the last time he'd seen Clara she had been, to his knowledge, the head cook at Lady Wellborough's.

'Never mind that Charlie, we all fall on hard times, there's no shame in your job or my need.'

'Ah, yer right there missus. There isn't a shop exactly here in Brighton but old Bill Fairbrother, 'e does the rounds when 'e's told there's a big affair being prepared for an' 'e goes along an' collects the leftovers, as you know. Well now 'is place is in the backs of Bread Street in Tichbourne. If yer wanter find me I'm in Jubilee.'

'Thank you Charlie. Got our family, brothers and sisters, down for the holidays next week. I'll go and see what I can find.'

'Tell Bill I sent yer dear. Good luck.'

Being the early bird in Bill's yard at the back of Bread Street, Clara arrived in time to find all manner of perfectly good food that would otherwise have gone to waste. She came away from that first visit to the second-hand food collector with nearly a whole shoulder of roast mutton and

160

a huge bag of boiled potatoes, a lump of good suet and an untouched vanilla blancmange, half a decorated salmon and half a chicken, all for twopence. When Clara returned, Rose was waiting to fly out of the door to her pub job, but was forced to stand aside as Clara came carefully through the front passageway heavily laden with bags and baskets.

'Don't want this milk blancmange to tip over,' she told Rose as she rested a bag with a bowl balanced inside on the end of the kitchen table.

'Blancmange? What y'er talkin' about gal?'

Clara emptied all the items out along the table to show what she had gleaned. Rose was astonished at the sight of all that food. 'Where'd yet get that from? Oh gosh, I can't stop I'll lose m' job, got ter run. Ta ta.'

When Rose got home that night it was past eleven o'clock and she was dog tired. But not too tired to wolf down some fried sliced potatoes Clara had ready in a pan over the fire.

'Out with it then,' said Rose, as she mopped up the last of the runny dripping with a hunk of bread, the only meal she had eaten that day.

Clara explained how she remembered Mrs Charlish telling her about the second-hand food shops in London. With the huge amounts of dishes prepared in the kitchens of the gentry to spread before their guests, many of these dishes were barely touched or returned to the kitchens unwanted. Sometimes the servants were given the food but more often that was not allowed.

Clara reminded Rose how they had seen the amounts Lady W ordered especially when guests

161

were staying. She said she herself had been involved in most elaborate dishes and quantities ordered even by the tight-fisted Rachel Anderson when guests came to dinner from town. That was when Mrs Charlish told her about the second-hand food shop in the Vauxhall Bridge Road that took the uneaten food from the kitchen she worked in at that London establishment.

Mrs Charlish said that in London collectors went round to the kitchens of big houses every day collecting leftover food, like the bone man collected fat and bones for the soap factory. Of course in London there were large hospitals that took food and some of the workhouses if they could afford to spare the money. It was the food shops that displayed some wonderful bargains. Roasted chickens with one piece cut off the breasts or one leg taken off. Beautiful pork pies with maybe one or two slices cut out.

Mrs Charlish sent good food from her own employer's kitchens if the next day's menu disregarded dishes already in the larder. It was rare that a dish would ever be offered for a second viewing. Some housewives never even realised they'd ordered so much to be prepared. It had all appeared for appearance itself. There were those households who forbade their staff from touching any food that had been to the family and guests' table. Rose and Clara both knew that servants' halls were provided the usual hash from the bone pickings or cheap cuts unpalatable to the family. Oh, it was all true – that's what Clara explained to Rose.

'But what has all this cost, Clara?'

'Penny ha'penny, no I lie, twopence; he found me half a chicken too. You can do a lot with a little I always say. I rendered the dripping for your fry up from the mutton fat and bone. An' a little taste of salmon each day will do wonders for the little chaps. Build their bones well.'

'Well waste not want not. You're a genius Clara, but what about next week when the boys bring the little 'uns, 'spect they'll want to stay more'n a day or two?'

'Yes, that's what was on my mind but don't worry. Bill Fairbrother told me there were going to be plenty of cooking going on this next weekend when the toffs have their pals down from London for the theatre. The Royal's busy and I know Hilda told me her ol' man's going to be busy at the Music Hall over the next month or two. Bill says to be there at his sheds early because most cooks send food down directly after clearing because they don't have space when they've more dishes to prepare for next day. The pig men collect at nights and mornings. If anything gets a bit spoilt they bag it themselves.'

'Heavens Clara, somebody's lookin' after us. Any of that blancmange you mentioned about?'

'Yes I've kept you the last of it. The boys have thoroughly enjoyed their share.'

It was the weekend and the following week she needed food for five children including two fast-growing brothers. A few days before the children arrived she stayed home with the two babies while Rose did more hours at the pub. But Clara wasn't idle, well whenever was she idle?

She moved the double bed she was sharing with

163

Rose while Tony wasn't about, into the little back room with the babies' two box cots. In a nearby second-hand shop she found four feather mattresses rolled up with a quantity of bed linen and pillows for a shilling, also a pile of old pictures for a farthing. The shop lad brought the bundles along the path on his truck, saving Clara many journeys. All the bedding was arranged over the chairs in the kitchen to dry near the fire while she cut out round the flowers and faces on the pictures. Remembering how effective Lally's painting on the walls at the tea rooms had been, Clara stuck the colourful cut-outs across the old creamy white walls in the front bedroom in the form of arches and swags. It looked very effective. Next morning in daylight Rose was astonished at the result.

'How d'yer get 'em to stay put?'

'Flour and water luv, don't you remember how Gran showed us.'

The sight of that pretty front bedroom with the piles of soft feather mattresses drew squeals of delight from Clara and Rose's young brothers and sisters when they arrived early on the Sunday morning.

The weather that week was the best it had been all season. Clara was able to take the children to the beach every day. Jack and Tom had only stayed for the Sunday because at sixteen and fourteen they were working lads. However they did enjoy watching the girls go by along the prom that day. Fanny was old enough to be a little helper, she was eleven. Harry and Nancy walked either side of little Albert, and Freddie, barely four years old, sat on the pram with Frankie and baby Leslie.

Edward was then a babe in arms so stayed at home with Emily who was pregnant again. Clara could cope, she was used to it. The little tribe skipping their way down Manchester Street and across to the beach each morning became a familiar sight.

As planned, Clara had nipped out early on one or two mornings up to Bill Fairbrother's, returning with enough food to fill all the extra tummies that week. On the beach they chewed on bread and cheese and apples, and once she bought them each a hokey pokey from the end of the Chain Pier. The children wanted to go along the pier every day but Clara rationed their jaunts. Keeping them all together and out from under the promenaders' feet was a stretch too far for one person on her own.

The great blessing of those lovely beach days was that all the children slept like tops every night.

The Willows

'Ah those children did enjoy their summer with Clara and Rose,' said Laura.

'Yes and thank goodness we weren't used when they were in Brighton,' Mrs Potter teapot added.

'No, don't suppose we'd be here now if Clara hadn't kept us out of the way up here on the shelves; Emily's youngsters were very boisterous,' Albert commented.

'An' when Jack and young Tom went back to start work, the behaviour, well, we could hear the thumping pillow fights in the mornings,' Laura laughed.

'And when Clara or Rose weren't in the kitchen

165

they were so noisy, I can't think how the neighbours didn't complain.'

'It's as I said,' Albert reminded them, 'it's much noisier in the town than we're used to out in the country at the Lamb. Even with the men's singing by the inglenook on winter evenings it's never as noisy.'

'Ah, I do miss the old place.'

'Sad about Granma Annie passing away,' said Mrs Potter.

'Yes. I think she knew her time was near when she packed us up and sent us over here to Clara,' Bea suggested.

Laura agreed. 'After all, we have been her cup and tea dish all these years.'

'Unkind of Elizabeth to keep the news from Clara and Rose,' said Albert.

'Well she's certainly succeeded in keeping Emily and the children away from the inn.'

'Yes but Clara and Rose were very close to their grandmother,' replied Vicky.

'I think that's probably why dear,' said Laura.

'Weren't they upset though? Poor Clara she never had chance to see her grandparents since the day she left the Lamb.'

'Maybe Elizabeth had read the letters she wrote to Ann.' Clara and her grandmother had written to each other regularly over the last two years.

'Well if Elizabeth has read all about Frank and the baby, no wonder she won't have Clara or Rose there now that Tony's buzzed off.'

'I think it's heartwrenching they've been kept apart. Ann and John had such a happy group of grand-children around them,' said Bea.

'No need to be quite so dramatic dear, worse things

166

can happen to families. It was hard work for them though, wasn't it Bea?' said Laura.

'Yes but they so enjoyed having the children and to know they were giving them good food and a healthy outdoor life. Ann often talked to Hetta about the poverty she had witnessed in their circumstances when Tom was unable to work,' said Mrs P.

'Well, it's all gone now,' Albert said glumly.

'Quiet when the children had gone home,' observed Sama.

'All I can say is I'm proud to watch how Clara and Rose are carrying on their grandparents' loving kindness to their young brothers and sisters,' said Mrs P. 'Those two gals are full of resourcefulness. Long as they can find the rent money and the babs get food, we know they won't let them go hungry.'

'Bravo to that,' came back the reply from Albert and all the other Willows on Rose's little kitchen shelves.

Clara

Emily and Tom came over to Brighton on the train after they had been to Granma Ann's funeral at Hooe church. It was the first time Tom had seen his two first grandsons, Frankie and Leslie. He had been told everything some time back so he was reconciled to past events by the time they met. Mother and father Dann stayed for the day and one night before they took the children back home to St Leonards.

Although in heavy funeral black for the death of her mother, Emily just had to go down to the seafront to watch the Daddy Long Legs. She had

167

not had time to see it when she had been on her flying visit to Clara after the birth of Frankie.

The ice was broken although in great sadness over the loss of Granma Pilbeam. Emily told Clara that Granfer had taken her aside and sent his love to her and Rose. He also said to remind Clara that he would be at Hailsham Market on the last Wednesday of the month if she was ever able to get the train across. 'Don't write because Elizabeth will make sure he doesn't get the letter.'

Reaching deep into her bag of family necessities – bibs, nappies, dummies, apples – Emily pulled out a small cup.

'Here, Granfer gave me Granma's christening cup for you Clara. It's got her name on it, look.'

Clara cried, but not in front of everybody, she didn't want to spoil the last day of their holidays.

Clara and Rose had been able to collect a real feast early on the Sunday morning from Bill's. Taking Frankie's pram they came home with their tins and boxes full of a whole chicken, lamb chops, a half pork pie and a whole apple pie all for threepence. Sunday dinner was their best meal that week, all the children agreed and their father topped it all by saying he'd had a 'real blow out'.

Clara had not given up making every effort to find a job where she could earn at least decent money. If only she could do that, it would release Rose from working long hours in that pub, then she could have time to find enough sewing work at home where she could look after their boys. But again, events changed all that.

Clara did find a job, a good position as cook in the household of a family in Adelaide Crescent. The only problem she had to consider was that they wanted her to live in. She didn't have to consider for very long because Rose decided the answer for her.

Tony wrote to say he'd found a job and got a flat for them and asked Rose to come back to him. Rose made the quick decision that little Leslie should have a father in his life. So there it was, the families were on the move once again.

'You must do what you think is best for Leslie and yourself Rose.'

'I do hate letting you down Clara.'

'I know dear, but you and I know that we could be told to leave this cottage any time if the agent realised Tony wasn't actually living here.'

'Well, you're right there. We've both lived a little on the edge recently.'

'Anyway, it's about time I got back to full-time cooking. My references from Mrs Charlish and dear old Lally Crimmins will be out of date. If that happens I would have to start as a kitchen maid to prove my credentials.'

'Been fun though 'asn't it gal?' Rose was always ready to say life was fun on the edge. ''Bout time you found a husband Clara.'

'No. I'd rather earn for myself. He'd have to be well off to allow me to cook the kinds of meals I'd like to make.'

'You'll get ter be a fat old cook,' Rose laughed.

'I won't. I like to feel good without those awful restricting heavy corsets. If I keep slim nobody will know I'm not wearing any. It's just too damned hot to be bundled up with tight things when you spend hours round a cooking fire.'

'I would be surprised if some chap doesn't snap you up gal. Look at yer. Not one of your elderly crabby old cooks. You're a good looker with loads of energy.'

'Maybe, but that middle-class family out Hove were far more interested in knowing I've been cook at Lady Wellborough's establishment. Think of the prestige they'd get out of that with their guests.'

'Yes, I can just see them round their over-decorated dining table all corseted up and unable to eat more than a morsel.'

'You might be right Rose, you've seen plenty of them undressed.'

'Cheeky,' chortled Rose.

'But I hope the missus isn't tight with the ingredients, you can't make a silk purse out of a sow's ear.'

'Hah, I bet our grandmother could 'ave!'

'Yes, dear old Gran.' They both stopped their laughter and sighed, thinking of their Grandmother Annie.

'I've decided to go over to see Granfer on my first day off,' said Clara. 'Oh I didn't tell you did I. The missus said I can take a whole day off so long as I leave two cold meals with soup or something ready for the kitchen girl to heat up. I'll get the train over to Hailsham. Frankie'll love to see all the animals at market.'

'Sounds lovely Clara, wish I could bring Leslie.'

'Maybe you can if you come down to Brighton of a week sometime when I'm going over on a

Wednesday. Do you know where Tony's got the flat?'

'I think he said something about it being near the big theatres. Coventry Street I think he said.'

'Oh, now I forgot to tell you in all the goings on. Yesterday when I went up to take Grandad Luckins his baccy, there was another old fella hanging over that wall. He said, "I don't know a Mr Luckins dearie." Then I heard a voice say, "Go on you'd better tell 'er Bert. He's been dead these past two weeks luv."'

'Oh no Clara, poor old chap.'

'Yes, but those old beggars have been telling me they'd take his little bit o' baccy in for him – I bet they've been keeping it. I must have been up there four times since he's passed on.'

'Well, just as well he's no longer with us I s'pose, 'cos you'd have a long walk across town from Adelaide to the top o' Elm Grove. It all works out doesn't it love?'

'Sad though, he was a dear old sort. I won't forget him, or Mrs Luckins for that matter. They were both real loves to me.'

All the while, the girls had been feeding the two little boys and chatting to them about a train ride for Leslie when Clara suddenly said, 'Ah now, I'd better not turn up in Adelaide Crescent with my chattels on a hand cart.'

Rose laughed herself silly at the thought of it. 'Why not take a hansom, Clara, you could 'ave 'im take your trunk on the back.'

Clara gave the idea a few minutes' thought then said, 'Mm no, not really. I've got more than would go in my trunk now. I'll order a carrier for my

171

things and take myself and Frankie on the omnibus. Yes I'd better get the carrier ordered tomorrow.'

After Clara had attended her interview at Adelaide Crescent she took the opportunity of walking to the nearest school up Holland Road. Frankie would soon be going to school so she wanted to be sure it was near enough for him. She had been given permission for her small son to share the bedroom that the missus had shown her at the top of the house and also to be in her sitting room along the passage from the kitchen in the basement. Had the family had a housekeeper Clara would not have had a sitting room to herself. She felt very lucky in the circumstances. Employers used this as a way of keeping their essential staff on the premises at their behest night and day.

Rose had no interest in taking any china with her to London. She said she had enough to cope with taking Tony's disc player and all those metal discs with her. Clara wrapped the willow china in newspaper and packed it snugly into her yellow tin trunk.

Tucked away underneath Clara's desk in her sitting room at Adelaide Crescent, the Willows didn't see the light of day for the next ten years.

5

Clara

Clara would tell you that life for her over the next ten years was uneventful. Yes, I suppose if you meant her personally, otherwise one would say it was anything but. To be fair though it must have been the security and the regular routine throughout those years working at Adelaide Crescent for the Whiteside family, so maybe that's what made her say nothing happened during those years.

When she and her small son Frankie arrived on the first day they found laid out on her bed two pretty floral dresses for afternoon wear, two blue and white striped ones for morning kitchen work and two French navy ones with white lace collars and cuffs for special evening duties. There were even two pairs of dungarees and shirts for Frankie on a tiny bed in the corner. The family wanted their new cook to feel so at home that she would want to stay.

Clara's bedroom at the top of the house had been cosily furnished with a tiled washstand, bowl, jug, bucket and chamber pot next to a roomy wardrobe. A sitting room next to the big kitchen had likewise been prepared with two comfortable chairs, a small eating table and chairs, a cupboard with shelves above, behind double glass doors and a well-appointed kneehole desk under the window

173

to catch the best light, where the menus and pro-visions orders could be written up. Pretty curtains at the windows and soft cushions on the armchairs gave young mother and son a warm welcome.

For a woman alone with a small child Clara had fallen into a lucky position. The job offered the grand sum of seven shillings and sixpence a week all found, food and lodgings. She might also have one half-day a week so long as cold meals and an easy to heat soup be left ready prepared. After the first month it was agreed Clara could have one whole day off to meet her grandfather at market every six weeks or so.

The family soon took Clara to their hearts. They liked her cooking and she liked them. The White-side family was mother, father and five young Whitesides, two small children and three young adults. Mr Whiteside's carriage took him to the station at ten o'clock on three mornings a week. He did something in town but he was generally home by six in the evening. Mrs Myrtle Whiteside was a buxom lady who spent her days writing music and playing a variety of musical instruments and occasionally meeting her friends, shopping in town. All five young people shared the rooms on the third floor, an arrangement that appeared to Clara to be working very successfully, because although down in the basement she couldn't hear the youngster' daytime life, when she put Frankie to bed or later when she passed by on her way up to the attic to her own bed, all she ever heard were happy murmuring voices coming from the four bedrooms.

On the second floor lived their two grandmothers. Mrs Whiteside had the grand front room and Mrs Hartfield two small rooms at the rear.

The first floor with the front balcony over-looking the crescent had folding doors that could be opened to reveal its full length front to back and was known as the music room, having a grand piano and plenty of space for music stands and comfortable chairs. This was the most used room in the house, often full of visitors with all manner of musical instruments being heard throughout the day and evening.

But Clara didn't have to concern herself with any of those areas. The family employed two up-stairs maids who slept in another attic room and a maid of all work who came in every day. All Clara had to do was produce meals to be served in the ground-floor dining room. Any further comestibles wanted would be taken to the family by the upstairs maids, Colleen or Madge.

The baker called twice a day, three days a week, so Clara didn't have to make bread every day. It was a great saving with nine in the family, es-pecially young adults with their growing appe-tites.

Mr Whiteside was a practical man who obviously realised he had a very demanding household, and therefore he had set up a kitchen capable of meet-ing their orders. Colleen told Clara in her first week that the last two cooks had walked out because they couldn't cope with the amount of meals they had been required to produce on an old-fashioned fire with hanging pots and a spit. Clara had a little laugh to herself as this story brought a vision of her own Granma Annie providing the inn's customers with all their needs until she finally got her own bread oven and range in their family kitchen behind the bar. It seemed that Mr Whiteside had caught sight of a splendid patent closed and open fire cooking range, in a showroom near his offices in Westminster, so decided to have one put in at Adelaide Crescent.

'So you're the lucky one because they're darned keen you should stay, but it won't be an easy job I'm tellin' yer Mrs Dann.' Coleen, although much older than Clara, respected the code of servants' hierarchy in addressing the cook as Mrs Dann. It hadn't escaped Clara's notice. This beautiful new range and the knowledge of the family's troubles with their previous cooks gave her the edge in asking for that extra time to visit grandfather, besides the fact that they were charmed to know their cook's family were in business.

How could four adults and five young people besides two maids and nursery helpers not be demanding, with all their comings and goings, let alone preferences and different times of meals for the varying ages and life needs? Two old ladies, five young appetites, and then there were the visiting musicians and the dinner parties, and all to be catered for by one cook and two maids. At least the upstairs maid had two sisters who came in to help out on dinner party days. Clara, for the security of a home for herself and Frankie, had taken on a huge job, and all for seven and six a week, which she thought to be a very good remuneration.

So there she was, settled in a job with a roof

over their heads and Frankie soon off to school. Meanwhile her little boy played on the sitting room floor or more often stood on a stool at the end of the kitchen table, wrapped around in an apron, with his own small utensils and mimicking his mother's every move.

'Why did you change the wooden spoon?'

Clara answered with, 'A wooden spoon opens up big holes in the mixture and lets in lots of air.'

'Why are you using a shiny spoon now Mum?'

'Because I'm folding the flour into the mixture, slicing fine cuts through the mix, taking the flour in without letting the air out.'

At four years old he wanted to know all the reasons. 'You used a wooden spoon in the saucepan.'

'That's because I don't use a metal spoon in a metal pan. It scrapes the surface and leaves scratches in the metal where food can lodge.'

'Why are you grunging up those little balls?'

Clara had to smile at Frankie's description. 'They are what are known as seeds. This is cumin and this one's coriander and they are grown in hot countries. Smell them. That's right.'

'But they don't have much smell.'

'Now, I've ground both types in my mortar with this pestle.' She held the mortar under his chin saying, 'take another sniff.'

'Wooh! That smells a lot.'

'This aroma is stronger now. And if you sizzle the powder in a little butter these flavourings will enhance a sauce for meat or fish. Take a taste. Store it in your taste memory.'

And so each day Frankie watched and asked. His mother patiently answered. He was her life;

177

the job and the home it gave them came second.

'Why are you adding flour when you beat that egg in?'

'Because I can see the mixture might curdle before I finish adding all the egg. I don't want that to happen because my cake won't rise.'

These were all small things he noticed. Frankie watched all the moves closely. Then he'd say 'Look, it's about to curdle.' So he kept her on her toes, something that always brought on her little chortling laugh.

'Why are you picking the mixture up high and dropping it like snow?'

'I'm making pastry. If I lift the mixture it collects the air. Look it makes it all lovely and fluffy. Then we'll mix icy cold water and a squeeze of lemon juice in to make dough. Give it a little knead, pat it to a neat round shape, lay it in a cold cloth on a plate. Then I'm going to put it outside on the shelf in the safe above the ice block. Just cool enough out there. The ice man will be along in the morning.'

'Why do you put the dough above the ice?'

'Because the dough needs a rest while the gluten has time to grow slowly. Gluten makes the pastry stretch and rise.'

'But why above the ice?'

'On the top shelf so there's nothing above that might drop on the pastry. You see we've got fresh meat in dishes at the bottom because we don't want any juices to drip on other foods.'

It was the ice box that thrilled Clara, more even than the brand new kitchen range. At last she would have an opportunity to make some of the ice creams Mrs Charlish had shown her at the Andersons'. That was of course if the family liked ice cream. Rachel Anderson used to have savoury ice creams, like tomato, served instead of heavy soups or spinach ice cream bordering a dish of salmon or apple-scented ices between rich meat courses. She would have to see what she could introduce to the Whitesides.

At the end of each day Clara finished off her kitchen cleaning by scrubbing down the big deal work table with salt and a good squeeze of half a lemon, flushing all the salt away, drying off with a clean cloth ready for the next morning. That table surface was as white as snow. It was usually too late in the evening for Frankie to help his mother, he'd long gone into his own little room near the kitchen where he kept his treasures. Frankie had noticed that following rough weather on a narrow area of beach he could find unusual stones with holes in them. Colleen noticed he'd gathered quite a heap so she brought an empty cigar box down from Mr Whiteside's study. Alongside his pebble collection Frankie had a few cigarette cards with colourful pictures of exotic scenes in hot countries.

'Perhaps one day I shall visit that place,' he told his mother, pointing out one especially sunny scene.

After he had started school he began to accumulate what seemed to Clara rather a lot of *The Boy's Own Paper*. Frankie could read very well even before he started school and he loved the stories. She often saw him sitting on the area steps reading aloud to a small group of lads. Colleen

179

and Madge, when they had a moment, sometimes stood out in the yard listening to the tales of adventure and smiling at the boys wriggling with excitement.

One Friday, Frankie presented Colleen with a copy of *Blackwoods* magazine. She took it with thanks, remarking to Clara what a thoughtful little chap he was. What Frankie didn't realise was that some adults couldn't read. Clara was keen that the two maids should not feel humiliated so she waited until the Saturday evening, when Colleen and Madge often came down to the kitchen to take a break, and asked Frankie if he would read them all a story from *Blackwoods*. She sat at the table with a tray of apples that she was peeling, passed a knife each to the two maids, with a wink, and poured cups of tea. When the story ended all three women complimented Frankie on his reading.

'Oh you do it so much better 'n' me lovey, you make the story come alive.'

'Yes, me too,' agreed Colleen. 'You'll have to give us another reading sometime when we've got a minute.'

'That was lovely dear.'

'Thank you,' smiled Clara. She thought he never knew the two ladies couldn't read.

Clara had been in Brighton longer than she had originally intended, and really missed the soft sounds of the marsh at dusk; standing silently watching the birds swoop up the last flies; seeing moths gather and glow worms start their bright green courting lights; the feel of a low breeze

180

gently swishing through the reeds bringing faint mysterious sounds across from the Downs. Looking up from the wide flat marshland on nights that were clear sweet and heavy with stars the sky and land were all one, the stars seemed like close neighbours. It was with their grandfather on the marsh they'd had this little ritual of saying goodnight to the sun and hallo to the moon.

Now surrounded with buildings in the town she could no longer hear the stars like you could on the marsh. Deep in the alleyways and curving streets all you could hear were voices; a shout of anger from a back yard, a raddled old woman sitting against a pub wall crying and hiccupping, laughter coming in gusts strained through the network of lanes.

In Adelaide Crescent few human sounds other than music from the Whitesides and their friends drifted from the windows on summer evenings. Some nights Clara would stand in the yard area listening to the waves rushing in and sucking out a long pull of pebbles on the shore edge.

Late one evening after her first large dinner party, when she felt Frankie had confidently settled in to his new home, Clara threw a shawl round her shoulders, walked out from her kitchen in the crescent down to the seafront and stood listening to the waves rhythmically beating on the shore. While gulls were taking their last sweeps through the skyscape she breathed the fresh night air, filling her lungs and enjoying a few moments of freedom. A deep voice close to her ear said, 'Move along my dear, your services aren't wanted here.' The policeman had crept up on her so

181

quietly that she jumped out of her skin.

'Hold on a minute. Why, it's Mrs Dann!' Clara turned to look through the darkness and could just make out the uniform. It was Jim Slater who lived in Regent Row. 'I do apologise, but it isn't right for you to be here so late and all alone Mrs Dann.'

Clara told him where she was working and the busy evening they'd just had. 'Tell Sara where I am. I hope the family's well Jim. Goodnight and thanks for the advice.'

'Goodnight Mrs Dann. I'll just stand here and watch you safe back inside.'

As she walked back up the crescent Clara thought how she could go anywhere alone on the marsh and stand still to listen to the earth drifting towards sleep. That night she made a mental note never to stand around wearing a shawl or she would be taken for a destitute or even a prostitute. That's towns for you, she thought.

Then there were the people. She had started off thinking townspeople rather sharp and gruff but soon found them so supportive and helpful. She also found out something else. Many townsfolk had the impression that 'thems with their country accents' were a little bit slow. And thinking that way they tried to diddle these slow country bumpkins. Trouble was thems country folks knew more than theys townies realised!

The first time it happened was when Clara opened the kitchen door to a man holding a pole with ready-skinned rabbits for sale.

'Rabbits Missus, eight pence a pair, if you will.'

Strangely these skinned animals were shorn of

their ears as well as their jackets. But he couldn't pull the wool over Clara's eyes. She knew a rabbit from a cat at a glance, no skinning could catch her out. The animals all looked fresh enough so she made a quick internal examination of each one and found only two rabbits.

'You can only 'ave one o' these Missus, for other's ordered. That's a white one see. These are nice ones,' he said, pointing to the top of the pole.

She'd already unhooked one of her choice from the bottom.

'Why d'yer want that one then?' asked the game seller.

Clara would only say, 'You offered me a rabbit and I took a rabbit,' and handed him threepence. 'Thank you,' she said, 'call again if you've got rabbits.' And she shut the door. She knew how much rabbits sold for in the town. She'd never tell him how she knew which from t'other. Thereafter he always let her make her own choice.

Town living had its compensations; the variety of friendly people and being beside the sea was an added bonus because, when she had time, Clara would walk for miles in the bracing air along the seafront either towards Shoreham harbour or east up to the cliffs at Black Rock and sometimes on to Rottingdean village.

Clara was able to make cakes for store, pickles, chutneys and preserves when the family were away on their frequent trips to London to hear the young musicians of the day. If a new composition was performed in the capital, off they would go to be there and then be able to discuss all the finer points with their friends at their own musical evenings when Mr Vaughan Williams and his friend Gustav Holst came to stay.

There were times when the whole family journeyed to Paris or even as far as Vienna just to be present to hear a new symphony or concert. It was on these occasions that Clara could take the long bus ride over to St Leonards to stay for a few days with her parents. Frankie enjoyed the ride and seeing new sights. He was never a great lover of the beach but he joined in exploration with his mother's youngest siblings, Edward and Albert, who were his own age.

Clara kept up her own spasmodic correspondence with Frank. He wrote to her regularly telling her about his journeys and the people he met. He told her about Cecil Rhodes and his own interests in the British South Africa Company. In one letter he mentioned how more British soldiers and Boer farmers died of disease than in the fighting. He couldn't always keep away from the conflict because he hated to see families suffering, whoever they were. He made money but he spent it too and he never missed sending a contribution to Frankie's future, sometimes not as much as others. Clara wrote back about twice a year. She had promised to keep him informed of Frankie's progress. As he had never had any contact with his father, young Frankie gave him very little thought. Clara told her son about Frank's letters but he showed little interest. Cooking was his interest. When the newspapers were full of the war in South Africa it never seemed to be of any relevance that his father was in South Africa.

Growing up in a big house full of people none of

whom seemed to give a thought to his position as the cook's son, he fitted in. The grandmothers, although of an earlier generation, found him a charming little chap who would run their messages more readily than their own grandchildren. These children played with Frankie as one of their own and stood up for him out in the gardens.

As the years went by, watching his mother cook became a much greater interest. He liked helping. In fact he was often another pair of much-needed hands.

Just a few months after Clara had started working for the Whitesides Rose walked unexpectedly into the basement kitchen. Two weeks would have been long enough for Rose.

'I've left 'im for good 'n' all Clara,' Rose told her sister. 'He'd got the filthiest pair of rooms over a rag 'n' bone shop. It smelt so yuk – awful! An' the wonderful job he described, turned out he only got paid out if the 'orses won.' Lowering her voice she went on, 'And I can't tell you the disgusting antics he wanted me to get up to in bed.' Shuddering at the thought she didn't intend to fully explain, she said, 'I couldn't stomach anymore of it.' Rose had walked in the back kitchen door in the middle of the morning saying, 'Don't worry ducks. I've found somewhere ter stay a night or two.'

Clara sat her sister down with a cup of tea and picked up little Leslie giving him a cuddle and a kiss with a comforting biscuit. He was silent. Frankie was at school so the little boy sat down on the floor and nibbled at his biscuit while Clara got on with the lunch preparations and listened

185

to his mum's plans.

'I'm so sorry luvvy. What do you intend to do?'

'Mrs B along in St James Street's given me a bed for a night or two an' I'm off to see about a sewing job. It'll 'ave ter be a live-in of course.'

Rose was as positive in her determination to plough her own furrow as Clara had been and it wasn't long before the dressmaking job she found had a flat with three rooms on the top floor above the owner of the dressmaking workrooms. So, like her sister she had a measure of both freedom and security. It wasn't safe for a woman alone with a child nor was it even legal for a woman to hold a rent book. At least this situation made it possible to give Leslie a more secure home because the owner's husband lived on the premises.

The sisters worked long hours but found time to visit each other and give their boys family roots. At the end of many a long day Clara would drop a postcard in the pillarbox to Rose and Rose would do the same to Clara. The messages would read, 'Finished that lacy blouse, the Guvner's ever so pleased an' Leslie got all his spellings right today.' Or 'Come over to tea on Sunday. Whitesides away so we can go to beach with boys.' Sometimes, 'Really thrilled, had a pay rise. Have got some extra trimmings for your new hat,' and, 'Had card from Mum and Dad. Fanny's working in Eastbourne now and Nancy's got her first job.'

'I've made a birthday cake for Leslie, I'll bring it Saturday.' They were short chatty notes for mutual support just keeping close sisters in touch.

Another family upset arrived one Saturday afternoon about eighteen months later, again quite out of the blue.

The Willows

'How did you come to be here at Deerfold Cottage, Bessie?' asked Geraldine, an elegant fruit bowl.

'When Leslie was a very old gentleman he used to give me to Galia to play with. She was a quiet little girl. Aw, about two years old I suppose. Well, she would sit on the mat in front of the gas fire in Leslie's tiny front parlour and he would give her some dried peas or lentils. She liked the sound of the hard dry peas running through her fingers and tinkling into me. When Leslie died in 1972 I was given to Galia and I've been here on the dresser ever since.'

'Do you remember who owned you before Leslie found you, Bessie?' asked Old Po.

'No I don't. Everything just seemed so dark. You know when Leslie found me in that cupboard he can't have been much older than Galia when I was given to her to play with.'

'You came from the Agricultural Show at Ardingly didn't you Geraldine?'

'Yes, Lily found me being used in a kitchen furniture manufacturer's display. That was in 1985, but before that I was at Lady M's manor at Chailey. That was throughout the 1930s and 40s.

'What a coincidence,' remarked Mrs P. 'So what about this other family upset?'

'I can tell that. I can tell all about that. Let me,' cried Bessie.

'Of course you can Bessie. You were there so why

not,' agreed Mrs P. The Willows were intrigued.

'Yes, and that's because my previous owner had left me in the landing cupboard outside Rose's top flat. When little Leslie found me he asked his mother if he could keep me because I was like the blue and white pattern on the china from his Great Granny Ann at the Lamb. Now about that Saturday afternoon at Rose's flat. Clara had brought Frankie to play with Leslie and the two sisters were having a cup of tea and a chat when the door knocker three floors down could be heard a rat-tat-tat.'

Who should it be but their sister Fanny? Well they were surprised to see her. Poor girl she looked worn out standing all alone with her suitcases one either side on the doorstep.

Fanny was eighteen years old but looked older and quite distraught. The sisters were shocked to see their young sister looking so unwell. They had been aware she had gone to work for the Rolland-son family in Eastbourne, a wealthy household that very frequently entertained important guests. The mother of the family decided she needed a second young maid to help her personal maid with her own and her daughter's clothes, so Fanny was being trained up to be a lady's maid. Although Fanny had been with the family for less than a year, her employer thought she was sufficiently well trained to act as personal maid to her son's new wife when she stayed with them over Christmas.

Not long into the New Year the son obtained a position with a business that necessitated him and his wife going to America for a year or so. Fanny was asked to accompany the couple to look after the young wife who was now pregnant. Emily and Tom were asked for their permission to let Fanny travel abroad as Fanny was barely eighteen years old. They gave it willingly, especially hoping it could open new future opportunities for their third daughter.

Settling Fanny with a calming hot drink, her sisters listened as Fanny unfolded the happenings of the past months. She told them first how the young wife was only twenty-four and the husband, her employer's son, was in his late thirties. On board the liner for America, Fanny said she was given a very nice small cabin only a few doors away from her master and mistress, and on the same corridor. The first night out, the husband came to Fanny's cabin. He actually entered with his own key and without a word he made her get into bed and pulled Fanny on top of him. She couldn't resist, she hadn't the strength. As he left he told her, 'Well, what do you think I had you brought along on this trip for, not for the good of my wife? She's pregnant and I need sex. Think yourself lucky, young woman, that you have such a nice cabin.'

What a shock! She didn't know how to face her mistress the next morning when she went in to help her dress. To make it worse the husband sat smoking and pretending to read the paper when he was really watching.

As the journey progressed across the Atlantic her employer came to her room every night and then sat watching the two women each morning. After a week of this the young wife told Fanny

189

she need not stay in the mornings, she would dress herself. The young lady obviously felt uncomfortable being watched so closely. Fanny told her sisters the husband would have none of it. 'What do you think I pay her for my dear? Let the girl dress you.' Then he looked at them both and said slowly in a sly tone of voice, 'I like watching two women handling each other,' making Fanny feel like vomiting.

One way she could delay his unwanted attentions was to take her mistress's clothes down to the ship's laundry in the evenings on the pretext that her employer was so fussy with her clothes, staying away from her cabin late into the night, washing and ironing the clothes herself. She was careful not to put the laundry workers against her but it was a relief to have others to talk to. Getting to know the staff and other travellers' servants she found her predicament not entirely unheard of. Although it gave her strength to cope it didn't help her feelings of horrible violation.

Fanny decided to enquire after a job on the liner for its return journey. The purser told her there was certainly an opportunity but she would need to get her personal arrangements in order. She'd have to secure her release from her present position and that could prove difficult because she was listed as Mr Rollandson's property. Fanny told how he reacted.

'Don't try to blackmail me girl,' the rapist hissed. 'You can tell my wife what you like. She won't believe you. And I will say you pushed yourself onto me.'

At eighteen and with so little knowledge of the

world Fanny talked to other servants in the laundry. Some sympathised while others had their own troubles.

'All I wanted,' Fanny said, 'was to come straight back home to my family.'

Then she went on to tell her sisters how a silly mistake on her employer's part opened the way for her to retrieve her passport. Her employer, Mr Rollandson, was caught cheating at cards. Word soon got round. He became distrusted by fellow passengers and those who frequented the card tables would no longer take a seat with him.

Fanny told her mistress that she was so homesick she wanted to leave her service when they docked in New York and return home. She also mentioned that the purser had said there was a job for her in the laundry which meant her employers wouldn't have to pay her return fare. Being young and pregnant herself the woman knew how Fanny felt, she too was lonely and homesick, and although sad to lose somebody from home she agreed and asked her husband's permission to release Fanny. He told his wife he'd take the cost out of the silly girl's wages.

'Oh I don't think you should do that my dear, Fanny has been so helpful to me. She's very young. I'm missing my family too and I hardly ever see you. I know how she feels.'

'Damn you women,' her husband shouted. 'Here take the money. That's what we owe her isn't it?' He threw the coins across the cabin.

'My dear, why are you so annoyed? We can find another maid in New York.'

Fanny was lucky she got away so easily. He

knew, though, that if he had made a fuss Fanny would have told the purser her full reason. In the circumstances the purser would have believed her.

Although Fanny worked hard on the journey back to England she enjoyed the freedom and new hope. When the liner called in at Newfoundland a flamboyant young man boarded, travelling steerage. He had a French accent and was really rather attractive. Although as Fanny told her sisters she definitely was not looking for a man after what she had so recently experienced. Nevertheless she liked him and enjoyed his company and all his ideas. He told her about what he planned to do when he got to France. It all sounded so exciting.

One of the old hands among the staff took Fanny aside and told her, 'I know him, he's no more French than I am. And there's another thing gal. Don't bother with him for anything to do with love.' Fanny at eighteen said she didn't know what he meant. Was the young man married, she asked?

'No,' the adviser said, 'that one prefers men.' Well she didn't know what that meant either, at that time.

'And don't you tell him I told you. Keep it to yourself or you'll get him in trouble.'

'Aw I wouldn't do that.' But Fanny spoke up for herself. 'One thing you should know. I'm not looking for a man. I had enough trouble with the employer I was working for on the outward journey.'

'Yes, I do know that me luv. We all did. That's why I didn't want to see you get into any further difficulties. Oh by the way, the purser knew it too. We did tell him, that's why you got this job.'

Fanny felt she'd found a second family including the non-Frenchman who preferred men.

It was no surprise to her two elder sisters that Fanny ended her tale with the words, 'Now I'm pregnant.'

The sisters cried and laughed together in Rose's little flat on the fourth floor above her employer's workroom on Queen's Road.

'Come on, dry those tears girls,' ordered Rose, 'there's only one way and that's to go straight to the 'orse's mouth.' With that statement she went out of the room and down the stairs leaving her sisters in suspense.

'What do you think she's up to?' Fanny asked.

'Don't worry dear. Our Rose is an organiser. She got me sorted out when I had my troubles,' Clara assured her.

'I don't know how you've both managed on your own.'

'We're not on our own girl. We've got each other and now we've got you.'

'Thanks Clara. Mum always called you her rock, taking care of us all.'

It was some time before Rose returned. When she did it was with good news.

'I've gotcher a job Fanny. I told the missus downstairs that you've been a lady's maid an' good with the ironing, so she says she can use you in the workroom.'

'But I haven't got anywhere to live Rose. I was on my way 'ome to Mum and Dad.'

'Course you got somewhere ter live – 'ere o'

193

course. Dear oh dear, I 'ad the same trouble with Clara. Now look, I 'ad ter tell the missus exactly what's 'appened to yer before I came an' told you about the job. Anyway Mr Jacobs 'e came in while we were talkin' an' 'eard it all. Says it's all right for you to share this flat with me. An' yer know what? 'E'd come back from London with a big order so 'e says you're just what they need in the workroom startin' next week.'

'What about the baby, Rose?'

'Oh don't worry we'll see about that when the time comes.'

'When do you expect it by the way?'

'Six months I think. Oh, I can't believe it. I can't tell you what a relief. I thought you'd throw me out.' Fanny's tears of relief flowed.

'Us, throw you out!' Rose squeaked in her disbelief, 'Oh Fanny, how could we? Haven't we had our troubles, you said so yourself. You 'ave a good cry luv, make yer feel better it will.'

'Yes, I know but what about your employers Rose, how could they take it so easily?'

'Fanny, half the women on earth would be out on their ears and walkin' the streets if it weren't for people who understood reality.'

'Nobody could say this baby was your fault. And who would want to have anything more to do with such a disgustingly selfish brute as your employer? It's his poor wife I feel sorry for,' remarked Clara, then added, 'Money isn't everything.'

'You can say that again Clara, but it ain't half useful.' A bit more laughter did a world of good.

'We've got each other to look after now,' Clara said. Then she promised to find out if Mrs Turk would attend Fanny when her time came.

'That's it then Fan,' said Rose, 'now we can all look forward. The guvnor's brought in some lovely material for next week's job,' she called out from the kitchen as she put the kettle on.

Fanny worked at her sewing job with Rose until her son Peter was born in Rose's flat, helped by Mrs Turk. Baby Peter was the last baby Mrs Turk delivered before retiring. Fanny was lucky to have her attend the birth. When old Mrs Turk had cleaned up and cleared away she cradled Peter in her arms telling him, 'That's me lot young lad, you're me last. I'm 'angin' up me apron today. You better grow up a big strong man an' do yer mother an' me proud.'

Living together above the workrooms Rose and Fanny were able to look after the two boys and carry on working. On Sundays they would take the omnibus or walk along the prom to Clara and have tea down in her sitting room behind the kitchen.

It was only natural living in such close company that the sisters had their disagreements but they were only minor ones, after all they were such different characters. Strong-minded Rose always quick to react; she lacked Clara's calm thoughtfulness. Fanny's character now matured within her sisters' protection, and she proved her quiet determination to succeed on a higher plain. For her part Clara wanted Frankie and Leslie to meet and know their heritage. When her visits to see Grandfather John at Hailsham cattle market came during the school holidays she took both the boys along with her. They loved that outing on the puffing-billy train and Grandfather John did so enjoy seeing both his great grandsons.

Fanny's 'non-Frenchman' had kept in touch. He sought her out when Peter was near-on three years old. Clara and Rose found him engaging company, but older than Fanny had described. He turned out to be a great help to Fanny. It was through Pierre Dupont that Fanny was to have her own business.

6

Clara

Rata tat tat. 'Morning Mrs Dann.' The baker always knocked on the door and waited to be invited in.

'Good morning Mr Cowley, come on in out of that rain now why don't you? Nice cup of tea Mr Cowley? I've just got the kettle singing.'

'Don't mind if I do Mrs Dann.'

From the first week Clara was at Adelaide Crescent Mr Cowley the baker called before breakfast and again before afternoon tea on Mondays, Thursdays and Saturdays, whatever the weather or time of year, great basket on his arm and more to choose from outside in the van, his patient horse waiting at the kerbside for his orders. On wet, cold days Thomas Cowley wore a black-caped Mackintosh covering his usual waistcoat, rolled-up shirt sleeves and long navy striped apron, and never without a neat collar and tie, he had respect for his customers. Order book and payment chits along with cash were in a double-pocket leather satchel strapped round his waist. Saturday was a busy day, no time for chat. Soon as produce was selected, his tea blown cool enough to drink, Thomas stood up saying, 'Well I must be off. Thanks for the cuppa Mrs Dann.'

'Bye, Mr Cowley.' The same opening and closing words had passed between Thomas Cowley and Clara Dann for the last eight years. It was very formal, except that in some involuntary way as it is with people who meet regularly, they knew a lot about each other's lives and background through their short snatches of conversation.

She knew he was a widower living in one room above his son-in-law's butcher's shop over towards Montpelier Road. He knew she was from St Leonards-on-Sea originally where her parents still lived and she had twelve brothers and sisters and that she regularly visited her ageing grandfather when he was attending the cattle market in Hailsham. He knew also that she had a young son who lived with her, and two sisters, also with sons, one living in Hove and the other near the railway station in Brighton. He could see she was generally fulfilled because she loved her cooking as much she did the little boy, but she was sorely overworked. That worried him although he realised it was none of his business. After all, everybody worked long hours and those living in service mostly worked longer hours than anybody.

Clara knew Mr Cowley didn't feel at home where he was. His daughter Ethel could be a real shrew at times and both Thomas and Ethel's husband Albert suffered equally from the woman's sharp tongue. Thomas's son, Dudley, would have given him a home but his wife was an ailing soul and couldn't have coped with a lodger in the house besides two youngsters. No, Thomas kept out of the flat above the butcher's shop as much as he could, making a life for himself by serving all the nice people who were his customers.

'Mummy, Mr Jones has sent me out of the gardens again.' A small dark-haired boy, neat in knickerbockers and hard white collar, called out as he ran down the area steps, tears barely held at bay.

'Oh dear, rules,' sighed Clara. Then another child's voice up by the railings shouted down, 'C'mon Frankie, take no notice of Jones. You're our friend and it's our gardens not his.'

'Yes, do come back,' called a small girl's voice, 'an' bring some buns and lemonade if you would. Don't be long, I'm starving.'

'Just a minute Frankie, I'll bring the lemonade. Mr Cowley's got some iced buns on his van I'm sure.' Turning to Thomas Cowley, who had just sat down to an afternoon cuppa on his Saturday teatime round, she said, 'Be a dear and let me have a half dozen more buns. Sorry to have to get you up those steps again. Pity that garden attendant can't overlook one small child, it does no harm, they're quite happy playing altogether.' To Frankie she called, 'I'm coming love. If I come too Mr Jones will have to let us in.'

Frankie was waiting patiently beside the baker's van when Clara came up the steps with a bottle of homemade lemonade and four china beakers. Mr Cowley followed saying, 'Now then young man what shall it be? There's a few iced buns left or eccles.' Before he could say more, Frankie answered firmly, 'We like iced buns best please Mr Cowley.'

'So it shall be then four nice icey-spiceys how's that, go down just right with lemon juicy?' Frankie smiled at the man's wordy old joking while his mother laughed her appreciation.

'Let's take all this into the garden then dear. You lead on.'

The Whiteside children, Judy and Georgie, came running across the grass to plunge their hands into the paper bag of sticky buns.

'Is there one for Tilly too?' asked Judy.

'Course,' replied Frankie, 'haven't forgotten Til.'

'Now, where're you going to sit and drink this lemonade?'

'Oh thank you Mrs Dann,' said George.

'Over here will be our cottage garden,' answered Judy, pointing to where little Joaney crouched by the hedge pretending to lay out a cloth and scatter cushions around. 'You sit there Tilly dear beside Aunty Joaney and your daddy Frank Dann can sit next to you. George and I will pour the tea and hand it round. Oh, George, do come on.' The children sat joining in the game and Clara set the bottle of lemonade and the beakers down between them.

'Thank you, Mrs Dann,' said Judy very formally.

'Pleasure Miss Judy,' replied Clara, also very formally and she even gave a little bobbing curtsey. As she walked back to the gate Mr Jones the attendant caught up with her and said, 'Now by rights your boy shouldn't be 'ere in the railed gardens, it's for residents only. If I let one in, all the riff raff'll think they can come 'ere.'

Clara stopped. 'My son is not riff raff Mr Jones, so don't call him that. You know perfectly well where we live and you also know Mrs Whiteside has given the children permission to take their friend Frankie to play in the gardens along with them.'

'Yes, Mrs Dann, but the other residents don't know that, and they complain when their children tell them a servant's boy is in the gardens.'

'Then you will have to tell them to refer their complaints to Mrs Whiteside, Mr Jones.'

'I can't speak to the residents like that. I'd lose my job,' whined Jones, indignant at her suggestion.

'Then you will have to think of another way Mr Jones. Let the children play. Life's too short to do all things grumbling. Good afternoon.'

Of course Clara knew she had no right to speak to the man like that. After all he had his job to do just like any other servant. One day maybe things would change, she thought.

Thomas had been standing in the road watching the scene. 'Do you always curtsey to the children?' he asked Clara as she came across the road.

'No!' she laughed. 'It's all just fun. Judy loves to play mother, she likes it all just so. Now come and finish your tea, you've had a long week, you must need that drink before you get on to your last calls.'

Before he left, Thomas asked Clara if she got an

hour off on Sunday at all. 'Would you care to take a walk out with me if it's fine tomorrow?' he asked.

'That would be nice. I could probably be out by half past four, just for a while though. The family have asked for a cooked tea for the children this Sunday.'

'Thank you Clara. I look forward to seeing you tomorrow.'

The man who lifted his brown bowler hat to her that sunny Sunday afternoon on the promenade was something quite different, unexpected in fact. Thomas Cowley was always neat and tidy but this man was a very good looker; a round, close-trimmed beard and narrow, slightly flyaway, soft moustache that didn't hide his lips. Clara had not noticed what attractive lips he had. Also really blue eyes and a head of thick dark-brown hair that it seemed a pity to obscure with a hat.

Here in full sunlight reflecting off a sparkling sea she wondered what she looked like straight out of a hot Sunday lunchtime kitchen, when he had had time to groom himself and put on a fulsome navy silk necktie and a well-cut brown jacket suit. She knew his age. He was then forty-nine, smooth-skinned with rather a serious look on his face.

Pushing a stray curl back under her floral straw hat Clara went towards him, her hand out ready to shake his. He simply took her hand and pulled it through under his arm. 'I thought you wouldn't come,' he said gently.

'Oh Thomas I wouldn't be so unkind.'

So, looking straight ahead, they just walked. He seemed struck dumb, lost for words. She barely came up to his shoulder.

'How long have you got Clara? I don't want to make you late.'

'An hour at most, but let's forget about that, it's just good to feel the sun and the fresh air.' Then quickly she added, glancing up at him, 'And it's not at all bad being on a handsome man's arm.' That broke the ice so they could both laugh.

They couldn't stroll on the Lawns, or take tea at one of the kiosks – Clara wasn't dressed well enough to get away with that, she had only had time to throw on an old cream summer jacket over her afternoon floral cotton. That said it all: 'servant'.

'Never mind that Clara, it makes little difference to me where we walk. It's lovely to be with you.'

Why had she never thought of Thomas Cowley in this way before? When he had made his deliveries he had always been businesslike and friendly and, in their passing conversations over the cup of something she always offered, he had been fairly offhand, say, resigned over the family circumstances he described. It was just rather reassuring for both of them to have a sympathetic ear. A bond had grown between them almost without their realising. Well, it had been more than eight years.

This bond took its time to grow still stronger over the course of the summer months. Clara organised the Whitesides' Sunday lunch to be cleared away more quickly so that she had an hour with Thomas walking along the prom or sitting in a shelter out of the rain. It was just comforting to be together. Sometimes Mrs Whiteside would ask for a savoury cooked meal on Sunday evening or one of the grandmothers would say she had a guest and 'Could a nice tea be sent up?'. Neither knew Clara took a bit of time off for herself on Sunday afternoons. Mrs Dann was the family cook and provided what they asked of her.

Rose had quickly sized up the situation and kept Frankie for the whole day, bringing him back after tea on Sunday. Previously Frankie had walked along Western Road to meet Leslie and Rose, and she would take the boys to church, leaving them at Sunday school while she stepped back to Queens Road to cook a Sunday dinner. It was a long walk for Frankie so Rose would sometimes take the boys along the seafront back to Adelaide on an open-top horse bus that picked up at the railway station, went down to Poole Valley and all along the front to Hove Lawns. The boys loved it. They always tried to go right to the front upstairs so they could look straight down on top of the driver. They had to keep quiet though or the driver would shout up to them, ''Ere you boyz, sit yer down or I'll 'ave yer orf me bus.'

'Aw right Bill,' Rose would call out, 'their mother's with 'em.'

Whether his name was Bill or not, Rose thought it sounded authoritative to take the upper hand straight off. She was right in most cases.

'Have you ever had your own home, your own kitchen, Clara?'

'Now you say it Thomas, no I suppose I haven't.'

'How about it then Clara?'

She stopped beating her batter and looked at him. He smiled. 'Would you think of marrying me dear?'

She couldn't say 'I hardly know you'. He hadn't ever even given her a kiss. Well you didn't in full daylight on a Sunday afternoon in the street.

He would have loved her to give him an answer there and then, but he could see she had a lot to consider. 'I'll leave it with you then. Well, I must be off. Thanks for the cuppa Mrs–' he grinned with embarrassment. 'Thank you Clara. See you on Saturday morning.'

'Bye Thomas.'

Clara stood distractedly looking into space. Her arm automatically carried on beating the mixture. Do I love him, she asked herself? Where would we live? And there was Frankie to consider. Her arm ached. Oh bother, it's a bit too thick. Adding a little more milk she told herself to put her mind on the job in hand or she'd be all behind and there were extras to prepare for store and preserves to make so she could get ahead. Christmas wasn't far off and the young Whitesides always came down to stir the puddings and secrete their sixpences when she wasn't looking. And what was it Mrs Whiteside had said this morning when they were sitting together over the weekend menu order? 'Oh I must tell you Clara, Mr Brangwyn did enjoy those biscuits you sent up last Sunday. I said he could have some to take next time he came. Can you do some extras next time Clara?'

Then as she left Clara's little sitting room

retreat Mrs Whiteside turned and, smiling at Clara, said, 'I really don't know what we'd do without you Clara. Thank you so much.'

Her arm stopped again. It would be very nice to have her own kitchen and just cook for herself. What a thought. Mmm ... more biscuits, plum jam and there are those blackberries still to do. A rat-tat on the door. Oh my goodness he's come back, she thought. The door opened a crack and a head came through.

'Just makin' sure your coal door's shut love,' the coalman called out. He always came down the area steps to make sure the cellar door was tight closed before sending his coal delivery down the coal hole in the pavement. 'Now keep this door closed on yer'self missus. This mornin' I'm sendin' down extra for all that Christmas bakin' you tell't me about the other day, all right?'

'Yes. And thank you, Charlie,' Clara called, nipping into the scullery for a cloth to soak at the sink before laying it along the bottom of the door. Coal dust flew everywhere and she didn't want it in her kitchen getting fine grit on the food. That meant pushing up the sash window tight closed as well.

What with the jam making and pot filling, waxing in the lids, the lunch to prepare and a hot pudding today, she mustn't forget to fill that bucket and slosh the steps and area yard down before the provision van came with dried fruit and sugar after lunch. She had already taken extra flour from Thomas's van that morning so she wouldn't be seeing him again until Saturday. No more thought of his offer passed through her mind for the rest of that day.

Clara had been walking out on Sunday afternoons all that summer. It had taken nine years. Thomas hadn't given it any thought himself, only but a year ago when he had seen Clara handling a tricky situation in the kindest of manner. Good heavens he had thought to himself, women could be so different. Ethel would have bitten everybody's heads off, turned everything against herself and come off badly in a deal and walked away worse off and still not admitting it.

His poor dear wife Maisie couldn't have been more different again. It had always been her way to see the best in people. Even when she wasn't well herself she'd gone to her parents' home in Worthing to help nurse her mother even though her own sister lived in the same street. But no, her sister Jess said her family needed her more. She hadn't got the time to look in constantly on their mother. Maisie's answer was that Jess had four children while she only had two who were old enough to look after themselves at ten and twelve, just for a few days, so she could nurse her own mother. So while Maisie's mother got better, Maisie overworked herself looking after her father and nursing her mother. Coming home with pneumonia, she died the following week. She was only thirty-three. Maisie had been four years older than Thomas when they married. Their boy Dudley was ten at the time. He missed his mother but for some reason Jess had offered to look after him so he'd stayed over in Worthing while Ethel kept house for her dad, seeing him off to work each morning in her own slapdash

206

thirteen-year-old way.

Adolescence came on Ethel early, making her appearance voluptuous and worth a real look from all the young men. Fortunately Ethel had already been seeing her monthly courses before her mother died so Thomas didn't have that to negotiate with the growing girl. Ethel never got over her mother's loss but neither did she want to be saddled with looking after her father for the rest of her life! By the time she was eighteen and working in the cash desk at Rolf's butcher's shop she knew where her aim lay. Mr Rolf's son, Albert, was in his middle twenties and still unmarried. He was expecting to take over the family business, so Albert was a good catch and Ethel made straight for him. He didn't have a chance. Albert hadn't bothered much with girlfriends but this one had plenty of meat on her. He fell, she caught. Ten years later and three children he often wondered how he hadn't noticed the way that tongue had cut into customers. All right for getting their money but the business never got their custom back.

Thomas hadn't gone to live with his daughter and new son-in-law right away. He'd never do that to a pair of newlyweds. He stayed on in the cottage he rented in Upper North Street for five years. It was hard, working long hours and looking after himself. He ate the odd pie off the van most days and that did for his dinner with an apple or sweet onion maybe. A cup of tea and a bun back at the bakery did the rest. Then most Sundays, Ethel had him up their place for a good meat Sunday dinner. One day Albert noticed Thomas had great holes in his socks and made his suggestion.

'Why don't you come and live with us Dad? We've got a spare room an' you can store your furniture in one of my sheds.' Albert had thought about it and considered his father-in-law would be a buffer between Ethel's tongue and his ear. 'Go on Dad, say yes. Make your life a lot easier.'

So Thomas agreed, and got the other half of the sharp tongue.

Recently instead of a snooze in the chair he had taken to going straight up from the Sunday dinner table, shaving, changing his clothes and going out. He didn't say where.

It was a Friday and Clara was joining Frankie on his walk to school because she had a bit of business to see to and would be passing his school. Frankie didn't mind because it gave him time to talk with Clara about a recipe he wanted to try so that he could take his teacher a piece of his cooking next Monday. Frankie at twelve had stayed on longer than he needed to because he had a job to go to after Christmas. As he shut the gate at the top of the area steps and started to walk up the crescent Frankie noticed a lady, well dressed in a good winter coat with a high fur collar almost hiding her face, only her eyes visible between collar and a large floppy hat.

'Hum, Mother, that lady over there. She's staring at you.'

Clara stopped a moment, looked and walked on. 'I've never seen her before, son.'

'Do you think she wants to ask directions?'

'Maybe, but we daren't stop or you'll be late if

we get caught up. There's plenty of other people about.'

'But she's still staring at us Mum.'

The woman started across towards them so they hung back, just a little, but before she got close she said, quite loudly, 'I just wanted to 'ave a look at what my father was seein' on Sunday afternoons.'

'Are you addressing my mother?' asked Frankie, formally but politely.

The woman didn't appear to take any notice but went on in the same tone. 'I wondered who he might be carryin' on with on Sundays. 'E 'asn't got any money if that's what yer think.'

Clara walked on and Frankie followed suit, leaving the woman standing in the middle of the road.

'She looks like a lady but she doesn't sound like one,' Frankie commented to his mother.

Clara knew who she was all right. Oh yes. This woman fitted Thomas's description perfectly.

'I'm going to make some cheese d'Artois,' Frankie explained. He'd forgotten about the shouting woman. 'Miss Todd says she likes savouries so I thought I would give her a taste of my cooking before I leave. What do you think, Mother?'

'That sounds just the thing, Frank. Will you want three different types of cheese or are you making layers between puff pastry?'

'Oh just one type, the cheesemonger calls on Saturday mornings doesn't he?'

'Yes, about half past eight dear.'

'I'll be down in good time then. Bye Ma.

Thanks for the chat.'

Frankie gave his mum an affectionate squeeze and a peck on the cheek. They were close but not sentimental. He saw himself more in the line of looking after her now. He'd be earning soon and intended to see she had a few nice things.

It wasn't the thought that this handsome middle-aged man was living where he didn't feel at home, although that was true. It was that Clara could see she and he hit it off. In fact she found herself proud to be on his arm during their walks.

On Friday night Clara called Frankie into her sitting room with a purpose. Usually he liked to meet his pals to play football up in Hove Park. The evenings were drawing in fast so time was short.

'Can you leave it 'til I get back Mum? I really want to have a kick about and see Bud about tomorrow's game at the Albion.'

So, much later that night, Clara told Frankie about Thomas's suggestion. Frankie sat back in the chair opposite his mother deep in thought. Then he said, 'Mum you've done your best for me. You know what I'm planning for my future and it will soon take me away from home. So if I'm unselfish I can only say that now's the time you can make new arrangements for your future.'

Frank Ashdown had finally got the message and unselfishly let her go her own way. Now his son was reacting similarly.

'Thing is, do you love him?' he asked.

'I can't tell, Frankie. Not yet. I'm not the young woman I was when I loved your father. It doesn't feel the same to me now. I haven't known that kind of love for so long. I'm different now. When you fall in love you'll know what I mean.'

'I've fallen in love with cooking, but I hope loving a person will be different.'

'Oh yes. Very, very different sweetheart, and I hope you do.'

'It would be good for you to have a home of your own, Mum. I know the Whitesides think the world of you but they don't have the reasoned thought a loving partner would have when yet another request comes down for your attention just when you are going up to bed.'

Frankie was more far-seeing than most lads of his age.

'Thank you dear.' Clara leaned forward and squeezed her son's hand. No more than that. He was coming into the years when he didn't want his mother constantly patting and pawing him the way she'd seen some mothers do – Rose, for instance.

He's right. I came into this job to have some measure of security for the pair of us. Now he's on the cusp of his own life – yes this is a chance for me to have a life of my own choosing.

On Saturday morning Thomas came through the door slowly, looking apprehensive. Clara looked round from her position at the range where she was stirring a sauce.

'Yes,' she said and went on stirring.

No sound came from behind her. Thomas hadn't moved. But for him the earth had. He was still trying to control his balance. She turned and walked towards the table with her pan and spoon to pour its contents into a bowl of soft fruit. Looking up again and smiling she repeated the word, 'Yes.' Thomas set his basket down on a chair behind the door and let out a huge sigh.

'Oh Clara, will you? I can't believe it.' He made to walk towards her then stopped himself. 'May I kiss you?' he asked.

'Of course. Come here.'

They embraced for the first time. He was shaking in his joy and relief. She found a man's arms round her for the first time, in love, not as her brothers sometimes did when they came. This time, this time, it was a man who loved her as a woman. It hadn't happened for nearly fourteen years. It seemed a huge cloud had lifted.

'I really do love you Clara. Thank you for saying yes.'

After a soothing sit down with a hot drink Thomas jumped up as if a new man inside him had been set free. 'My gawd, I don't know how I'm going to get through my customers for the rest of today.' He made a dash for the door, then turned back and gave Clara a kiss on the cheek. Going through the doorway he realised he'd left his basket and had to turn back. 'There, what did I tell you, I'm good for nothing now! Oh, and will I see you tomorrow? I've such a lot to tell you dear.'

'Tomorrow. Now go on Thomas Cowley, back to work – you'll do.'

She laughed to see him as he went up the steep steps two at a time.

When Sunday dawned, Frankie told his mother

he'd arranged to stay at Adelaide Crescent all day. 'Auntie Rose understood. I'm going to help you with the dinner then I'll wash up so you can get off early to meet Mr Cowley.' He'd got it all worked out.

With autumn well on, the family expected a good substantial roast of mutton with lots of vegetables, roast potatoes and a steamed plum and apple pudding with custard. Cooking for four adults, five young people, three servants and a young son, the pair were kept busy until half past two. On Sundays the same food was provided for all, family and servants alike.

'Now then mother you go up and get changed, I'll wash up and don't worry about getting back. If they send down for tea I can see to that.'

'That's an awful lot of china and glass to get through Frankie.'

'Well, you do it, so I can. And anyway Coleen and Madge are both going to help me.'

'That's very good of Coleen, it's not usually her job though.'

'Don't you fret, Mother,' Frankie told her as he ushered her firmly through the door. He was already inches taller than Clara; it was quite noticeable, and it made him add, 'My little mother,' with a cheeky laugh.

She was early and looking her best. Thomas was already there and coming towards her saying, 'Clara, I do apologise for Ethel. She was so rude. I...'

Clara raised her hand to silence his apologies. 'That's Ethel, Thomas. Let's forget her right now or she'll spoil our enjoyment of life.'

'Yes,' Thomas replied, relieved. 'You are very sensible, let's forget her. I've more to tell than expected my dear.'

'Go on then.'

So as they walked arm in arm Thomas explained how the bakery was opening a new branch in Kemp Town and he would be Chief Roundsman Manager covering Sussex Square, Lewes Crescent and Arundel Road, right up to Roedean School. He told her how he would be training the new roundsman for his patch in Hove and would be having a whole day off on a Wednesday quite soon.

'Ah, wait a bit,' Clara said. 'That's rather sooner than I can make plans for, Tom.'

'I thought you'd say that. Sorry I didn't mean to press you Clara.'

'It's not my choice you see dear. I do have to give three months' notice, and Christmas is nearly upon us. I couldn't leave the family before Christmas. When do you start your new duties?'

'Not until after Christmas but I will be organising the roundsmen and going to the houses to get the new customers.'

'Have you told Ethel and Albert anything yet?'

'No nothing, let her nose carry on twitching. We'll settle our plans before I tell anyone else.'

'Could you stay where you are until after Christmas, Tom?'

'Well I might not have to. There's a nice little flat and it's got two bedrooms, over the stables in St Mark's Mews where the vans are kept. None of the stable lads need it so I've asked the guvner if I could have first option. That's why I was going to say to you we could move in soon. But I see your point. You can't do that. There's nothing to stop me getting it all done up and my furniture moved in. Yes, that would be practical. What do you think about that Clara?'

'It would be a help Tom. That Wednesday you say you've got off work. Would you consider coming with me over to meet Grandfather?'

'That would be nice. I'd like that.'

The pair talked for so long that dusk was setting in before they realised how far they had walked. They'd passed Ovingdean village and were almost at Rottingdean on the cliff path.

'I've laid tea out in the sitting room Tom so let's wend our way back. And there's still a lot we need to talk over.'

Where to get wed? It couldn't be a church wedding so the simplest was the Registry Office at Hove Town Hall.

'I'm sorry Clara.'

'What's to be sorry about Tom? How we do it isn't important. That's just a certificate, a piece of paper. Life together and what we make of it, that's what's important to me.'

'There's a good school in Arundel Road, so Frankie will be all right.'

'He's leaving school at Christmas Tom. So that won't be needed. And he's got his plans to take up a kitchen job at the Grand. He'll be living in. I'd like us to keep a room for him. You won't mind will you?'

'Good heavens, Clara, he's your boy. Of course I don't mind. I'm pleased he's so loving and kind to your plans, and mine. He's part of your life, so

215

he'll be part of mine soon.'

Tom had never seen Clara's sitting room along the passage from the kitchen.

'Oh this is nice, Clara. Is the furniture yours?'

'No Tom, I've just got crockery and bedding linens of my own so I'm glad to hear about your furniture.'

'I've made a list of what I've got in store in Albert's shed so if you'd like to go through it...'

'Tom, you're lovely, you think of everything. Thank you.'

'Well let's hope we can have that flat. Maybe in a couple of weeks I can take you to see it.'

'So, three months' time then?'

As she watched Tom go up the area steps late on that Sunday night Clara thought, no time like the present, and sat down at her desk to write her letter to Mr and Mrs Whiteside explaining how she would be getting married in January and therefore would be leaving their service. Coleen delivered the envelope on Mrs Whiteside's breakfast tray on the Monday morning.

Mr Whiteside was late for the office on that day and Mrs Whiteside did not rush down to Clara with her weekly menu order at the usual time. Routine in the house had come to a sudden halt. It wasn't until half past ten that Mrs Whiteside entered Clara's sitting room with her household book and sat herself down at the table as usual.

'Congratulations Clara. Mr Whiteside and I hope you will be very happy,' she said, with a kind smile. 'Although I have to say,' she went on, 'we couldn't be more unhappy that you want to leave us. Is there no chance of you staying?'

'No. We will be moving over to Kemp Town, Madam.'

'Oh well. Thank you for being considerate about Christmas.' And so, putting aside the personal, routine took over, with the week's menu orders to discuss and a review of Christmas preparations already underway. Before leaving, Mrs Whiteside asked, 'Would you kindly help me assess a new cook, Clara? I would appreciate your help.'

Throughout the day discreet taps on the door brought visits from all three of the children, who made sure she knew their loss, coming right into the kitchen and throwing their arms round her waist pleading, 'Do you have to get married, Clara?'

'Couldn't you stay with us, Clara?'

'Couldn't you marry me, Clara then you could stay,' begged young George.

'Will Frankie be getting married too?' asked little Joaney. 'I do hope he won't.'

Even the elderly grandmothers each sent down formal messages by the upstairs staff to say how much they would miss her.

Rose and Fanny had kept abreast of Clara's meetings with 'her chap' as they called Tom. They hadn't met him yet, that was all to come. Clara wanted to be in control of her own decisions although she knew her sisters would never try to stop her happiness. She just wanted to be quite sure for herself.

A letter came, addressed to 'Mrs Dann, Cook'. Clara read the letter with mounting disgust. Its handwriting got more erratic and large as the pages progressed. She was thankful she'd opened it in the privacy of her sitting room with the door closed because the language she was reading was so gross. In fact some words she had actually never seen before, although it was obvious what they meant. The stupid, horrible woman had even ended it with her name. Clara sat for a long time in shock – all those filth and allusions to bodily parts! As she quietly folded the notepaper sheets, Clara began to laugh in disbelief that the idea had even crossed her mind that somebody might have overheard what she had been reading. 'Silly Clara,' she said to herself. 'No,' she continued, 'I'm not letting Tom know about this, it's too revolting.' Whatever would he think to even know his own daughter could write such horrible things about her father? He'd be so ashamed and Clara was damn sure she wouldn't allow him to be embarrassed. Goodness knows what her poor dead mother Maisie would have said.

Resolved to keep to her decision that Ethel should never be allowed to put a canker into their lives, Clara went through to the kitchen, lifted the lid on the range fire box and plunged the sheets of paper deep into the hot coals. She would never let on that she ever received any letter.

Tom was so pleased to be invited to meet Grandfather Pilbeam. Early on the Wednesday morning the pair sat comfortably together, each quiet in their own thoughts, on the upper deck of the motor omnibus waiting to move off from Poole Valley bus station. It wasn't until the bus ground its way up the hill to the pretty village of Falmer that any conversation got started. Clara took a white napkin-wrapped parcel from her basket and offered Tom an egg sandwich.

'Breakfast Tom, I don't expect you've eaten this morning yet.'

He laughed. 'How did you know?'

'Just intuition dear,' she replied, 'it's a long journey over to Hailsham so we might as well make ourselves comfortable.' Out of the basket came a glass bottle and two small cups. 'Tea?' she asked. 'Afraid it's cold but it's sweet.'

'This is like a Sunday school treat, makes me feel like a nipper again.'

'Good,' she said, 'and why not?'

As the bus trundled over the cobbles into Lewes, Clara pointed out a narrow turning where her eldest brother Jack lived, off to the left round behind the castle. 'He's only been there a few months, got married to Pearl in July. Pearl was in service, housemaid, over at The Grange.'

After changing buses at the bottom of School Hill they crossed the bridge over the Ouse, Clara telling Tom that Jack worked at the brewery on the left at the end of the High Street. As they went left round Cliffe the bus conductor called up, 'Anybody for Newhaven 'cos we're goin' to Ringmer me dears. Right, off we go then.' Taking Malling Hill towards Ringmer, the road undulated gently, winding its way down into Laughton, then the long road across to Lower Dicker passing the smoking chimney at the pottery, on through Horsebridge by the flour mill and across the Cuckmere river this time, into Hailsham. There the bus had to wend its way slowly through the throng of farmers and animals gathered for the auction.

Tom had been thoroughly engrossed in the landscape and all the little stories Clara had told him, while drawing his attention to the sights. He knew West Sussex best, it was where he grew up, so that would be a treat he looked forward to giving Clara one day. Now he was deep in thought as the bus inched into the town. He was apprehensive. Would the old gentleman approve of him he wondered? Twenty years older than Clara and a widower with two grown children.

Tom stood back when Clara tapped her grandfather's elbow. As he turned, he lifted off his old tweed hat at the sight of a lady. Tom was surprised to see he had such a full head of flowing white hair.

'Clara Ann, my lovely. 'Ow are thee gal?' At once, Clara was enveloped in the arms of this great bear of a man who was giving her a hug and a kiss. 'Oh 'tis good ter see thee. 'Ow's Frankie, is he with thee?' And what a loud deep voice he had. What with the 'thees' and 'thous' and the curls running down his temples into mutton chop sideburns, they could have walked back into the eighteenth century. John was wearing his shepherds' smock that day for this particular market meet. Oh Lordy, the man even stood head and shoulders above the crowd, an old leather satchel slung over his shoulders and a tall crook. All Tom could think was the line from the psalm, 'The Lord is my Shepherd'.

Then Clara stood on her toes to speak to the old man and he looked up sharp across to Tom, who stepped forward.

'Granfer, this is Tom.' The hand took a hold full square and honest as the words that accompanied it, "'Tis a glad day to meet thee Tom.'

'Good to meet you, sir,' replied Tom, lifting his bowler in respect.

'Come now, will 'ee take a sup?'

'I certainly will,' replied Tom. 'Thank you.'

Most of the older men in the gathering knew Clara, saying, 'Hallo my dear' or 'There 'tis my duckie, 'ow are thee?' and 'Good ter see thee, Clara.'

Sitting outside the Market Inn, the sun at its height, Old John had his hat pulled low over his eyes. Clara likewise had tipped her straw hat over her face. At home among them all, she was back to her country roots.

'Here we are, John.' The barmaid plonked three tankards on the table in front of them. 'Two pints and one half. Oh it's you, Clara love. Goin' on well are yer dear?'

'Yes I'm well, Lucy, thanks.'

All the while, John's weatherbeaten face smiled on his granddaughter. 'She's the spirit of my Annie,' he said to Tom. 'Your health, sir.'

A shepherd dressed in his smock like John's spoke as he went into the bar, 'Don't often see thee sitting with a pot middle 'o' day, Johnnie.'

'Aar, it's the only way to get this young woman off her feet for a while. Busy cook she be, makin' 'er rest 'ere a while.' A soft bleating sound came from John's satchel.

'Granf. I should have known you'd have a lamb in there.'

John gently scooped the baby lamb from the

221

bag. 'Little ol' bab, couldn't leave 'im. Found 'im after the sale.'

'I know what you're gonna ast me for – just a mo,' said Lucy who was soon back with a drop of milk in a small cup.

'Thanks, Lucy.' Clara took the cup and dipped her little finger in the milk. The baby lamb lay on her arm as she dripped the milk in its mouth. Soon she was having trouble taking her finger away. The cup empty, the bab fell asleep back in its nest in the satchel. What a scene of pastoral warmth. Tom felt from this family a deep sense of rest.

John was to be given a ride back to the Lamb on another farmer's wagon today. He was in his late seventies and although robust he had spent a very long busy day since rising before four that morning to drive his animals to market. His sheepdogs were telling him they were keen to get away. While Clara gave them each a fond farewell John turned to her, saying, 'Well you've had your hard times my lass, you deserve it a little easier.' And to Tom he said, 'No doubt you've known some solitary years since your dear wife passed on. I know I have. Take this offer you've both been given. And don't let any person sully your days.' He shook Tom's hand and then gave Clara a cuddle with a few words in her ear.

'C'mon now my fellers,' he called to his dogs. 'We must be away.' He waved and turned to the wagon, mounting the board like a twenty-year-old. His dogs jumped up behind seating themselves just a space away from the owner's farm dogs. After all, they were the visiting passengers and respected their own inferior situation.

'Is your grandfather a mind reader?' Tom asked when they were safely on the already crowded bus.

'I know what you mean Tom. Maybe it's that you gave a funny look when you said you had a son and ... daughter. He's had a similar problem. So he caught the expression.'

'Yes. Now I know where you get your philosophy from. I'm glad – your attitude sounds real sensible to me.'

It had been a lovely day for them both. A relief but very fulfilling for Thomas, and a joy for Clara to have the two men she loved, meet and show liking one for the other.

As the bus made its way back to Brighton along the lanes and through the villages, stopping at a farm here or the church there, locals came and went, their friendly banter knitting a pattern of family ties across the Sussex landscape.

'Ah so the miller at Cherry Clack's your uncle, well now, my cousin's married his daughter.' Or 'You come from Petworth you say? My father-in-law still lives there, old Mr Davies.'

'That's my first wife Maisie's uncle,' said Tom, amazed. 'He's over ninety now. Still walks his fields every day my sister says.'

'Oh I'll tell the wife. She'll be tickled pink, tata then.'

Left alone Clara and Tom cuddled up in their seat. 'We've got relatives before we're relatives ourselves m'dear.' Tom laughed.

On a Saturday afternoon in January 1902, Clara

and her new husband Thomas Cowley emerged into soft rainy air. Family and friends, dressed in Sunday best with the extra flower buttonhole and feather trim, cheered and laughed under a collection of umbrellas.

Followed by parents and children, Clara and Tom walked the short distance along the road to the café next door to Fanny's new hat shop. Rose and Fanny had made sure their sister's outfit was the best they could make up. Clara always looked well in light turquoise blue. Rose was able to acquire just the colour in heavy silk crepe from the wholesaler. The dress had a slim line from high lace-edged collar to the floor with a matching coat fastened to one side at the hip. Fanny made the latest style in hats, large brim that dipped on each side of the face. As Clara was only five feet tall, Fanny made the hat in a lighter blue than the dress, with a swag of flowers across the brim.

Clara was very conscious of looking so fashionable while she was 'only a cook/housekeeper' but the staff at the Whitesides' had reassured her that she looked a 'picture'. And there they all were, waving from the edge of pavement across the road alongside the Whiteside children with their governess, she in her black dress and little shining black hat wiping a tear from her eye, while the smallest little Joaney doused her own head with rose petals from a paper bag as she blew kisses with the other hand.

An arch of silver and white paper chains greeted the couple at the door. Festoons of bells and horseshoes in blue and silver seemed to be floating and twisting all around the room. Clara stopped to take in the whole scene lest she forget any detail. She squeezed Tom's arm with a thrill of childish excitement. All this for us, she thought.

Tom wouldn't hear of Clara doing the catering. Somebody must have overheard that short conversation because a message came down to the kitchen to say Mr and Mrs Whiteside would like to pay for tea at that little café if Clara would agree. 'It's our wedding gift to you both.' And of course Coleen had gone straight back upstairs to relay Clara's thanks.

The company was full of fun and chat and reminiscences, meeting new relations, hugging brothers and sisters, uncles and cousins, five of Clara's brothers and sisters, but not Mum and Dad Emily and Tom, they still had youngest ones at home and the cost to travel for all of them was too much. Anyway the couple hoped to be going over to St Leonards next week for a night or two.

Albert provoked plenty of laughter, using his Best Man's privilege to include his own cheeky comments when reading out the letters of good wishes. Ethel, reluctant guest, sat mute. Nobody spoke to her; the barrier she'd raised was too great and nobody wanted to risk verbal sparring. Albert did his best under his wife's scrutiny. He'd always liked his father-in-law and wouldn't let him down. He'd told Tom that Clara looked like the ideal woman for him, lucky man.

This was the first experience Clara had had of a delicious tea carefully served that she had not produced herself or helped to serve. She didn't even have to be restrained from 'doing her bit' because she was so engrossed with talking to them all, Jack and his wife, Tom and Harry and of course Rose and Fanny. Their middle sister Nancy was in service and couldn't get away, it wasn't her weekend half-day so she'd had just to send her love with her brothers. 'Anyway she spends her half-days with some Italian waiter she met. 'Is father's got an ice-cream cart on the beach at Eastbourne,' Harry told the family.

Everybody's stories were brought up to date, who was doing what and where they were. It would all be relayed home to their parents with Tom and Harry, at which point a tiny hollow place in Clara's heart was filled by their brother Fred, dead these two years in South Africa. Gifts passing across from Jack, Rose and Fanny brought her mind back to the moment as she watched her siblings renewing their bonds. Then she returned to herself again, making sure Pearl, Jack's wife, wasn't left out by drawing her into their group. Clara learned she was to be an aunt again and responded with love and advice to her sister-in-law. She'd be on hand to help when her time came she assured Pearl, who herself had no mother. So that was settled, the sisters closed ranks again around their new sibling, making Jack comment to Thomas how proud he was of being part of a unit of thirteen now ballooning out, soon to be eighteen.

'How do you get there Jack?' cracked Thomas.

'Well there's you and yours today and my new addition in six months, makes eighteen.'

Thomas stood beside his son Dudley, a married man with a son and small daughter.

226

'I'm really pleased for you, Dad. Sybil and I can't understand why Ethel is so anti.'

'She'll come round my boy. Don't worry for me.'

'No I don't Dad, but she's said some real nasty things and I wouldn't want her to hurt your Clara – not like the way she tried it on me when Mum died.'

Tom was surprised and wondered what was coming. Dudley went on. 'You see that's why I stayed over in Worthing with Aunty Jess. I just couldn't take Ethel's constant bitchin' about you letting Mum go out helping others then and getting ill herself.' Sybil had wended her way across to where the two men stood talking. Dudley pulled a chair up for his wife as she wasn't very strong and looked tired. 'Oh duckie,' she said, 'don't worry your father with all that now. It's gone and forgotten. Aunt Jessie said your mum would have gone to Worthing to nurse her mother whoever had tried to stop her.'

'No you're right Syb. Sorry Dad. Syb and I were just sayin' what a lovely young bride you've got.'

Thomas stood tall and proud watching Clara, her golden hair glistening, set off so well by the pale turquoise she was wearing.

Rose and Fanny were motioning to Sybil to join all the girls surrounding Clara. The cake was soon to be cut so the women were heads together making plans to have regular meetings and ask Clara to make her wishes.

'What's Ethel doing over there alone?' asked Rose, who immediately walked across and without a word took Ethel under the arm guiding her into the group.

'How about you hosting our first get together Ethel, you're central for us all?' Fanny put her arm around Ethel's waist.

'Hostess always gets a little gift from the company. This time it's a discount on a hat from my shop. How about that Ethel love?'

Ethel was really taken aback. 'Is that your shop? I was told some French woman had opened there.'

'*Mais oui, Madame.* I look forward to serving your fancy.'

Fanny had cultivated a lovely accent. Pierre had trained her well. Clara's hat matching her wedding outfit was so flattering; Ethel, tight-lipped, had been jealous at first sight. Now she began to thaw a little. Clara's sisters were 'on the job', they couldn't win all the time but they've had a good try!

Eastern Road was in deep darkness by the time Tom and Clara arrived at their new home.

The next morning being a Sunday, Tom left Clara to sleep while he had a go, in his own fashion, at preparing breakfast.

When Clara finally woke it was almost midday. She lay listening to the horses in the yard snorting and giving the odd gentle whinny. She pulled the covers up round her cheeks; the air was cold and the light dim. It was January after all. Tom put his head round the door.

'Awake now love? Would you like a cup of tea, Madam?'

228

'Don't spoil me Tom. I'll get used to it!' she exclaimed.

'Just enjoy it Clara, you've worked long hours. Now take some time for yourself.' He sat on the bed beside her as she drank her tea and they talked over the events of the previous day and the friendly party.

'Do you want breakfast or luncheon, My Lady?'

'I think I would like you to show me round the mansion first, Mr Cowley.'

Clara hadn't lain abed like this since – since the last time she had slept in her little room under the eaves at the Lamb Inn.

'Oh Tom I quite forgot. You remember when we went to meet Grandfather at market? Well, before we left, after I told him we were getting wed, he put this packet in my purse.'

'You haven't even opened it Clara.'

'No, I thought I knew what it might be so I kept it for us both to open.' Inside the packet Clara found four gold sovereigns. 'His secret,' Clara whispered.

'What a dear man, we must thank him.'

'No, no they mustn't find out. Aunt Elizabeth opens all the post. No dear. Grandfather knows and anyway I'll thank him when I next go over to market.'

'Where did all these pots and pans come from, Tom?' Clara asked. The preparations for Christmas at the Whitesides' along with stocking up the family's larder with the special things they liked, not forgetting her time given to helping interview

229

a new cook, had left Clara little time for her own life apart from a quick look at the flat in St Mark's Mews when it was empty.

'You know who gave us those?' asked Tom.

'No, tell.'

'Albert.'

'Oh how kind of him.'

'Yes an' all off his own bat. I was loading the last pieces of furniture onto the van when Albert lifts this great box on the back. "Last one," he says. I told him, "No, that's not mine." "Yes," he says. "Look, it's got your name on it. 'Spect it's sommat you've forgotten after all this time." "No," I says. "Look here," says Albert, "I'll be glad to get my shed back and I don't want any more of your rubbish left 'ere." An' he winks hard because I just see Ethel coming out into the yard. So I quick up 'n' says, "Of course – yes – forget my own hat if I had one." Albert just smiled and walked off.'

'Tom, they're not cheap ones. Look at this. And a whole set too.'

'Well obviously Ethel knows nothing about it so don't go thanking her dear.'

'It's the first time I'll have cooked using my very own saucepans.'

'Wonderful, isn't it? Life's full of twists and turns, love.'

Clara was in heaven. Her own home and lots to sort out. Tom had done a grand job painting the walls and making the bed. Clara had all day to unpack boxes, lingering over the lovely Spode blue-ware meat dish Aunt Hetta had sent for a wedding present. As Clara put the linens away and jollied up the fire to make the room just that little bit more warm and comfortable, she thought of Hetta being Grandma Annie's longest-living friend. Dear Aunt Hetta, she would never forget the mutual support the two women had given each other.

The kitchen-cum-living room had a small open fireplace to cook on and there was a deep sink downstairs to do her washing in beside the copper where the horses' mash was prepared. A tin bath hung on the wall outside next to a box lavatory. But they had it all to themselves, including a smaller room where they could put a bed for Frankie. He had already started his job in the kitchens at the Grand Hotel and he was living in, so it was easier for Clara to move on from her job and have the flat shipshape for when he did have time to come home. Just on the end of the mews a gap between the stables was fenced off, leaving a piece of unused land that was theirs to grow vegetables and even string a rope across for drying washing.

Clara felt she couldn't have asked for anything better. The last parcel to unpack was from the Whitesides' two grandmothers. A hand-written card said, 'You brought such light into our lives.' Nestling inside layers of tissue was an elegant table oil lamp with a blue glass bowl and a pretty etched globe.

Clara's eyes shone as she said, 'The dear old things, always so proper, always sent down their thanks.'

It did look fine set on Thomas's shiny round dining table. The table looked rather grand set in the middle of the room, its deep golden sheen

231

shining in the afternoon sun. Clara put the elegant blue glass oil lamp in its centre and stood back to look at her first home. The first room she could call her own. Thomas put his arms round his new wife, so pleased to see the look on her face.

'Oh Tom, it does look rather splendid doesn't it?'

He laughed and said, 'Something old from me, something blue from you, in a borrowed room all surrounded in our new love, there now, how about that for a bit of poetry?'

She reached up to give him a kiss, saying with a laugh, 'Tom, you get cheekier the longer I know you. Come on, let's have our tea.'

Surrounded by whitewashed brick walls, and standing on a piece of plain red carpet, the tea table was laid with two cups and saucers, a milk jug and sugar bowl, teapot and slop basin holding the tea strainer, all arranged around the central oil lamp, lit early for the occasion – its light making the newly washed willow pattern china sparkle again for the first time in eight years.

'Just look at that, Granny, don't they look lovely again,' Clara whispered under her breath, smiling at the thought of grandmother's afternoon 'cup o' tay.'

With Clara's china on the table and a plate of cakes, bread and butter, it did all look rather good; their very own first tea of married life.

After tea they walked down to the seafront the way they would on many a Sunday evening. On this January evening the light was fading fast, the air was cool, smelling of salty sea. A quiet evening. They seemed to stand still for hours, watching the water ebb and flow leaving little frothy bubbles on the shoreline, suspended in a time bubble of their own like two people at the end of a long journey into a peaceful loving relationship. Around Clara and Tom there was always this gentle quiet atmosphere.

Come Monday it was back to work for Tom, a new round and a bit more responsibility. Nobody said anything about taking holidays, let alone honeymoons!

During the weekdays Clara kept their beautiful table thickly covered with blankets and an oilcloth, as she had to do everything on that table; cooking, ironing, eating. There wasn't room for another table. She couldn't complain, the room was big enough for the table, four small dining chairs and two old armchairs, left by previous occupants on either side of the fire, that she kept covered to avoid splatterings while she was cooking. Later she made them respectable with covers and cushions. An old built-in dresser cupboard and shelves were perfectly adequate for two people, eventually to display the Willows. When Tom came home at half past six, she had a tasty filling meal on the table.

After he'd eaten he sat back saying, 'Well missus if yer can produce a meal like that every night, I'll think about offerin' you the job.'

'Get on with yer – you're a comedian you are, Thomas.'

'And another thing,' he said, 'I've got a bit of a surprise for you. I've been given all next weekend off so we'll be able to stay over at St Leonards for a night after all.'

233

Married life brought such an enormous contrast to Clara's days. She only had one person to make breakfast for and see off to work.

'C'mon you don't have to get up so early. I can get myself something, a crust and a cup of tea. You enjoy the rest.'

'No, I'm used to early starts Tom. If you've got to get up I will join you. There's plenty to keep me busy when you've gone. I will make some hooked rugs 'n' maybe start my own quilt.'

Of course there wasn't really plenty to keep her busy. Not for such a long day starting at half past four. The pair of them only needed one set of clothing a day and she only had two people to cook dinner for. Clara even found her gaze far away and her hands quite still as her mind wandered over the happenings of the past few weeks – making herself chuckle heartily, remembering when Mrs Whiteside interviewed the young cook who, on being questioned on how she made her custard sauces, said she always used 'Alfred Bird's custard powder'. The woman quickly found herself outside in the street.

'Well, I never did!' Mrs Whiteside almost spluttered in disgust. 'How dare a servant call Mr Bird by his Christian name. What is the world coming to?'

So after a couple of weeks, Clara gave Tom some news when he got home from work.

'Tom, I've been thinking. I can't spend my time being lady muck with spare time on my hands. I've decided to find a job. We need the money and it would be nice to have some savings in case

234

of difficult times.'

'A man doesn't like to think 'is wife's got to go out to work. You don't have to, you know.'

'No, I know that, but I would like to do my share.'

He relented. He wanted her to be happy. Tom's life had improved a hundredfold. To come home to a really well-cooked meal in a calm atmosphere was better than he had ever expected life would bring him again.

Clara found a pleasant tea room in Kemp Town where she had noticed parents taking their daughters when they visited on school half-days. There were two or three private boarding schools in the area for boys and for girls besides Roedean and that wasn't far away on the next hill. Taking her old references from Lady Wellborough and the Blue Rooms, also the 'Character' given her when she left the Whitesides, Clara called in one morning early before the service was busy.

'Well, we do want a pastry cook but it's not full time. We only need somebody four mornings, including Saturdays.'

'That's just what I was hoping for,' replied Clara.

'Then that will suit us both, Mrs Cowley. When can you start?'

'Would tomorrow suit you Miss Burgess?'

'Very nicely indeed.'

'Tomorrow then.'

'That was quick,' said Tom when she told him.

'Ideal I'd say, a bit of luck. Easy to walk to and it won't interfere with me getting your dinner in the evenings.'

'Pity you've got to work on a Saturday though, just when I wanted you to enjoy being a house-wife.'

'You work on a Saturday, so I shall.'

'Well, that's settled then,' he said with a smile. 'Got me all organised.'

'Got meself organised you mean. Come on, it's a lovely evening, let's go down to the front for a walk.' As the spring came and the evenings length-ened, Clara and Tom would often walk further along the Kings Road or down to King's Cliff along under the covered walk to the Aquarium. Other times, they'd go down Rifle Butt road and down onto the undercliff.

The Willows

'It wasn't long after Tom started delivering in Kemp Town that my owner's family was preparing to move away from Brighton. Our housekeeper met Thomas at the kitchen door to take the usual order of bread just as one of the parlourmaids carrying me came through into the yard. I'm Leonard by the way,' the speaker told the younger Willows.

'"Where are you off to with that muffin dish?" Mrs Rowe called after the parlour maid.

'"Missus says to throw it out. They won't be needin' it in Lunnon."

'"Whatever does she mean?"

'"Says it's too rustic for town entertainin', Mrs Rowe."

'"What a waste," the housekeeper remarked.

'"Ere, 'old on a mo', can I take it, Mrs Rowe? My

wife really likes the willow pattern. It's a shame to break it, throw it out like."

"'Why of course Mr Cowley – give it 'ere girl. Needs a good wash."

'So that's how I came to be living with Clara and Tom in their first little place. Tom would bring home the leftover muffins off his van on Saturday night. On Sunday Clara soaked them in milk an' toasted them for Sunday tea, an' I kept them warm on the table,' Leonard informed everybody, looking very pleased with himself.

''Ow do yer do that then Len?' asked the triplets.

'They put 'ot water into my double plate,' Leonard told them, pointing to the small funnel and rubber stopper on his side. 'Look see, water goes in there.'

'I always wondered what that was for,' said Dixie pepper pot.

'Shouldn't you 'ave a lid, Len?' asked Pixie.

'No, 'e's never 'ad one,' Mrs P intervened.

'No I've never 'ad one.' Leonard winked. 'Though why she thinks she knows better'n me I don't know,' he muttered under his breath, while the little triple cruet set sniggered.

Seeing that Mrs P had heard Leonard's side, one of the teacups stepped in saying, 'Do you remember what Frankie told Tom when he was over for tea one Sunday Mrs P?' Not letting Mrs P reply, the teacup carried on, '"Seeing mother cooking in the Whitesides' great kitchen inspired me, but what I see her achieve, on just a small open fire, amazes me."'

'Yes, I remember that myself,' cut in Leonard. 'Baking cakes, making pancakes, steaming a whole meal of meat pudding and separate vegetables all on one small open fire. What a miracle – he was right –

237

a true achievement.'
What more could Mrs P say after that?

Clara

Clara and Rose sometimes met when Rose had an afternoon off and the pair walked along to Fanny's shop together. Arm in arm they chatted as they stepped out, diverting every now and then to look in a shop window or wave to acknowledge a friendly call from an old friend, maybe a carter or bus conductor. It was rare for them to stop and go into any of the shops; there wasn't the money to buy much more than necessities. They made their own clothes and shoes lasted a long time as Tom mended all their heels and soles.

One day a week, when she didn't have to bake at the shop, Clara walked along to the Grand Hotel with Frankie's clean washing and picked up his dirties. The pair usually only had a few minutes' chat to catch up on personal events. He'd started off as a kitchen boy but was already promoted to vegetable preparation. Clara was pleased to see her son happy. He seemed to get on with everyone very well.

She wrote to Frank to tell him his son had left school and what he was doing, saying he had grown into a fine young man. She even sent him a photograph, the second. The first had been of a youngster in school clothes, typical small boy. This time Frankie had a picture taken of himself in his kitchen whites for a special occasion when the hotel had a promotional line up. Almost as a

238

PS Clara mentioned that she was now married and gave her new name and address.

Tom knew all about Frank and encouraged Clara to keep in contact for Frankie's sake.

Frank never referred to Clara's married state in his letters. He carried on their spasmodic correspondence as usual along with the regular money order. He could have transferred money directly into Frankie's bank account but then he'd have no need to correspond with Clara so he kept to the original agreement to keep in touch.

Eight months after Clara and Thomas were wed, Clara found she was pregnant. Only this time she didn't feel at all well, right from the beginning. Leaving herself aside, Clara focused her attention on her sister Fanny.

7

The Willows

'Moi, s'il vous plait,' *called a small voice.* 'My turn now please.'

'Hey what's that?'

'What's she talkin' about?'

'Never noticed 'er before.'

'Wot they use you for then luv?'

'Hat pins,' *replied Hannah, a bit put out.*

''At pins? Wot's 'at pins?'

'Now come on boys, don't show yer ignorance. Be good mannered ter the lady, ask 'er nicely.'

'Sorry Uncle Bert,' piped three voices in unison. They came from Pixie, Dixie and Dido, the cheeky little cruet set, salt, pepper and mustard. Dixie pepper pot cleared his throat. 'An' wot may we arst are 'at pins dearie?'

Uncle Bert's eyes rose to the ceiling. 'Oh dear,' he said under his breath – resigned to their awkward manners.

'I'm a hat pin pot and my name's Hannah.'

'An' Hannah has stood quietly behind you cheeky beggars for some years,' Big Pol pointed out.

'Well, did you know what she did for a livin' then Polly?'

'Yes, course I did,' lied Polly blatantly, her nose in the air.

'Well wot's 'at pins then?'

'You must ask the lady.' Big Pol sniffed. 'I'm surprised Lily hasn't put any hat pins in you Hannah, to show off your skill.' Big Pol gave a huge wink.

'I can tell you what they are,' announced Mrs P. 'I don't expect Lily has got any. Hat pins aren't used much these days. Hat pins are long sharp pins with fancy ends. Women used to wear big hats, and they fixed pins through the crown into their hair to stop the wind blowing the hat off their heads.'

'She has. I know,' called Ruby teapot, 'Lily's got some 'cos I've seen them in her straw sun hat.'

'Yes, that's right,' agreed Hannah, 'and the pins have pretty knobs on them.'

'What kind of knobs on your pins then Hannah?' asked Florrie water jug.

'Well, some knobs were very swanky, great swirls of sparkling brilliants. Others were valuable pink pearls, while there were collections of bright-coloured feathers.

240

I looked quite a sight when I was filled with a good selection of pins. My first owner used to keep me on a shelf beneath her hat mirror in her entrance hall where everybody admired my display as they passed by.'

'How did you come to be here with us then Hannah?' asked Ruby teapot.

'My owner was Pierre Dupont's grandmother.'

'You mean the Pierre that Fanny got to know on that liner, the one who boarded at Newfoundland?'

'That's him.'

'Ooh 'er, how exciting! Do tell us about him Hannah,' called Florrie. 'Was he really handsome?'

'Was he Fanny's gentleman friend then Hannah?' asked Ruby.

'No. It was never like that then. Pierre could see what a good needlewoman Fanny was. He thought she'd had a real rotten time on that liner so he decided he could help her out and help his own business enterprise at the same time.'

'Well, go on then,' encouraged the triplets.

'Oh gawd, there they go again,' sighed Uncle Bert.

'You know that man who gave Fanny the advice about Pierre, he told her he didn't think he was really French. Well, he wasn't. This is what happened. Pierre's mother was the wife of a ship's captain who fell in love with a Russian prince.'

All the Willows turned to face the storyteller. It sounded like something juicy was about to be told.

'Marsie, that's the captain's wife, accompanied her husband on a sea journey to Odessa. The ship was carrying machinery from England. When they docked she went ashore with her husband to call on the British Consul in Odessa. Marsie became friends with the Consul's wife who was pleased to entertain a woman from home. She invited Marsie to stay at the Legation while her husband's ship was unloading and taking on grain for the return journey to England. Her husband agreed readily, seeing how well the two ladies enjoyed each other's company. Marsie revelled in dressing romantically for the receptions. The Consul and his wife hosted garden parties and card playing and even a grand ball. It was at the ball that Marsie danced with a handsome foreigner and they very soon fell in love. When her husband's ship was ready to sail, Marsie persuaded him to let her stay on. Of course he knew nothing about the Russian prince so again he agreed, as he knew he would soon be return-ing with his second cargo.

'The prince immediately carried Marsie off to his estate where they luxuriated in lovemaking miles away from prying eyes. Well, of course Marsie finds herself pregnant. It's her first so she doesn't realise how far into the pregnancy she is because it doesn't show very much. Anyway, she and the prince are convinced it's his, and he and she go on with all their shenanigans all over the place. He takes her on long journeys to palaces in far places, they dress up and dance and make love and drink too much vodka, until one night she has a stomach ache and out pops this beautiful baby, as sandy-haired as her Scots husband. Nothing could have been more opposite to the black hair, raven beard and jet moustache her handsome prince displayed. Besides, the baby arrived just six months after the pair met in Odessa and the baby was quite obviously full term.

'Reluctantly Marsie's prince delivered the captain's wife back to the British Legation in Odessa in time for

242

mother and baby as if they had been there all the time waiting for the ship to return. Very soon after Marsie and her husband got back to England he died, leaving Marsie and the baby destitute. By this time the prince had moved to Paris but he did not invite Marsie to join him. He did however provide the capital for her to have her own millinery workroom and shop in a fashionable part of London. And that's where I come in.

'Marsie's mother, back in England, had kept me on her shelf beneath her hat mirror, just inside her front door, for some years. When Marsie set up her milliner's shop she unpacked the few things her mother had left her when she died and I joined the small crowd of hat pin stands and vases in her shop called Marsie et Cie.'

'What's that mean?'

'Lord, save us!' Uncle Bert sighed.

'It means "Marsie and Son", my dears,' Hannah told the boys. 'Madam Marsie walked the deep pile carpet down the centre of the showroom carrying a tall silver-topped cane. On either side of the long room two tiers of deep drawers contained a wide variety of hats, styles in all sorts of sizes. The walls above the drawers, which resembled lady's knee-holed dressing cabinets, were mirrored either side the length of the room. At intervals along under the mirrors stood an array of tastefully displayed hats on elegant chrome and glass stands, each with a small group of hat pins.

'As lady clients entered from the fashionable shopping arcade, Madam Marsie would thump her cane on the floor for the attention of an assistant calling "forward" as she herself led the client towards a vacant set of soft, low-backed armchairs. The assistant's first priority was to light the shaded candles around the mirrored posi-

243

tion. The customer's countenance was caressed by the lighting as she and her friends were ushered to their seats.

'The assistant, or sometimes more than one, would attend to their client, opening drawers fetching out hats. By the way the drawers didn't pull out, the fronts let down to show their contents. Rejected styles were never left around but arranged gently on stands awaiting final elimination. All was arranged like a stage set to enhance client's best features.

'"We must not confuse our ladies", Marsie would tell her assistants. "We must guide."

'We pots holding our display of hat pins were offered as an extra, the assistants showing their clients how much safer they would feel when using pins. Of course the assistants earned more if they sold these pins. When they saw a favoured pin chosen, they showed matching sets, bringing them out of small drawers to the side. Three pins was the ideal option recommended.

'As the nineteen-hundreds moved towards nineteen-ten, hats got bigger and hat pins became more elaborate, besides being double-ended to anchor the great "garden displays" onto women's heads.'

'Wot d'yer mean, garden displays? Wot, on their 'eads?' interjected Big Pol, who had never seen women wearing such hats in her days at the Lamb Inn.

'Yes,' answered Hannah. 'Some of the hats carried very flamboyant flower displays including stuffed birds too!'

'What a carry on!' remarked Ol' Po.

'Over the years Marsie regularly paid the prince a visit in his Paris home, taking Pierre with her. Pierre got on well with his surrogate father. When he was older the boy sometimes went to stay with him in

244

Paris. This is when he learned to speak French like a native. It was altogether a lucky situation for Pierre. Marsie was happy and very satisfied with her lot. She never had a husband at home and was therefore able to give all her time to the millinery workroom, creating new designs for her shop. When she felt the need, she went to Paris to be with the man she loved. Her part-time husband, you'd call him.

'When Fanny met Pierre on the liner he had been to North America to view the furs for winter hats and muffs. When he got home he heard that the prince was in poor health so he went on to Paris and stayed through the last months of the Russian prince's life.

'Some months later, after the prince had passed away, Pierre heard he had been left some money from the estate of Prince Rimgolski. This is how Pierre was able to do Fanny a good turn. He proposed to open another hat shop, this time in Hove, and he wanted Fanny to manage it for him. He would have the salon fitted out in similar mode to his mother's premises in London and to start with, her workrooms would supply the stock.

'"How would that suit you Fanny?" he asked. At first she was overwhelmed.

'"I've never thought of managing a business Pierre."

'"It would be your own one day Fanny. Just think of that. And maybe, just maybe, your lad would like to be trained in the trade."

'"Do you really think I could do it? Where are you thinking would be a good position Pierre?"

'"I think Hove, near Palmeira Square. I know there are some of Maman's customers with houses in the square and some in Lewes Crescent. But I think Hove.

You could have a flat over the showroom. Wouldn't you like that Fan my dear?"

'"What an opportunity," Rose said. "You can't say no, Fanny. Go on take it."

'"I have," Fanny told her sisters. They named the shop Jolene et Cie.

'I came to Hove with a selection of other fittings and decorations from Marsie et Cie and when the shop in Hove finally closed in the late 1950s, when hats had gone out of fashion for a time, Fanny's boy Peter gave me to his god-daughter Jolie. When she retired and moved to Cyprus in 2003 she didn't want to keep anything she did not use every day so she gave me to Lily. And here I am.'

'I bet you saw some preening women and strange faces in your time Hannah.'

'Hah, you're right there Polly. I could tell some tales about the posh and not so bloomin' posh. Yes, there's another whole lot of tales there.'

'Did Fanny walk the walk with a silver-topped cane like Marsie?'

'No. Fan was far too down to earth. But she did make sure her clients were elegantly served. Her lady assistants all wore pretty lavender dresses down to the floor, with lace cuffs. Their hair was well brushed, hands and nails always carefully manicured. And she also made sure each assistant sat down when they weren't serving, to rest their feet. Fanny had a chiropodist look at everybody's feet once a month too.'

'You know where she got that from doncher?' Big Pol remarked.

'Granma Annie. Remember what she used to say to all the children? "Keep your heads and feet warm and dry".'

'Yes, you're right there,' Mrs P agreed.

'There was something else different about Fanny's hat shop. Clients couldn't run up accounts. Before she opened, Marsie told her to start the way she meant to go on. So, when a new customer came to the salon and was seated at her sales position, a neat little card centre front on the dressing table said, "Please do not ask for an account as we do not wish to disappoint. We accept cheques or cash only. We will deliver."

'It was a very new departure for those days. Very few women carried cash and the gentry expected to have their purchases written down on their account and sent for payment monthly. Often these bills never got paid. Marsie told Fanny, "If you don't get payment it's not worth having the customer. Customers don't think of it that way. They think the very sight of them entering your premises brings you prestige. Have none of it dear."

'So, on the rare occasions that a lady asked for a purchase to be put on her account, Fanny would quietly tell her, "I'm sorry Madam, but the prince would not allow it."

'"I had this hat made for me at Prince Jolene Rimgolski." That was the prestige on offer.'

'What a story Hannah,' said Uncle Bert. 'Aren't you glad you asked about those hat pins boys?'

'S'pose so,' they said, a little grumpily. 'Not very exciting though.'

'I think Hannah's story was very exciting,' pronounced Big Pol.

'Well, if you think that Polly, I can tell you something else,' offered Hannah. 'One afternoon two young matron ladies came into the salon and behind them, being pushed by a servant, a ladies maid I think, came

247

an elderly lady in a bath chair.

'"Here Mother, we thought you would like to see the hats, such a lovely selection all together."

'"Yes, Dorothea, but the girl could have brought a selection to the house."

'"Now come along Mother it's a lovely day and the outing's doing you good."

'"Well, it's certainly a change from trundling along the windy seafront every day."

'"There now, would you like to take the middle place in front of the mirror? Maude and I will sit either side?"

'"Is the milliner here?" called Old Mrs Rollandson in a commanding voice. "I do not want some girl who doesn't know what she's doing."

'As Fanny walked up to stand behind her customer's chair she recognised the lady sitting to the right of the mirror. The lady immediately recognised her. Fanny wished the floor could swallow her up, but abruptly changed her mind, smiled and nodded to Dorothea Rollandson who smiled back. Neither woman acknowledged the reason they knew each other. That became apparent rather more quickly than expected.

'Meanwhile the old lady in her bath chair had been peering intently through her lorgnette at a small photograph that was in fact leaning against me, where I was standing in front of the mirror. Earlier in the afternoon Peter had run home from school and straight into the salon – something he was not normally allowed to do. He was so excited to bring a small photo of himself home from school. There being no customers in the premises at that moment, Fanny sat down at the mirror to take a closer look at the photo, her son standing at her knee. The assistants came gathering round, telling Peter what a handsome picture he made. In all the chatter and compliments the photo was left standing against me on the dressing table,' Hannah told the Willows.

'The first thing Mrs Rollandson said was, "How did this photograph of my Roland come to be here? Look Dorothea, Maude. That's Roland when he was a small boy, how odd."

'"No Mother. You're right it certainly does look like him but it's not."

'Maude, Roland's sister, looked from her sister-in-law to Fanny and immediately sized up the situation. She knew her brother only too well.

'Nothing more was said. Fanny served her customers and all three ladies purchased summer hats. Dorothea Rollandson asked when Fanny's winter styles would be available to view. She would return she said. It seems Maude lived in Palmeira Square and her mother and Dorothea were staying for a short visit from Eastbourne.'

'Poor Fanny, she must have been embarrassed,' said Polly.

'Quite,' chipped in Mrs P, 'don't suppose she wanted anything to do with that family again.'

'You're right Mrs P,' said Hannah. 'But it didn't end there. Dorothea Rollandson did return, the next day in fact. "I'm going back to Eastbourne tomorrow Fanny," she said. "I can't tell you how sorry I was when the true story all came out and I discovered your ordeal. Mr Rollandson has been a disgrace to our marriage. I know it's not the thing to talk of your husband in this way. I can't leave him. You were lucky you could get away."

'And I'll tell you another thing. Between you and

me,' Hannah lowered her voice. 'I heard her say—'

'Hey, we can't hear wot you're sayin' over here.'

'Come on Han, speak up, you don't have to be so conspiratorial.'

'I overheard Mrs Rollandson tell Fanny that the young woman her husband hired as soon as they got to New York didn't stay a week.'

'Oh, I'm not surprised,' chortled Big Pol.

'No, an' that's not all. The girl was so damn mad about his use of her that she gave him a black eye, an' even shouted to his wife about wot he was up to. "I'm no whore," she told them both. "You hired me to take care of your wife an' baby." Mrs R told Fanny that the girl told her agency about Roland, and they found it very difficult to hire a nursemaid after that.

'Well, Fanny listened to all this in silence 'til Dorothea Rollandson broke down in tears, thanking Fanny for listening because she hadn't been able to talk to the family about it all. Then she asked after little Peter and do you know, she handed Fanny a purse of money? Quite a lot of money, and told her she'd sold two rings. "Put the money in an account for Peter for me please. I'm telling Roland my rings have been stolen or lost somewhere. It's the only way I can make, at least some amends Fanny." Then she left. Never saw her again.'

'Poor young woman,' said Florrie.

8

Clara

Clara looked down at the shrivelled, raspberry-coloured little face in the shawl lying on her arm. She felt none of the exhilaration and joy of achievement she'd experienced with Frankie's birth. This little soul was quiet, sleeping most of the twenty-four hours. Clara wasn't complaining because after eight days she still had not been allowed to put a foot to the floor. Her labour had been long and gruelling for them both. Poor Tom thought he'd lost them.

Her first visitor after Tom was young Frankie. He'd been as worried as Tom. Clara had already started her birth pangs when he called in on his half-day the previous week. Not hearing any news of a birth, he hot-footed from the hotel on his next half-day to find Freddy had only just been born. Even Tom had not yet been allowed into the bedroom. Clara didn't see the two men in the kitchen, their heads together, fighting back the tears of relief for wife and mother.

Frankie followed Tom a little later, albeit warned by the laying-in woman, 'Only a minute mind, poor woman's worn out.' He produced quite a bundle which he opened out on the end of the bed revealing a beautifully patterned white lacy shawl, a set of baby clothes, bonnet, mitts and booties.

'Oh and a couple of pairs of socks for Dad,' he added.

'Frankie, whenever did you get the time?' Clara asked. She knew he must have made them because she had taught him to knit when he was very young.

'Well, I've had six months. When we have our breaks most of us sit out in the yard. I find it relaxing doing my knitting. The others smoke; I don't know how they can taste what they are cooking. And no, they don't laugh at my knitting,' Frankie added with a chuckle. 'They wouldn't dare, the odd pair of socks gets them over all their jibes.' Just like Frankie, thought Clara, won't let anybody put him off.

Rose and Fanny gave their time unstintingly, one or the other taking it in turns coming across town on the bus each day to see that Clara and the baby were well looked after, doing the washing and ironing, fetching in all that was needed. They'd found a neighbour who could cook and bring a hot meal in daily, and grateful Tom gave her a free day-old loaf off the van for her own large family. Of course nobody had to know about that.

'I'm so sorry Tom. I wish I hadn't brought this worry on you.'

Tom wouldn't hear that kind of talk. 'Now you stop thinking that way Clara. We've done this together. We'll get through, you'll see.'

No sight or sound had been heard from Ethel. Albert, bless him, left a good joint of mutton on the kitchen table one morning besides many a titbit on other days. The first time, Mrs Moss came running up the stairs to tell Clara about the 'wunnerful meat'.

'That'll be our son-in-law, Mrs Moss, he's a dear. You take it for making our dinners, use it for all of us; your growing lads could do with some too.'

Clara wasn't able to get up and work this time so she was very grateful that Mrs Moss continued to come in every day to help, and it didn't need saying the food was a godsend. Mary Moss was a strong woman, she had to be with five boys to feed on a meagre pay packet, already halved by her poorly paid stableman husband's tendency to roll home by way of the pub.

At thirty-four, and with only two children, Clara felt her body could only cope as if she were eighty-four. This pregnancy had knocked the stuffing out of her. She got through with Mary's help. She never forgot Mary Moss.

Tom worked very long hours. He was up and away before five in the morning and never back before seven in the evening, six days a week, on his feet all day. His round had widened and if any roundsman was ill, it was his job to share out the customers with the other men, or do it himself. There really was no way of shortening his hours without being demoted and getting considerably less pay. At least in this position he didn't have to groom his horse; that care and preparation was all done at the stables.

Baby Frederick did not thrive. He was slow to make progress in any way. He wasn't a grisly baby, just quiet and watchful, slept a lot, taking his feed but not with any enthusiasm. Clara had little milk, but fortunately the baby seemed content to accept what was on offer and leave it at that.

Rose and Clara, with Tom, and Leslie when he wasn't staying with his great grandfather over at the Lamb, had tea together on Sunday afternoons at one or the other's homes, just as the two girls had done ever since Rose returned to live in Brighton. When Fanny could get away from business along at Palmeira she and Peter joined them. They were a united little group.

After a year, no, nearly eighteen months, Clara's energy returned and at about the same time, Tom saw a possibility of changing his round to one in the centre of town. Although he would lose his wealthy family houses in Kemp Town, Sussex Square and Arundel Terrace, a central round was more compact allowing him a shorter day. Clara was sad to think she'd have to leave their cosy flat over the stables but Tom's wellbeing was far more important, so when he came home saying he had found a cottage to rent in St George's Mews between Trafalgar Street and Gloucester Street that was absolutely central for the bakery and stables and all his new customers, Clara replied, 'Come on then love, let's take a look this very evening shall we?'

There was just one unoccupied cottage set in a terraced line of two-up, two-down each with its own small backyard and a shared lavvy. Between their yards and the high flint wall backing the buildings in Sydney Street there was a patch of rough weedy ground slung with a line, its length held high by a wooden prop, providing a communal drying area. The sun had short access to these back ways but someone had taken notice, for a row of bamboo sticks was pushed into the soil by the wall at the far end already showing a burgeoning array of runner beans. Clara felt the country ways alive before her eyes. It relieved her heart even in this confined space.

The terrace fronted onto a cobbled yard surrounded by workshops housing a variety of businesses. Straight across the yard, opposite, was a piano repairer and tuner, Mr Alfred Moffat. To his right was an iron gate and railing repair shop and a harness makers. To the left, across the cornerways beside the archway leading out into Gloucester Street, was a printer's workshop making large, colourful lithograph posters that were stuck up on the walls outside in the yard giving the place a jaunty air. A large poster for Bird's Custard Powder faced down the row, showing a chef in his whites with the words 'What no eggs?' and opposite, a smaller one just inside the passage for Whiteways Cyders. Clara loved these pictures on the walls and later found it fun to see the new sample prints come out of the works.

The house was unoccupied so Tom was able to fetch the key, allowing them to look round. The front door opened straight into the main living room where the strong smell of mice sent them gasping. The brick floor was treacherous with black grease causing careful stepping through the one room into the scullery, its stone-flagged floor also needing a good clean. The grate beside the small oven range showed rust and soot from the chimney spread across the floor. Upstairs the two bedrooms were cleanish and dry although the walls were stained revealing evidence of a rotten roof. Looking up inside at the rafters through the fanlight Tom could see repairs had been made. While he checked from the outside, a neighbour came into the yard to say the roof had recently been repaired. He knew it was well done because he'd been employed to do it himself and had worked across his cottage too, he told Tom, so he'd made sure the repairs were waterproof.

Before she would move in Clara managed to get permission to go in and give the floors a mighty good scrub. Throwing all her cleaning water out across the scullery floor she swept the last of the muck out into the yard and away down the draining channel running along behind their house and the houses in Sydney Street.

When she and Tom moved in with baby Freddy on the following Saturday afternoon, her cleaning venture had dried out and refreshed the atmosphere. Tom acquired some sizeable pieces of sisal matting to cover the brick floor so the living room had already been given quite a cosy feel.

The neighbours hadn't bothered Clara as she busied herself cleaning the floors before moving-in day but when she and Tom arrived with their bits of furniture, all hands came out from the other houses to help heave the heavy table and manhandle their bed up the narrow boarded stairway. The neighbours either side each introduced themselves as they worked, Clemmie and Joe, Jenny Starr with her two girls cooing over Freddy's perambulator as they walked him round the mews, Rod and Maudie with their three eager young boys came out to help. A happy crowd soon making light work of the operation, consequently the move in was done in a trice. Jenny swept the cobbles out front as the horse van left. You'd hardly know a change had happened. Friends were made and in good neighbourliness they melted away back behind their own front doors, leaving the new incumbents to themselves. Before Tom could close the front door the rent man had his foot over the step asking to check their rent book for receipt of their first week's payment.

Clara was down to the scullery at half past four next morning to make Tom's tea only to find a mouse scuttling round under the sink. She shooed it out of the back door with her broom where the rodent was immediately pounced upon by a small tabby cat.

'See yer've met our resident mouser then missus?' Jenny Starr called from where she was emptying her night bucket in the lavvy.

'Sweet little cat,' said Clara. 'I saw her sitting on the windowsill last night.'

'She won't let yer down. Best let 'er stay.'

'Oh I'll let her stay all right,' replied Clara, calling to the small tabby cat with its rosebud pink nose, 'Hallo Trilby love, sweet little dear.'

Ethel opened the door and walked straight in. She hadn't knocked. Well, why should she? It was her father's home. The room was rather cramped with furniture. There was the familiar round table with four chairs tucked up tight against its rim and that ridiculously over-elegant blue-glass paraffin lamp at its centre. Two soft chairs

257

pressed either side of the little fireplace and even a built in dresser. You couldn't get anything more in that room. Ethel's fingers swept across her mother's shiny table and lifted to inspect for dust, her eyes roving the room, looking to find fault somewhere. A body could be heard overhead moving round in the bedroom but there was no sound from the child. The door at the bottom of the stairs swung open into the scullery, a bucket came into view followed by a pile of bedclothes, lastly Clara taking her laundry across to the stone sink where she had a bowl ready. Lifting a large kettle from the kitchen fire to pour its hot water into the washbowl, Clara almost dropped it as she caught sight of Ethel standing silently in the doorway between the two rooms.

'Oh Ethel, you gave me a fright standing there. I didn't hear you knock.'

'Thought I'd see my father's home, and I didn't knock.'

What could you say? Ethel was so consistently irritating it was best not to react. You only got more back.

'How's the child?' she asked. It was a throwaway comment, just something to say as she remained standing in the doorway looking round, taking everything in.

'He's very well, thank you,' Clara replied, 'Sleeping just now, I won't disturb him.'

'Oh, no need to bother,' came the brisk reply. 'How's father?'

'Come and see him when he's home Ethel. You know we've always said you and Albert are welcome for Sunday tea anytime.'

'Not with a house full of kids. Your Rose and Fanny still come do they?'

'Yes Ethel, we're a very close family.'

'Must be a tight fit in here then?'

'We've room to accommodate all who come. Your father would be pleased to see you. Dudley and Sybil were over from Worthing last weekend.'

'He didn't say he'd be here,' Ethel shot back, biting her tongue on her annoyance.

'I didn't know,' said Clara. 'It's up to them. They seem very happy. Syb looks healthy and full of life.'

'Well I thought they might have looked in on us.'

'Do you ever go over there Ethel?'

'Never bin asked.'

No, thought Clara, I'm not surprised. She knew Dudley had had his fill of his sister as a young woman full of sour backlashing words. Sybil said she couldn't even manage half an hour of Ethel's spiteful manner.

'Oh well, must be off, valuable customers to visit.' Then turning while fumbling in her fancy shopping bag, 'Forgot. This for yer,' she said pulling a newspaper-wrapped bundle out and thumping it down on the draining board. A small tabby cat with a cherry-coloured nose sidled in the back door at that very moment and jumped up beside the parcel. Ethel recoiled, muttering sharply, 'Ugh don't let that animal get into my parcel. What's in there's better for dogs than cats,' then stopped her mouth before going on rapidly to say, 'Of course we always used to have a dog when mother was alive; a much better pet for adults of course.'

'Our Trilby's a good mouser, a real worker aren't you love? She's no lap cat.' Clara could have said she had grown up at the Lamb Inn knowing more dogs around the family who were all working adults. But what was the use.

'So long, tell Dad I've been in.' The front door slammed behind her.

Clara watched as Ethel paused briefly in front of the window inspecting the curtains from the outside then stomped away towards the arch and into Gloucester Street. Taking a deep breath Clara got on with her washing to get it out on the line before the sun went off the yard. It wasn't until she came back in from hanging out their personal linens that she remembered the parcel. A pile of old dried-up bones.

'Not even any marrow bones among them,' she said to Tom that evening. 'She couldn't have found anything meaner to bring as a gift. I don't know how she does it Tom. I'd be too embarrassed knowing how much good meat Albert has to bone out for all those orders up the Dyke Road.'

Tom gave a wry laugh. 'A few old bones are better than a long lambasting from her sharp tongue gal.'

'Oh, you're not wrong there luv,' Clara replied as she kissed the top of his head on her way out to the scullery with their empty dinner plates.

'They'll get you an extra copper from the bone man won't they?' Tom called over his shoulder towards the scullery.

'Always look on the up side. That's my Tom.'

Now Clara and Tom were living in the centre of

the town, Frankie could call in more frequently. On his first visit he brought a gift for their new home. It was a meat safe to hang on the wall outside in the back yard. Clara was thrilled, just what she needed. When he didn't have to get back on duty until the breakfast service, Frankie was able to stay for his evening meal and a long chat with Tom and Clara.

One afternoon when Clara had been delivering Frankie's washing to the hotel, the Head Chef had come across the yard to tell her he'd never had such a keen youngster to train up. It wasn't long after that Frankie moved to being a commis and started going to evening classes at the Technical College opposite the Level. He was well on his way to becoming a sous chef so he knew he would have to make a move. He wanted more experience, he told Clara and Tom before he could apply for head chef or go to another big establishment. Clara was so pleased her son was enjoying his work.

The move down into the town had been a good one for both her men. Tom had shorter distances to cover on his rounds each day and Frankie was able to have a few hours relaxation after classes and talk over his plans. The next thing Frankie wanted to do was to go to Paris to learn different methods. He didn't want responsibility, he told his mother, until he'd really had a lot more experience.

Clara suggested it was now time to start using the bank account his father had been adding to all these years. At least it would pay his travelling and a few necessities.

'I'll need some clothes and new whites too, Mum.'

'Then that's what it's for son.'

'What about you, Mother? I don't see you taking time for a rest now and again.'

'Don't worry about me. Tom and I have each other an' I've put out a few hints. Tell you about it all next time you're in.'

Frankie was off to work in a small hotel in Mayfair for six weeks, 'While the elite were in town,' he joked, 'Next year Paris. How about that, little mother?'

'You mind all those dubious women we hear about.' Clara gave him a sneaky little pat on his backside on his way out.

'Bye then, I'll pick up my washing before I go.' It wasn't very far up the hill to Queens Road through Air Street and down into the back of the Grand Hotel in Cannon Street. Frankie hadn't had a girlfriend – he was still a youngster but he did meet a young lady when he worked in London for that short time. She was a Scot who had come to London to get away from the overcrowded tenement living.

Clara's letter to Frank that year told him about his son's plans for gaining more experience. She explained how he had worked in a Mayfair hotel kitchen and how he would soon be off to Paris. She said he had used some of the money in his account to fund his travel and clothing and enclosed a photo of Frankie in his new kitchen whites. She said nothing about Freddy, only sending her new address, commenting on it being more central for Tom's bakery round.

'I hope Frank realises you've done a grand job for young Frankie, Clara. He's growing into a man to be proud of.'

Clara's mind travelled back over the years full of happy memories. No, he was no longer the little boy watching and copying her every move in the kitchen, he was now flying away. Her one real satisfaction was he had a skill that would earn him his living. More than that, he was healthy and strong.

Now she had a new family, a new responsibility and this time a husband by her side. Tom loved his little boy. Freddy wrapped his arms round his daddy's legs as soon as he got through the door. Although it was early evening, Clara allowed Freddy to stay up to have time with Tom. Invariably Freddy would have slept all afternoon so an hour or two with his father in the evenings sent the little lad to bed happy and he slept right through until well into the morning.

Clara was more concerned for Tom who was tired when he got home, but no, he gave his time to the boy, even bouncing him on his knee while he ate his dinner. While at the table they had a rag book or two, but Freddy showed absolutely no interest, he just wanted to hear his father's voice. So it was upstairs to bed with a story by candlelight. More than once in a while Clara would find Tom had fallen asleep, his head on the pillow beside little Freddy. Often the child would be wide awake, quiet and smiling, stroking his dad's greying hair.

Clara guessed from the moment Freddy came into the world that life might be difficult for him to keep up but he would get there in his own time. Clara was never impatient with Freddy. She always said, 'He did his best.'

As soon as they had settled in, Clara's younger brothers and sisters made regular weekend and school holiday visits to Brighton. They hadn't been so welcome at the Lamb Inn as when Granma Annie was alive. The eight oldest of Emily and Tom's children were grown and out to work by the time Clara had enough space to have them. While still at school Edith, Mary and Robert had weekend jobs so it was mostly only the two youngest, Edward and Albert, who came for the long summer holidays. Nancy had stayed at Adelaide Crescent for her last holiday before she married her Italian and went to live in Soho. Bouncy Nancy turned out to be the perfect foil to a fiery Valentino.

Jack was married and had started a family with Pearl and they were living up behind the castle in Lewes. Harry had gone to the navy and Thomas had followed Great Uncle Albert into the tea business out in India. James was working in a small country provisions shop and, as he told Clara, when he stayed at St George's mews for his interview at Hudson's the grocers shop in East Street, 'My aim's to join Tom in the tea trade, eventually.' Clara enjoyed having them all to stay at one time or another.

Young Edith and Mary were so close in age they went everywhere together. The first time the pair stayed with Clara and Tom they talked all about the Lamb and the marsh where they had been with Edward and Albert the summer before. They, like all the others, loved their days with Grand-father. They'd only stayed a week mind, no more long summer stays. Elizabeth wouldn't stand for that now she was in charge. When Clara took Edith and Mary along to their sister Fanny's milli-ner's shop they instantly knew what they wanted to do in life. As luck would have it Pierre was visiting that week. He was charmed to think the girls were so keen.

The next holiday saw them staying with Fanny and having a grand time helping out in the work-shop. When first one then the other left school at twelve and thirteen they went to London to work in Marsie's milliner's workshop. Edith was really good with the designing side and Mary leaned towards assisting customers in the salon, much more her style. Before they both married, they'd pop down to Brighton as often as possible to visit their sisters and show off their smart London creations. Clara and Rose would see them off at Brighton station as they skipped and waved their way arm in arm along the platform.

If truth be told, Mary was more interested in looking in on young Frankie. There was never a dull moment for Clara. She loved seeing any member of the family whenever they came to stay or just called by. Like Jack, who would occasion-ally have to come over to Brighton on brewery business. One day he called in, sitting high up on top of a great brewery dray, causing huge excite-ment for the local children. And didn't that give a fine boost for Freddy when they heard whose uncle brought such enormous horses along the mews.

It was on that visit that Jack brought some pots of geranium cuttings. Clara put them outside on the windowsill where they thrived in the sheltered mews. From that summer on, their front looked very gay with the line of pillar-box red blooms and complementary lush green leaves. When the rent man called on Friday he stood back and stared at the cottage. Handing the signed rent book back into Clara's hand he remarked, 'Your cottage looks extra attractive behind those flowers. We'll have to put the rent up.' Clara's heart sank. You could never tell what was a hint or a joke with this man, he was a law unto himself.

The only brother who had, so far, never left their parents in St Leonards was Robert. He had come eleventh in the family and had a deformed foot. When Clara had made her visits home to see her parents she always failed to persuade the young man to come back with her for a holiday. People were so unkind to anybody with a limp and Robert's built-up shoe never did anything but draw attention to his awkward walk. There was nothing wrong with his hands or brain. In fact a local accountant's office took him on. He was very quick with figures. Nevertheless he was asked not to walk through the outer office if a client should be there. Nobody complained about that treatment in those days. You just shut your mouth, did as requested and kept your job.

Tom really didn't want Clara going out to work. She had little Freddy to look after, so she had to be at home. It was his duty to be the breadwinner. On the other hand, Tom had to work long hours to bring home about nineteen shillings and six-pence a week, now this new round only paid eighteen shillings, and it took all of this to keep them both and the baby, pay the rent and buy their few necessities. Her strength now renewed, Clara couldn't waste a good pair of hands and lots of ideas.

Albert had said in the past if she wanted bones for soup she knew where to find them. It wasn't as easy as that. When she and Tom lived at the far end of Eastern Road, Albert could drop off a few helpful items as he passed that way delivering to the Roedean area, but to walk into the butchery yard to pick up off-cuts and bones when Ethel kept her eye on every scrap of meat cut from the carcasses was near impossible.

Over the years Ethel had developed a keen knowledge of the butcher's craft. She made it her business to know exactly the yield of each animal in joints and pieces, fat, offal and bones. Little passed her by. She worked out the profit and wanted to know why her targets hadn't been met at the till takings each week. Even her best cus-tomers in the Dyke Road and St Ann's Wells knew they had to pay their bills when issued.

Clara had noticed there were often more than twenty men and boys working daily around the St George's Mews yard. A cup of sustaining hot soup for a halfpenny or a basin for a penny would go down well. She decided she wouldn't waste her energy climbing up over Clifton Hill to Mont-pelier for free soup bones. She'd go once or twice a week over to the meat market, off Grenville Place, at closing time, say six o'clock or six thirty in the morning where for a halfpenny or two she could get the trimmings and cheap ends of meat as well as bones. Every morning she nipped the other side of the Victoria Gardens into Circus Street to pick up, or even glean for free, the last of the vegetables in the wholesale market at the close of business. Among the market men standing outside the pubs or in the steamy windowed cafes eating their breakfasts, Clara became known as 'Ruthy', after Ruth in the Bible story who gleaned the ears of corn from the fields.

'Yer want a barrer luv? There's lots more needs clearin' up,' some called, but Clara would only ever take two canvas shopping bags. She wouldn't be greedy, there was enough for all. Plenty of people in those days were very needy having to feed big families, like her own Mother had with thirteen, and her with a husband who so often had been unable to work. Clara was mindful of her own husband Tom, no longer a young man – she never knew if the time would come when they'd be glad of a few savings.

Clara would return home with her bags full of lovely leaves trimmed from cabbage heads being shaped for the top layer of a show box, or all sorts of vegetables just broken or misshapen. Items others had dismissed were gathered by an extra pair of hands who had recognised Clara the first morning she went to the market. It was Sydney who had been kitchen boy at Lady Wellborough's back in 1889.

'Mrs Dann,' he greeted Clara. 'What brings you here?' Sydney was now head porter for one of the wholesalers.

Clara halloo'd him in return saying, 'It's Mrs Cowley now dear. Good to see you Sydney. You look well love.' She told him briefly of her circumstances. He saw her all right. Sydney hadn't forgotten Clara's kindness.

While Clara went to market her neighbour Jenny, Mrs Starr, would mind baby Freddy in return for a basin of good soup for her family's dinner. Clara had always been known for her imaginative blends for soups and stews. Her answer to that was, 'Need makes you inventive.' Some days she offered meat and potato, on other days a vegetable soup, but always the mix was different with the addition of lentils or garlic cooked whole and mashed fine and smooth. In her tiny back yard she had a growing collection of herbs in pots, pans and buckets – parsley, thyme, sage, winter and summer savouries. Even on the flint wall there grew swathes of golden marjoram with mint along the brick-topped edge throughout the summer months.

Now was the time she made full use of the larger pans Albert had given them. Some days, when the winter weather drew in, she needed more saucepan space so a trip to the rag and bone yard unearthed a great iron pot with a well-fitting tin lid. Just the smell of her soup attracted more young workmen, until she realised if the Council got wind of what seemed like a business, she might find the rent man kicking them out of the house.

It just happened she was in the piano repairer's giving Alfred Moffat his basin of soup one cold autumn day when they were both surprised by heavy boots coming to a slithering halt outside in the yard.

'Here it is lads. I knew it. It's that mouth-watering smell.' The small door at the side opened cautiously and a nose came through, sniffing the air. 'Hey missus, is it you sellin' soup?' called a voice, followed by a poor-looking lad. 'I wouldn't half like a drop o' that.'

Alf Moffat smiled and nodded his head towards Clara. Before they knew it, five more boys fell in the door behind the first one. 'Oh my goodness,' exclaimed Clara.

'You'll have ter open a caff my love,' laughed Alf.

'Look lads, I can only do you a small cup each today, I'm nearly out. Oh, an' you'll have to bring your own basin another time.' Then she looked round at Alf. 'But I don't know if I dare take on anymore from our cottage.'

Alfred Moffat quickly summed up Clara's situation. 'Look 'ere lads, Mrs Cowley has only made what she had orders for. Now if you come back here next week we'll be ready for you. That right, Mrs Cowley?' Alf said, looking to Clara. She nodded. 'An' she'll serve you in here.'

Clara quickly called to them, 'Wait a minute. How many of you are there?' She went outside with the lads and to her amazement there were at least twenty other men and boys in St George's yard looking to find the door through which their leaders had disappeared. 'Ah, well now?' They all looked eagerly towards her.

Jenny Starr was on her doorstep wondering what the crowd was for. 'These lads work round in

Gloucester and Trafalgar, Clara.'

'Oh my! Bring a cup each on Monday and I'll see what I can manage.' A cheer went up. 'Hold on now, not so loud, we can't feed the whole town!'

Meanwhile Alf Moffat opened the big door on the other side of his lock-up workshop. Behind was quite a sizeable partitioned office area. 'My wife used to keep this for the times customers would call in. She did the books over there. Look there's a nice fireplace. You can bring a pot or two of soup and ladle it out here on business premises. What d'yer think? Will that fit the bill duck?'

'You're a brick, Alfred Moffat and no mistake,' Clara told him, but followed with a laugh saying, 'but I've got to make all that extra soup first!'

Jenny took a hold of Clara's elbow as she carried her empty soup pan back across the yard. 'Clara love, you're a good lookin' woman. Mind what yer do. 'Er along the yard 'ad a right old time fighting off rent collector when she moved in. Said 'e'd take extra payment upstairs 'cos she was hanging out too much washin'.' As she finished, Jenny tapped the side of her nose and raised her eyebrows. Clara listened and kept her neighbour's advice in mind.

Fortunately the following day was Friday so there'd be more meat and bone trimmings at the wholesale market. Clara took a bit of her savings and another two bags on Freddy's empty pram. The men at the abattoir said, 'Business must be boomin' love. We'll 'ave ter come an' try yer cookin'.'

271

She did the same at the vegetable market and spent the weekend cutting and chopping while the bones bubbled gently in the stock pots. By Monday morning Clara had put her two kitchen knives to the steel over and over again. Their work over for the time being, the small paring knife and large chopping blade were stored away in the slotted canvas bag Rose had made for Clara to hang alongside the steel on the wall behind the back door.

Clara had four huge pots of soup and plenty of stock on the go for, as she was well aware, this wasn't going to be a one-day wonder. However, there was a limit to what she could manage on her small coal range.

Clara realised she'd got herself in an unexpected situation here. These men were in need of nourishment. They worked long hours, few had any midday food. She had given hope and now had to fulfil that expectancy or she would feel so guilty. With the winter coming on, the only concession most men gave to the cold was to wind a thin twisted scarf round their neck and across over their chest. Few owned coats, even fewer had anything different to wear summer come winter. Even her own husband's only cold weather addition was just a tweed jacket under his baker's apron.

On the Friday and Saturday she told her existing customers she would be serving them first all next week, then see how many new people came over the following week. If they were men from the surrounding workshops she could serve them and maybe manage up to forty servings; beyond that she couldn't maintain production. Clara did her best for the sake of these hopeful men. Over that first winter Clara did produce enough soup each day to serve between thirty and forty lads and men. At times she'd only been able to do onion soup thickened with barley but they'd always said how grateful they were for whatever she made.

Last winter had been very sharp so Clara was determined to make sure the cottage would be warmer before the cold weather came round again. The walls were very thin, only a single brick depth, and with the front door opening directly into the only living room, the cold air rushed in making it difficult to keep any warmth in the place, let alone the wind driving snow in under the door.

Taking her stock bones into Charlie's in Jubilee Street one evening, she overheard him calling to his lad across the yard that he would be off extra early next day as he'd been told there was a big house opposite the Preston Park being cleared out.

'Might 'ave some good finds there. I'll be takin' the horse 'n' cart. You'll have ter use the 'and barrer tomorrow Jim.'

'Hmm,' thought Clara. 'I'll look in later tomorrow and see what Charlie gets.'

The next day Clara took a few shillings from her soup money and acquired two heavy woven curtains and a curtain rail and rings. Charlie even delivered them.

'Housekeeper said those curtains had some bloke's name, Morris something?'

That rang a bell. 'D'you mean William Morris, Charlie?'

'Yeah, that's the one.'

Clara remembered how a Mr William Morris, an artist designer, had sometimes been a visitor at the Whitesides', in Adelaide Crescent.

The wooden rail was long enough for Clara to hang the curtaining all across the front door as well as the window. Rose neatened the new curtains up on the machine. The bundle cost Clara a whole two shillings but it was worth it.

'We'll be real snug this winter then young 'un, your ma's never lost her eye for a good bargain,' Tom told Freddy.

Come the spring and summer, the numbers to serve dropped back to the original fifteen to twenty workers, so she kept her soup making down to those numbers. Often during the summer Clara would only cook and serve on just one or two days a week. With young Freddy now toddling about, albeit quietly, around her skirts and dabbling with little mud pies out on the cobbled yard, Clara was satisfied to make up to about three shillings and sixpence a week as she originally intended.

Tom never had holidays. Sunday was his only day off. As they were already at the seaside their occasional day out was to visit his son in Worthing. Clara's little stash of earnings paid for the bus ride across West Sussex and a few little gifts for Dudley and Sybil's growing family.

Dudley worked at a market garden where they grew tomatoes. The soil in the area produced tomatoes with the most delicious flavour. No seasoning was needed; the flesh of those tomatoes was perfect as they came. Tom and Clara looked forward to their summer visits to Worthing, having tea outside Dudley's flint cottage in the garden sheltered by high laurel hedges.

The well at the bottom of the garden gave clear, sweet water with a little effervescent sparkle. Clara suggested perhaps the move to this house with its pure water coming off the Downs could be the reason Sybil had regained her health. Thinking of the low-lying area where the young couple had lived when they first married, Dudley said she might well be right. The water from the shared well they'd previously used always had an odd smell.

While Clara's two youngest brothers, Edward and Albert, were still schoolboys they spent some of their holidays with Clara and Tom, sharing Freddy's little bedroom. They had only known a few carefree days at the Lamb Inn rambling over the marshland with their elder brother James and once with Leslie. It was a time they often talked about. Clara made it up to them as well as she could, taking them to the beach when they were young. She told them all about the sea life, finding winkles at Black Rock, collecting little fish and shellfish at the fish market under the arches then cooking up fishy soup with soda bread. They made paper kites with coloured bows down the tails to fly up along the cliffs at Black Rock. She would say the boys' visits made her youthful days last into her forties. Just like the days when she was a young carer with all her older siblings on the marsh.

Leslie was the one who now kept Rose and Clara in touch with their grandfather. Since her son was ten, Rose had allowed him to travel alone over to stay with John at the Lamb. His mother had taken him before on visits so he knew his uncles, Edward, who was the same age as Leslie, and Albert a year younger. But this would be the first time he'd spent the summer with them. The three boys enjoyed walking and learning about farming on the marsh with the old man. Now in his early eighties he didn't walk the distances so the boys often had the chance to drive the pony and trap over to Bexhill or into Pevensey, where once John would have scorned to ride such a short distance. He even let them help Bill the potman, who was still living at the Lamb, tap and taste the ales. It was then that they learned why so many huntsmen and walkers made a beeline to stop off at the Lamb. The ale was smooth and hoppy while the stout was rich, dark and malty.

These days the local baker provided the inn with crusty loaves and the butcher made the sausages and smoked the hams. Elizabeth couldn't match her mother's cooking. She never even tried. It wasn't that she was in her mother's shadow and couldn't keep up with her fame – there were only a few old men who remembered Ann's tasty generous fare and Elizabeth didn't care much for them. 'The sooner the old'uns went and stopped cluttering up the place the better,' she said. The reason Elizabeth was tolerant of her nephews and her niece, Rose's boy, was they kept the 'Old Man' as she called John, occupied and out of the place. She would rather have all those young healthy cycling club people to meet at the Lamb and bring their money with them.

Old John told the boys wonderful stories of stout Jack Hares, rounding off his tales with a song or two. When Leslie came home he was full of his time with his uncles and grandfather.

'Granfer's got a really deep voice, Mum, and he's got silver cups and a clock on the mantel-shelf for training puppy hounds for the hunts-men.'

'Does he still sit in his old chair in the chimney corner Les?' asked Clara.

'Yes, an' yer know that grandfather clock, well he said it belonged to Granny Ann's father.'

'That would be James wouldn't it Clara?' Rose asked.

'Yes. I remember Gran telling me how James made the case for a man who walked all across England with his clock mechanisms slung on his shoulders, one on his back and another on his chest. Bit like a yoke only the opposite way round, held over his shoulders with a leather harness. He had two other bags, one on each shoulder to carry his toiletries and a change of shirt and in the other bag he had his clock-making tools. Gran said the clock man left a clock face and mechanism with her father to set it into a particular-sized case. Apparently the order was for a man who was taking his family to live in another country and wanted a good English clock to go with them. The clockmaker said he'd return in a month's time when he was to take the clock to the port. He left a deposit for the clock case but didn't say which port or who the purchaser was. The clockman never returned and the clock stood in her father's workshop for years. As he had no idea where the owner might be sailing to, he couldn't know which port he might have been leaving from. The clockman was never seen again.

'What happened to him Auntie?'

'Nobody in the area knew anything. Maybe he had an accident and died. We'll never know. Anyway, when John and Ann took over the licence at the Lamb, Ann's mother persuaded James to clear that clock out of the workshop. 'Give it to John and Ann, it'll look real nice at the Inn,' she said.

'Cor Auntie, what a long story. I mean all those years.'

'That grandfather clock must have been built in the 1830s or 40s Les.'

'When Granfer told us stories by the inglenook, lots of people stayed to listen. It got quite crowded.'

'It always used to be like that when we were kiddies didn't it?' said Rose looking round at Clara.

'Auntie Clara, did Granfer let you all taste the ales?'

'Not if Granny Ann was about! Ha!' That made the sisters laugh.

'Granma Annie was a kind loving Gran, always busy but she was hot on good manners and discipline with us grandchildren.'

'Oh yes,' agreed Rose.

'She was generous with her time for all of us though,' Clara went on. 'As she worked in the kitchen and yard with the small animals and out in her vegetable garden, she told us how to do this and how best to grow that and when to sow

278

the seeds at full moon because the ground was warm and damp. We loved it didn't we Rose?'

'Yes. I always had a bit of lace making or knittin' in my hands while I watched her do the bakin',' added Rose. 'Gran told how it was done. She'd draw a little extra drop of icy cold water up from the well when she made her pastries, worked a treat. Made all the difference it did.'

'Sad getting old, because Granfer used to walk out long distances when he was younger. If we weren't with Gran we went far and wide along with Granfer. Walked miles we did, in all weathers.'

'Not me,' laughed Rose. 'I liked sittin' on the back step in the sun doin' my lace. There was always a tiny one to watch over while Granny got on with her work.'

'Some of the younger ones tried to keep up with Granfer – remember he was over six feet tall and had a long gait. He got along faster 'n us but he often picked up two smaller ones. He was a powerful strong man you know. He'd p'raps be carrying Harry and Fanny, one on each shoulder, with the rest of us doing catch up when he stopped to scan the fields. He bred cattle for himself and for other people too so he had further than just his own acres where he looked after the animals. Like Gran, he told us about his sheep; which were yearlings and which had been castrated. He'd point out the pregnant ones and say exactly when they would drop their lambs. Yes, and he told us about Jack Hare. He called one Harry Hare.'

'No Mum, you got 'is name wrong. Granfer told us all about Harold Hare and the smoot,' cut

279

in young Leslie.

'Oh yes – course it was Harold Hare.'

'Did he show you where they were?'

'Where what were, Auntie?'

'The smoots.'

'No, where?'

'Get Uncle Jack to show you love. He goes over with his two little'uns sometimes, doesn't he? Get mummy to find out when he's going and you could meet him when they get on the train at Lewes.'

'That's a good idea,' Clara hadn't thought of that. 'Yes, I'll drop him a card.'

'Jack and I used to keep the smoots clear of mud and rubbish after the winter high waters, always left the grasses to hide them of course. Did Granfer tell you how we used to make baskets with the withies?'

'Yes, an' he showed us his eel traps too. We're going fishin' with him next time I go over. An' he showed me how to drive the pony 'n' trap. Oh, and Mum, a man came with a motor car! He says they'll be a picture of Grandfather in the car printed in the *Observer* newspaper, an' he showed Granfer how to drive. We went over to Pevensey village with Granfer driving. Gosh it were real excitin'. No horse!'

Just as Leslie was finishing his story about the motor car ride, the boy next door gasped out in surprise – he'd been standing by the door waiting for Les to finish telling about his holiday. 'Come on Les come an' tell us about the horseless carriage – did yet really ride in it?' As Leslie ran to the door he stopped and turned. 'Forgot. Granfer sends his love to yer both. An' Auntie, Granfer said to say hallo to Uncle Tom.' Half way through the door he turned again. 'Oh yeah, an' 'e said to give you a wink too, Auntie.' They heard the boys in the street shout, 'Is yer grandad a toff then Les?'

'No 'e's an innkeeper.'

'Blimey Jim, Les's old man's got a boozer. Does 'e let yer drink, Les?'

'Nah,' replied Les, his accent sliding into street lad.

'Rotten old devil.'

'Why?'

'Well don't 'e even let y'er 'ave 'n 'alf Les?' Their voices faded as the ball was kicked further down the street.

'Oh dear, the language!'

'Never mind Clara, as long as 'e keeps it for out in the street I'm not going to make him look a sissy in front of the lads.'

Later, after Sunday tea when Fanny and Peter were with them, Clara told more of their roaming with Grandfather Pilbeam. She said how he'd made them part of his life, showing them the freedom and freshness of the marshland, the gull and the heron flying across what he called the endless heavens.

'"Lookee", he'd say, "watch, look how his great wings lift then lazy beat the air down – up and away he goes, yes, slow 'n' easy." He told us about managing the water courses and how the flow was controlled at the sluices to irrigate certain fields at the right moment of need. Showed us great con-gregations of beautiful lilies growing tall and bright white. Also he'd say where and when the rushes were cut and dried for different uses.'

'But did he let you do things Granny didn't like, Auntie?'

'No, why? What makes you ask that Les?'

'Well Mum said this morning he only let you try the ale if Granny wasn't there.'

'Oh no luvvy no, it wasn't like that. Both Gran and Granfer had seen some young men drink too much and get into the kind of state where they couldn't work, and if you can't work you can't earn your living so you needed to avoid strong drink.'

'They told us, best not to start young,' said Rose.

'And Gran believed in self-discipline. No, we'd see them give each other a little conspiratorial wink, but Granfer would let us taste the ale. When you are very young it usually tastes horribly bitter for young tongues, so you don't like it. Best way to put you off.'

'Besides getting horribly sick,' Rose commented.

'Ah! Yes, you're right there. You remember when Tom was quite small, he hid down in the cellar one night and drank too much. Dear oh dear, he was ill, never touched a drink since, young scamp.'

'Still, did 'im good though, didn't it Clara?'

'Is that why Granfer said to give you a wink Auntie? Did you get sick on drink too?'

'Oh no love, what a mix up – I didn't get sick, nothing to do with winking dear.'

'My dad got sick when we lived in Lundun though didn't 'e Mummy?'

'Yes, Leslie, he did an' that's why we had to leave him luv.'

Leslie turned to his cousin Peter and said under

his breath, 'Mum got sick as well.'

Rose overheard. 'Now that's enough Leslie. Mummy was ill, that's why she was sick.'

'Oh there's Freddy needing his tea,' said Clara, 'come and help me boys. Give mummy a minute to do the washing up. We'll fetch baby down and let's see if he'll play with you for a bit.'

'At least I don't 'ave ter worry about that any-more,' Rose remarked when Clara told her she was pregnant again. She tried to keep her condition from Tom for as long as she could, knowing he would make her stop all the soup making and lifting heavy pots. Frankie was away working in Paris so she didn't let him know because it would just give him months of worry. By the time he came back the baby would be born.

Of course, Tom noticed before she was ready to tell him and he was worried for her. As she was serving fewer customers during the summer months, it was decided she could cope with the work. Clara felt well all through. Thanks to a neighbour who recommended the midwife who had seen all five of her children into the world, Clara came through this confinement very happily.

Jenny kept a birthing chair hanging on the wall in the back yard shed along with what she called a 'gator'. Clara didn't know what that was.

'Yer know, luv, cleans yer out afore 'n' after.'

She had a lot to learn from these women, neighbours who looked out for one another. She'd been too young to know the intimate private details of women's lives when her mother was having her babies. Clara discovered Jenny meant an irrigator, an enamel jug with a small spout at the bottom and a rubber tube kept separate and clean.

'Simple see,' said Jenny holding the vessel up high.

James was born healthy and well in November 1907. He took his feed quickly and always seemed overflowing with vigorous energy. From his first moments he was full of smiles.

Alfred Moffat looked into the perambulator one morning and remarked, 'My goodness Clara, this one's going to be a right little comedian.' He didn't know then how true his words were.

Frankie wrote to say he was staying in Paris for another year, sending a silver and ivory teething ring for his new brother. Freddy was four and very interested in the new addition to the family. Jimmie was Freddy's opposite, bright as a button and way ahead of what his older brother had been doing by the time he was ten months old. His rapid progress actually had a good effect on Freddy who, seeing the way Jim was doing everything, copied and joined in the fun. Before Jim was ten months old, Clara gave birth to a daughter in August 1908. The baby was so small and neat that everybody said she looked like a little dolly. The name stuck and Dolly she was, to the family, for the rest of her life.

Jim and Dolly could pass as twins. Poor Freddy rather had his nose put out of joint with Dolly's arrival. Dolly copied Jimmie much more quickly than their elder brother was doing and often left him behind. Freddy didn't seem to have a physical disability, he was just very slow to react, to get off the mark. It got so that his two younger siblings ran either side of him as if he were the younger. When he got annoyed at his own inability they cuddled him saying 'Silly Freddy'. Unfortunately he began to react by pinching and punching.

What a handful these three were, two tiny little mites making mud pies and constantly egging their big brother on. Freddy had started school along at St Bartholomew's but he didn't like leaving home; it was much more fun playing where nobody smacked his legs for lagging behind his classmates.

One of the workmen from the metalworking shop made a folding fence that hooked onto the front wall by the front door like a big playpen. It kept young Jimmie and Dolly from wandering into the way of delivery carts and horses' hooves. The pair were little rascals banging their small pans and spoons. Even when Clara loaded them onto the old pram to meet Freddy from school they bounced and threw themselves around, frequently breaking a spring. Clara tried singing softly to them to calm them down but as soon as they picked up the song, they sang at the tops of their voices. Naturally our budding comedian picked up all the naughty words he overheard the workmen say. Then Dolly would answer back with a garbled version.

'Bugger it,' Jim would shout.

'Dudder rich,' echoed Dolly in an effort to get the sound right with a second try.

'Sod it.' Jim would laugh in delight.

'Sod ick,' Dolly squealed.

Clara would stop the pram, and instead of telling them sharply, 'No you mustn't say those words,' she'd tell them, 'Bother it. Say bother it.' But she always made it sound funnier than the sound of bugger it. Or she'd say 'Silly wolly woolly wow' making a funnier sound for the children to copy, then follow it up by patting her hand over her mouth, eyebrows raised to the sky, as if she was about to get into trouble. They thought that even funnier. Clara recalled all those little ploys she'd had to use with her young brothers and sisters whose language often had to be curtailed when they brought town swear words into the country. Granma Annie wouldn't have any men swearing in front of women and children, and would have been very embarrassed to hear her own grandchildren's repeated airings, particularly from the fishermen's wives down on the beach.

Tom was thrilled with his new young family and so pleased that Clara seemed to thrive once more. Occasionally the children would meet him for the last few visits on his round on Saturday afternoons and he would allow them up onto the car in front of his van. Jim always wanted to take the horse's reins and Freddy liked to feed the horse while little Violet May (Dolly) just sat on her daddy's knee for a few moments, enjoying looking down from high up in the baker's van.

Frankie came home on a flying visit to find not just one new baby, but another. Freddy was excited to show Jim somebody he knew that Jim hadn't met. Frankie bounced them on his knees and played growly bears with them on the floor under the table. He and Clara had a session in the kitchen making cakes and Frankie showed Freddy how to make special tiny crispy biscuits for his baby brother and sister.

'Now Freddy – we call these Freddy bikkies 'cos they are Freddy specials only big boys can make.'

The flying visit was because Frankie was moving on to another hotel kitchen outside Paris. Then he told Clara he and a friend had been asked by a businessman to travel to South Africa to open a new hotel restaurant in Cape Town. He said this man wanted young blood and he'd pay their fares if they would give at least a couple of years to the job.

'What do you think, Mother?'

'I think it would be a wonderful experience for a young man who's unattached.'

'Oh good, I hoped you'd approve. Mr Lovegrove is going to send our tickets when the building is well on the way, so we don't have to hang around with nothing to do when we get there.'

One evening, after Frankie and Les had met up for a drink, he told Clara that Les was thinking of cutting loose and going to work in London.

'Well, he should get away from home now. It's not good for him to spend all his time with his mother.'

'Yes I told him that Mum. But he doesn't want to hurt Aunt Rose's feelings.'

'But he must have a life of his own. He's a good athlete. Often goes running up over the Downs with a group. Belongs to the youth club – they go camping. He took his friends cycling over to the Lamb earlier this summer.'

'Yeah, he told me, said Granfer made 'em all laugh a lot.'

Clara knew she would miss Frankie but it was good for him to travel. When she knew the definite times of sailing to South Africa, she would tell Frank in her next letter. Maybe there would be a chance for Frankie to meet his father.

The Willows

'I know Frankie didn't think much of that idea,' said Bessie. 'You see I was sitting on the windowsill in Leslie's room when they were talking over Leslie's plans to go away to work in London and Frankie asked if he'd got any plans to meet his father, Tony.'

'Don't know yet,' Les replied. He was getting his jacket out from the wardrobe and as he turned round, pulling his coat on, he said, 'What about you Frank? You know your ma will write to your father and tell him what you're doing now. Do you think you'll meet him?'

'I don't care a damn whether I meet him or not, Les,' Frankie replied.

Leslie looked very surprised. 'Why's that then?'

'He could have come back home and married my mother. Remember I saw her all my young life working long hours to keep the two of us. Oh, it wasn't just money, Les. She had to tell untruths about where Dad was otherwise we would have been flung out for her being a fallen woman, so she had to keep up all that pretence. I can't remember us at the tea shop, I was too young, but since I've worked in kitchens I know how hard it must have been for her carrying a baby on her back as well as baking in a hot kitchen from early morning till gone half past six, besides stopping throughout the day to feed me herself. Les, I've witnessed those long working hours and worked them myself, and I didn't have a baby on my back.

'You know what, when Tom and Mum finally found each other, I can't tell you how relieved I felt for her. She's been so happy being loved and cared for.' Frankie felt all this so strongly that Les didn't like to interrupt. 'It wasn't that she was unhappy. We were lucky to be at Adelaide Crescent working for the Whitesides. Their home was always full of music and singing, and laughter too. They all got along so well. Mum used to sing while she was cooking. No, it's having another human being to share your life and worries with. You can't exactly do that with a small child.'

'But Mum says he writes regular to Aunt Clara, and he really loved her,' Les said.

'Then he should have come and supported her! She's been withered out of the family and kept away from her beloved grandfather by Aunt Lizzie. I'd like to have known him like you, but Lizzie gave me the cold shoulder that one time I went over there with you.'

'Sorry mate. I didn't know you felt like that about him.'

'I only know my father as a letter writer, Les.'

'Les didn't tell his mother Rose how Frankie felt,' said Bessie. 'Same as he didn't tell her that Tony had been in touch with him. I saw Leslie writing to his father on a number of occasions.'

'That puts a very different side to Clara and Rose's stories doesn't it?' Albert said to Victoria.

'Well it's only to be expected,' added Uncle Bert. *'Youngsters do like to know about their background. I'll tell you sometime about where I came from.'*

Clara

Waving goodbye to his mother, Frankie noticed how her golden hair reflected the light shining down through the glass roof above the platforms at Brighton station. Clara had hidden the natural pain of parting behind a loving smile and a 'Have a wonderful, wonderful time son,' as they kissed each other goodbye.

Walking away out of the station, pushing her two youngest in their perambulator, Clara would normally have called in on Rose, but knowing Leslie hadn't yet told his mother of his plans, she decided against. The sisters had never kept secrets from each other. Anyway, Rose would be busy in the workroom. Instead Clara walked on down Queens Road towards the sea glittering in the distance beyond the tall spire of St Paul's church on the right at the bottom of West Street.

The two little ones woke up as she turned towards the Palace Pier. Above their heads a group of seagulls wheeled and squawked, fighting over scraps being thrown by an old lady wearing widow's weeds. It crossed Clara's mind how much the black bombazine would be to buy when a member of your family dies.

Frankie and Leslie took the train over to Newhaven together. Frankie boarded the ferry across to France while Leslie travelled on to stay a few days with Grandfather Pilbeam. He found Old John was often in great pain with arthritis and taking to his bed. People were missing him in his usual seat by the inglenook. Leslie reported to his mother and Clara how the arthritic flare-ups were leaving Grandfather very weakened.

Clara felt agonised that she was unable to visit John. She knew she could, at a pinch, get Jenny to look after the children for a day. On the other hand it was doubtful whether Elizabeth would even allow her through the door to see her grandfather. She had written to him, but Leslie had to make sure he brought the letter back after he had read it to John in private.

Soon after Frankie had left to return to his job in the Paris hotel, Leslie told his mother he had found a job in London. He said he would be staying in Soho, at Aunty Nancy's flat to start with. Rose was shocked. 'You're not leaving me?' she blurted out. 'After all the upbringing I've given you. I can't believe it of you.'

Leslie had told Frankie he wouldn't find it easy to get away. 'I want a new experience,' he told Rose. 'Working in the council offices was boring. There were no prospects and no wage rise until somebody older retired.'

He had his bag packed and would be away the next morning early. Rose couldn't believe it. She kept saying how abandoned she felt. Leslie promised that as soon as he settled into the job he would get home at weekends.

'How can you Leslie, if you're going to be working in a restaurant? They'll want you on duty at weekends.'

'I'll come down on my day off, Mother.'

'Then I'll be working if it's in the week. I don't know how you could do this to me, son.'

'Please Mother, don't make it difficult for me. All your brothers and sisters have left home and they're doing all sorts of interesting work.'

'But you've got such a secure home with me, love.'

Leslie left the next morning on an earlier train than planned. He knew if he gave her another hour, Rose would find a way to stop him.

Nancy and Valentino were now running their own Italian restaurant in Soho where they lived up above on the third floor. Valentino cooked and Nancy managed out front. Leslie had asked for a job just so as to get himself started. On his first evening he joined the front of house staff and soon picked up the routine with guidance from two Italian lads of his own age, full of chat and jokes but very professional in front of the customers. By the end of the week Les had learned a few new words, which he tried out on Nancy in case the rascals were teaching him to swear in Italian. Les had a great sense of humour and in this new company it could blossom.

Early on the first Saturday morning when the staff were just up and about, preparing to cater for a special family party booked for midday through until midnight, there was a rap on the flat's street door beside the restaurant. One of the waiters passing through the corridor heard and went to investigate.

'Les there's a lady here, says she's come to see you.'

Rose stood at the bottom of the stairs in her hat and coat, an overnight case in one hand and an umbrella in the other. 'Expected you 'ome last night son.'

At the sound of his mother's voice out in the passage, Leslie looked up abruptly from where he stood, laying a table with a red chequered cloth. Across the room behind the counter Nancy summed up the situation in an instant. She knew her elder sister's character and it wouldn't have changed. 'Why, hallo Rose,' she said. 'What brings you here? A bit of a bad moment, we've got a wedding party arriving in an hour.'

A voice called from the kitchen, 'Where are you all?' Then Valentino appeared in the kitchen door-way. First he saw five people rooted like statues, and a shadowy fifth away in the corridor he took as being a new hired help. 'Ah, is our washer up. Come through missus, come through.'

Rose caught on quicker than all of them. She dumped her bag and umbrella on the bottom stair, hung her coat over the banister, and rolling up her sleeves she walked through to the kitchen all businesslike with her black straw fixed firmly on her head by two bobbly hat pins. She would not be set aside that easily.

In July 1910 Clara was perched on the windowsill outside shelling peas while two-year-old Dolly followed Jim, who was running to meet Nobby Hollands the postman. He didn't often come along the mews to the houses' side but when he did it was always for Clara. Nobody in the other three families could read or write. This morning, though, he wouldn't hand over the post to Jim for the last few yards of its journey to his mummy. Clara caught the difference in the postman's body language immediately. It made her put her bowl of peas down on the step and stand up, wiping her hands down the sides of her pinny, ready to meet him.

The small white envelope he handed her was edged with a black band. Her heart squeezed her breath a tad as she accepted the unknown.

Little Jimmie looked up at her expectantly – he hadn't seen this reaction to the postman before. They usually shared a joke and a light-hearted farewell. Now the man just gave a kind smile and turned away, leaving Clara with her news. Jim was distracted by a beautiful big beetle scurrying across the shiny cobbles. Two little squealing children quickly followed its progress.

The 'In Memoriam' card read, 'John Pilbeam passed away on June 18th.'

Clara turned her back on the happy squeals of her children and the hammering on metal and tapping tones from Alfred's piano tuning, into the solitude of her scullery where she pushed the singing kettle across the coals and took down Granma Annie's cup and tea dish. Setting it on the round table in the front room, she poured boiling water onto a few fresh tea leaves in the tiny breakfast teapot. Sitting down in front of teapot, jug, cup and dish at the table, Clara went into a silent world alone.

Emily hadn't realised her daughters had not been asked to the funeral, let alone been told of their grandfather's death. Sipping the tea from

Annie's 'tay dish', Clara tried to hold back the tears. Tears that she'd hoped she had put behind her through all the years of cold rebuff, now, with the belated news of grandfather's passing, came flooding back. She sat quietly with the small black-edged card on the table between her fingertips. A distant yip and squeal made her focus her attention onto Laura and Bea, taking the pair out to the scullery washing them carefully and replacing them in their place on the dresser. Granma Annie's influence was telling her not to let this news dash her spirit – not for long. 'Let the joyful memories live on,' she'd say.

The following day Clara received a copy of the local Bexhill paper dated 24 July 1910 from her mother. It contained photos and a long obituary with the opening words 'Famous Looker of the marshes has gone to his rest.'

Along with the newspaper, Emily enclosed a few sprigs of lavender from her mother's garden border. 'I laid a nosegay on the top of Father's coffin as it stood in the aisle. When the bearers carried him out to the churchyard, the scent of lavender lingered in the air. She was there with us too.'

Clara's heart was full of tears. So many people had loved John, they thought so highly of him. He had been one of the grand old men of his time, they said. When she read the obituary she could picture the scene at his burial, with the morning sun shining across from the sea, the coffin being carried up the church pathway between swathes of tall nodding daisies.

Her grandfather had never seen Jim and Dolly.

Only twice had she been able to take Freddy to market to meet him. Now that life had passed, his precious light had gone out and she felt empty.

Her mother told her later how Elizabeth could never let it go. Clara was worse than a fallen woman, a harlot. Even at the funeral, Clara had been snubbed. Over the years Elizabeth had always found a way of spitting her personal animosity back at her sister. Other times she'd spoken in a low rasping voice as if to keen the shame within because Emily's gross production of children cast a shadow over her importance in social standing. One way or another, she blocked Clara's contact with her grandparents and the inn.

Just a year after Clara was ordered from the Andersons' household and had moved to Brighton, Granma Ann had died. She was spent. She'd had a full life. John was bereft. The pair had loved each other from the day they first met. They had worked together in harmony throughout the years to bring up a healthy family, supporting a growing band of grandchildren and serve customers in a warm welcoming atmosphere at the Lamb. In Ann's last few months Elizabeth almost dashed the welcoming atmosphere her parents had established, but she never dashed Ann's spirit. In her final days Ann told John how much she had enjoyed her life, especially all the years at his side. Clara never did get back to see her beloved grandmother.

John managed alone through the years with the help of Bill his potman and Elizabeth's grudging hour or two in the kitchen, ordering the one or two fostered youngsters about. However, something made her realise that as the eldest, she should inherit the property. Her parents had given enough over the years, caring for her sister Em's brood and the help they'd provided to Lottie's husband's transport business venture. So she persuaded her husband to move to live at the inn and take over its day-to-day business, saying her father was getting too old to manage. Elizabeth wanted to make sure of her inheritance – more than a major share – if in situ, she would already be in control.

John made her wait a long time. He lived on until his eighty-seventh year. Meantime the inn would have closed for the lack of customers had it not been for those who called to see Old John to hear his tales of life on the marsh as he sat welcoming them from his high-back chair beside the inglenook fire. So long as John was there the hearty welcome remained. During the weeks he was confined to his bed with arthritic pain, Elizabeth and her waspish attitude and rules – 'Wipe yer boots,' 'Don't spit,' and 'Take that 'ackin corf outside with yer' – almost did for the place. Then when John did reappear she'd tell customers, 'Yer set too long, yer makin' the ole man tired,' and, 'I've got no time makin' yer vittles.'

The cycling clubs still met during the summer months and were at the inn even on the day John died. They had been coming for so many years. When he died that June day it was in fact his eighty-seventh birthday, and he passed away in the very room in which he was born. It was obvious the inn had lost the one spirit that had made the place magical. Visitors said he had always put the topping on a grand day out. But now Elizabeth's influence had devalued the very inheritance she had been determined as eldest child to take for herself.

The Will John had made and left in safe keeping, just prior to Horace kindly telling his father-in-law he and Lizzie would move to the inn and look after him, was fair. She and Horace did get a major share but by that time, the business had diminished so much the inn was sold out to a brewery. A portrait of John that had hung on the wall at the end of the bar for the last twenty years of his life had not been mentioned as an item in the Will. This was the last irritant that caused hot dispute as to who should take ownership. Emily said it never came her way. In fact she didn't know which way it went.

Chancing to look back that day she rode away on the carrier's cart, she saw Grandfather John standing tall on a raised 'eye' so as to be seen, waving his goodbye as the sun rose over the marsh. The sight so moved her she could hardly bear to think of it and all the pain she had caused.

The portrait did come to life again.

The Willows

'What does it mean, "Come to life again"?' An urgent whisper flew round the kitchen. 'Who has?' chorused the younger Willows.

'Wake up! Who do you think the story's been about?' Big Pol asked sarcastically, ''Ol' nick? That's him over there beside the pastel portrait of Lily's Grandson.'

'Where? Who?' squeaked new bowls and dishes.

'Grandfather John,' answered Mrs P in a very important voice. 'The miniature on the wall beside our dresser is the portrait of Clara's grandfather painted by her granddaughter Lily. I for one had quite a shock when I saw that face appear again after all these years. I really did think he had come alive.'

'True,' agreed Big Pol. 'It's the spittin' image.'

'Sad that Clara's father died just a few months after Great Grandfather,' added Mrs P.

9

The Willows

'I can't keep quiet any longer; I've got to tell you my story now. I've only realised whose family I've joined since you've mentioned St George's Mews. I had to wait and listen to make sure he's the same Tom Cowley your Clara married. When you told about their move to their mews cottage, I knew I was really part of your family stories from further back, well before Lily and Paul bought me from that antique shop opposite the church in Goudhurst. Mind you, I'd been a bit battered about by then. Paul could appreciate a good china repair job since he worked for the "Restorique" in Brighton in the nineteen-fifties. He told Lily I was worth buying for the quality of my restoration job. Paid sixty pounds for me they did.'

'Calm down! You'll bounce yerself right off the shelf, Bertie. Get yerself more damaged,' warned Ol' Po.

'What's all this about you knowing Clara and Tom Cowley?' asked Mrs P rather crossly. She liked to think she knew everybody's stories.

'Oh I never met them. No, my owner told us about Tom and Clara Cowley. She said, well she whispered so's we could all but barely hear her words, "If you want to find me I'll be at St George's Mews with Tom and Clara Cowley." And that was only an after-thought. She turned back to tell us, "that's in Brighton you know."

'And we never saw her again, our Mrs Sinden. Never even knew her first name in all those years.'

'We can tell you that,' offered Laura and Bea.

'Yes, we can too,' said Mrs P. 'But now you've started, Bertie you'd better tell us your part in Maud Sinden's life.'

A shocked 'Well!' exploded in unison from two deeply annoyed voices. 'We were going to tell Mrs Sinden's Christian name.'

'And we know all about her exciting adventure,' added Bea.

'Never mind dears, the limelight will still be yours. I'll tell you my story then you can tell me yours from St George's mews. How about that?' Bert reassured them.

Satisfaction restored, the Willows sat back in anticipation of Uncle Bert tureen's tale.

'Betcher didn't know I was born out of a mail order catalogue.'

The boys looked sideways at Uncle Bert, sniggering at the very idea. 'Nar! Yer too old for that, Uncle. They didn't 'ave mail order back in the dark ages did they?'

'Yep boys, they really did. Gamages, Army and Navy, those big department stores, they all 'ad catalogues. Folks going overseas to the colonies an' that like, they'd choose what they needed to furnish their homes. It all got packed up in a warehouse an' put on a big ship goin' to the country where the family ordered their purchases to be delivered.'

Dixie and Pixie and Dido were now all ears. 'Where did you go to Uncle Bert?' asked the cruet triplets.

'Gaw, where we landed was hot just like an oven. But that weren't the end of it. We were all piled into a wagon behind something we heard called an outspan. What a journey that was, joggling and bumping, fit to break us all.' Uncle Bert's eyes looked far away into the distance, his words slowing.

'What's an outspan Uncle?'

Bert roused himself with a rattle of the china ladle resting under his lid before he answered. 'It's a long line of wagons, pulled in those days by oxen, being driven out from Cape Town in South Africa, going inland up into rougher and rougher country.'

'You can say that again,' Mispah put in.

'Yes, well you've been there haven't you? It seemed like weeks being rumbled along in all that heat, didn't it? When we finally arrived at the family home we waited a long time before our boxes were unpacked. We were in a steamy kitchen with voices all around but what worried me was I couldn't understand what they were saying. Suddenly a really shocking thing happened. The pair of hands that unwrapped my packaging were as black as your hat. I thought, oh dear he hasn't washed his hands – then I could see he hadn't washed his face!'

By this time the triplets were wide-eyed with amaze-

301

ment. The room filled with laughter.

'Well,' said Uncle Bert, getting on the defensive. 'It was the first time I'd ever seen humans with different coloured skin. I just thought, oh my, wherever have we come to? We got used to our new surroundings though. The servants in our family's big house were a friendly lot and really careful. Course, when we were served at table we were handled by white-gloved hands, it was the fashion in those days you see.

'The missus was so excited; everybody enjoyed unpacking and lifting us out of the wrappings, finding piece after piece of china all covered with pictures. The dining room where they took us to display on a big sideboard was cool and dark. When we were used in the evenings the room was lit by candlelight.'

'Who's we, Uncle?'

'Why all the other members of our dinner service of course. Oh, very proper our household was, everything had its own function and in its rightful place. I sat in the centre of the sideboard with two smaller lidded tureens each with its own ladle inside, just like I've got here. We didn't have a china cruet set, far too rustic, we had a set of cut-glass bottles standing on a silver holder. Each bottle contained a different condiment including one each for pepper and salt. Today we would say, quite a line up.'

'Quite a line up,' echoed a sleepy slur.

''Spect he's still in the dark,' remarked Dido, cheekiest salt dish of the lot.

'Well, Uncle Bert doesn't get used much at all these days,' Dixie and Pixie agreed.

'These days,' they repeated again, tipping their heads together mockingly and closing their eyes as Uncle Bert opened one eye a peep, murmuring, 'Those were the

302

days.' Then, both eyes opened wide and in a loud voice as if he was shouting to the kitchen to jump to its orders, 'You could tell the time of the year from the soups that were served out of me. Game, like venison, springbok or oxtail. The Master, his name was Norman, had to have what he was used to at 'ome in England. In spring it was vegetable, maybe artichoke or sweet potato, then later, turtle as a julienne. Mrs tried an iced julienne one time but that got thrown across the room, plate 'n' all. Poor ol' soup dish got badly chipped. There weren't any changes after that. Always steak and kidney pudding, great roasts carried in on the meat dishes for Master to carve. Then one day, Master went on business to Jo'burg. We heard he'd had a heart attack and died. Weren't any family meals for a while. The missus just used the supper set on a tray in her little sittin' room or on the verandah. We stood untouched. The whole household was sad. Then missus decided to move back to England. We'd been at the farm for near on thirty years. Our owner packed us all herself. It took days and days, wrapping and packing, selecting shapes that fitted closely to avoid movement. A methodical woman with everything she touched. The locals respected her an' she them.

'They wanted her to stay, she had been a mother to all their families over the years, knew them all. Both she and Master worked side by side with the servants, they were born on the land. This woman had spread a calm, kind, togetherness and now she was leaving them. When she came out as a new bride she was just twenty. The locals and their families had grown alongside the young Sindens. Played together, made music and danced together. They'd been such happy years ... and now she was fifty, the children had all gone their own ways. She was lonely for the husband and the life she had lost.

'The final box was filled, closed and sealed and we went up onto wagons again. We could hardly remember the time we had arrived, but now we were on our way down to the port from the great rail junction at Bulawayo, a lot smoother and swifter than the outspan.

'Back in England she had her living to earn. "Mrs Sinden, Housekeeper" went on the lookout for a job. Well, it was obvious, that's what she'd been doing for the past thirty years. She didn't really know England anymore but surely a professional family somewhere would be in need of a housekeeper? The agency in Regent Street welcomed her with open arms and soon we were all on our way to Sussex. "Yes," she had said, "I'm prepared to travel down to Sussex, that's where I came from originally."

'Young Mr Cedric Barton and his new bride, Constance, had unexpectedly inherited Ashlar House, a beautifully proportioned flint-built place snuggling in a sweeping wooded valley deep in the Sussex Downs. Neither of them had ever expected to have such a large house and they hadn't even started a family. The garden, now overgrown, looked as if it were protecting this family home. Mrs Sinden sounded just the experienced woman they needed. This young couple didn't know we were all included in the one package, housekeeper and effects.

'When we arrived at Ashlar House on a horseless van in the late spring of 1907, Mrs Sinden was telling the driver that the old queen was on the throne the last time she was in England more than thirty years ago. The lazy sound of tyres crunching to a standstill on the

304

beach gravel drive had long died away and Mrs Sinden had suddenly become mute. From her seat high up in the van's cab, she looked down onto a garden almost enveloping the buildings in a riot of neglected foliage in every shade of green. Mind-your-own-business outlined – nay, almost covered – the ancient yellowing flagstones around the house, even creeping up the wall surrounding the front porch. New young leaves sprouted on the tips of the low branches of huge beech trees. Tall dark-green poplars. Olive-green, purple-green, blue-green, sappy-green leaves beginning to push all aside with little droplets of sparkling dew deep in their centres. Feathery forms mingled among smooth dark-green mother-in-law's tongue; spiky, frothy, grey-green fennel rising high above bushy silver cotton lavender; feverfew in yellow-green skirts. This garden was a medley of greens turned riot. Descending from the cab Mrs Sinden was exclaiming on what a very wet spring it must have been to have caused such luscious early growth.

'What a wonderful vegetable garden we could have,' she was saying as she took the proffered small white hand in both her own, so large and capable.

'Could we really, Mrs Sinden? How do you do. I'm Constance Barton.'

'Oh my dear, I'm so sorry! How rude of me, rushing on with my ideas before we've been introduced.'

'Ah, it must be Mrs Sinden,' called Cedric as he came round the corner of the house. 'Welcome to Ashlar House. You look as if you have brought your whole household with you.'

'Yes, just like a garden snail,' laughed Mrs Sinden, ''fraid so dear, I have no other abode. Still I expect you're used to snails here. But tell me. Your house

305

name, Ashlar, what does it mean?'

'They say it's the way the walls are built with flints dressed in square blocks.'

'Ah, yes!' Maud Sinden clasped her hands in amused agreement, 'There's a word for everything, isn't there?' They all laughed as Constance led the way through the glass vestibule doors into the wide entrance hall and across its black and white tiled marble floor. Confronted by a striking ship's figurehead in the form of a fish cum woman, even though the faded paint and peeling gold lining was dulled with age, Maud was stopped in her tracks. 'Well,' she gasped, 'I was struck by the green welcome outside but now I'm brought to halt by this whelming sentinel.' The well-worn carving set a pose as if floating across an archway that divided the entry from the inner sanctum. Flickering green lights lazily seeped through the frosted glass panelled door at the far end of the passage, suggesting another delightful garden beyond. All three stood for a few moments allowing Maud to contemplate her new surroundings as Cedric Barton explained, 'We have been told the skipper of a coaster once lived here. Apparently he brought this old figurehead up the Cuckmere on one of his delivery trips. They say that's when the river was regularly navigable up to Lewes.'

Through into the kitchen it was dark, but not hot like our dark dining room back in Africa. With deep scrapings and screeching of old wood against stone mullions, Mrs Sinden pulled open the tall window shutters revealing a spacious high-ceilinged kitchen. The walls were limewashed white. The grubby well-worn boarded floor showed that it used to be scrubbed. The pantries, milk room and preserves stores had shiny flagstones. Slate shelves in the salting larders needed flushing down and by the strong smell of soot, the chimneys needed sweeping. Observing Mrs Sinden's critical eye, Cedric said, 'The house hasn't been lived in for some years.'

'But it feels welcoming,' she replied.

It wasn't until all the surfaces were cleaned in the kitchen and the fires lit that we were unpacked – much to the huge delight of the young Bartons who were thrilled to see us all blue and white and shining. The kitchen suddenly came alive. There was no money to decorate the house in those first years. All but the most pressing repairs had to wait. Only the soft furnishings and china Mrs Sinden had brought with her gave the house that instant 'lived-in feeling' – everything else still had an unused musty smell.

Cedric and Constance were at the start of their life together and Mrs Sinden saw no place for herself other than cooking and housekeeping. We Willows were her family. First thing she would say was, 'Now Bertie, what soups shall we make this week?' The missus always planned ahead and talked her thoughts through us. Her stock pot was just called simply 'Stocky'. 'Can you take a little more today, Stocky dear?' If she slammed Stocky's lid shut hard, maybe she was cross about something, missus would turn saying, 'Oh sorry Stocky, I heard that ouch.' The thing was, Mrs Sinden had not only lost her husband, but also her farm. Her children, well, they were leading their own lives, one in Australia and the other in Malaya. No she wasn't odd, she was a very resourceful woman. We knew her well, so when she said, 'Remember what Charlie used to do as his Special?' we knew Charlie was her cook on the farm. She had taught Charlie to cook the way her husband wanted his food, 'Meat in the centre and all the vegetables packed around the pot. No water. Seal the lid and put it in to roast in the big slow oven overnight. Oh, the juices were magnificent. You liked that didn't you Bertie?' she'd say, looking across at me an' wavin' her long-handled wooden spoon, 'Lovely rich dark and thick gravy ... yum.'

Ashlar House faced south onto gardens terraced down into a sheltered wooded valley, collecting the light throughout the whole length of the day. It would be hot in summer but not as hot as Africa. The evenings were still closing in fairly early. Here in this valley it was cool and still damp from all the rains. It wasn't long before our missus was all but lost deep in the gardens. The Bartons soon treated their housekeeper like a mother, learning by her side how to set seeds, prick out the tiny plants and pot up. It was easier to have pots along the terrace outside the kitchen to start tomato plants, peppers and okra. Runner beans and lots of little lettuces were set in rows. Spinach was on its way, all before separate allotments on the lower terraces were cleared and dug over ready for bigger storage crops. The young couple hadn't mentioned it to Mrs Sinden but this was their honeymoon and they were enjoying their newly acquired property like small excited children.

When Cedric had to go back to his work in London he was relieved to feel he could leave his young wife in the safe companionship of the older woman. We Willows watched the family's progress.

Their house wasn't the only residence in the valley, there were a dozen or so, each one tucked away in dips in the hillside and down twisty turning lanes. Some were quite large houses, other small and compact, even

308

two little rows with cottage gardens. There was also a public house, a post office and a dairy shop in a farmyard.

Mrs Sinden got to know many of the gardeners at the neighbouring houses. Walking around the lanes collecting herbage for the pot she stopped to talk, swapping garden hints, listening to the history of the area, learning who had lived at Ashlar House years before. There were only four head gardeners in the valley who supervised other workers in the gardens belonging to the wealthiest house owners. A few were wealthy – very wealthy indeed. Rather like our Mr Cedric, their owners were often away or abroad on business. Their wives and families went to 'town' on shopping trips. Some took cruises around the 'Med' at intervals. When they were in residence they were more often in each other's homes playing cards or mahjong or making up bridge parties. Except for a few servants the houses were frequently empty of human movement.

Mrs Sinden had taken to rummaging round in the unused rooms and attic spaces at Ashlar House on the days Constance wasn't being hostess to her women neighbours. The house was still fully furnished from the days of the previous occupants who had preferred plain white china, a whole service of which Mrs Sinden discovered stacked on shelves in the cellar beneath the kitchen.

While Constance was out at a musical evening, Mrs S brought a few of the white items up onto the kitchen table. When Constance saw them she suggested it would be sensible to use this china for every day, while the blue and white china was kept safe from daily wear and tear. We Willows were all duly relocated to the highest shelves, leaving the bottom shelves and dresser top for the recently discovered plain household china.

One morning the little tureen next to me said, 'Thomas, my twin tureen had a heavy object wrapped in tissue put inside him overnight.' Thomas stood on her other side. Well, I thought that was a bit odd. Then from the shelf just above me a whisper came down to say Rachel sugar bowl had found her lid quietly lifted in the night and she too now had an item inside wrapped in tissue paper.

We thought no more of it until a week or two later when, in the early hours of the morning, my lid was quietly raised, five small tissue-wrapped parcels were deposited and my lid lowered back gently into place. It was too dark for me to see who had done it. But I had my suspicions.

Some months went by, then one Friday evening as her husband arrived home from his week in town, we heard Constance telling Cedric excitedly all about how the police had been called to the Rosebergs' manor house because Madame Roseberg discovered on her return from Paris that various pieces of jewellery were missing from her dressing table drawer. Then no more was said.

Life went on in the usual casual way, all the doors and windows flung wide, the warm summer air wafting through the house, seeds and petals floating in onto the floors and surfaces. Constance and Mrs S flung down their sun hats inside the doorway while armfuls of flowers were arranged into pots and vases, bringing the garden into every room. Sometimes folks from the other houses gathered at Ashlar House for their bridge sessions then the ladies would take tea on the terrace with Constance. Of course Mrs S never joined them. No, she was considered one of the servant class.

The visitors talked openly of their likes and dislikes about the ways of this or that servant in their own houses, not a thought that Mrs S might feel uncomfortable – she wasn't noticed or even considered to be listening.

'Of course the house is always open,' one high-pitched lady was saying. 'Nobody comes into the valley who we don't know. There's always the servants about of course but I lock my best jewellery away and Juliette puts my treasure box in the safe if I'm not taking it travelling with me.'

'Well there's somebody very light-fingered around somewhere. I have a beautifully delicate carving of a boatman that I found in China way back. In fact now I think of it.' Here the speaker slowed and frowned as if in a revelation of memory. 'I haven't seen its colleagues recently.'

The company stopped what they were doing and listened, just as if she'd said something extra poignant.

'Oh you're getting old my dear – admit it, Shirley, do.'

'I know. You've been telling me that since you were born, Beatrice.'

'Well, at least your own sister can say that, none of us could, now could we?' The company laughed at that and went back to their cards.

Returning from a trip to London with Cedric, Constance brought home a set of fine bone china teacups and saucers together with their teapot, jug, sugar bowl and slop basin. They fitted in rather well, having a design of lines with swirling leaves and flowers, bringing familiar garden shapes into the house.

311

It was the teapot of this Liberty set who remarked that she thought the conversation going on around Mrs S as she was pouring and handing round the teacups, was becoming rather pointed. 'Just as if they wanted to provoke Mrs S into saying or doing something.'

'Or not doing something,' one of the companion cups joined in.

'Yes. Yes I think you could be right there,' the leafy-patterned teapot agreed.

Around that time we noticed a ghostly figure moving and crouching in the shrubs near the kitchen windows. The figure was seen many nights after the pointed nature of the conversations had been witnessed at the last bridge party held at Ashlar House.

On the nights when the figure was about in the garden, no more items arrived on the dresser, until one night, quite late into the early hours, a shadowing figure stood up on a chair and leant across, dumping tissue-wrapped items as if in a hurry. Some were bigger, some very small, and all weights from lead heavy to light as a feather were dropped into almost every piece of willow china that either had a lid or was deep like a jug. We were amazed and intrigued, to say the least.

Just three days later, Constance walked into the kitchen followed by two dark-suited gentlemen. Mrs S was at the sink clearing away vegetable parings ready for the compost heap. As she picked up her sun hat to go out into the garden Constance stopped her, saying, 'Just a moment Mrs Sinden, these gentlemen would like to speak with you. Can you give them a minute?'

Putting the bowl of peelings down on the draining board, Mrs S dried her hands and turned towards the men, her hand out ready to shake theirs. Neither

312

responded, their hands were not offered. In fact it was obvious they expected a bowed head or at least a bobbed curtsey from a servant woman.

'Gentlemen, this is my housekeeper, Mrs Sinden. This is Detective Jack and Constable Sidebound.'

Mrs S smiled at the constable. He was the local man but he turned away, looking rather uncomfortable.

'Mrs Sinden, you may be aware there have been some unusual losses from the houses in this valley,' said the detective.

'Well yes, but that was some months back I heard of that happening.'

'Mrs Sinden, I've given the police permission to search our bedrooms. Would you be willing to allow them to do the same to yours?' Constance asked.

'Of course. The police must not be hindered from carrying out their duty. The door's not locked, please, go in.' Mrs Sinden turned away to carry on with her business of throwing out the peelings.

'Er, Mrs Sinden,' the detective called. Mrs Sinden paused by the back door, plate of peelings in her hand. 'I would rather you stay in the kitchen where my officer can see you.'

'Why yes, if that's what you would prefer.'

So she stayed while Constance showed the detective upstairs to point out the various bedrooms. Mrs Sinden busied herself with pastry making, inviting the uncomfortable looking police constable to search the kitchen if that's what he had to do.

'Don't mind me, dear. I shall just get on with this,' she told him.

Constable Sidebound opened a few cupboards. Then he reached up to open one or two of the higher ones, but being rather short for a policeman he didn't bother

313

with anything above his eye level. A broom cupboard out in the pantry passage and a larder full of inviting smells caught his interest, but no more. Footsteps were heard coming softly down the stairs causing the constable to swiftly return to stand at attention beside the door leading to the dining room.

'Mrs Sinden,' the detective said, 'do you recognise this?' In his hand he held out a small tissue-wrapped item.

'Yes,' replied Mrs S. 'It looks like the tissue I keep to wrap round the silver cutlery when it's been cleaned ready for storage.'

'Then would I expect to find this kind of tissue in any other house in this area?'

'Oh more than in this area sir, I would say in every household that has good silverware.'

'But what about the item wrapped inside this piece of tissue?'

Mrs S came forward to look, as it was still tightly covered, and waited for the detective to open the wrapping. Leaning forward she saw a small silver item and at once answered, 'That's a dear little nutmeg holder. The chain and loop is for a gentleman to attach it to his watch chain.' Looking up at the now very stern face she carried on, 'My grandfather used to have one, there's a small grater inside. Grandfather used to like a touch of nutmeg in his mulled wine.'

'Is this item yours then? Is that what you are telling me?'

'Oh no, I've just seen these before.'

'So how did this one come to be under your bed?'

Mrs S looked from the nutmeg grater to the policeman to the nutmeg grater again, saying, 'I've no idea.'

'Madam, we have been watching movements in this valley recently and we notice you are often out in the gardens here in the evenings and sometimes quite late at night.' As he said this, the police constable called from just outside the door to the vegetable garden. 'Sir, I think I've found something here.'

The detective moved towards the voice. Mrs S looked for the first time at Constance, who seemed to avoid her eye and moved away jerkily to follow the detective. The police constable was pointing to the soil in a pot of parsley and to another where a basil plant now wilted slightly. Taking a penknife out of his trouser pocket the detective dug its longest blade into the loosened soil in the first pot, bringing out a bracelet, its gemstones glowing deep red in the sunlight. Surprise registered on both women's faces. Into the second pot the knife dug, this time not too deep, and retrieved a man's sapphire and diamond stick pin.

Mrs Sinden's face was blank.

Constance looked sadly at her housekeeper.

'Mrs Sinden I'm asking you to come to the station with me please,' said the detective. 'I'm sorry about this madam,' turning to Constance, 'I'm afraid you'll have to manage without your housekeeper until we have completed our investigations.'

Mrs Sinden wasn't allowed to take anything with her.

It was a long time before we saw her again. Four years went by.

Cedric and Constance started a family. They had twins only six months after the stealing incident. Then a year later, a girl followed very closely by a single boy. Constance was kept very busy although she had a nanny and a new cook. A happy family was gathering around us all but disaster struck, and the little girl died. Apparently she had found a silver whistle and sucked it in down her throat so quickly that the chain attached to a large piece of coral broke away – the rough end of the chain scratched the child's gullet, piercing the membranes badly on its way down.

The nanny hadn't seen it happen and, as she had not even come across the whistle on a chain before, she assumed the coral on the broken chain was all that had existed. It seems the brother indicated that the little girl had found the silver item tucked under the edge of the carpet in Constance's dressing room. Such was the sadness and despair that Cedric took his wife and family abroad to forget and recover. The house was silent, the cook was dismissed and the nursemaid turned out without a 'Character'.

All was quiet at Ashlar House.

We Willows felt utterly abandoned.

The autumn set in and the house lost its glow except for a few sunny afternoons when the low sun reflected the red and gold autumn leaves through the windows. When dull weather took over, even the spiders retreated into the old crevices. The odd mouse ran across the kitchen floor. A soft scraping sound told us the mouse had tried to edge open the flat wooden lid across the bread crock. No more sound came from that direction. The mouse had either discovered the crock was empty or he'd fallen in.

Dog foxes barked and owls hooted at night. Occasionally the postman delivered something onto the doormat during a morning. Otherwise little moved, and sounds were few for weeks.

A slow squeak from a damp-tightened door told us

somebody was inside the house. Then, after a pause, footsteps with a positive objective came straight into the kitchen and across to the dresser. Someone lifted the heavy sloping lid on the big willow-patterned cheese dish, lifted it high. With a sigh of relief they put it right down again. I immediately knew who it was. Cedric had left his copy of The Times on the kitchen table and this was brought into use, opened and fully laid out across the table. The cheese dish was wrapped in one sheet and placed in a big old shopping bag.

Then the large sloping lid was turned upside down ready to wrap but before this, a parcel was carefully removed from inside. I remembered having seen this parcel before. It was a small leather pouch that Mrs S had secured up under the lid when the family was at the farm. Now she shook a number of little stones onto the palm of her hand. After counting them she put them away again back in the pouch. Then, letting down her hair, Mrs Sinden plaited the little bag up inside her bun, winding it back tightly against the nape of her neck and finally folding a scarf round her head, finishing it off at the side, African style.

The cheese dish lid was then wrapped, and stowed with its plate in the shopping bag ready to leave. Coming back to the dresser, our Mrs S raised her hand and touched me lightly saying, 'Goodbye my friends, I shall miss you all.'

I couldn't let her go. We had a lot to tell. I had to tell her to lift my lid. I had to. I thought as hard as I could. Wait! Stop! Look, please look inside me. Please!

Mrs Sinden slowly put her shopping bag back down on the floor, then lifted my lid and felt around inside. She immediately withdrew her hand as if she'd been bitten. Over to the table she went to fetch a chair.

317

Standing up on its seat she could look inside me, at once seeing the tissue-wrapped parcels. Taking hold of two items she went across to the table and opened them. Then she must have realised the whole story and came back to the dresser, retrieving more than eighty parcels from inside all us Willows 'stored for safety' up on the higher shelves.

But I noticed that after opening those first two items she became very careful, only looking inside the paper wrappings at the contents then each was tightly re-wrapped. Pulling an old sack from under the kitchen sink she placed all the re-wrapped items inside then pushed the bundle into the big old shopping bag. She'd obviously had a change of mind because the cheese dish came back into its place on the dresser to stay with us. All tidied in the kitchen, and shopping bag in her hand again, Mrs S sighed.

'Well, there we are, all done. I'm sad to leave you. If you want to find me,' she said with a chuckle, 'I'll be at the Cowleys' in St George's Mews. Oh, and that's in Brighton.' Then she left, as quietly as she had come.

A sigh of relief and yet expectancy floated from Willow to Willow as Uncle Bert finished his reminiscence.

'Now Laura, Bea, it's your turn. Tell us what happened next.'

'Ooh! Ooh!' A gentle little thrill of glee came from up on the shelf around a group of small cream jugs while the Willows settled for the next episode.

'Our story begins in St George's Mews, before Mrs Sinden came back to retrieve her property,' Laura began.

Bea picked up the narrative. 'It was an autumn evening. Clara had put Jim and Dolly to bed and

318

Freddy had followed them up; they'd had a busy day. Clara could tell they were already asleep by the time she reached the bottom stair. As it was still fairly light she didn't bother to put a taper to the lamp on the table centre. Tom was sitting over his last cup of tea, reading the local paper so she brought her sewing basket out and began to darn a sock.

'A gentle tap on the door made them both look up. As Tom was nearer he went to see who it was. For a few moments there was no sound of voices at all. From where Clara sat she couldn't see who stood outside because her view was masked by the heavy bunched curtain, still looped back that evening to let in all the light.

'We could see from the dresser though,' added Laura.

'Yes,' Bea carried on. 'A lady stood outside wearing a tatty old coat, her hair wispy grey around her face, a scarf falling back loose. It was light enough outside to see the woman's chalky grey face. Tom seemed unmoving; of course we couldn't see his face. But the woman, who had as yet said nothing, remained looking hopefully at him.'

'Maud?' A moment's silence. 'Is it you, Maud?' Tom asked.

'I'm not Miss Thatcham now, Tom.' The voice showed some of the relief on her face. 'That was a long time ago. I'm Maud Sinden.' Even then the pair didn't move.

'Ask her in Tom,' called Clara, breaking the tension. Tom pulled a chair out from the table for Maud to sit down. 'This is my wife, Clara,' he offered.

The two women smiled at each other. Clara could now see how sickly grey their visitor's face looked. 'I'll

319

make us a fresh pot of tea. Tom, take Mrs Sinden's coat, love.'

Tom seemed nonplussed, a searching look on his face. When Clara came back into the room with the teapot and milk jug on a tray, Maud Sinden was seated at the table but her coat remained firmly buttoned.

'I know you can't quite place me, can you Mr Cowley. You were a year older than me at the village school in Petworth. My father worked at Petworth House for Lord Egremont.'

'Oh, Mr Thatcham! Yes, I do just remember you Maud, your brother was my age. What's he doing now?'

'Yes, Charlie. He's sheep farming in Australia, well that's the last I heard. He has a wife and family in New South Wales.'

Maud picked up her teacup in both hands cradling it close. Clara was surprised it wasn't too hot for the woman to hold but she seemed half mesmerised, looking at the willow china on the dresser. Tom noticed how her hands shook as she drank the whole contents down in one gulp. Putting the cup down, she seemed to rouse herself.

'I had better tell you what brings me to your door.'

'Tom, Clara, I've just come out of the Holloway prison for women offenders.' Maud Sinden stopped to let them take in the first part of her introduction. By the look of their guest, Clara was not surprised.

Tom reacted immediately with concern for his one-time neighbour. 'Oh my dear girl, whatever has happened in your life and how did you find us?'

'I would like to tell you what's happened if I may. But first I must tell you why I have come to you.'

Clara put her hand over Maud's. 'Take your time,'

she said with a reassuring smile.

Maud slid the scarf from the back of her head, rolled it and put it in her coat pocket.

'It was just days ago that a new inmate came into the prison. The woman told everybody in a loud voice she was from "good old Brighton by the sea". Like all of us she was dishevelled, we had each been subjected to a good roughing-up on our passage from court into prison custody. However, this woman had both eyes blacked and chunks of hair missing. Although she can't have been much over twenty, the teeth that remained in her jaw were only a few black stumps. Her explanation was she'd fought off a toff who'd followed her home. "Bad luck for 'im," she told us, "knocked 'is block orf I did. Nar 'e's only got one eye an' 'arf an ear. I got 'is dosh tho. I gave 'im back 'is wallet. Trouble is bloody ol' bastard tells the court 'e 'ad ten times as much money as I pinched orf 'im, besides saying I took 'is watch 'n' chain. Well I seen a fella take that after I'd laid 'im out. Now I'm 'ere worse luck an' just as I'd got me eye on a bit of all right too."

'Of course with this snippet of information the young newcomer knew she had the floor. All the women liked a nice bit of man story. "I was barmaidin' at a pub down the end of Elder Street, the Old Hoss they call it, bin there donkeys. Well, a few weeks ago we 'as a new baker call. The missus sells just bread 'n' beer, always 'as. Anyway this 'ere baker looks a bit of all right. Thought I could get 'im upstairs sometime, so I ast 'im where 'e comes from and 'e says Petworth – well that's a bloody long way ter come sellin' bread ain't it? But 'e wouldn't tell me where 'e lived. Well, the missus she's very posh under it all, gets to callin' the roundsmen what deliver Mister this and Mister that, so I knows

321

he's Mr Cowley, but I find out 'is name's Tom, so I start callin' 'im that. 'E don't seem ter mind. So I follows 'im. Then I find I didn't 'ave ter – 'cos when I takes a jug o' beer round ter Mum's sister Jen, there 'e was in front of me going through the arch into St George's Mews an' three little bleeders come runnin' out from next door callin' out 'Daddy, Daddy' an jumpin' all over 'im. Nice lookin' wife. Pity, still it wouldn't 'ave stopped me. But I got locked up before I'd 'ad me chance."

'Oh, I can't tell you, Tom, how that lassie's story gave me hope. I don't know anybody else in England I could go to. I knew I would be released very soon, my term was nearing its end and I just had nowhere to go and no money, nothing. Only these clothes I stand up in. But now I was able with some authority to say I would be going to Brighton to family, the prison authority gave me a train ticket.'

Tom and Clara could see Maud had spent all her energy on telling her story. They helped her over to an armchair. With a blanket swaddled around her legs and up to her chin, she was soon away to sleep.

Later, when they were in bed, Tom asked Clara whether she minded having somebody who'd been in prison in the house. 'You didn't show any surprise.'

'No Tom I didn't. The woman looks like she's been through a really bad experience. If I hadn't had Rose and all the strangers who helped me, I don't know where I'd be. She's snatching at a lifeline, Tom. We must help her.'

Maud woke with a start the following afternoon. She lay in the chair wondering what had woken her, trying to make out where she was. The quiet made her sit up with a jerk. On the table close by was a woolly-cosied teapot, cup and saucer, sugar bowl and a milk jug covered with a beaded net. She thought she must be dreaming. Laid out on the armchair opposite were a coat and a dress with a paper bag. On the floor were two pairs of shoes beside her own broken-down pair set on the edge of the fender. So she wasn't dreaming. Easing herself off the chair she felt the teapot, it was hot. Someone knew how welcome a really good cup of tea was after four years of dishwater. Beneath a cotton napkin lay a slice of fruit cake: heaven. She'd landed.

The afternoon sun filtered through the lace curtains sending a dappled pattern across the room. Maud lay back in the armchair to enjoy the nectar in her cup, letting her eyes watch the movement of dust particles lazily spiralling in the sunlight. Biting into the delicious cake, she sighed as she savoured it. Ambrosia! It was just like she used to make for the Bartons, and her own family of course.

She hadn't expected to hear anything from the Bartons. They must have thought she was guilty just like the rest of the folks in the valley. Through all those long days and nights in prison, Maud had taxed her brain over and over again, trying to think who had taken all the items people had complained went missing. There was a slow movement of the door handle, the front door opened a crack sending a sudden shaft of light across the room. Three small heads each with dark curly hair came slyly into the room like little birds bobbing in a nest, heads held up high, peering across the table to see if the new auntie was awake. Clara followed them in.

'Oh you are awake. We didn't disturb you then. Now say hallo then go and wash your hands ready for tea. This is Dolly, and here's Jimmie and this big man is our eldest son Freddy.'

'Hallo,' came three whispers; three pairs of twinkling eyes told that there was more behind the whispers. Maud smiled and winked as they scampered away to the scullery.

'How are you feeling, Maud?'

'Blessed,' was the reply. 'Thank you, Clara.'

'Good. You take your time. I'm giving the children their tea now in here so if you feel like freshening up there's a kettle and a bowl in the sink with soap and a towel. Oh an' I forgot – so sorry. The lavatory, it's out back. Oh dear. I do hope you're all right.'

'Don't worry dear. I found the offices earlier.'

'There are clean undies in the bag. My sister fished the dress and coat out of her workroom closets. She's a dressmaker, and we found a couple of pairs of shoes that might fit.'

'Clara, I'm overwhelmed.'

'Don't you worry, we're here to help. I've made the bed up for you in the children's room. They are going to enjoy camping out in our room for a bit. So make yourself comfortable. There is a washstand up there so you could take the kettle up.'

'Oh please, don't turn the little ones out of their beds. I'm very used to a room full of women.'

'No, you have your privacy. I don't doubt you've got to make some readjustments.'

It was dark by the time Tom came home that evening. Clara tapped on Maud's bedroom door saying she was about to put a meal on the table.

'Oh goodness, I'm so pleased to see you looking better, Maud. How do you feel?' asked Tom.

'Thank you. I feel rested.'

At the meal table Maud noticed the small collection

of opened letters standing between two jugs on the dresser. The envelopes had South African stamps on. So she commented on them.

'Oh they're from our son. He's in Cape Town. He's a chef in a hotel out there,' Clara told her.

After their meal Maud said she would like to tell them about the events that originally brought her home to Sussex and how she came to be in prison. Mrs Sinden related her story about Africa, the family and her husband's sudden death. Then all about Ashlar House along the Downs east of Brighton.

'I've left my clothes at the bottom of the stairs, Clara. Is there somewhere they can be burned? You know, they're the dress I used in the kitchen garden in the mornings together with these old rundown gardening shoes. When the police took me away I was given no time to change or fetch my belongings. The old coat was one I kept hanging just beside the back door for wet gardening days and I was only able to slip that off the hook on my way past. Luckily they hadn't already handcuffed me. Awful – nobody listens to a servant even though the law of the land says a person is innocent until proven guilty.' Maud shook her head at the memories of her despair.

'Seemed as if it was already decided I had done the deed,' Maud told Clara. 'A lot of small jewellery and valuable items had gone missing from all the houses in the valley. Any of the servants could have been guilty. I suppose I was different. I wasn't one of the young servants. I was older and walked round talking to all the gardeners – probably sounded like I had some authority – well, having had my own farm and gardens for all those years, it came naturally that way.'

She told how the young couple left her to run the

house and garden – she had a free hand. Said they must have thought it was her but she had no idea who could have put the little silver nutmeg under her bed. She'd wondered if it could have been Constance, but then she dismissed the thought. The girl was so young and full of life. She had so much. No idea how the other items got into the herb pots though. Of course it would have been easy for anybody to put them there.

'*I didn't leave my home in Africa completely destitute. Norman and I had collected some savings over our years together, a small insurance policy really, something for our old age. Well, I was too bereft at the time to think of negotiating money. I thought I would sell the property and come home. So I spent my time gradually packing everything carefully and it wasn't until I was on board ship nearing port that I gave much thought to where I would live, and I remembered my financial wherewithal had been packed deep in my cases of china. I had nowhere to go in England where I could have unpacked to find which case contained what I needed, and no money for rent and food. I was forced to look for a job, get settled, then plan to get my money into an account. The job at Ashlar House came with immediate fulfilment, just what I needed.*

'*Well, the house and garden were idyllic in themselves. I didn't bother with money. I had no need at that time, so I left things where they rested for two years. I got on with my housekeeping for a nice young couple. All the talk of little thefts here and there had been going round the village for weeks, I'd got like that I wasn't listening anymore. It hadn't got much to do with me and Constance had never said she'd noticed anything missing. I would have seen if a stranger had been in the house especially up in the bedrooms. Any-*

way Constance hadn't any jewellery worth having – the young couple always seemed pretty hard up. Come to think of it, Cedric paid me a pittance when he remembered to. He paid all the bills so I had no house-keeping money to handle.'

Although it was getting very late in the evening and Tom had to be up early for his work, they let Maud talk on because the woman so obviously had a need to talk over her ordeal.

'When Constance came into the kitchen with the besuited man and the local constable, I was quite non-chalant about them searching my room. It was an awful shock that in the space of just fifteen minutes I was accused and taken away. My feet barely touched the ground. In what seemed no time at all I found myself in prison. One day I had a lovely big airy kitchen and a lush vegetable garden, and the next I was in this dark, noisy, bad-smelling spiral of landings full of women in cells behind bars, me included.

'The only money I have is still in Ashlar House, so I need to find a way to recover it.'

At last it was out, off her chest.

Next day Clara was into her regular routine back in the kitchen preparing a soup for a few of the workmen. She had seen the children off to school, keen to do all her marketing, and as there was no sign of Maud she thought she must still be fast asleep upstairs.

The mews was used to thumps and knocks and the sounds of hammering and sawing besides the tap tap tapping from one note to the next coming from Alfred Moffat tuning a piano he had rebuilt for a customer. Doors were ajar along the row of houses, it was a lovely morning.

Sawing and hammering in the distance floated to

the ear but the tuning had ceased. Alf must have finished that job. Suddenly the air was full of a piano being played with great urgency. After a few minutes men came sauntering out of their workshops to stand, wiping their hands with bits of rag while staring towards Mr Moffat's half-open workshop doors. Even the regular deep rumble of the printer's press ceased. Women came from the houses opposite, looking to see what it was all about. Nobody had ever heard such piano playing. A horse at the end of the mews had to be firmly restrained from bolting.

Alfred Moffat came out into the yard smiling as he turned to gently pull open the two big doors, revealing a woman sitting at a grand piano, quite lost in the music she was playing.

'It's your visitor.' Jen touched Clara on the arm, because Clara was as surprised as anyone at what she was seeing and hearing.

Alfred walked across to the woman and said, 'It's Rachmaninov.'

Clara answered, 'It's Maud Sinden.'

'No, I mean what she's playing. Isn't she good?'

'How do we know?' whispered Bill Rattan the elderly printer. 'Never 'eard music like that before.'

'She's a goer ain't she Mr Moffat?' added Joe Blundell the saddler. They'd all wandered across the yard to know what Alfred Moffat was up to.

'You 'ad her locked up in there long Alf?'

'Shush!' Annie Belle from Gloucester Street put a finger against her mouth.

Maud hadn't noticed the crowd. Clara whisked off back into the scullery, remembering her soup would be boiling over.

The Prelude in C sharp minor finished, Maud

bowed her head down and breathed deep. Then an appreciative clatter of applause zipped her back to reality. Shocked, she stood up and seeing a crowd of happy smiling people, realised how bashful she felt.

Alfred put his arm round her shoulders. 'Feel better now, my dear?' asked the sensitive gentle man.

Clara looking from afar could see the years and cares had fallen from Maud's face. Maud smiled and looked around the faces. 'Thank you.' Just a simple thank you.

'Lovely, missus, we enjoyed that.'

'You can do us some more o' that any time.'

People dispersed, talking happily to each other on their way back to their work.

'Where did you learn that piece?' asked Alf.

'Norman and I heard a young woman playing that at a recital in a friend's house in Johannesburg.'

'So you learned it from sheet music?'

'No, I just remembered it.'

'Good heavens. There aren't many of you about.'

'Of who, Mr Moffat?'

'Why, those who can hear a piece of music played and then be able to reproduce it in the way you have just done.'

'I thought that was quite natural.'

'Well, you're very welcome to play the pianos we have here before they go back to their owners.'

During the morning the postman had brought a letter from Frankie saying he expected to be sailing home in a month or so. Clara read it out to Maud and the two women spent the afternoon knitting and discussing their offspring who were living their lives in other countries. It made Maud remember there was more in her life than this recent few years of misfortune.

329

'Talking about our children and their far flung existences did me good this afternoon, Clara.'

What a difference Tom saw in the face that looked up as he walked in after work that evening. Maud was sat in the armchair still at the knitting she and Clara had shared in the afternoon. Tom commented how Maud looked 'a veritable new woman'. Clara told him that was what playing the piano and knitting did for the soul.

'Trilby's certainly decided you're one of the family, Maud.'

'Yes, nothing like being cosied up to by the family pets,' replied Maude.

'She's another working woman!' chortled Clara.

'So what's to be done about you recovering your property then, Maud?' Tom asked as soon as he had finished his dinner.

'I feel at a crossroads just for the moment. Don't know quite which angle to strike from, if you see what I mean, and I don't want to keep your children from their own bedroom.'

'Don't you worry about that my dear, something will come along.'

As luck would have it something did come along in the form of an old newspaper. But not straight off, no, it was another week before Tom said, 'Didn't you mention the young couple you worked for were called Barton?'

'Yes, that's right. Why?'

'Look at this Maud, "Child's death caused by swallowing a whistle". It's the headline look, and the parents, their name's Barton, Cedric and Constance.'

'My goodness, it's them. They've got a family in the last four years, Oh, what a sad story.'

'Yes, but look here, see what it says in the last paragraph: "Husband is taking wife and their other children away on holiday abroad to get over the shock."'

'You're right. How old's this paper Tom?'

'Let's see now, I've had to turn this bundle out of Bessie's stable, those lads get so untidy. Ah, here – it's the Mid Sussex Times. Aw, nearly three weeks old though.'

'Mmm but see, it says they're going to France so they would probably be away more than two weeks. Well let's hope so. I must work out carefully what to do. This could be the answer I've been searching for. If the house is empty so much the better!'

'Now, careful Maud, you mustn't be seen. Do you want me to come with you?'

'No. I won't involve you and Clara, no more than you're helping as it is!'

'You've been a great help to me, Maud, love. You've made a grand job of the children's winter woollies, got them done quicker than I could have on my own.'

'Well I hope turning up this old paper helps,' added Tom hopefully.

'Yes Tom, I think it does,' she answered thoughtfully. 'Much the best thing. I don't want to meet them again. I'm going to sleep on it.'

Maud was downstairs early the next morning. 'Clara, do you have any more of those useful cotton shopping bags I've seen you taking to market?'

'You can use these two. I've been to the wholesaler's this week. I won't need them till Saturday.'

'You don't have any others at all?'

'Well I've got a thicker, larger one – it's a bit stronger for carrying heavy items.'

'Ah now that would be ideal and maybe I could use the light cotton one. That would roll up into my coat pocket.'

'Yes certainly.'

'And I'm going to have to ask you if you could lend me a few pence for a bus fare.'

'How much do you need?' Clara asked as she looked in her purse.

'I really don't know. I shall be catching a bus over to Seaford then another back, maybe through Lewes. What do you think? I've got just a sixpence left I had when I came from Holloway.'

'I can give you another ten pence, that should see you through. Do you want me to make you a few sandwiches because that journey's going to take you away all day?'

'All night as well I'm thinking, Clara.'

Clara looked surprised but did not ask.

'Yes please, the sandwiches will be welcome, something to put in the bag.'

As she was cutting slices off the loaf Maud said quietly to Clara, 'I'm not telling you anymore dear because I don't want you implicated if anything should go wrong. I shall be gone overnight and may even be a little longer.' Clara said nothing but showed Maud where the spare key was kept outside the front door.

'I know,' said Clara, noting Maud's look of surprise, 'it is unusual to find cottages like these having a front door key. Alf Moffat told us this is where the foreman of the carpenter's shop lived; he kept a lot of his tools here. So this is why our door has a lock, and we've got used to using it.

The two women embraced, saying their goodbyes inside the house. Maud sallied forth carrying the big *shopping bag.*

When Maud returned from her mystery journey on the evening of the following day, she told Clara and Tom the details of her adventure.

'I have been very concerned not to have you implicated in anyway so when I left, carrying your big old shopping bag, Clara, I walked up to the station intending to go in and disappear into the crowd waiting for the London train. Instead, as I went through a twitten up near the station I took the cotton bag out of my coat pocket, transferred the folded large bag into the smaller one with the sandwiches on the top. As it was a warm day, I took my coat off, laid it over my arm and walked briskly off down Queen's Road and North Street. I crossed the Steine because I decided not to get on the bus at the Poole Valley Terminus and walked up along the seafront towards Black Rock. As I got to the bottom of Rock Gardens a bus came along. I got on and asked for Seaford. 'Going to stay with my sister,' I told the bus conductor. They want to know everything about their passengers and I thought that sowed a good story.

'I got off for Bishopstone, walked inland and stopped well away from the church to eat a sandwich. Then I stuffed the big bag into my skirt band to make myself look fat, and packed the rest of the sandwiches neatly into the cotton bag, putting it in my coat pocket. With the coat buttoned up, I thought I must look old and bent. I carried on walking slowly up over the Downs, crossing to pick up the chalk track to Hindover and on down to the river, crossing at the narrow stretch near Alfriston church. I wanted to get to where I could see Ashlar House from on high.

'Climbing up through the trees, the growth had become very much denser and overgrown than when I was there last. Nevertheless I found a good position to view the house along a firebreak and sat down to watch and wait. I hadn't seen anybody since walking the steep track over the Downs, although knowing any countryside, I must have been sighted by someone.

As usual in the autumn, many of the houses in the valley were unoccupied, the men away shooting game in the Highlands. Ashlar House appeared completely deserted. No evening lights lit in the servants' quarters that I was able to see.

'I used to love that deep verdant valley towered over by stands of deciduous trees and plantations of evergreens on its high hills. The houses were linked by narrow sandy lanes bordered with ditches, their slow-moving dark water masked under trailing grasses. As usual little moved as the hot afternoon silence smothered the atmosphere. As dusk gathered on the terraces at Hillside Place, drinks were being served to the women and their voices echoed across the valley. I know they would stay on to play bridge or mahjong late into the evening.

'As I had expected, the women walked arm in arm back to their minor manor houses, talking about their bridge partners, keeping to the middle of the lane. That night the pale moon reflected its ghostly glow on the sandy surface showing the walkers their way. Nobody walked towards Ashlar House, subsequently no light was showing in any window. It gave me a good guide that the house must be closed up while the family was still abroad. But to be sure I left it until all lights were extinguished in the valley before I ventured carefully down through the trees. There had been few dogs in any of the households when I worked there four years back and there certainly were no sounds of barking this evening. The key to the garden door into the family quarters was where it was always kept. I let myself in, closing the door behind me and stood waiting just in case somebody was a caretaker in residence. Not a creak or a sound of life came to my ears. Quickly going through towards the kitchen, I noticed all the inner doors left open as before.

'There on the dresser were my dear Willows, high up on the shelves, the plain white crockery ready for use at hand level and nobody had changed the position of my great old cheese dish. Laying out my bag on the table I went across to the dresser, lifted the lid on my cheese dish, felt up inside – and there it was. Taking the dish to the table, I turned the sloping lid on its back to retrieve my small bag of diamonds. I had to check the contents straightaway. Thank goodness; just as when Norman and I deposited our last acquisition, there they all were, glistening in the moonlight. Five beautifully cut and polished diamonds that Norman had registered with De Beers. Norman knew Joe Robinson, the best cutter in the State; his work had raised their value astronomically.

'This small collection should never be found on my person, but that's where they had to be for the next few days. I've never forgotten seeing an African woman hide her own wealth, so I did the same. The small leather pouch went into a fine hair net and this I rolled inside and under my hair plaited against my neck. A thin woollen scarf, looking old and worn with no bright feature, covered my head, wound and fastened just above the ear like African woman do, giving that final trim to the side. I wanted to appear young and upstanding, a new woman for my journey back. Not the old, bent, fat woman people would describe if they'd seen me in the afternoon.

'An old copy of The Times had been left on the table. I wrapped the cheese dish and lid ready to stow in the large shopping bag. Cheese dish had done us well over the last twenty or so years. It made a really good hiding place. The sloping lid on a cheese dish gets lifted and set straight down, few turn them up, and if anybody did, I'd tell them the bag held chips of charcoal to keep the contents sweet.

'My job done I was ready to go, except I did have one more little thing to do. Reaching up I touched the tips of my fingers to Bertie, my lovely big tureen. "Goodbye Bertie, my dear. I shall miss you all." Then something crossed my mind. I don't know what made me do it but I put the shopping bag gently down on the floor, stretched up and opened Bertie's lid, just a little and reached my hand inside – was it just intuition or did something else tell me? I don't know. I could feel the edges of some tissue-wrapped lumps. Fetching a chair to stand on, I was at eye level with the big tureen, and the moon was higher now, allowing me to clearly see four wrapped parcels. Taking them to the kitchen table, I peeled the tissue back on the first one revealing a gold necklace. It spilled out rippling its links through my fingers into a glowing heap. From the second package rolled a lipstick case, gold and platinum, patterned with a ruby set in the top of its lid. The third, a tiny rouge pot, glass with a chased silver cover. The last, a semi-circular hair comb, little diamonds flashing around its rim.

'Here were some of the items I had heard the tea drinkers complain they'd mislaid. Returning to the dresser, I began my haul. By the time I'd put my hand into each Willow I had a collection of eighty-four parcels on the table. I looked into only a few more parcels. I didn't need to see further – they must all have been there. Except, I thought sadly, for the silver whistle that killed the poor little girl.

'I couldn't stand there at the table any longer. If caught, I would be implicated in no uncertain manner, but what to do? Revenge would be useless. How could I prove my innocence?

'I couldn't put all those items back and anyway, left in my willow pattern china, I felt it did implicate me. Looking at it all lying there the word "swag" came to mind! Ah but then I thought, this is just like something out of the Boys' Own Paper. Of course, that's it! I'll take a risk. I found an old hessian sack under the sink, still there where I kept them after we had emptied out the seed potatoes. I placed all the tissue parcels inside and rolled it closed into a tight lump. I pushed the sack down in the large shopping bag. It just fitted. Sorry cheese dish, you're staying after all, I thought. I put it back in position on the shelf.

'Goodbye everybody, I thought, nothing obvious missing. Nobody will ever know it was me.

'Now it was getting very late but I had to get away. The moon was past its zenith, high and bright, a harvest moon, nearer waxing than waning. I estimated it was between half past midnight and one o'clock. This was the northern hemisphere of my childhood, a rather comforting place to be. The past years of my married life had revolved under southern heavens. The moonlight made it easy for me to see and pull down a few branches of damsons along with the very last of the blackberries. I laid these on top of the sack of parcels.

'Walking back up the hill and out onto the Downs, the chalk paths shone like white ribbons. It was a long walk over Lullington Heath to the main road the other side of Wilmington but I had the rest of the night and besides, I was determined to sleep with a man I know. His far-sighted opinion could be very helpful.

'Getting comfy into a corner of the old flint workings, I felt lucky the weather was still so clement for September. I slept like a top. In fact I woke up later than I had wanted to, and the sun was shining directly onto me and my bedfellow. I could just make out the partially obscured lines of chalk leading down one stave, across to an elbow, then to a shoulder. I was just about to make my way on downhill when I caught sight of a dark figure bending over only a few yards away. Gave me quite a start, him being so close. I held my breath and kept very still. The man hadn't noticed me, he was so intent on watching for the rabbits his ferret was chasing out of a netted hole between his knees. When a sharp movement revealed a darting rabbit, he swiftly whacked each catch on the head, stowed them in a deep pocket, then gathered his net and walked away with his ferret slinking under his collar. But I remained where I was for some time until I saw him again fading into the distance well off my path. At the bottom of the hill I drank from a cool spring. There's nothing more refreshing as the cold, hard, sharp taste of water through chalk.

'I caught the bus at the crossroads and the conductor even said to me, "You're out early young woman." What a complement after a night out on the heath with the Long Man! I felt very satisfied as the bus rocked gently along through Firle and Glynde villages, skirting Mount Caburn, and down under the

338

chalk pits into Cliffe High Street and over the bridge. School Hill had always seemed to me a real trudge up to the crossroads, then onto the long downhill stretch along the dip in the Downs into Brighton. The journey gave me time to think through my plans for the future.

'Oh I forgot to tell you,' said Maud, 'I've hidden the "swag" near my gentleman friend. He'll look after my haul until I decide what should become of it.'

The next day Maud packed her few belongings and left Brighton on the train for London.

Two weeks later a letter arrived. Clara waited to open it until Tom came home. As he sat opposite her at the table eating his evening meal, she slit the envelope with a knife and pulled out the heavy letter paper. Folded inside was a big white five-pound note.

'She shouldn't have done that. It's a fortune,' Tom exclaimed through a mouthful of toad in the hole.

'Don't speak with your mouth full, Tom Cowley,' Clara laughed at her husband.

Maud's letter, dated October 1913, carried her grateful thanks for all their patience and the kind support they had given at her time of great need. The letter went on to say that she'd visited Hatton Garden and De Beers had given her a good price for the diamonds. Clara read out, 'As you read this letter I will be on my way to Australia. I intend to find my brother Harry and his family. Best wishes to you and yours, Maud Sinden.'

'You know, Tom, I've a great admiration for that woman. She's been brave and courageous in the face of injustice. And you're right, we didn't need her to send us anything, but she needed to.'

'Yes, well, she's far too honourable not to,' replied

Tom, 'and it must give her pleasure to say thank you in this way. Every evenin' when I got home I could see the little girl I knew back forty years ago, blossoming in Maude's face.'

'Yes. My heart went out to her that first evening. Let's hope she finds her brother; they say it's a vast country.' Clara was sewing up the seams on the cardigans Maud had finished knitting for Dolly the evening before she left Brighton. 'There, that's done,' she said half to herself. 'Now let's get this pinafore finished and she'll be all ready to go off to school with Jimmie. What did you say love?'

'I was saying, Charlie was a good sort. Maud coming here brought all those memories back. We had some happy times when we were lads together. She'll find 'im. I should think he'd be a well-liked man so somebody will know him and point her in the right direction.'

'Tom,' Clara said with a cautious tone.

'Yes love?' Tom wondered what was to come next.

'Would you think it extravagant if I suggested we all have new winter shoes this Christmas?'

'Why wait for Christmas?' he answered, a smile on his face.

'What a lovely story Bert,' sighed Big Pol.

'H'm, what a coincidence Lily and Paul found Uncle Bert in that antique shop in Goudhurst,' said Ol' Po.

'Yes, very true,' replied Uncle Bert. 'But I can tell you there's more coincidence to come on that episode. I haven't finished yet.'

'Oh tell, tell!' squealed Little Polly milk jug.

'Yes please do' said Ruby tea pot.

340

'No. I won't be pressed. There are others who've tales to tell yet. Be patient, mine will come all in good time.' Uncle Bert's lid slid into place with a clatter.

'That's it then, he's asleep,' announced Big Pol. 'Now you will have to wait.'

10

Clara

'Hallo little mother!' Frankie roared happily, dropping his heavy bag down inside the front door. Picking Clara up, he swung her round in a big fat hug. Clara laughed with joy as her son set her down with care in the cluttered front room.

'Ah, it's great to be home,' he sighed.

Clara was full to overflowing, stepping back a little to gaze at Frankie's face. 'You look wonderful. Travelling has done you good.'

'And having a real family has done you good, little mother. You look blooming. Now, where are those cheeky rascals?' Frankie had heard the giggles and scuffles behind the scullery door but made to look away into the mews. Jimmie and Dolly had been peeping through the door jamb, watching their mother being picked up and swung round by this man. They'd never seen their father Tom being quite so demonstrative. Now it was their turn and they came bursting excitedly through into the room.

Dolly turned shy, hiding behind her mother's

long skirts while little Jim came on full tilt into his half-brother's arms and was carried aloft with a delighted squeal. He was six years old now, but although he'd been only two at the time Frankie was last home, he always said he could just remember seeing Frankie and Leslie walking off down the station platform.

'So here's a man still full of wriggling, giggling cheek.' Keeping his hold on Jim by his side, Frankie stooped down to the little boy's height, putting an encouraging hand out to Dolly and saying, 'Is this the baby you had with you when we last met, Jim?'

'Yep,' replied the child.

'Come little sweet,' Frankie coaxed. 'Your turn. Give us a big cuddle.'

She responded immediately although at just five years old, it was the first time she'd met her brother.

'Still the little Dolly, then.' Violet May was proud of her family name. Although her mother endeavoured to dress her like a little girl in white pinafores, they never stayed white for long. Dolly was a small girl caught in a boy's world all day. The moment she was outside that front door, the glossily brushed dark hair and the pretty bow went the way of the starched white pinafore and she became one of them – a scruff. The school photographs live on to tell the tale.

'How's our Freddy Ma?'

'Oh, not so bad. He loves school, can't keep him away.'

'Ah yes, just a mo. There's something I promised this chap I would give you as soon as I got home.' Rummaging in the front pocket of his haversack, Frankie produced a small round parcel. 'Now, what was it he told me to say?'

As Clara quizzically peeled away the wrapping paper, it came back to him. 'Ah ah, that's it. Funny word, he said tell your mother "Mispah".'

Clara's heart almost jumped out of her chest. Frankie grabbed her as she reached for a chair. 'Here, steady on. Sit down. What's all this about?'

Leaning against the table, Clara slowly finished unwrapping the parcel and cupped a very small blue and white willow pattern plate in the palms of both hands. Three pairs of eyes watched, one with concern, the other two with eager if not a little deflated surprise.

'What was the chap like?'

'What chap?' In his concern for his mother's sudden unexpected reaction, Frankie had completely put aside the giver of the parcel.

'The man who gave you this?' Taking it out of her hands, Frankie the chef and recent hotel entrepreneur, recognised the small item of china as a table place setting. Noticing it had her name written on its guest strip in pencil, which had obviously been there some long time, he asked, 'Where did he get this then? It's got your name on it.' He didn't wait for an answer. 'Hmm,' he mused. 'An Englishman, I suppose he must have been in his forties. Now I come to think of it, when we first met he said he knew Sussex well. He was sitting at the end of the bar in the evenings where I used to drop in after I'd finished late service. He seemed to be well known; everyone called him Andy.'

Clara's eyes glistened with rising tears as she looked up at her son.

'Oh Ma.' He stooped down beside her, 'I'm sorry. It's made you cry, whatever is it?'

'Is that all he said,' she asked, 'just Mispah?'

'On my last night before leaving the Cape, when I said I wouldn't be in again, this chap reached inside his jacket and took the parcel out and said, "Give this to your mother. Make sure you do it as soon as you see her. Don't forget now. Just say to her, Mispah". Then he got up and walked out of the bar.'

'Sit down my love. That man was your father.'

Frankie took her trembling hands in his. Mispah sat on the table between them. 'So that's why he said, "Goodbye son," as he went out the door. Oh Mum, I wish I'd known! He was so interesting. For those few evenings, he told me all about working up country in the mining. How he'd first ridden alongside an outspan from the square in the town. He even offered if I'd like to join him on his next trip out. But, well, we were still working long hours to get things just right before we left. I couldn't take that length of time away. After he left, the barman said that was the longest Mr Andy had stayed down in Cape Town – usually off back on business after no more 'n' a night or so's stay.'

Clara took a deep breath and wiped her eyes. Standing up, she popped a piece of the white tissue paper wrapping on the top of her head and, smoothing her apron down by her sides said, in a prim voice, 'Would sir like to order tea now?'

'Oh, get on with you, you old flopper,' Frankie

chuckled. Both children drew in air, exploding their tension with laughter. The mother they knew had returned.

'Certainly sir, I'll just be a few moments. I'm afraid it's a little early for muffins, the man doesn't call out till four o'clock round here.' And off she went into the scullery to put the kettle on, followed by her little helper while the scallywag stayed watching his brother drag the rest of his bags inside the front door. Clara would often act out some little scene when a happier distraction from a tight spot was needed. She had been called little mother over the years, originally by her own siblings and now by her eldest son. At 41 she had a trim figure, her natural auburn curls piled up on her head just like Queen Alexandra, both diminutive women who both wore similar high collars and floor-length skirts. Of course, in addition, Clara regularly wore a full-length white pinafore over the top.

With the willow pattern tea pot, cups and saucers on the round table, Clara poured the two of them a cup of tea while Jim and Dolly stood against the table, each with a glass of lemon barley. Now that their mother appeared to be her old self again, and their drinks rapidly finished, the pair skipped off out to play. Clara knew the time had come to reveal the story more fully to her son.

'We'd known each other all our young lives. It wasn't until we met again after Frank returned from university that we gradually realised how connected we felt. Of course Gran had taken me aside and warned me not to get involved. Frank had found us children when he was only about seven years old. He seemed such a lonely boy, so he got to be with us every moment he could. We were over at the Lamb all summers and often weekends through the year, sometimes at Christmas times too. Frank even rode his horse over to St Leonards one day onto the beach. His horse loved the long gallop. My mum, she was worried because he was still only a young boy; she thought if his mother knew how far he'd gone away from home, she'd stop him mixing with the local children altogether.

'But I'm afraid to tell you, dear, that Frank and I developed a passion for each other. Well, you see, at that age it is so difficult to deny.'

'Ma, don't be ashamed. I wouldn't be here otherwise, now would I? And I'm enjoying every moment of my life.'

'You're just like him. If he was enjoying something he'd go all out for it, loved life. When I overheard raised voices that afternoon, arguing – doors banging, then all the toil and bustle going on in the stables with the big family coach being brought out and what with all the orders Mrs Anderson was calling in the hall, I just had that awful sinking feeling I'd never see him again.'

'I never understood why you said he had gone away,' Frankie said.

'Well, I didn't know at the time just how much he'd told his parents. He was so full of it, overjoyed at our friendship and love. I had no idea really how rapid and thorough their reactions were, and obviously neither had he.

'It all seemed to happen so suddenly. The way his mother invaded the kitchen and berated me –

he didn't know about that. I went straight away and wrote my name on this place setting – it was the first thing that came into my head. Then I caught Frank in the hallway where he was putting on his greatcoat. At the time he thought he was being asked to go across the Channel to finalise a business deal for his father, because that trip had been on the cards for some time. When he wrote to me, it was from the cargo vessel he said was in the Bay of Biscay out near Spain. I didn't get that first letter for weeks.'

'But then you were left all on your own with a problem to tackle.'

'My problem, but being on my own, well, I suppose you could say it was for the best. Granny must have been suspicious but said nothing. She gave me that money to help my journey. Mum and Dad hadn't known what had really been going on. But Mum wasn't silly. I had to deal with my own fate and I was determined not to bring bad odour onto them from the neighbours, and of course they had customers to serve at the inn.

'I've always kept in touch with Frank. Tom said I should for your sake and his. As you know, Frank has added a small regular amount to the account that has helped you to do some of the things you've wanted to do.'

'Yes, but I still think he should have married you.'

'That was my decision, Frankie. I said no because I didn't want to go to a country that seemed so alien for women.'

'He should have come back then. It's not that difficult to travel between countries.'

'I think by the time he'd finally got there and travelled to where the trade was, he found he'd have to stay on the spot to make it all work. He did keep asking me to join him. After about five or six years he just lived his life, and stayed where he was. Anyway that's how it all came over in his letters.'

Clara took Mispah to the dresser and placed it on a shelf at her eye level. Turning back to Frankie as he sat there, teacup in hand, deep in thought, she said, 'I didn't ever expect to see this little Willow again. It gave me quite a shock.'

She was about to recite its meaning, but her words were drowned out of the air by the front door flying open, back against the wall, and by the appearance of a thin figure just too tall to get through without bending. In fact, when he un-ravelled himself into the room he towered over all.

Frankie stood to meet the newcomer who looked abashed at his own performance. Silence, or was it just a pause before Frankie asked his mother, 'Is this Freddy? Freddy, is it you?'

The boy was taller than his elder brother. As he slowly recognised Frankie, a happy look of aban-donment came across his face and gave a sound like, 'Yarrow, it is Frankie. Yippee you're home.'

Frankie shot an enquiring look across at his mother. She smiled saying, 'He's grown like this only in the last year. It's been a nightmare keep-ing up with the new clothes he needs. He's over six feet tall.' Freddy was all gangly and awkward, tripping as he flung his arms around Frankie's shoulders.

'Hallo that man. Well, look at you, great fella,'

Frankie said.

Freddy seemed proud to be addressed that way, although he was soon distracted asking, 'Can I 'ave a cup o' that tea, Ma. Got any cake?'

When Clara went upstairs to show Frankie where he'd be sleeping she spoke quietly, saying how Tom had had to cut the footboard off Freddy's bed and make up an extra length.

'But we've stopped mentioning the fact in front of the boy anymore because he's beginning to be ostracised by the other boys in his class. He's barely twelve. Pity, because he was really settled in and loving all the lessons. No Frank, he's not changed. Freddy will never be the bright little button Jim is. Still, they get along well. Now this is your bed. Jim sleeps at the other end of Freddy, and Dolly's in with us for the time being.'

'Thanks, Mum. Whatever happens you always make us all feel welcome and loved. You're wonderful.' Then after a pause, 'Damn it. I wish I'd known. I'd have told him what he's missed.'

'Better not say things like that in front of Tom, dear.'

'No. You know I wouldn't hurt his feelings. Tom! He's been the dad I never knew. And he loves my mum.' Frankie put his arm round Clara and kissed the top of her head. 'You'll do,' he said.

Frankie told Tom how he and his friend George had fulfilled the task they had taken on to get the new hotel up and running smoothly for the owner who had paid their fares out to the Cape. He and George had each taken a short time away to see something of the surrounding country and he said he had enjoyed the experience but now he wanted to get back home. That country, Frankie said, wasn't for him, relationships felt strained and rather overbearing, white people didn't like Boers, and both Boers and English treated the locals badly. He felt he'd been away long enough, he said. Paris had been a new and exciting time but he didn't want to settle abroad.

'What are your plans then Frank?'

'I'm going in to the Grand tomorrow. See what's on offer there. But I'm thinking I should be after a better position now. Head chef in a London establishment maybe, I've had offers but I want to look them over. Have a chat with chefs here in Brighton.'

'Take a bit of time off?' asked Tom.

'Maybe, thought I'd do a bit of walking across Sussex. How about joining me for a break, Dad?'

'Not me, not walkin'. I'm walking up hill 'n' down dale every day. Sit on a bus maybe. Nar, you don't want me. I'd slow yer down. Leslie'd be more your companion. He's young and fit. Ask him.'

'Yes. I might do that. I hear he's joined the Territorials to do with the Engineers in London near where he works? Does he write to you and Mum?'

'No, 'e's livin' in Putney and still working at Aunt Nancy's place in Soho. You know, his mother packed up their home here an' followed 'im to London?'

'No! Well I never. The blighter never said.'

'I'm not surprised, Frank. She went up there after 'im the very first weekend. Nance wrote tellin' us how embarrassed the lad was when his mother walked into the restaurant. Apparently as her luck would have it their washer up hadn't turned up that day an' they had a big Italian family do to cater for. Knowing Rose, she rolled her sleeves up and mucked in. Les was on tables learning from the other waiters.'

Clara came in the room at this point, having finally got the young ones in bed, and took up the story. 'Nancy said she could hardly put Rose back on the train at that time of night so they had her stay over and of course she helped all through the Sunday, clearing and getting the place ready to open for business on the Monday.

'Les said he'd rather walk with his mother to carry her bag back to Victoria and see her safely off on the last train that Sunday night. They never probed him, but a couple of months later he told Nance and Valentino that his mother had found a terraced cottage in Putney so he'd be leaving the restaurant and coming in each day if that was all right with them. They felt so sorry for the boy. He'd had no chance to have a young life of his own.

'Nance had written to me the first time to see if I could drop Rose the hint to let the lad have a life. I did try but she said he was all she'd got since Tony left. And anyway Les would never be able to manage on his own. Well, I said he wasn't on his own exactly when he was living above the restaurant with the family but no, she wouldn't have it. Said Soho was full of red lights and some tart might get a' hold of 'im.'

'What? Without him noticing?' chipped in

Frankie. They all had a laugh at that. 'I'll go and dig him out when I go up to town. Maybe that's why he's joined a real man's training unit. They go off on manoeuvres, don't they?'

'Rose has been a bit cool with your mother since,' Tom told Frankie.

'I know Les was having trouble wondering how to break the news to his mother when I went back to Paris this last time. He did say, "I wish my mother was like yours." I told him, you've got to live your own life, Les.'

'Fanny has lost patience with Rose. Peter's already away at Pierre's workrooms in London training in the trade. She says he's off to Paris soon and he's younger than you and Les.'

'Good luck to him. He'll do well that lad.'

'I must away up them stairs, early start. Night Frankie,' said Tom. 'Don't be long love. Talk about me being on me feet all day. That mother of yours never stops.'

Frankie helped Clara wash up the supper crocks.

'Thanks for what you told me today Mum, I wish you and Dad could have a weekend off. What if I looked after the youngsters to give you a break, might as well take the opportunity while I'm here, why not?'

'Well, I don't know. Who'd do Tom's round on the Saturday.'

Frankie was more than good at cooking, he was a doer. If a job needed tackling or an idea made to work, Frankie was on the job. Before he went over to the Grand that morning, he penned a letter off to Worthing to Dudley and Sybil. He explained his idea for Tom and Clara to have a weekend off, asking could they help him make it possible by inviting the pair to stay with them, just for a Saturday night. Make a break of it sort of thing. He would be at home to take care of the three young ones.

To Tom's surprise he had a letter from his son the next day asking if he and Clara would join them in Worthing for the weekend after next to celebrate their wedding anniversary. A short holiday, Dudley called it. Good heavens, they'd all forgotten Tom and Clara's anniversary.

'Wait a minute, that's not for a few weeks yet,' said Tom.

'Never mind, the idea's a splendid one,' Frankie told Tom. Clever old Dudley! Frankie hadn't thought of that one. 'Well, what do you think, Dad?' he asked.

'I don't know lad. I've nobody to do my round.'

'Who would do it if you couldn't?'

'I suppose old Neville might step in, he's done the round with me sometimes but he's retired now. He's seventy-five yer know. An' I'd 'ave to pay 'im.'

'Don't worry about that. What would you have to pay him? I'll pay it. I've got the money. Come on now. Mother needs the rest as much as you. Will you let us do this for you?' Whoops, he nearly let the cat out of the bag.

'See what Neville says. It's only one day and I expect the old chap could do with the money.'

'Yes, I've no doubt. The only reason he's not in the workhouse is his wife's a lot younger than 'im. She still works at that clothing manufacturer's up near the station where yer Aunt Rose worked.'

Frankie and the children waved their parents off as the omnibus pulled out onto the seafront from Poole Valley. Such an unexpected jaunt was as much an excitement for the children as it was for Tom and Clara. They were looking forward to a lovely long sit down while they watched the world go by. The children felt very important seeing their parents dressed in their Sunday best on a Saturday and because the neighbours said they'd never heard the like, 'A workin' man 'avin an' 'oliday. That was for the likes of the toffs.'

As the bus went out of sight into the distance along the seafront, Frankie rubbed his hands together saying, 'Right now lads an' lassie, what would you like to do today?'

'Paddle in the sea.'

'Go on the pier.'

''Ave some ice cream.'

'If we do all that today you'll have to think of something else for tomorrow. I've got a picnic here in my haversack so off we go and see what we can find. Follow the leader.' Dolly ran to take hold of her brother's hand, leaving one tiny boy and one very tall boy to bring up the rear with the odd kick and push that Frankie ignored.

Clara and Tom hardly passed a word between them for some time. Quiet closeness was enough. The view of sea to one side and familiar terraces of stately houses and hotels to the other, was quite absorbing.

'You know, Clara, we haven't sat on our own together like this for near-on fourteen years.'

'Done a lot of other things though haven't we love?'

Tom loosened his hard collar just a little. 'Let's enjoy ourselves then, gal.'

Holding hands they were like excited tourists pointing things out from one side of the bus to the other. Climbing inland towards the windmill at Blatchington, and on passing the ancient round tower of Sompting church, the bus journey taking them up hill and down dale was a joy, just watching the world go by. People got on and off, pursuing their peaceful lives.

'There they are, look. That's where they said to get off. Come on love.'

Tom got up and rang the bell, going down the stairs first holding his hand up to help his wife. Dudley, Sybil and the two children were standing at the end of the lane to meet them. It was beautiful weather, coming up to the middle of the day. Sybil had brought an old pushchair to carry their case on as they all sauntered off up the lane towards their village. The Cock and Pheasant was open so the men went in and got themselves a pint, each bringing out shandies for Clara and Sybil sitting on the bench outside, with orange squash for the children, who sat on the grass. Quiet little children, a boy and a younger daughter, soon little Suzy had a daisy chain necklace while Tom showed his grandson Danny how to make a grass whistle.

Clara and Sybil finished their drinks and carried on walking along the lane to the cottage, the men coming along later with the little lad. Dinner around the kitchen table was followed by two chairs in the sunny garden. Clara and Tom felt they were being treated like royalty.

In the early evening, the whole family went to see a picture show in the village hall. The place was packed with locals. It seemed a wealthy newcomer was something to do with the film industry and brought as yet unseen films to try out on audiences. The village hall must have rocked with noisy surprised laughter because at one point the door was flung open, letting in the bright sunset. Everybody at once shouted to shut that door. Standing silhouetted in the doorway was a very old man who shouted back, 'What in tarnation's going on in here? Sounds like a chicken house.'

'Shut that door!' Good manners had flown out of the window in their eager haste to witness the antics on screen. Although great guffaws of laughter predominated that evening there were tears too, for that poor little man who always seemed to be in trouble.

Everybody must have slept well that night because the sun was up and shining through the curtains so bright when they woke. Tom said he would have been out for hours by that time. Sybil fed them a grand old Sunday roast then wouldn't let anybody wash up.

'Sorry. No sleeping after yer dinner today. We're off to a special do this afternoon. Aunty Jessie's having a get together for her new baby granddaughter out at Tarring. She's got a few musicians from around the village and they are having a bit of dancing in the garden. It's a christening.'

Sybil had kept the secret to herself when she knew Tom and Clara would be with them. She

356

knew if the children heard about it, they'd say something. It would get out.

A huge cheer came from the company standing in the garden with their cups of tea, waiting while the accordion player and the violinist helped a percussion player to set up his drums.

'Tom, Clara, we didn't know you'd be coming.' Jessie, Tom's sister-in-law, Maisie's sister, was overjoyed to see him after all these years. 'Oh, Tom, you look so well. Clara, you've certainly done a good job.'

'Where's the young 'uns?'

And that's when Frankie's undercover plot came out.

On the bus journey home that evening, Tom and Clara talked the hind legs off a donkey although they were both dead tired. Healthy, happy tired. They'd had more than a breath of fresh air.

'I know what the neighbours will say. You two look well, no wonder the toffs are so healthy.'

All talk exhausted, Clara slipped her arm through Tom's. The rest of the journey they each spent in their own quiet thoughts. They were the last to descend the stairs. Walking arm in arm away from the bus Tom remarked with a sigh, 'Ah. That was a right treat. He's a good lad is Frankie.'

Frankie and the three young Cowleys had fared just as well as their parents – a paddle and ice cream on Saturday morning followed by tea on the pier in the afternoon. On Sunday, Frankie had them up and out early to walk the cliff path to Rottingdean with a picnic on the beach. Then up over the hills way across to Falmer village and back down through Stanmer Park and along the valley into Brighton, the last lap carrying little Dolly on his back.

Tom and Clara hadn't expected to be met from the bus that evening although when they got home in the gathering dusk to St George's Mews all was so quiet they thought their young family had run away. They found the house in darkness and Frankie asleep in an armchair beside the fireplace. He hadn't lit the lamp because, as he told them later, it was only half past four when they got back home. Dolly was so fast asleep, he'd laid her on her bed fully clothed with a blanket. Little Jimmie drank some lemon barley and was so tired he had to be carried up to his bed. And Freddy had gone straight upstairs when they got home and was already snoring when Jimmie was tucked in to the foot of his extra-long bed.

'I came back down intending to make myself a cuppa and the next thing I knew, you two walked in the door.'

'I can see what you were doing when you sat in that chair,' laughed Clara, pointing at Frankie's feet.

'Oh goodness I was just taking my shoes off – one on and one off. I must have gone out like a light. Oh, sorry, there's sand all over my shoes.'

'Well, looks like you've had a busy weekend lad.'

It wasn't until the Monday teatime that they had time to tell each other about all their exciting exploits. Nobody noticed what they ate for tea, so when Clara said, 'Is everyone finished?' Jimmie said, 'Finished what?'

'Your tea, luvvy,' his mother answered.

'Hadn't noticed, Ma.'

Freddy punched the little boy on the ear, making Jimmie squeal.

'Now then lad, not quite so hard. He's only a little whippersnapper,' Frankie rebuked him.

'Well, 'e's cheeky 'e is,' came the slow Freddy reply.

'But it's not nasty, Freddy – just humorous. Not naughty, so a little gentle bump would be enough.'

Clara and Dolly had left the room taking the dirty dishes to the scullery when Frankie spoke to Freddy. He'd noticed how Freddy over-reacted with his younger siblings. As he said to Clara later, 'You know, Mum, he's quite spiteful with them at times, pinching and punching. Dad's not home enough to see what's happening. I've seen a lot this weekend. His actions need curbing before he really does some hurt.'

Clara had noticed, but of course she had always tried to shelter him. She knew he was slow. 'I think he gets frustrated, Frankie. The others are so quick, usually they get out of his way. They seem to know the trick is to move fast.'

'Yes I can see how canny they are, but he's not silly Mum, he's just slow and he catches them out. Especially now he's so tall – he's got a very long reach on him. Tell me you haven't got some bruises on your upper arms Mother.'

'Oh dear, how did you guess?'

'I've seen him give you a sharp little punch here and there. I know he's only twelve but he must be stopped.'

Before he went off to his new job in the West End of London, Frankie took Freddy to a picture show. Walking back home he asked the boy, 'Do your classmates ever hit you Freddy?'

Freddy thought for a long while, seeming to fight with his conscience and his words before he blurted out, 'They hit me so I hit them.' Then he said, all pleased with himself, 'I can hit them down on top of their heads – an' it 'urts too.'

'Do they hurt you, Freddy?'

'Not much.'

'Then you must not hurt them. Big men have to be gentler than little men. And another thing, you must never hit our mother, ever again. She belongs to us all, so you'd be hurting my mother too. Can you remember that, Freddy?'

'Yes all right. But I've seen boys hit their mothers down the mews,' he shot back – his robust retort was a surprise.

'But you are a nice kind boy, Freddy. They are not. In our family we don't hit each other. You've never seen our father hit Mummy have you?'

'No.'

'Well then. Remember that. We don't hit each other.'

Coming in from her marketing one morning some weeks later, Clara was unpacking her vegetables in the scullery when she stopped to listen. No, surely she was hearing things, but there it was again. Leaving the bag of vegetables she went quietly across the scullery, carefully lifted the latch of the door to the staircase and listened. Yes. She was right. She could hear real crying and sniffles coming from upstairs. Tiptoeing as silently as possible up the wooden stairs she peeped through the door to the bedroom that Freddy and Jimmie shared. Freddy was curled up on the bed, his body shaking with deep hiccupping sobs.

'Oh luvvy, whatever is it?'

A tear-soaked face turned to her followed by the slow words, 'They hurt me, Mummy.' Gulping and hiccupping he stuttered out, 'They said I'm not all there. They keep shoutin' it at me Mummy.'

'What made them do it to you, Freddy?' she asked as she sat beside the boy cuddling his head to her chest. He curled up like a baby in her lap, all six feet of arms and legs – a gangly twelve-year-old whose classmates were undernourished boys, none of whom had yet topped four foot ten. Clara had feared these times would come, when Freddy would be made fully aware of his difference. In her heart she could never see him have his own happy family life. Up until now his teachers had been kind and supportive, allowing him to develop in his own time. And as long as he had all the love she and Tom could give him at home, she hoped it would keep the door firmly closed against any adult taking advantage of his need for love. But it could arise, they wouldn't be here to protect him all his life. A sharp rap on the front door gave them both a start.

'Stay here my love. I'll be back in a jiff.' She tucked a blanket tightly round her son.

It was Father Grantly from school. 'Has young Freddy come home, Mrs Cowley?'

'Come in Father. Will you have a cup of tea?'

'Thank you, I will. I saw what happened, Mrs Cowley. Children can be so cruel. Anything unusual is a threat.' Father Grantly had a parcel under his arm. 'Now I don't want to make you feel uncomfortable but we see Freddy is in need of clothes to fit his rapid growth. It may be difficult for you to find the wherewithal to accommodate the lad.'

Clara had never experienced such thoughtful attention from the church before, but she didn't voice this. 'Thank you for the thought Father. Yes this will be a great help.'

'Mrs Cowley, soup for clothes helps the world go round. Thank you.' He smiled his recognition, then louder to be heard above stairs. 'Tell young Freddy to bring the jam jars I sent him to collect into school this afternoon. I expect the job took him longer than expected. Good morning.'

'Goodbye,' Clara replied.

Freddy came out from behind the scullery door. 'I've only got two jam jars left, Mum. They smashed the others I got.'

'There's more under the sink, love. Come on, let's get my old shopping bag filled. A cold-water splash and you'll feel as good as new. Remember how I told you Grandfather John used to do it.' That made the boy laugh. 'Laughter's a wonderful thing for the soul, Freddy my love. I've got a nice jacket potato in the coals. You need a bit of dinner inside you before you go back.'

After he'd eaten, Clara took a comb to his hair as he sat at the table. 'Remember Grandfather John was a very tall man and he laughed along with everybody. I expect you are going to be as

362

tall as him, Freddy.'

As Freddy went to pick up the bag of glass jars, Clara laid a paper bag on the top. 'Now when you get to the playground, you can tell the boys a man gave you these apples to go with the jars. You give them one each. They're only little apples but it'll make them lads feel they can join in your good luck.'

'But Mum, they punched me.'

'Forget the nasty things they do, Freddy. You just show them what a generous chap you are. That's what a grown-up would do. And you are grown-up now. You're in men's long trousers.'

'Is that what Father Grantly brought?'

'Yes. So there you are then. They're not Dad's left-offs, these are yours.'

Clara watched her boy walk away towards St Bartholomew's with the heavy bag slung over his shoulder in a real workman way. 'Put the bag down gently Freddy, remember it's glass.' He might be too tall to walk under the passage at the end of the mews without bending his head but he was still only a lad. Nature had snatched his childhood so suddenly.

Before Clara retreated back inside to get on with her work, Jenny from next door put her head out of the upstairs window to say, 'Your snooty sister-in-law called round over the weekend, Clara.'

'Oh my, what did she want?'

'Didn't say. Was annoyed to find yer door locked. Heard the knocking an' put my 'ead out this winder, said you'd all gone on holiday. "Holiday?" she shouts. "What is the world comin' to?" I 'ad ter laugh, should've seen her face. Like a bucket crushed under an 'orse's 'oof.'

When Clara told Tom that night he said how Albert had stopped his van and come across to him when he was delivering up near Buckingham Street that morning. 'He says to me, "What's this I 'ear? I thought you were away on holiday." No I'm 'ere ain't I, I says. "Ethel's bin on at me ter take 'er away on holiday, says if workmen can take holidays so can businessmen." I thought meself, I'm ready for the next question. "Where yer bin then?" he asks. Only across to Le Touquet for the races, I says, with me nose in the air. "Blimey Tom, comin' it a bit aren't yer?" he says, all surprised like.'

Tom went on, 'Housekeeper at one of my customers up in Sussex Square used to tell me when the family was away stayin' at their house over in Le Touquet for the races and the casino. So I laid it on thick. You should have seen poor Albert's face! I don't 'spect he really believed me.'

'Oh Tom, you are naughty,' Clara laughed. 'That'll upset Ethel, now Albert will have to take her somewhere really posh!'

'Only if 'e tells 'er what I said, love.'

'She'll winkle it out of him Tom, you can be sure of that.'

'Ooh dear,' replied Tom looking guilty but oh so sly.

In Frankie's first letter from London he told how he'd not realised how much the talk of war was in the air in the capital. He'd heard rumours and that's what had caused all the bad feeling between the British and German communities overseas. He went on to say how he had met the girl he'd taken out last time he worked in Mayfair. They were getting on well. Her name was Marjorie. Oh, and did they know that Les had a really lovely lady friend? Probably they didn't, Frankie remarked, because Les hasn't told his mother yet. This girl's a real good looker.

Another letter told Tom and Clara how Frankie saw less of Leslie because his training with the Royal Engineers was taking up all his time off.

Yet another said, 'Les is over there already. He says he's part of the Expeditionary Force. Seems I will have to go soon.'

To top it all, just before Christmas 1914 Freddy came running in the door calling, 'Mum, Mum, a lady has just hit me in the chest and told me I'm unpat … unpat… She pushed this white feather into my jumper. What's she mean?'

'Unpatriotic dear – is that what the word was?'

'Sounded like that.'

'Oh dear, Tom, I never expected his sudden growth to get him in this kind of difficulty. I said to one woman, he's only thirteen, madam. She told me it was no use my lying for him. He ought to be man enough to go. He's big enough. The trouble is in the long trousers nobody's convinced he's only coming up thirteen.'

'You can't be with him every moment of his life, Clara. He's going to have to stand on his own two feet and stick up for himself.'

The very next day Freddy seemed even quieter than usual when Jimmie and Dolly chatted on about school to their mother. Clara waited. She could see something was on Freddy's mind. When Tom came in, he came out with it all in a rush.

'I went cross-eyed Dad. It frightened the lady away.'

'Slow down old chap. Now what happened?'

This time haltingly. 'A lady came right up to me and...' he was stuttering now, 'she, she banged me on the chest with another one of those feathers. I loo ... looked hard at her then went cross-eyed. She squealed and ran away.'

Tom and Clara couldn't stop their laughter, however Tom said, 'Good idea lad, but before you do that again, make sure you step back and leave a good space between you and the lady.'

'Why, Dad?'

'Well people might think you've hit the lady if she screams like you say.'

'All right, I'll remember that too.' Freddy was always slow and deliberate in his replies unless there was something he had to get out before it slipped from his mind.

Times were suddenly harder for Tom because all the younger roundsmen had volunteered. They all said they'd be back in the New Year, and most businesses said they would keep their jobs open for them, but that didn't help the older men already getting on in years and not wanting to do longer hours. Somebody had to make the deliveries. The only solution was to employ twelve- and thirteen-year-olds who could only assist, not take over rounds of their own. Tom did think maybe he could try Freddy on a Saturday to start with but he found Freddy couldn't keep his mind on the job. He could be sent to deliver one order to a single house but couldn't remember what a customer said if she asked for something extra, and Saturdays were a crucial day for making extra sales and therefore adding a bit more to the wage packet. Then Freddy would forget which house to return to if he did remember the order. If a note was left, he had to find Tom to read it, for Freddy had not succeeded in reading more than his name and address by the time he was thirteen.

Then he'd get lost. Something would take his eye. Maybe an unusual-looking cat or a different flower outside a house and Freddy was distracted. Once he followed a cat, 'Just to stroke it Dad.' Tom's round had taken them further from the centre of the town than Freddy was used to. When the cat finally had enough of being stroked, he jumped up and over a wall. Freddy looked around and didn't recognise where he was. So he wandered off in search of the baker's van. Seeing this wandering young man who looked so lost, an elderly lady asked where he wanted to go. Freddy told her he was looking for a baker's van. Unfortunately she sent him further away in the opposite direction – the way she had just come and where she'd noticed another baker's van standing in the road.

It was a Saturday evening and almost dark when Clara and Dolly finally found Freddy wandering along Queen's Park Road. How he had got there they never knew because Tom's round was on the other side of the London Road. Jimmie had looked all along the streets as far as Dyke Road before he gave up. What made Clara go in the direction she did, she never knew. Luckily she followed her intuition.

When the war started, Jimmie and Dolly were eight and seven respectively. Both full of vigorous life they had no fear – they were fun-loving, cheeky young scamps who ranged far and wide together. It seemed there was no lane or twitten they hadn't investigated, no court or terrace they had not explored or been chased from.

Neither was a brilliant scholar but both could read and write by seven years old. Dolly's hand-writing had special character. Clara had sent them on errands with money and expected change. She maintained it was the best way to learn. She was right and it worked. There were no flies on Jimmie or Dolly as far as money was concerned.

The one calming influence was Tom. Not that Clara was his opposite, just that Tom was from an older generation than Clara. She could see he was tiring much more quickly than before, so it became her way to tell the children, 'Let Dad have a snooze,' or 'tiptoe in, Daddy's fallen asleep in the chair, try not to wake him.' For some time Clara had been giving Tom his breakfast in bed on a Sunday. It was his only day off and the one time she could make sure he had his rest.

Nevertheless as soon as the younger pair knew he was awake, they would be in bed either side of him with a story book, or asking him to tell them about his horse or about when he was a little boy.

The Willows

'Do you remember that Sunday morning when Tom woke later than normal?' Victoria asked Albert, 'The time Jimmie ran into the bedroom just as Clara had given Tom his first cup of tea.'

'Ah yes, and Dolly came tumbling up behind him, her hair all wet and her face smeared with mud.'

'Oh dear, oh dear, where have you two been?' their father asked. 'I thought it was church this morning not a mud fight.' Tom always managed to get humour into any situation with the children.

When Clara saw Dolly's straw hat she was ever so cross. 'I spent all last evening trying to make you look like a lady and now those pretty silk flowers are a bedraggled mess.'

'She slapped it on Dudridge's wall, Mum,' Jimmie spoke up.

'Well you knocked it off my head into a puddle, Jimmie.'

'An' you thought that hot wall would dry it quick.'

'You said it would.'

'Now now, young 'uns, better go downstairs and peel spuds and help do the veg for Mum's Sunday dinner. Go on now. Skedaddle!'

'Oh must I? I didn't do it,' Jim mewed, wriggling and giggling.

'Seems to me you're both in on this, go and help your mother or there's no dinner.'

Clump, clump, clump down the stairs. Freddy had heard it all from the bottom of the stairs so he laughed and poked them as they came through the door. And that's what got Freddy disliked because he wouldn't stop. He still didn't remember about overreacting. He could be very spiteful. The days when Freddy would tuck up beside daddy on a Sunday morning were long gone, although he did love to hear the well-read story books.

Tom was always fair with giving his time because Freddy was the first one to get back home after Sunday school. Tom got to know that Freddy did it to get his father to explain what was happening in the picture on that stamp the priest stuck in his Sunday school attendance book each week. That was because Freddy couldn't understand all the high-flown language the priest said. Tom told him straight what the characters in the pictures were doing and explained the story. It certainly did the trick because Freddy was able to join in the family talk round the Sunday dinner table, and especially as Tom would be ready sitting on the back doorstep with the shoe polish box out so that he could be polishing his shoes when Freddy ran in the front door.

'Come on then son, sit down here beside me and we'll take a look at that picture you've won.' He made it Freddy's special time, looking through his book of picture stamps. One for each week Freddy had attended Sunday school.

Clara would call out to Jimmie and Dolly when they came bursting in a bit later, 'Now then you two, in here, keep out of the scullery. The men have got business to talk over on the back doorstep.'

Then there was the Sunday morning Freddy came in all full of questions, only to find Tom sitting at the table with tears running down his cheeks. The last delivery had come at ten o'clock on the Saturday evening. A bit unusual to have a letter along St George's Mews at all, let alone that late, but seeing the postmark, 'Worthing', Clara had a suspicion she knew what it might be. Tom was fast asleep. He'd come in extra late from work that evening, nearly nine o'clock and by half past nine he'd said, 'I'm going up love. I can't keep my eyes open.'

'You go on love, you look like you need the sleep.'

Clara decided to keep the letter until the morning. Whatever it contained, Tom couldn't do anything about it that time of night. And if it was bad news, why wake him. Let him have his rest.

It was bad news.

Clara

'He didn't have to go. Not at his age.' The tears streamed down Tom's face unchecked. He couldn't help himself. 'I never expected my boy would go before me. And there was no need. No need at all, poor Sybil. Oh dear, and the children. Dear me, how will she cope?'

Clara was concerned for her sister-in-law. There was Tom's sister-in-law fairly near but she wasn't a young woman. Sybil had no family, no brothers and sisters, and her parents had been gone many years.

'She says here he was shot by mistake at training camp. What a waste, what a waste,' Tom sighed. 'I didn't think I'd ever react like this, love. Sorry.'

Clara put her arm round his shoulders. 'Whenever you heard this it would be shattering news, dear. You've had a terrible shock Tom. It's natural. You can't help how you're reacting.'

371

'It was meant to be, that lovely sunny weekend we had together wasn't it?'

'Yes, love. At least you both had that together.' Clara couldn't help but emphasise the brighter side of life. This was such a crushing blow for Tom. He'd always thought such a lot of his son, Dudley.

The front door burst open, Freddy was through straight up against the table with his Sunday school stamp book waving in front of him. 'Look Dad. I know what this is! Look.' His voice faded away. His was a surprise, a different kind of shock. He'd never seen his father in tears before. Freddy couldn't find any more words, so he just sat down opposite Tom and cried at the sight that confronted him. Nobody spoke.

The next four years seemed colourless, sombre grey. The adults went on with their regular routine. Tom did his bakery round, often coming home mourning the loss of yet another young life they'd never see again.

Clara experienced a stomach-tightening fear as she opened a letter from Frankie saying he was posted, but he didn't say where. Rose wrote to say Leslie sent cards regularly to her and that a young woman had turned up on the doorstep one day asking her to please let her know if Rose heard news of Leslie because the War Office only made contact with the closest relative. So Leslie still hadn't let his mother know about his love. Frankie had mentioned that her name was Charmian Judge, in one of his letters home.

'Poor girl,' Clara said to Tom. 'Les really ought to have introduced her to his mother before he went overseas.' Tom said it didn't sound like the lad had had the time.

'Be kind, Rose. I know how the girl feels,' Clara wrote to her sister, 'don't leave her out in the cold. Share him. I'm sure Leslie would appreciate it.' That didn't go down too well with her possessive sister, but needed saying.

Leslie sent a card occasionally to Aunt Clara but she wasn't able to write back, he never gave an address. It wouldn't be wise to write a letter to Leslie at Rose's address, his mother would only open it and that would cause ructions.

With all the young men away in France, it didn't take long to find Freddy a job when he left school. Odd jobs like boot cleaning at one of the smaller hotels suited him well. He went off to work full of his new life but the hotel soon suggested he lived in because they needed him to work late and early. Freddy seemed willing as it wasn't far away so he often came home for tea with his mum, and to bring and collect his washing. He often forgot, so Tom got him an old worn-leather music case from Alf Moffat. Before he returned to work next time, Clara handed him the case saying, 'Here Freddy, never leave the hotel to come home without your music case.' Freddy looked puzzled. 'Make sure your dirty washing's inside. Mum will exchange it for your clean washed clothes.'

It did the trick and it also created a bit of joshing from the other young chaps working at the hotel. 'Off t'yer music lesson again Fred?' they'd call out. At least if he'd forgotten the bag he'd be reminded to fetch it before he got too far. But, as Clara wrote to Frankie, 'My heart aches for Freddy. On so many occasions he's come home with his washing and I can see he's been bullied and pushed about. He never says, but there's the tell-tale bruises and angry marks on his arms where he's been punched and there's the pants he rinsed out so I won't see he's had an accident. He must be so frightened at times. Dad says don't go and complain to management, it'll only make it worse for the lad.'

As for Jimmie and Dolly, they scrambled and skipped their way through those four years, their awareness breaking in and out of the adults' sad moods. Life was a pageant to them.

'What's all this?' Clara asked, looking hard at Dolly.

'She bumped 'er 'ead,' Jimmie answered.

'No, I'm not looking at her head. What are all these white dog hairs down the front of Dolly's coat. Where did they come from?'

'Dolly bumped her head,' repeated Jimmie, 'so the hurdy gurdy man gave 'er a cuddle an' sat Twister on her lap while 'e rubbed her head better.' Having finally got that out, Clara and Tom turned to Dolly.

'I fell over,' was her bald reply.

'But the hurdy gurdy man's up by the Clock Tower. What in the world were you doing up there?'

'Listening,' the children said in unison as if their mother must be stupid. After all what else would you be sitting on the pavement beside the

374

hurdy gurdy doing but listening?

'Oh an' Dolly started dancin' to the music an' tripped up,' Jimmie enlarged on the story.

Clara turned to Tom. 'That's right, up at the Clock Tower, Tom.'

'Clara, these two probably know more about the courts and twittens around the town than we do.'

'An' we like his dog Twister too, Daddy,' Jim said. Tom raised his eyes and shrugged.

'Let's get that coat off then Miss, we'll take it out in the yard and give it a good hard brushing. I don't know what Trilby will make of all these dog hairs though.'

Dolly followed Jimmie into all his scrapes. He had his pals but she was as scruffy and daring as they were. She could match them with scabby knees, broken nails and a head topped by straight tufts and clumps of hair, in stark contrast to her brother's shiny curls. The only time they sat still was inside the overwhelming high void that was St Bartholomew's church. Dolly gazed into the gigantic space where the priests and nuns seemed to float, the fabric of their billowing black robes wafting incense through the air.

The pair loved the church school one day and hated it the next. Dolly despised the little girls in her class who came to school in the mornings dressed up in sparkling white starched lacy-edged pinafores and went home still sparkling white and lacy at the end of the day, not a curl on their heads out of place. Even worse, on school photograph day, a great display of beads also came out on show. Jimmie didn't care.

The one thing the pair did notice, along with every adult, was the distant boom of the great guns across in France. One morning before Tom went off to work, he and Clara were sitting at the table with their breakfast cup of tea. There was a distant rumble like thunder – you couldn't quite tell whether it was in the ground or in the air.

Tom said, 'There they go at it again.'

Clara's answer was, 'I'm just glad that Grandfather never lived to hear such horror. Church bells would have been the loudest sound he ever heard in his lifetime.'

11

Clara

In their early years together when Tom and Clara lived in Kemp Town, it was Tom's job to expand the bakery's rounds among the wealthy households beyond Sussex Square, Lewes Crescent and Arundel Terrace. The new rich, moving into houses further out along towards Ovingdean and Rottingdean tended not to have large retinues of servants with cooks who baked for the family seven days a week. These customers expected fresh bread and cakes every day and especially late on Saturdays, consequently Tom's week ended later and later.

Before the children arrived, the couple often enjoyed their omnibus rides on Sundays out to

Lewes to have tea with Clara's brother and sister-in-law, Jack and Pearl, or over to Worthing to Tom's son Dudley and his wife Sybil. Tom particularly appreciated the bus rides, 'for the long sit down'. Although they loved the Sunday journeys they reciprocated when Tom's grandchildren came with their parents or Jack and Pearl brought their little ones to Brighton for the day. Tom would go for a lunchtime drink with the men while Clara prepared Sunday dinner. The first time the men went off to the pub, they didn't return when Clara had said the meal would be ready. That day both families had come over from Worthing and Lewes, a lovely gathering. So when the four children were needing to eat, and Sybil and Pearl were looking forward to enjoying a meal cooked for them, no fathers reappeared.

Clara said, 'I'm not going to the pub to rake the men out and neither are you two. It's beneath our dignity. If they can't come back in time after we've worked on our day off, they can have cold food.'

'Clara, aren't yer bein' a bit bold?' her sister-in-law warned.

'No Pearl, I'm not. My grandparents believed it took two to manage a business and keep their family together. I know Tom and your husbands need a day off, but so do we women.'

'You're right Clara, but it's always the men who are head of the household, isn't it?'

'Let them think they are Syb. It was Tom whose idea it was that I shouldn't be a servant anymore. I'm not a servant now. C'mon, we'll have our dinner while it's lovely 'n' fresh cooked.'

So the women and children enjoyed their hot dinner. When they'd finished they piled the washing up in the scullery and left three plates of food on the table for the men when they decided to return. Luckily it was a beautiful sunny day so the three women took the children down onto the beach.

Steak and kidney pudding, boiled potatoes and cabbage congealing in its gravy, alongside three bowls of cold apple pie and custard with a skin, wasn't what the men had expected. When they all met up again at tea time, the women found the men asleep in the armchairs. It was not a man's job to wash up, although they had cleared the table. And that was a first!

The children jumped all over their fathers and grandfather, waking them with a start, a groan and a growl.

'Where've you been?' The children wanted to know. 'We've bin paddlin', you should've come.'

Tom told them they'd been paddlin' too, but got lost in the crowd. 'We'll come with you next time.'

Tea with bread, butter and cakes from Clara's oven calmed the situation. The children had loved their day out. Clara and Tom waved their relations off on their buses down at the Valley. Tom turned to Clara and said, 'Let's blow the air clear love. I'll see that won't happen again.'

As they walked arm in arm back up through Kemp Town to their flat, Tom told her she'd missed out on the expectations of the working man. Clara couldn't believe her ears. What did he mean?

'You've always worked for the gentry. They expect you to have their meals ready on time and they were usually there at table regular, weren't they?'

'Yes, of course,' she replied.

'They also called upon your time because they considered it belonged to them.'

'I suppose that's true, Tom. But what are you meaning?'

'A working man gets one day a week and expects to do what he wants on his day off. I thought you might have heard Jack and Dudley shouting the odds right down there on the beach. Dear oh dear, were they angry!'

'Were they?'

'You're not used to the working man,' Tom exclaimed. 'A woman's place is to get her husband's dinner. They couldn't believe what you did. My father would have beaten Mum if she had left him to get his own food.'

'Would he? How barbaric.'

'Clara, you've been in service too long. But let's get over this. I know how you feel. You need your time off too. I'll make sure we do something different next time when they come. Summer will be here. We'll all go out with a picnic.'

'Bit unusual for working class men ain't it, Tom?'

'Nar then, don't you be so cheeky my wench.'

'Ha, if it's a wench you're after, I'm well past that age.'

Maybe Tom was one of the old school but he was mature enough to see other people's point of view, and he could see a housewife needed her rest day too.

When they moved to St George's Mews down in the centre of the town, Tom's rounds took him daily up the steep hills stretching out around through the streets of terraced houses that had grown up over the previous twenty to thirty years, to house a growing population of workers at the railway carriage works and shunting yards. These growing families bought larger quantities of bread, although fewer cakes, and didn't expect deliveries after midday on a Saturday. Being able to finish by one o'clock on Saturdays allowed Tom to return to the routine of his younger days. After a quick bite at home he would go up to the barbers in Sydney Street to have a close shave, beard and hair trim. The barber had a notice on the wall above the mirror saying 'Our shaves are bridegroom close'. After his shave and trim, Tom went to the slipper baths in North Road, before the war when there was the Sunday excursion to look forward to. The barber and bath made Saturday afternoon even more enjoyable.

Now with Dudley gone and Sybil moved away with the children back to her old home in Somerset, he told himself to make the most of this luxury particularly as Clara used to say she had a new bridegroom every Saturday night. It always amused him, that little quip. While he shaved every evening after work, the light in the scullery was not enough for him to make much of a job of it himself. The bakery expected their roundsmen to keep themselves smart.

Tom had been given to believe his service to the bakery in establishing new customers, widening the business and managing the rounds in the eastern part of the town, would bring him part ownership of the family business. But instead, his cousin took on a new partner and Tom never heard anymore of his prospects. Nevertheless, his secret disappointment never changed his attitude to the service he gave his customers.

Tom had always been an early riser, going downstairs at four thirty in the morning to stir the fire in the small range and put the kettle on to boil while he dressed in the warm kitchen. Clara followed soon after, making the tea and making sure her husband ate some breakfast. Theirs was a quiet, loving and comfortable relationship. He left for the bakery yard to feed and water his horse and stock the wagon ready to be out on his round by five thirty. Clara rarely returned to bed. She was able to do heavy washing or baking unhindered in the hours before the children woke. And there were the stock bones and vegetables to collect for her lunchtime broth for the workmen in the yard.

From the very first week of the war, in August 1914, Tom had listened daily and sympathised with women on their doorsteps. Various members of the families he served, stopped him in the street to talk about the loss of yet another son, husband or loved one. None knew he'd lost his own loved and sorely missed son. That remained a gaping hollow deep down inside where he dare not allow himself to go.

As time went by, Tom worried about the terrible demise in the male population. Some weeks his hours were longer when yet another roundsman went off to fight. Then great gaps where there were no customers at all, where whole areas went quiet as families moved away because their bread-winner had been killed. Widows had to leave their houses, children were dispersed among other family members, or even abandoned to roam the streets and sleep in neighbours' yards. A woman from Gloucester Street who lost her husband and oldest son was thrown out of the rented house, and went demented with sorrow. Her children scattered, begging and hiding until the town authority rounded them up. An elderly couple in Bridgen Street left a note on their door saying 'no more bread' and another in the milk bottle, 'no more milk', then starved themselves to death behind locked doors. Both their sons had been killed and they hadn't even told the neighbours. In Albion Hill, a tiny baby was heard whimpering in a darkened house days after his mother had cut her wrists when she'd read the telegram informing her of her husband's death.

Even the horses left to pull the delivery carts were getting too old and weak. On top of all that, a spate of horse stealing broke out. It meant the few men left working the rounds in the central part of town had to take turns to sleep at the stables. Even though padlocks were used on all the gates and doors, thieves got in during the night because carcasses of the horses stolen from a nearby dairy were discovered in a slaughter yard being cut up for their meat.

On the home front in 1915, Clara went along to the Town Hall and volunteered to help with packing first aid kits. Rolling bandages and cutting lint and gauze dressing patches made her feel she was doing a bit more than sitting at home alone knitting socks and mufflers. Each woman on the team had to take their own large white apron and roll their hair away in a tight scarf. Tom didn't like that much. 'Putting away all that lovely hair,' he'd said. Never mind, she was performing an essential service for the boys. After all, she told her husband, my brothers are out there too. He didn't really approve of her working. He believed the husband should be the breadwinner. Growing up among country folk, Clara knew it was normal for wives to work alongside their husbands, taking part in the family income. Naturally Tom didn't say no to the bit extra Clara made with her lunchtime cups of broth for the workmen. She was determined her children would have shoes and clean clothes, even if they were second-hand. Some neighbours' children had no shoes and their mothers didn't know how to alter and darn to give hand-me-downs a second or even third life.

With the war situation becoming ever more worrying, the loss of life affected every family in one way or another, Clara had to be satisfied with the little that society allowed women to participate in when they also had a husband and children to care for.

Although she was more active in a practical sense than many women, she preferred not to take part in such antagonistic activities as those that the Suffragettes performed. Her ways were positively aimed at earning to aid her family circumstances at home and for the men fighting away from their homes. She was uncomfortable with the loud, unladylike antics the Suffragettes displayed even though she agreed with their. cause. It was the class attitude she found obnoxious. As when the likes of Mrs. Miss or the Honourable came swanning into the workroom to roll a few bandages that all needed re-rolling after they'd left, having declared total exhaustion when they'd given barely half an hour, only to be praised to the high heavens and rewarded with a medal and their faces in the local newspaper. That's what made Clara and other working class mothers so exasperated. But she held her tongue – an untimely comment could have you put in prison. Better to keep her family with a mother, best to keep your thoughts to yourself.

Now her life was fuller than ever, with two young children at home and Freddy often much in need of her support, and her daily broth in demand by about twenty older workmen in the yard, and that included her three neighbours on Monday wash day who each took their turn to heat the washing water in their coppers, leaving Clara to carry on with the broth making. Jenny would take on the heavy soiled rubbing while Clemmie took her turn to thump the dolly or use the wash board. All hands were needed working along the backyards to twist and pull the bed linens ready for the wringer. Besides the sun for bleaching, they prayed for windy days for drying, otherwise their families would be grumbling about damp washing flapping round their ears indoors all week. As they were doing their Monday morning's washing Clara would often think of her mother Emily and her neighbours who washed sheets and pillow cases all week long for the local hotels. It was one way the women could earn a few pence. Besides her bandage rolling three afternoons a week, Clara took time to write to Rose in Putney and to as many of her large extended family. She was still their 'little mother'.

This was nothing new to Clara. Running the Whitesides' kitchen had been a busy full-time existence and before that she'd coped with all the baking at the Blue Rooms tea shop, even when she was pregnant. Ah, but then in those days she was younger. Other women might look old and raddled in their mid thirties, but Clara looked the picture of health. Tom was now sixty-six and people thought this straight-backed man with his clear eyes and skin was only in his forties.

What Clara knew was how to feed her family fresh, health-giving meals. Granma Annie and Mrs Charlish had taught her well. Besides, she'd always kept her eyes and ears open to news especially if it was about food production. In 1901 she'd heard about the discovery of what were called vitamins, from the reports she saw in the day-old newspapers that came down to the kitchen at the Whitesides'. At the public reading rooms she'd read the reports on the newly discovered food constituents in *The Times* newspaper and various magazines. Clara had a little chuckle to herself because Granma Annie would often say to the gathered grandchildren, 'Here's something that will make your bones grow stronger.' Or 'Here we are, good greens, this'll give your skin a bright glow.'

When they came down to live in the centre of the town, Clara had noticed children scratching their skin. Parts of the old town centre were tightly packed flint and crumbling brick cottages around small crowded courts. Arched byways under some upper floors connected by narrow twittens were often dark, airless and smelled bad, unlike the Kemp Town and Queens Park areas where the houses and stable yards were large and wide and youngsters had room to play free in the clearer air. Wherever you went in Brighton, the air was dirty with smoke in the winter months, although the west wind off the sea tended to keep the atmosphere fairly clear – except, that is, in the close-packed old town area. There was good water off the chalk Downs in abundance but some women didn't wash or keep their children clean. A good number of mothers still went by the old ways, wrapping their children in larded rag body belts throughout the winter. Clara could see you could hardly blame these women; they did their best in brutally poor circumstances. She herself showed her own children how to keep clean, especially their hands and faces. It could be quite an uphill struggle with Jimmie and Dolly at times. More important, she warned her three to keep their distance when they saw other children scratching. Impetigo was rife at times and as people scratched, they shed the yellow crusty skin from the pustules that the scars produced. She'd never turn a child away but it was always a drink sitting outside on the cobbles. Their own cottage was cramped enough and impetigo was highly contagious, you had to look after your own, teach them good sense. 'Never drink out of anyone else's cup,' she warned.

One thing Clara had always believed in was cod liver oil. Although money was so often in short supply, Clara knew how to stretch everything as far as it would go. You didn't need piles of food to keep well, 'What you need is the right food,' she'd tell the family. Meals were small and nourishing, you could always fill up with porridge and the potato bread she made on wash days when the range fire was built up for hot water. It was, Freddy said, the real reason he came home, 'For a good meal Mum, the hotel staff food was little better than pig swill.' And Clara discovered her belief in cod liver oil was right. It wasn't long after she had finally persuaded Freddy to have a teaspoonful each day that his memory for words and ability to keep his mind on the job in hand changed out of all recognition. He would never be a bright lad but his life was transformed, with confidence in his own ability to cope once he'd given in to Clara and started taking the oil, even though he didn't like the taste. He was converted. It certainly kept Tom in good health. Out in all weathers every day, he'd hardly ever had a cold. His hair and beard remained thick and glossy after it was well into steely grey. He looked handsome, still unbent and with cheeks pink and weather bright.

Clara even shortened her skirts in the latest fashion, but not too much. Oh no, ladies who rolled bandages were not to be of that class. But as to what class they meant, Clara said she didn't know. The tarts on some street corners had showed off their ankles for years and now the well-off fashionable ladies did also. Clara felt a bit of an in-between. Tom told her he preferred her demure, and not to give anybody reason for criticism. Especially after he'd come in late from work one evening having seen a woman at the end of the mews flopping her breasts out to Alf Moffat. Poor old Alf was shocked and chased the woman off shouting, 'We don't want wimmin like you down 'ere givin' our workshops a bad name – be orf with yer.' Later Alf realised who the woman was. On the quiet, Clara also knew who she was, so the next day she left a jug of soup and a stale loaf off Tom's van on the woman's kitchen table, including a penny Alf had pressed into Clara's hand – 'Poor woman,' he said, 'an' she's got four littl'uns and old grandparents to care for. Living in the cottage the old grandfather rents is the only reason she and the kiddies have a roof over their heads.'

Clara had noted the bare kitchen. She knew the husband had been killed in 1914. Nobody was well off down their way. Those that could, tried to help – to do their bit you would say.

News from across the Channel came regularly from Leslie to his mother, Rose, in long, albeit heavily censored letters and a series of colourful silk-embroidered postcards. Clara was delighted when she received one of the beautiful cards from her nephew. Frankie wasn't over in France so he didn't have those cards to send – his letters were on thin paper containing the part of his news he was able to get through the censors.

'Amazing what you find yourself caught up in

during war time,' he commented. 'Don't ask, I can't tell you more.' No more information came from Frankie. 'You'll be seeing my pal Arthur Levett. He's being sent back to Blighty, had his foot shot off. Go and see him for me will you, Mother?' When she did find Arthur, he hadn't lost his foot, well, not all of it. He told Clara that Frankie was with the army in Dublin. Clara had been too busy with her own life and family affairs to read the newspaper hoardings.

Rose had kept Clara regularly in touch with Leslie's news, then suddenly his letters stopped and Rose became frantic, sending Clara two and three letters a day until she had news that Leslie had been wounded. Rather badly in fact, being returned to England with a nasty lump of shrapnel in his chest. For some time, nobody knew exactly where he was or even if he would live. He was unable to write so it was a while before his story came to light.

It happened in the Ypres salient in November 1917. Leslie was in the Royal Engineers, taking part in Haig's offensive; it was their job to clear debris from roadways and rebuild bridges. Their work was mostly carried out during the hours of darkness, especially where they were near to the front lines. On this particular night, they'd been kept busy clearing huge unwieldy pieces of immobilised equipment strewn along a large area. Their aim was to get a road through by daylight. The work was taking longer than expected because they couldn't get their heavy moving gear into place. The light came up before their objective was complete. Leslie and his unit tried to heave away one last blockage but, unusually for that November, the day dawned bright clear, almost a spring-like dawn. While the men were struggling in their determination, the pilot of a spotter plane caught sight of them still out in the open and near to a German line. They should have left immediately. They did not. So, before Leslie and his pals did leave the site and run for cover, another plane came over dropping bombs onto the road, making a series of craters, destroying their hard work and setting their aim back at least two days. All six men in the unit were injured. Four died and two were badly wounded; one of those was Leslie. They lay in the ditch they had been making until darkness came ten hours later. It was in those hours that the four men died. Stretcher bearers could only proceed past forward positions under the cover of darkness and in this case, near silence with guarded torchlight.

Weeks later Leslie was able to write to Rose himself. He was in hospital somewhere in Scotland. He told her he was 'going on well' but would have to remain in hospital as the wound in his back was deep and had not yet started to heal. He had a drain in the wound, which was receiving constant attention to avoid infection, he told her. Not to worry because the nurses were wonderful. It was at this time that Leslie started to end his letters with 'Chin chin' and he carried on doing it for the rest of his life.

Rose's letters to Clara passed on news of Leslie's progress, but she was bothered that the busy nurses weren't feeding him enough or, she maintained, he'd be getting better more quickly. 'Oh why this, or oh why that,' Rose kept questioning, until finally she snapped. That day Clara had a letter from Rose posted on the station just before she boarded the morning train, telling how she'd found out the name of the hospital and was on her way to Edinburgh to sort them all out.

'Typical Rose,' Clara said to Tom as she read Rose's letter to him that evening. 'I can just see her. Coat on, hat firmly on her head, storming off. I bet they'll be pleased to see her. The Scots can be pretty Joe Blunt.' And so they were it seems.

Rose arrived at the hospital to find her boy had only the previous day been sent down to the south coast to convalesce. To Bexhill, the report said. Rose kicked up a hell of a stink. Was she mad! Was she?

'But Mrs Collins,' the Sister said. 'You should have written before you set out on such a journey. We'd have told you to wait, you would have not needed to waste your time and money.'

Forty-eight hours later, Rose walked into the convalescent home for wounded soldiers in Bexhill to find her son on a stretcher bed out on the lawn in the sun. Beside him was a visitor.

'Sorry, only one visitor at a time,' the Sister told Rose.

'But I'm his mother and I've come on a very long journey to see my son.'

'Well now, there's a few minutes left of the visiting hour. I'll see if the young lady is willing to let you have the remaining time.'

Rose was mad all over again. 'I had just five minutes with him,' she told Clara.

'No, we won't let you stay any longer, even

391

though you are his mother. He's been very ill, Mrs Collins and he needs his rest. Come again next Sunday.'

'I refused to leave,' Rose said, 'not until I was allowed to speak to the doctor.'

Tom and Clara sat at the table opposite Rose listening silently as she railed against authority and the hospital services in particular.

'He gave me permission to visit for half an hour tomorrow. I don't know what I would have done if he hadn't. So here I am. Let me sleep in the armchair tonight, Clara. I'll be away early in the morning but you're nearer than it is to go all the way back to Putney.'

Rose and Clara had time for a short sister-to-sister chat. But it struck Clara that Rose was angling to move away from Putney and London altogether, mainly to distance Leslie from the lady friend. She didn't ask anything about the young woman but she was sad for Leslie, especially after all he'd been through. Knowing her sister, she could see she'd get her own way in the end.

Next morning as Rose was pushing Kirby grips into the knot of hair high upon the nape of her neck, she half turned to Clara saying, 'An' yer know what, Clara? The young hussy had her hair loose hanging down all round her shoulders. An' during the daytime, at that!'

The war was taking its toll with everybody. It seemed to be grinding on with no let-up in the numbers of men's lives being lost. Now another killer was visiting the families, this one was at home, and like 'over there' it had no class boundaries. The newspapers had been commenting for some time on how there were more and more deaths among the men from the influenza than from wounds inflicted by guns and gassing. As 1916 changed to 1917 and on into 1918, the numbers of Tom's customers dying from the flu was reaching significant numbers.

If only this horrible war would stop, people were complaining. All the huge patriotic enthusiasm of 1914 had drained away, everybody had had enough. Most families were at their lowest ebb in 1918. Only the destitute felt a little hope when food cards were issued in March of that year. There were so many other worries piling up all around. By the end of 1918 with the prospect of another winter to get through, it was hard to rejoice when the church bells rang out as the guns silenced. So many and so much had been lost and was still being lost.

Clara could see a great change had come over her husband. With two young children still to feed, Tom could not think of retirement, they had no money for that luxury even though he was nearly seventy. Clara did her utmost to keep him as well as she could, like giving him his breakfast in bed on Sunday mornings. Dolly and Jimmie still sat beside him to hear what he'd done during the week. It was a close family time. Tom listened to their excited banter, noting between the real truths the scrapes they'd just avoided. Clara was watchful because he would always let Dolly have a taste of his boiled egg.

'Tom, you eat your egg. Dolly and Jim have had theirs.' So she decided to wait until the pair had gone to Sunday school before taking his egg and toast up to him.

Their mews cottage didn't have a foot scraper set into the wall beside the front door like they did in the better houses in Gloucester Street, and when Clara put a tough mat on the cobblestones outside their front door, it prompted some passerby to remark loudly, 'The neighbours are gettin' a bit above 'emselves.' The mat barely lasted 24 hours before it was pinched.

Each evening during those winter months she'd hang Tom's work clothes, especially his greatcoat, in the scullery near the banked-up range fire. Remembering the layers of capes the old coach drivers used to wear in the days of her youth, Clara had got some oiled cloth and made a shoulder cape for Tom to take on the van ready to tie on when the rain came down. She did her best to keep everybody well in a house where everyone came straight into the one living room through the front door, straight out of the weather, bringing in the last dirty crusts of snow and muck on their boots and drips off cold, wet coats.

Tom shook and shrugged as much of the wet from his cape outside the front door and shuddered as he came in out of the icy slush and rain. 'When will this everlasting downpour stop?' he grumbled, moving carefully through a dimly lit living room into the scullery.

'Here, let me.' Clara went behind him to lift the cape off his shoulders, shaking it outside the door in the yard. 'Off with that sodden coat.' Hanging the heavy coat on the back door, she gave him a towel for his head and face. 'At least this rain is

394

clearing the last of the snow away,' she said.

'Young 'uns are quiet,' he said through the warmth the towel was bringing to his bearded face.

'They're in bed.'

'What's up? Not well?' He looked concerned at her abrupt answer.

'No, punishment.' Clara turned away, busying herself to make his pot of tea to avoid his seeing the tears forming in her eyes.

'Now what they been up to?' She turned and looked directly at him. 'Oh no, love. What's the matter? Come 'ere, give us a cuddle.'

'No, Tom. I'm too angry for that.' He looked at his wife questioningly and she inclined her head towards the living room. Taking a peek into the room he couldn't see much, for there was only a single candle on the dresser.

'I thought it was a bit dim when I came through.' Clara could see he hadn't noticed the reason. Then the penny dropped. 'Where's the la... Oh no, they haven't broken your lovely wedding present? Oh Clara! Oh dear! How did that happen?'

'Playing ball across the table,' she said with a brisk clip to her words, immediately backed up with reasoning on their behalf. 'You know what awful weather it's been, they've been shut in for days, just got silly and over-excited. Lucky I hadn't refilled with paraffin this morning.'

'No chance of repairing it?'

'No, gone to smithereens.'

'Who was responsible?'

'Both. I've made them go to bed with no supper. They've got to learn.'

'Come on, let's have our food. I'm not going up to them. No more words will make it better.'

The blue-glass paraffin lamp had given Clara such pride to own. Apart from spreading the family table with such good light for sewing and reading, it had been a gift to her in recognition of the esteem from the Whiteside family, thanking her for the years of loyal service. She was proud of that. Tom knew they could never afford its like again.

'I know it's only an object, Tom,' Clara said while they sat at the table eating their meal, 'but it feels like a part of my life has gone.'

'I feel that too, love. It's not many employers who'd say thank you like that, especially you having left them. Oh well,' he sighed, 'I'd better see if I can find something that will come somewhere near the light it gave. We've been spoilt all these years.'

A thudding of heavy boots out in the yard and a rattle on the door knocker made Tom jump to his feet. Lifting the edge of the curtain, 'Who's that this time o' night?' he called, peering at the two soldiers silhouetted against the gas lamp high on Alf Moffat's workshop wall opposite. Tom couldn't let soldiers wait out in the cold. Pulling back the heavy drapes from across the door, he opened it wide and saw two hopeful faces, great packs on their backs, standing in the rain.

He'd said, 'Come on in lads,' before he knew who they were. Hardly had the second figure come through into the living room than he heard Clara cry out from behind him, her voice full of excited joy.

'Albert!' Never mind the wet clothes! Her arms were round him in a great hug, 'Oh my lovely boy.' As she stepped back to look at her youngest brother, she realised Edward was there too. 'Eddy, Eddy! Dear me.' He got the next big hug. Clara's apron was wet through; she didn't care. 'Oh it's so wonderful to see you both.'

Tom was shaking their hands; he just hadn't expected to see family. The pair looked so much older now than the seventeen- and eighteen-year-olds who went away to war.

Clara was overwhelmed with joy, fetching dry towels to mop the wet off their faces and hair. 'Rattle up the fire, Tom. Fate knew you two were coming tonight. I made extra broth today so there's plenty left over. Sit you down dears. I'll be back in a trice.'

And so she was. Two bowls of steaming vegetable soup and a loaf of new bread heated up above the range fire.

'I've given the lads a warm from the medicine cupboard, Clara,' Tom said as Clara came back into the room.

'Couldn't have thought of better myself,' she replied. Tom winked at the brothers. 'Clara Ann's still our "little mother".' Trilby had already picked the first lap to sit on. She'd commandeer the other before the night was out. Eddy played with her, and Albert was still and peaceful to sleep with.

'You look well,' Tom told them. 'Uninjured we hope?'

'Pure bloody luck,' answered Eddy between mouthfuls. 'Cor that's 'ot,' he exploded. Albert was tucking in. No time to talk just yet. The brothers had been lucky to stay together all through the battles. They had been young errand boys at the local cottage hospital when the war broke out and immediately volunteered to go over the Channel to serve as stretcher bearers.

Clara and Tom had heard from Emily that that was what the boys were doing. To be quite honest, Tom never mentioned his concern to Clara, but he didn't expect to see them again. ''Bout the most dangerous job to do wasn't it lads?' he asked.

'Yep,' replied Albert. It raised the spirits to hear such a light-hearted reply from one who must have seen the worst.

'I know what you're thinking, Tom,' said Eddy, 'there's no hidin' it. The job was terrifying at times, ghastly too. We had to be light-hearted when we could, it was the only way.'

'It's a damn miracle we didn't get injured. Most of our mates were killed.'

Clara was watching and listening. Her brothers looked more than ten years older – maybe more even than she knew they were.

When they'd told Clara their plans to drop in to see friends and family in Brighton then walk most of the way back home to St Leonards, she said nothing except, 'Come on then, Tom. You've a four-thirty start in the morning. Here's some blankets and it's these two armchairs by the fire for the rest of tonight. There'll be beds upstairs for as long as you want to stay, from tomorrow night.'

'Ah, lovely, better 'n the Dorchester,' Albert said, putting on a posh voice as he shimmied himself deep in his chair.

'Ooh, love yer both, come 'ere.' She couldn't get enough of them; they laughed and returned all her cuddles and kisses. 'Thank God, you're both home safe.'

The tears flowed as she went up to bed. Mustn't be too soppy with them she thought. It was so strange to see her baby brother with a moustache.

'Does yer heart good to see them tho' doesn't it, love?' Tom said before he fell asleep.

Clara thought it was a relief to see Tom's worry lines relax in the few hours noggin' and natter with two young men, looking ahead into their lives. Yes, a blessed lift for her husband's flagging spirit.

It was nearly five o'clock before Tom hurried down into the kitchen. The fire was bright, the teapot covered with its cosy on the table and milk in the cups. A small figure stood beside the fire, hands behind his back.

'Sorry Daddy,' came a subdued voice.

Tom was in a hurry. He daren't be late. He'd been warned there'd be another man short on the rounds this day. As he scrambled into his clothes and drank his cup of tea, Jimmie held out a piece of bread and butter. 'Shall I take a cup up to Mum, Daddy?'

'Why not? I'll be off now. Just remember this. You're the eldest and old enough to know better. You're too boisterous, lad. That was a precious gift and Mum treasured it. I'll see you all later. And thanks for the tea. I know you're a good boy.'

The Willows

'That pair could be such wild little things. She was ten, he eleven. Violet May followed everything Jimmie did, so he'd get more extreme. Not naughty mind, just pushing to greater deeds.' The knowing comment came from Mrs P.

'He was showing off. If he'd had brothers at home they would have tempered his ways,' added Rosie.

'Yes, but there were. Frankie had tried and Freddy wasn't capable. Not like Clara's big family. No checks and balances of characters,' sighed Mrs P. 'Not only that, you know how Tom worried so about there being fewer men to keep the community together. He said it seemed the whole of society was in danger of becoming a strengthless brew.

'Tom paid five shillings for a new oil lamp to replace the one the children had broken. Jimmie stood awkward beside his father in the shop until he spotted something up on a shelf.

'"Can I buy that chamberstick for Mum?" he asked his father. "It's short and stubby and won't get knocked over like the tall ones, an' she needs another one up in the bedroom while Albert and Eddy are using ours." His father was watching the shopkeeper carefully wrapping the new oil lamp.

'"It's a Willow pattern one," persisted Jimmie.

'"That one's tuppence, an' I'll throw the snuffer in for the same price," the shopkeeper told Jimmie, who immediately smacked his two pennies savings down on the counter. '"Please Dad?" he asked again.

'"Yes Jim. Mum will be pleased with that."

'"I wish I could have bought her the oil lamp, Dad."

'"It'll be some years before you can afford that kind of money son. But never mind, you've thought of your mother – she'll like that tubby little candlestick."

'There you are, 1919 – that's when I came into the family,' said Tubby, 'Eddy and Albert stayed two more nights an' I remember their happy talk.'

'Fanny was thrilled to see them when they called into her hat shop along in Hove,' added Hannah hat pin pot, 'but Peter, he was away in London training to manage the milliner's workshop and they heard Leslie had finally been discharged into his mother's care. So they didn't see either nephew or cousin on this visit.'

Clara

Jimmie and Dolly revelled in their uncles' company; they were so proud to have two soldiers of their own in their house. When it was time to leave, the lads marched off along the mews waving to everybody who'd come out of the workshops cheering them goodbye. On their way down towards the Steine they caught sight of Tom on one of his rounds, so they flung their arms around him, causing passing strangers to shout, 'Cheerio lads,' and 'Wonderful to have yer 'ome boys.'

Giving them a bag of sticky currant buns for the journey, Tom clapped each on the back saying, 'Come again soon. Yer sister thinks the world of yer.'

'Our Clara's got lucky after all, hasn't she, Ed? Grand chap, Tom.'

'Yep.'

'You still thinking of droppin' in at Westham on

401

our way through then Al?'

'Maybe.' Albert hesitated.

The Willows

'*I must have been sitting up there on that beam for a good ten years. Nobody noticed I was there. Nobody who would have known was around anymore,' mused a soft voice in the background.*

'*What's that you say Tommy?' called Uncle Bert from his place on the dresser. Big Pol leaned over to where she could see the small willow pattern pie dish sitting beside the sink, half full of old milk bottle tops and discarded silver foil.*

'*Yeah of course, Tommy, I'd forgotten you were at the Lamb. What 'appened to you then? You didn't get collected up with us and given to Clara. I don't remember how you got here.*'

'*Hooray, a story,' shouted the cruet set. They had only been at Deerfold since 1985 so they were keen to hear about Tommy's previous homes.*

'*We're all ears,' mumbled Ol' Po.*

'*Ha! Give yer clients a shock seeing yer bowl full o' ears Po!*'

'*No cheek now, Polly gal. Go on then Tommy, tell us all about it.*'

'*Around February 1919 it was. The barn door was always left hangin' 'alf open them times. I spied a couple of soldiers swinging along the lane headin' up to the inn. It was lunchtime and a few of the locals had already wandered in for a half.*'

'*What were yer doin' in a barn then, Tommy?' interrupted one of the triplets. 'You bein' a pie dish n' all.*'

'One of the buildings around the inn yard it was. The Lamb Inn, you know, Great-Great-Grandfather Johnny Pilbeam's place on the marsh. That barn used ter house the milk cow, an' some of Annie's sheep at times and her little "gorls", the chickens. They'd be in an' out the stalls. Up above were a hay store and up the end feed were kept. Clara Ann's brothers slung a rope over the beam when they were young boys, used ter swing up an' sit astride the beams, foolin' about an' tellin' jokes on wet days. Quite a hidey hole they had there. They'd be half asleep some afternoons cuddlin' the cats, those that would tolerate human touch, that is. After all they were mostly feral those cats. Some took food grabbing tit-bits from the youngsters' fingers but otherwise they'd back off smartish. Others, the lazy ones, would curl up among the children especially on the summer nights when Granma would let the boys sleep out camping in the barn, just on hot, dry nights of course. Young Albert was the only one who kept still long enough to accommodate a fluffy partner all the night through. Eddy, he actively put them off, never encouraged much close contact.'

'Interestin' you should say that,' cut in Big Pol. 'I remember hearing Eddy's eldest son talking to Lily when he visited us here at Deerfold. He said his father never gave him and his brothers and sisters any loving cuddles when they were little children.'

'That was a few years back wasn't it, Pol?' remembered Ol' Po. 'That must've been sometime in the 1980s.'

'Come on, Tommy, go on with your story,' called out one of the little jugs. 'You still 'aven't told us 'ow you came to be out on a beam.'

'Started on the days when the local chaps brought

403

their terriers to a Meet it was. They all gathered in the yard chattin' like and the terriers were chasin' the cats an' of course all their food got gobbled up so the boys took me up on to one of the big cross beams in the barn so's the cats' grub was safe from those blinkin' terriers. Then I was forgotten wasn't I? Got left up there. It was when the two soldiers came out from the bar with their beer tankards and started talkin' over old times that I realised who they were, 'cos one said, "Not like Gramps used ter keep it."

'The other replied, "No. Bit warm 'n' weak."

'"Bet this bloke waters it down."

'"Still, it's better 'n a kick in the arse."

'Oh dear oh lor.' I about fell off the beam with excitement! They was Clara Ann's brothers, Albert and Eddy. I watched as the two young men leaned back leisurely against the wooden board wall, bits of rotting straw spread around.

'"After the mud of Flanders, even dry rotting straw's a luxury," Albert muttered.

'"Huh! Specially with no orders being shouted over our heads," Eddy laughed. They looked as if they were in bliss. I supposed they were feeling the quiet comfort of their childhood holidays. "Oh yeah, I forgot, some chap off the boat threw this bundle at me, said I needed it."

'"What's that then?" Eddy had pulled a brown envelope from his breast pocket flicking it across to his brother. Lazily Albert drew out a handful of coloured picture cards, shifting suddenly onto one elbow to take a better view. "Blimey boy, have yer looked at these?"

'"No, I told yer I forgot 'em." Eddy swivelled round on the greasy stalks, "What's up mate, you all right?"

'"Oh I'd say." Looking over Albert's shoulder Eddy

remarked, "Ah, I see. Yeah the chaps sometimes did that."

'"Not surprised with this lot ter look at." Albert adjusted his crotch and fell back into the deepening cradle, his wriggling body was getting all he could from the vision.

'"Yeah, she's a bit of all right she is." After a while, Eddy picked up the discarded cards.

'"This one's better than those." Albert sighed, holding one picture card above him as he lay enjoying his last moments of pleasure.

'"Give 'em 'ere then." They tussled a bit for it, Albert finally letting his brother have the card. Out of the corner of his eye he waited for the results. Nothing. Eddy looked through all six and put them into their envelope, buttoning the packet back into his pocket. Albert exploded, sitting bolt upright. '"What no…?"

'"Sorry Albi, I know the other lads reacted like you. But ever since Rus got his head tossed off his shoulders an' fell into me lap I've 'ad it. Jus' goes through me mind over n' over."

'Albert raised his hand. "Don't. I don't want to see it Ed. It gets me too. I know, I know. Bugger it. You think of the life they'll miss. Christ, Eddy, you've got to push it out of yer 'ead."

'"That's what the lads told me as gave us those cards, said if I didn't, I'd miss my future too!"

'"S'right." By now Albert was really deflated. They both sat forward draining their beer. Eddy spat the last bitter dregs. '"Naw, not like Gramps kept. Damn that buggering war."

'"Oh my word, take a look up there Ed." Albert had caught sight of something on one of the rafters. As he clambered onto the old pen boarding to reach above

405

his head Eddy recognised me. "The old cat dish!" they chorused.

'"Damn it boy, you're right." Albert gasped, jumping down holding his discovery.

'They blew away the chaff and scraped out a little of the years of congealed gunge, and my blue and white pattern saw the light again.

'"Ha, would you believe it!" For a few moments the brothers stood steeped in their memories.

'"Sunny ones?" asked Eddy.

'"Safe and sleepy." Albert answered with a gentle smile. "Yer know what, Ed, I'll take this to Clara next time I'm over ter Brighton. She'll love it."

'"You're right there." They both laughed at the thought. In those few minutes I felt I'd been welcomed like a part of the family and all sadness had been clean wiped away.

'"Thank yer landlord," they called, stomping their pots on the bar counter beside the newly installed pump handles.

'"Them flashy engines hasn't made 'is beer any better," remarked Eddy.

'With me stowed in Albert's pack, the pair swung away side by side down the lane towards Bexhill. Four years in the army had stamped its mark on Albert and Eddy's marching steps.

'That's how I left the Lamb Inn during the year 1919. But you'll have to wait to hear how I ended up here at Deerfold.'

12

Clara

Throughout her darkest night, Tubby's candle glowed. The room seemed crushed in silence.

Clara gently pulled the sheet edge across Tom's lifeless face. It was a reflex action. That's what you did when someone died. No. She couldn't do it. Uncovering his face, she smoothed the sweat-soaked sheet back and tucked the bedding in to make him comfortable the way she always had. Why put him away so soon, she thought. He can't have got very far yet.

Tom's alarm clock told her it was only half past four. The darkness was still pressing as she closed the curtains. Clara sank back into the wicker easy chair beside the bed where she had sat all night, even two whole days and nights. She had kept their low-ceilinged front bedroom well ventilated. Taking a deep, slow breath, she gazed at her dead husband's face and let the memories flood her mind, fill her vision.

The doctor had finally arrived, puffing up the narrow stairs, at half past ten last night. A weary, middle-aged, wing-collared man. He stayed all of five minutes.

'You've done well to keep him alive this long,' he informed Clara, when she told him Tom had taken to his bed two days ago on the Friday night as soon as he had arrived home from work.

'I could see he was more than just tired,' she whispered, half to herself, as the doctor felt Tom's pulse, then looked under his patient's eyelids and reported no hope.

'Just carry on keeping him comfortable.'

Oh, had this man become so inured to the sight of impending death, Clara thought as she followed him down the stairs. 'Is there nothing I can do, Doctor?' she asked.

He stopped momentarily and turned at the bottom stair. 'My dear, we have no cure for this. I have seen more than a hundred in your husband's situation this weekend alone. I won't give you hope where there is none. I can see you have nursed him lovingly.'

Taking her purse down from the dresser shelf Clara asked what she owed him.

'Look after yourself now. That's my payment.' Almost before he had finished the sentence, he'd closed the door gently behind him.

Climbing wearily back up the narrow, well-worn stairs she said, 'That was kind of him wasn't it, Tom?' Clara spoke to her husband as she always had. After all he was still there. Her dearest love, their life together had been blessed with such sweet harmony. He had looked after her so well. She'd been his wife for just seventeen years. When they married, he had been a widower of fifty-one in that flush of handsome, middle-aged virility a man gets in maturity. She hoped she had given him happiness. Well, she knew she had. Even her step-daughter had grudgingly told her so one evening when she had called in, as her father stepped through the door home from work, crouching low to balance one little child on his back, another tinier one under his arm and a small boy hanging onto his other hand. They were all four laughing 'fit to bust' he said as he set them all down to mill round his legs while he washed his hands and face at the scullery sink.

'Never heard Father laugh so much since Mother passed away,' Ethel blurted out. 'Don't let him overdo it. He's not a young man you know, Clara. Well, I must go. Bye, Dad.' Ethel didn't laugh. Life to Ethel was no laughing matter.

Tom had overheard his daughter's warning words, 'don't let him overdo it'. 'Tch! You can't overdo love. She wants to show her husband a bit of love for all that scent he must buy her. Place smells like a tart's boudoir when my daughter's been here,' he remarked.

Ethel always brought that kind of sarcasm out of Tom. He was never that way really. Laying the towel on the back of the chair, Tom put his arms round Clara and gave her a loving kiss. She responded, giving him a kiss, whispering in his ear, 'How many tart's boudoirs have you been in, Tom?'

'Countless.' He laughed. 'Had a busy day, love?'

'No more than you have dearest.' They stayed in their comforting embrace for a long moment. The children knew they would, so kept to the scullery. Freddy used to grab and hold the two exuberant babes until they realised this was a regular happening. Mummy and Daddy always had a loving cuddle when Daddy got in from work. They waited eagerly because they knew he would soon say, 'Come on, your turn now my little ones.' Tom had few worldly goods. No money. What he had he gave in abundance; love and kindness worth more than any riches.

Yesterday as Clara had held a feeding cup to Tom's parched lips, he had taken her arm and looked into her eyes. His words were a hardly audible croak, telling her he loved her and 'Thank you'. His head fell back, the effort had exhausted him. They were the last words he could manage. Right to the very end, she thought. Made his last effort to tell her he loved her.

'Remember how you used to sit down in my kitchen at the Whitesides' and give that deep sigh with your first mouthful of tea? Quite spent you were, last thing on a Saturday. But I could see you were at a real low ebb at that time. Remember that afternoon while you were sat at the end of the table? Colleen and Madge were there helping with preparations for an evening dinner party for the Whitesides and Colleen called out, "'Ere he comes, proper little bandbox our Frankie, don't 'e always look the young gentleman now?" The maids loved him comin' in when they were setting up the dining room an' him on his way back to the hotel. Always gave me a big hug before he left for work. I was so relieved when you said what a "fine young man" I had. That was some time before you asked me. Never showed you had a bad opinion of me. Thank you, Tom, I loved you for that. Even then, before you asked me. Before I even thought of ever marrying anybody.

'We did laugh on that first outing together didn't we? I couldn't believe my eyes how handsome you were dressed up, without that brown overall and striped apron with your money bag 'n' all. I was ever so proud to be on your arm, ever so proud.' Clara's voice trailed away.

'Oh, and weren't we happy our first months together in our little flat at Sussex Mews? I didn't know I could be so happy. The freedom of having my own front door, my own kitchen. You gave me that, Tom. You kept your promise. I felt like I was a child again roaming at will on the marsh. No. I felt like a queen, cooking for the one person I loved.

'And those evenings at the Old Oxford Playhouse before the children arrived in our lives. We did have some lovely times, didn't we? Nobody to ask me to bring them yet another tray of tea or stay back to make one more meal on my afternoon off.'

Silence overtook her, changing suddenly into an icy suffocating blanket of despair. Hot tears flowed. 'Oh, my God, what are we going to do without you? What am I going to do?'

A bubble of air rattled in Tom's throat and slipped, his lips jerking. Clara came out of her painful despair. Hope momentarily filled her eyes, before experience reminded her she had seen it all before when helping her own mother and grandmother perform their family duties. 'My poor darling, you've had a gruelling two days. You did try, dear. I know you struggled to stay with us. I wish I could have taken those heavy aching spasms from you.

411

'Oh Christ how I hate this damnable flu! It's nearly spring and I thought we'd managed to get through.' Clara had watched in horror as Thomas's life was sucked slowly from his body down into an endless dark pit, her inability to reach like finger-tip to finger-tip just beyond touch, as he sank deeper. The horror of that hateful flu would never leave her.

Tom had his own anger at the leaders who had taken all the young men to their deaths and the despair and hurt it had poured on the wives, children and families at home. The wasteful draining away of innocent men who had been so eager to defend their country. That had all seeped away from him, replaced by sorrow in his eyes, apologising for having to leave. It was a horror for both of them – for everyone.

She couldn't believe it had finally caught her family, so rapidly doing its worst. No warning, like an invisible cloak descending, destroying. Light was beginning to filter through the curtains. Clara hadn't noticed that the candle had guttered out long since while she had been talking to Tom, going through her memories with him as if he was her recovering patient. She fell into a fitful doze. It didn't last long.

A couple of taps on the door at the bottom of the stairs, followed by a quiet voice jolted her into awareness.

'You all right gal?' Jenny from next door gently pushed open the bedroom door. 'Can I come in luvvy?' Clara covered Tom's face.

'Come in, yes Jenny. It's all over.'

'Oh, so sorry my dear! I did wonder. I've sent

412

the children off to school. They've had a good breakfast. They're all right,' Jenny whispered.

The two women stood side by side in silent thought until Jenny felt she could be practical once more. Not wanting to miss catching the busy doctor, she touched Clara's elbow to bring her attention round. 'I saw Dr John's bike outside Joe's cottage. I'll fetch 'im shall I? Then he can give you a certificate.'

Pausing at the top of the stairs, she said, 'An' I'll go 'ome an' pick up my bag an' we'll take care of Tom together dear, between us. Don't worry, the kettles are on. I banked up the fire for you late last night.'

Clara whispered her thanks, wondering what she would do without good neighbours. Jenny was everyone's treasure, midwife, general nurse to all the families in and around the mews and the men in the workshops too. They often needed first aid care. She was the one person they'd call to attend an injury. Jenny saw the beginning and end of most of their lives, together with the closest member of their family. Nobody asked after her needs – she'd only respond with, 'Oh, don't worry luv, I'm all right.' Clara knew different. What you did for Jenny had to be without words, like it never happened.

It was Jenny who had persuaded Tom to stay home the night Dolly was born. Made him boil kettles and bring all she needed up to the bedroom door. Although he had been four times a father, two with his first wife then Freddie and Jimmie with Clara, this was the first time Thomas was allowed into the room only minutes after the

413

birth and had his baby put into his arms. He said she looked 'like a little dolly'.

Now, in that same room, Jenny and Clara, hushed and gentle, were giving Thomas the last domestic service behind closed curtains. Such a contrast from that joyful morning only eleven years before when he had thrown the same curtains open on a new life and let in the August sunshine.

When the room was cleared of everything attached to the two nights and days of illness, and Thomas was dressed in his Sunday suit, a fresh candle was lit and left burning on the night table. As directed by the doctor, the sheets and pillow slips were burned outside in the backyard before the two women sat down at the scullery table with a cup of tea.

'You've always got a pretty blue 'n' white cup 'n saucer for any who comes Clara,' Jenny commented, mostly to keep Clara's mind on other things a while longer.

'Turn yer cup over, I'll read yer leaves.' It was Clara's turn to indulge her neighbour this time. As she upended her own cup into the saucer, Grandfather John's words came into her head. With a chuckle he'd say, 'If you believe that you believe anything. Believe in yerself my gal. Keep strong.'

Just as she was about to tell Jenny's leaves, Freddy came bursting in through the front room, clapping the scullery door back against the staircase wall.

'Can I go up an' see Dad?'

'Sweetheart ... Daddy hasn't managed to get

414

through the night.'

Freddy pulled away from Clara. His voice rose, struck with hurt. 'But Mum, you said you'd tell me! Mummy, Mummee!' Denial started in his voice – he'd been betrayed – he couldn't believe they'd do that to him. He didn't understand.

'He's only just gone, Freddy.'

'Your dad couldn't wait any longer, Freddy luv,' Jenny offered. Oh dear, that was a wrong thing to say, because Freddy wanted to know why when his dad knew he would be back from his job as early as he could get away from the hotel.

'He asked that you take this certificate along to Mr Jessup for him, dear. You're the man in our family now, Freddy,' Clara cajoled. 'Give the paper to Mr Jessup, Daddy says, he'll know what to do. Come straight back,' she added. Although he was sixteen, she knew he could be easily distracted. 'Then you can go up to see Dad, you'll be his first visitor, dear.'

Trust somewhat restored, Freddy wasn't slow to catch on this time. 'Yes, I'll be first won't I?' Off he shot.

'Cap on Freddy, an' be sure to take it off in front of Mr Jessup before you give the paper,' she called after him.

As Jenny washed up the cups in the sink, Clara went to make sure the downstairs front room curtains were properly closed, then she and Jenny moved the chairs to stand against the walls. Clara collected up the few pieces of family detritus. There was a little petticoat she'd just finished for Dolly, although her daughter had given it a surly look saying she'd rather have a lace collar better 'n' Carol Sutton wore when they took the class photograph. Thomas had told his daughter that Mummy couldn't afford the kind of lace the Suttons went in for. Maybe she could learn to do tattin' like his own mother had done, then she could have a better collar.

Jimmie said, 'That silly gerul Sutton looked a chump in her fancy lace-edged collar 'n' pants anyway.'

Jenny broke through Clara's thoughts by saying, 'I'll see Jimmie 'n' Dolly have a bite when they get back midday an' Freddy too. And you need something, missus.'

'Oh I won't...'

'Now don't you be tellin' me what a mouthful of bread 'n' scrape will do. I'll not let you make yourself ill.'

Freddy collided with Jenny in the doorway as he came through, flinging his cap onto the hook behind the scullery door before he noticed his bad manners. 'Oh sorry, Mrs Starr.' Then he stood still facing Clara with a hopeful look, eyebrows raised.

'Come on love,' she smiled, opening the door at the bottom of the stairs. He followed her up. At the top, Freddy suddenly held back. 'Where is he?' Of course, this was the first time he had seen a dead person, so Clara went in ahead. However, another member of the family had got there before Freddy. Trilby was sitting on the chair Clara had so recently vacated beside the bed, just as if she had taken over the vigil.

'Oh look,' said Clara with some relief. 'Trilby's keeping Dad company.' It broke the tension for Freddy who immediately stroked the cat whis-

416

pering, 'Thank you' in her ear. While Freddy's attention was taken by the cat, Clara turned the sheet back from Thomas's face.

'Mum, why does Dad look better but he died?'

'All his cares are over, Freddy. That's what happens, dear.'

'Will I look like that when I'm dead?' he asked.

Clara found herself shuddering, surprised at his question. It made her hesitate, but not too long. 'Yes, my love. I'm sure you will. You're handsome like your father, Freddy dear.'

The sound of wood scraping on wood and a hiss of 'Take care' alerted her to the men on their way up the stairs with the coffin. 'Oh dear, they could have waited,' she thought.

'We'll take over missus. Go with yer ma, young feller. We'll bring yer pa down in a mo.'

Before Clara could edge her way past the men and the coffin, there came a sharp knock on the now open front door and a rasping voice called out, 'Come down please, missus.' No consideration for the bereaved or sensitivity in the presence of death. Clara had hardly reached the last stair as the speaker came unbidden through the living room into the scullery.

'I've 'eard the news. Now I see your man paid the rent last Friday night as usual.' In recent years Thomas had taken to calling into the rent office to settle up the weekly rent on his way home with his wage packet on Fridays after work. 'So you've got 'til Thursday mornin' to be out.'

'Surely Friday night?' Clara said bleakly. 'And today's Monday.'

'Well, you can't take on the rent book missus,

you know that, so you'll 'ave ter go.'

'Can't you give me a bit more time, stretch a point, Mr Tollin?'

'Well, let's say Saturday morning,' he answered, looking Clara slowly up and down. Clara winced at the look on his face.

'We'll 'ave none of that talk, Jack Tollin.' A low, determined voice, uttering commanding words, made him jump and whirl round. 'Monday next, leave 'er till then, and none of your old shenanigans.'

'I'll be losin' money,' his voice rose, 'I can't do that.'

'I'll pay the difference,' Clara cut in.

'You can't, yer name's not on the rent book,' the rent man snapped.

'No yer won't, Clara, 'e can let yer stay just one weekend,' Jenny ordered, then facing Tollin, 'You know the gal's got three young 'uns to find a roof for.'

'Yeah, Mrs Starr but unless 'e's left 'er well orf she ain't got no income an' I'm losing money.'

Jenny stared into his face, making the man suddenly uncomfortable.

'Oh, all right, Monday mornin' eight o'clock. Out sharp!' As he backed through the room, Jenny's penetrating gaze didn't leave him until he disappeared through the front door.

'Selfish bastard!' Jenny's breathy comment hung in the horrible man's wake as Clara sank onto a chair behind the door.

Even then he had the audacity to poke his head back through the front door, delivering acid words scouring through his teeth. 'Make sure you

418

get this funeral cleared outta here by the end of this week, lads.' Tollin's eye caught Mr Jessup's as he was emerging from the scullery ahead of his men carrying the coffin.

'Tish man! Have you no respect?' hissed the funeral manager, almost losing his composure. 'Off with you.' Jessup held his hand up to slow the men and coffin behind. 'Damned rent collectors,' he seethed, trying to smile some comfort to the widow. 'Bane of our lives.'

When the week's rental payment ran out, Clara was thinking she and the children had no roof over their heads. Hold on, Clara, Grandfather said in her head. Somebody beside her cleared his throat.

'Oh, sorry Mr Jessup, I was lost for a moment there.'

'That's all right, Mrs Cowley, I understand. Now it's a bit unusual but as there isn't space enough in your front room here to move the table away, we've had to rest the coffin on the table. I've covered it fully with a cloth to touch the floor all round. I hope that's all right for you.'

Clara stood up. Her husband was in the room. She hadn't even noticed his arrival.

'Yes, yes, Mr Jessup. I knew you would do the right thing. Thank you.'

'If you would like one of us to come to keep watch, please say.'

'Thank you, I'll let you know.'

'Yes, well, I know you will be having a lot to do this week. Coming and going. So don't you worry, please ask. That's our job.'

When the men had gone, Clara sat again on the

419

chair against the wall behind the front door which was now closed. Freddy came down the stairs with the little willow chamber stick, the remnants of the candle still burning. Setting it on the table beside the coffin he sat himself on the chair next to his mother and put his arm round her shoulders.

Back home from school to have a bite of food at midday Jimmie and Dolly, wide eyed, dry of tears, struck dumb for the first time in their lives, kneeled up on chairs either side of the coffin to look into their father's face. Clara felt it would not be fair to deprive them of their last sight of him.

Brother Jack, in Brighton on his regular delivery day for the brewery, came in the early afternoon and suggested he take Jimmie and Dolly home with him to Lewes until Friday. He'd bring them back when he and Pearl came for the funeral. By the end of the week he rather wished he hadn't offered. They were a couple of real handfuls. Grief must have made them even more reckless. Jack and Pearl's own children loved every minute of that week. Never forgot the exciting scrapes that caught them up in a trail of mischief. Clara missed the little ones, but admitted it was a help to be alone.

Upstairs in the front bedroom, sleep found no place in Clara's frame on Monday night. She didn't know if she should keep watch beside the coffin or try to get some rest on her bed. What happened surprised her in the extreme. Awaking from a fitful doze as midnight was striking across the air from St Peter's, she found anger, seemingly unbidden, flooding her mind like boiling oil. Rage gave her body huge strength.

Rage at Tom for leaving her like this – how could he be so thoughtless, cruel even? How could he hurt her so much? The strength pouring into her body made her want to smash everything. Hit the walls with clenched fists. No, that wasn't enough, she couldn't restrain herself, she wanted to break things. Wrenching at the pillows where his head had lain, she hurled them against the wall again and again until the feathers flew. No, that wasn't enough. The clock was his, so she threw that against the wall, then smashed it again and again into the night table, all the while quite clearly knowing this action was hurting herself too. She was too wild with fury to control her actions. So what did she care, she'd trash his small leather purse to nothing, nothing. What did he care where she and the children would find to live or that a woman couldn't hold a rent book in her own name? What did he care? What did anyone care? She knew she was screaming although it didn't seem to be coming from her throat. These harsh sounds were far away. Like an animal, she thought. What did any man care?

The rage went deeper, possessed her more and more.

Frank – he didn't care either. Oh yes, she knew, he felt guilty didn't he? Still writing to her after all these years. Two or three letters a year, telling her about his life. Hardly anything since the war started though. Then she was pounding the feather mattress until her fists were sore and the mattress a shredded lump. Well, that's all these two men were worth.

In her maturity she knew that with Frank she hadn't been angry at him, she'd been angry with herself, in just as full a measure at her own naïve surrender to youthful awakening emotions. This time with Tom, it wasn't altogether anger that was making her yell and scream in deep-throated roars. Now it was the feeling of frustration, like a solid, blank, iron wall facing her at every turn, causing her chest to tighten, constricting her breathing.

Were there no answers?

A light had gone out of her life.

She was all alone again.

Sorrow waning, hurt made the tears run until there were no more left and she lay dried out and pained, each shallow intake of breath jerking her whole body until she was empty with exhaustion. She had nursed the man she loved, fighting with him to keep his life. They had both lost the fight. Weak and vulnerable with no sleep, she was now faced with eviction.

Spent, Clara trailed her lifeless mind downstairs to sit beside the coffin, laying her head against its side. Jenny slipped in the back door bringing the scent of seaweed on the air. Five o'clock light was just streaking the sky. She sat for a while beside the sleeping Clara who, on waking, smelling the clear sea air, seemed to be surprised to see where she was.

'Allo luv,' Jenny whispered. Clara's face showed the fight she had been through. 'Don't fret, yer 'ad ter clear it outta yer system, it 'appens that

422

way to us all.'

Clara realised her crashing about must have been heard all along the mews, when she'd thought it had only been in her own head.

Tuesday morning was hitting like a drunkard's hangover until Jenny made Clara take a raw egg in milk and honey. 'Now then gal, there's work ter do.'

Clara took a very deep breath. 'Yes you're right. I'll get Mr Jessup to watch.'

'That's my Clara. Up yer go, get yerself dressed. The big kettle's singing on the side, dear.'

Locking the doors, Clara stood in the shallow tub the family had always used in the scullery. As the fire was giving off a good heat she washed her hair, eyes closed, rinsing off the soap, letting jugful after jugful of water cascade down over her tired shoulders, breasts, abdomen, streaming down her legs. She breathed deeply, letting the water wash the tensions away until the bowl was full to the brim.

Going through her mind was the thought that, whatever her personal emotions might be, she had to make a good impression at every agency she visited. Nobody wanted a servant bringing problems to their house. As she possessed no current written 'Character', it was all the more essential not to look like a woman beaten down, unable to be on top of events.

A cascade of water sloshed against the window, a man choked, spat, heaved a breath and swore. 'Oh, didn't see you there,' Jenny's voice squawked. Clara jerked out of her thoughts and snatched up a towel. Through a crack in the curtains she recognised the shadow of Jack Tollin out in the yard. Dear Jenny, there was no mistaking her voice but now Clara realised how vulnerable she was without a man in the house.

Taking a deep breath, she started dressing herself carefully in her best frock, her coat and hat well brushed, gloves on, shoes well polished.

For the next three days she walked from one end of Brighton to the other and into Hove visiting every agency, scanning cards in shop windows, reading 'Domestics wanted' advertisements. She wrote letters to all the members of Tom's family and her own. Dropping in on her way past Albert's butcher's shop to let them know the time of the funeral, she received a short sharp, 'We'll be there,' from Ethel. No kind words or condolences passed Ethel's lips. Stepping back into the street, Clara heard Ethel remark, 'Well, after all, I've lost my father for the second time, haven't I?'

That night sleep once more eluded Clara, although thankfully there was no repetition of all the violent feelings. Sitting beside the coffin she took up her knitting, trying to keep the needles from clicking as she made a boy's pullover. By morning she'd unpicked every inch.

Wednesday brought the same, 'Sorry no vacancies', followed again by a disturbed night of nightmares and dreams. She was glad to find herself awake in the morning and free of the muddles going on in her head.

Thursday and still no live-in jobs. Had the world and society changed so much since she left in 1902? Surely not, surely there had to be cooks in the big houses from Kemp Town through to

Hove. Could things have changed that much?

Rose said to come to her if she wasn't able to find a job, there would always be a roof over their heads in Putney. Leslie and his mother rented a whole house, not big, but they did have a spare bedroom. But that would be an even bigger wrench for Dolly and Jimmie, and what would she do so far away from Freddy? Even without a job to go to, Clara had to clear the house of furniture and at least it would bring a few coppers. Jack Newman promised to take the lot for five bob, but would leave the removal until Saturday morning after the funeral or there'd be no table or chairs for the funeral tea.

Friday arrived, bringing a lively pair forgetful of the coffin in the front room.

'It's all arranged, Clara,' Jack couldn't tell his sister this good news quickly enough. 'Jim's got a job. Bed 'n' board too.'

'Mum, I went over to Lancing up with Bill on the dray. He let me hold the draught horse's reins. It was good fun.'

Clara stood wide-eyed, unable to get a word in.

'That's right,' agreed her brother, the pair were so keen to tell her the good news. Then age and maturity took over. 'Oh, sorry Clara,' Jack sobered and explained, 'we heard they needed a boot boy at Lancing College an' Bill was delivering this week so he took young Jim with 'im up on the dray. The school caretaker, nice fella, understood about the circumstances an' said Jim could start Saturday, so's 'e could go to 'is father's funeral.'

'Bless you Jack. Bless both of you.' Clara embraced her brother in real thankfulness. Giving her sister-in-law a hug, she said, 'I can't thank you enough for looking after these two.' Then she gave a knowing smile to show they must have been a handful for Jack and Pearl.

As Clara gave her son a cuddle and a 'well done dear,' and straightened his collar and picked up the brush to smarten up his Sunday hat, tears were welling in Jimmie's eyes.

'Where will you be, Mum?' he asked in a shaky voice.

'Don't know yet luv, but don't you worry, we'll be all right.'

Family, neighbours and friends all dressed in their mourning black were gathering out in the mews. Although there was none of the stiff bombazine from before the war, nevertheless, all wanted to show their respect to a well-loved family man. Highly polished shoes, well brushed hats and buttoned-up dove-grey gloves had been taken from their deep stored recesses. It was the order of the day.

Jack, Albert and Edward, joined by Ethel's husband Albert, carried the coffin to the hearse. Leslie touched his uncle's coffin in respect as it passed in token, as his chest wound was still too weak to allow him to be a pall bearer. All the men stood bare-headed; the women curtseyed. The crowd parted to make way for the black-plumed horses as their polished hooves slid and clicked their way slowly between the figures out of the mews.

In the street more people lined the way, black over all. Thomas's customers, workmates and friends following the relatives walking behind the coffin down to St Peter's Church. Clara was surprised to see the roads in their path were covered in straw. Her first thought was that somebody must have died. This tradition of laying straw to damp the sounds of the horses' hooves was usually only done for dignitaries or royalty. Then, as the bystanders stopped, the men baring their heads and women giving a little bob, she realised it was for her Tom.

Outside the church, after the short service, she noticed Albert Moffat walking rapidly towards the church across from Trafalgar Street. Clara remembered he had not attended the funeral, and when he smiled and winked at her she thought he must have been drinking – but no, not Albert. Gently taking her elbow, he whispered in her ear, 'My apologies, I had a long-standing piano-tuning booking to attend out Hove.' He could hardly contain himself. 'Clara I think I've found you a job and somewhere to live.'

The news quite took Clara's breath away. Jimmie overheard and smiled so brightly, then remembered it was at his father's funeral he mustn't leap for joy – although he wanted to.

'I just couldn't wait to tell you. I've been to a client, a man I've known for years. His housekeeper walked out early this morning. He's a dental surgeon – needs somebody mature very quickly. Understands your circumstances but wants to interview you tomorrow morning. Receptionist, housekeeper, live-in, all found.'

Clara wanted to cry. Her hopes were raised but – no. She mustn't expect too much. What about Dolly? She'd quite forgotten her eleven-year-old daughter. When the coffin had emerged from the front door, its lid closed and strewn with the little bunches of flowers she and Clara had gathered, Dolly's young heart broke.

Cousin Leslie standing behind the little girl, his head bowed, saw her sudden movement and caught the edge of her collar as she went to rush at the coffin.

'Hold on,' he whispered, 'take my hand.' Crying into his wounded side, she gave vent to her sorrow, and couldn't stop. Nodding to Clara, he turned the child slowly away from the procession in the opposite direction through the passage under the arch into Gloucester Street.

The pair had a day Dolly never forgot. Ice cream and Brighton rock on the pier, pennies in slots and laugher, lemonade, none of yer silly old cups o' tea, running along the promenade throwing stones into the sea.

While the relatives sat talking in the front room in the evening, Dolly was being sick in the privy out in the backyard. But it had all been worth it. 'Been worth it,' the words she still used into her eighties. 'Dear Les was so kind.'

The Willows

'So you were there then?' asked Big Pol. 'Saw it all?'

'Yes. Tears of such deep sadness are hard to bear witness. I hadn't known the family long. Bedrooms, where I'd spent most of my life, reveal some of the greatest despairs and heart-searching. Often near insanity like my previous owner. Well, maybe he

wasn't insane. More like out of his mind with not knowing where to go next. That's how I found myself on sale in the hardware shop where young Jimmie saw me.'

'Lucky you were keeping watch downstairs beside the coffin when Clara went through her heart-searching up in that bedchamber, old cock,' Uncle Tom remarked.

'Yep, wouldn't be here now had I been within hand's reach up there.'

'Damn war caused some havoc,' the candle snuffer mused.

'Course, you must have been there together.'

'Still were, when the family sat talking over old times after the funeral tea. We were sitting over on the dresser. Fullest the house had ever been, I'd say. By dusk most of the family had gone 'ome 'cept for Rose an' Fanny. Albert and Edward were still there an' Leslie too.'

Clara

'Do you remember those little boats we used to make, Eddie?' Leslie asked.

'Yes, bits o' bark we found fallen off the tree trunks that year. An' you used reed stalks to make the masts.'

'An' my handkerchief for a sail...'

'Nar – wasn't, don't yer remember 'ow Gran were none too pleased about the holes for the guy ropes you an' Harry made in the corners?'

'I bet there's no sign of the old salt barges now.'

'They were called punts, weren't they?' said Rose.

'We walked that way on the way 'ome few months back. There are still signs of the odd punt covered with green moss but most have slipped deep into the tree roots now.'

'One night us boys nipped out of the barn an' slept on one of those punts, the water lappin' all around. When the tide started to turn it were like a plug were pulled. 'Course it's all silted up now.'

'I loved those summer nights we were allowed to sleep in the barn. You could hear rustling from little creatures moving around.'

'Oh gosh! I nearly jumped out a my skin the time I went back to the kitchen to get you all some more lemonade,' Fanny said. 'On my way back one of the sheep coughed just like an old codger. Ooh nearly 'ad a heart attack.'

'Sheep in the yard, at night?'

'Yes, don't you remember? The previous winter there were those really cold snaps. Some of the smallholders only had a few sheep survive so they brought them down to the inn. Granfer penned them at the end of the yard. The shearers stayed for a week doin' all the sheep thereabouts, saved them moving from farm to farm for just the odd one or two head at each stop.'

'Them young shearers slept out under the stars, lovely fun.'

'Caught some extra language those times didn't we, Les?'

'Well you boys may have, we had to sleep up in Clara's little room when the shearers arrived, an' Lilian's mother made her go all the way 'ome each night.'

'Aunt Lottie didn't want 'er wonderful daughter

mixin' with Emily's young rabble any longer than she could 'elp it more like,' said Albert as he and Eddie pulled on their coats.

Leslie and Jim accompanied their two cousins and uncles on their walk up to the station.

'Oh dash it,' Albert said as they walked through the passage out of the mews. 'I forgot to bring that old cat dish for Clara.'

'What's that all about?' asked Jim, so they told how they had found the old dish again after all these years.

'Your turn next ter get wed then, Albert?' asked Leslie.

'Yes, he found his old flame again, dropped in on 'er over at Westham we did. Not a bad looker either,' said Eddie.

'Might as well get me feet under the table before too long – settle down!'

The women were round the sink in the scullery, helping Clara to wash and pack her last few bits of crockery. Clara was saying, 'Ah the lads didn't realise why Lilian really had to leave.' Fanny, being younger, didn't know either.

Rose explained how Lilian had been the first of the cousins to start her menses. 'She was only twelve years old,' she said. 'Oh, and wasn't Gran annoyed.'

'Why?' asked Fanny.

'Well, Aunt Lottie hadn't told Lilian about it all so Lilian was quite upset. Gran sat us all down – Jack as well, him being the oldest brother – and explained all about what most men dismissed as wimmin's troubles.'

'I kept quiet,' Clara said, chuckling. 'Because

431

our mother hadn't told us either, had she Rose?'

'No. But I expect she thought we knew, what with all the babies there were round us.'

'Our mother put a lot onto Gran. It's no wonder she went twenty years before Granfer.'

'Anyway, Gran told Jack that as the men dealt with all the birthing in the animal sheds, next time he and all the lads were helping his granfer, he might well tell his brothers this is the way it happens with all us boys 'n' gals.'

'I remember looking across at Jack. He just said, "s'right Gran – good idea."'

'Yes, made me laugh that did – took all the embarrassment away, even for Lilian.'

'One thing Gran did tell us gals when we were on our own tho'. Do you remember how she started tearing an old cotton sheet into strips? We wondered what she was up to. Then she sewed them into narrow bags sewn closed at one end, made tape loops, one each end, then stuffed them with chopped-up old cotton material and wool. Not all wool, she said because it's not absorbent. Dried moss is best. Empty it out each time before washing the bags then fill them again ready for each month. There now. You all know how to make your own. Very practical, our Gran, wasn't she.'

'Trouble with Lilian's father, he would make silly remarks about "women's swooning days",' groaned Clara. 'Yes, then she ends up with old George Deeplove for a father-in-law, he couldn't be trusted,' she went on. 'I remember Gran tellin' us to make sure we girls were never left alone in his company. The old devil was everlastin' trying

432

to grab a hold of yer where 'e shouldn't.'

'That's why I always stayed back doin' my lace.'

'Oh Rose, I never knew.' Fanny was surprised. 'I thought you were taking care of us littler ones.'

'Yes, that as well, Gran had enough ter do an' I liked helping Gran work on her patchwork,' Rose added. 'You remember that rustling silk I was making into the petticoats for Miss Thora that time in eighty-nine?'

'Oh yes, wasn't it lovely. Oh my Rose, you had a wonderful workroom there.'

'Well, I did as you suggested. I sent some pieces by post to Granny an' I think they must have been about the last pieces she put into her quilt.'

'I am pleased you told me that. Granny must have been so thrilled to have something so new.'

'It was such a heart-warming comfortable feeling to see Granma and Aunt Hetta sitting side by side affront of the fire, working on that family patchwork. I was sad to see them with the flour sacks backing it off. It made you realise it was a story coming to an end.' Clara sighed.

'Peace drained out of the world after Granfer died,' mused Clara. 'I'm glad he wasn't alive to hear the booming of those great guns over in France. They said the sound rolled through the earth and air like great ripples across the marsh.'

Rose said, 'Loudest sound he ever heard in his time must have been the church bells.'

'Yes you're right, Rose. That's exactly what I said to Tom when we heard them.'

'Good luck with yer job, Jimmie luv. An' you, good luck with the interview, Clara. Come in an' see us after yer've bin,' Fanny reminded Clara.

'Leslie an' I will still be at Fanny's 'til Sunday morning, Clara, so we'll expect to see you. Any help yer need we'll be here,' Rose told her sister.

All three women embraced. The sisters' bond was as strong as ever.

'Now you sure you'll be all right on yer own here tonight Clara? I'll stay if you want me to,' Rose offered.

'No, you go with Fanny. I'll be right as rain here. Better be off or you'll miss your bus.'

That night, lying in the darkness, Clara felt Tom near, telling her he was at peace. Jim, back from his walk, was spending his last night in the tiny back bedroom he'd slept in all his twelve years. Dolly, finally purged, was asleep, snoring gently in the tiny alcove above the scullery. It had been quite a squeeze when all five, sometimes six, had lived in the cottage. But space didn't matter. They had been happy together. That's what mattered.

Warm thoughts of the family she and Tom had so enjoyed raising together, flowed through her whole being. At last sleep came to Clara.

Saturday morning, Clara and Jimmie were down in the scullery first and found their little lady mouser with the rosebud-pink nose lying near the range as if fast asleep. Trilby had died in the night. She had given the family fourteen years of mousing, five sets of kittens under the scullery sink, and all her love.

Jimmie dropped to his knees and took her still-warm soft little body in his arms. 'Now Daddy's gone, she's followed him,' he said.

Clara saw that her youngest boy had started on his road to maturity in the last five days. 'She was always such an affectionate little creature to us all,' she said. 'I'm glad she's gone to your dad. I was wondering how I could ever leave her here.'

The children buried the little body wrapped in a cotton cloth, at the back of the cottages beside the flint wall, in a grassy patch that always caught the evening sun, her last snoozing place of each day.

'She's having a rest now after her busy life,' Clara told Dolly.

'But now we're unhappy, Mum,' Dolly said.

'You're unhappy for yourselves, Dolly. Mustn't be unhappy for Trilby, she's having that well-deserved snooze. Her job's done.'

'Hope we'll meet her again when our job's done, Mum,' Jimmie replied.

'Ah yes, now you've got your job to do first my son. Come on, I've packed collars and socks and your working shirt in the small case love. We'd best get off down the Valley ter catch that bus.'

Fighting back her tears, Clara waved to Jimmie as he stood on the open deck at the back of the bus, holding his little cardboard case in one hand and brushing away his own tears with the other arm. Off to start his first job, boot boy at Lancing College.

Dolly squealed, jumping up and down. 'See you next Saturday Jimmee!' she shouted over the roar and grind of the big old green bus's gears.

'Make 'em laugh Jimmie,' called Clara through now free-flowing tears.

A small smile crossed Jimmie's face, holding

back his sorrow. Clara's heart broke for her young son. This really was the breaking away of her little brood.

Albert Moffat had given Clara a business card that announced in copperplate, *Mr Algernon Hobden Parker. Dental Surgeon*, with an address just to the north of Western Road in Hove.

'It's up by St Ann's Well Gardens,' Albert directed. 'Twelve o'clock sharp. He'll be expectin' yer. Good luck my dear. Dolly will be all right here with me. I'll see she gets some dinner, Clara, don't worry. Now off yer go gal, do yer best – I know yer will.'

Jenny gave her neighbour a kiss on the cheek, along with a playful shove – she wasn't looking forward to the mews without her good neighbour.

'An' you say this Mr Algernon Wotsisname only asked you to smile?'

'Yes,' Clara replied. 'Then he asked me what time I would put a steak and kidney pudding on to steam to have it ready for serving at one o'clock luncheon, next Saturday.'

Opposite stood her two sisters, wide-eyed and incredulous. 'That all?' they barked in unison.

Clara couldn't help laughing at her sisters' reaction. Only five minutes earlier she had come in at a fast trot, quite unceremoniously, through the elegant glass door, forgetting there might be clients trying on hats. Thankfully the shop was empty. It was too early for ladies to be promenading towards an afternoon of shopping. Empty, that is, except for Fanny and Rose, side by side behind

436

the glass counter looking through the current issue of *Milliners' World*.

Clara dropped her handbag and umbrella on the floor and sat down firmly on the chair beside the counter. Peach-silk shaded lights above cast a soft glow across her flushed cheeks.

'I think Alf Moffat must have told him about my circumstances and my cooking because he didn't ask me anymore, just ushered me down the stairs to show me the kitchen, apologising for the chaos his last housekeeper had left. Lovely bright, airy kitchen, looks like it's got all the latest equipment. I told him I could only call myself a 'Cook Ordinary'. I hadn't worked in the kitchen of the gentry for seventeen years.

'"Thank you, Mrs Cowley," he said, then he mentioned I could ask for anything I might need. There's a comfortably furnished sitting room and a separate bedroom all along the same basement level, with a storeroom and wash house out back. I couldn't ask for more. It's a miracle!'

Seeming to have said all this in one breath, Clara paused to consider this miracle she'd just described. Taking in another breath she added, 'I start Monday as soon as I can get settled in.'

'He's giving you a whole month's trial?' asked Rose, incredulous.

'Well, he said I might not like it in his house.'

'YOU might not like it? He's the employer. What about him!'

'I know, I was surprised, I hope he likes me and my cooking because I've got nowhere else to go if he's not satisfied.'

Then as an afterthought, Clara told her sisters

437

what she'd planned about Dolly's presence.

'I thought if Dolly went to school then came home there in the afternoon, he wouldn't see her slip in the back gate.'

'You sure that's the best way to do it, Clara? After all it's a lie.'

'I'll take my chance to ask him when the time is right,' Clara said. 'Keep our fingers crossed, eh?'

Meanwhile she had a roof over her head, she reasoned. Then rather to herself, she mused,

'Now I must drop a card to Jimmie to tell him all's well, then hot foot down home to let the second-hand man in to clear the furniture. Safe journey home, Rose.' The three women gave each other hugs.

'So long, thanks for all you've done gals.'

They all laughed in mutual relief.

'She didn't even tell us what he's payin',' commented Rose to Fanny as they watched Clara march off into Western Road, her head full of what had happened that morning and what she had to do next.

She could have stepped on a bus but she needed to save every penny. No wages until the end of the month. Sadly, the round dining table would have to go and the two easy fireside chairs, but the bit she got for them would tide her over. As she walked through Kensington Gardens on down towards St George's Mews she thanked her lucky stars for Alf Moffat's client, remembering her first sight of Mr Algernon Hobden Parker as he opened his own front door. Well, actually the inner door, its beautiful glass panel etched with the words 'Dental Surgery' surrounded by an elaborate pattern of intertwined leaves cut into a smoky back-ground, reminding her of Mr William Morris's curtains that the Whitesides had at their windows in Adelaide Crescent.

The door had opened to reveal a tall, distin-guished man with dark-brown hair flecked grey at the temples. He wore a well-cut fine tweed three-piece suit. Round collar with a large floppy bur-gundy-coloured bow tie. It was unusual for such a man to open his own front door; then his house-keeper walking out was an unusual happening too.

Clara stopped in mid-thought and stared.

The front door was slightly ajar. She looked either way along the passage then back the way she had come along the mews. It was Saturday afternoon, the workshops had closed for the weekend and there were no workmen about.

Standing slightly back, she pushed the door open a little way and bent forward to peek inside as if she didn't belong. The table wasn't in the centre of the room. Surprising, she hadn't told the dealer he could come while she was out. Turning away towards the passage into Gloucester Street she almost collided with her neighbour.

'Oh, Jenny, you gave me a start! I was just coming to ask if the furniture man...'

'No, he 'asn't. *She's* bin.'

'Who?'

'Your step-daughter, that's oo,' answered Jenny abruptly. But seeing Clara's face fall she softened her attitude, saying, 'I know gal. You'd hoped to get a bit for that furniture to take yer through. 'Bout an hour ago I heard all this kafuffle and a man's voice outside saying "You sure you agreed you're 'avin' this table?" Then I saw the van aways up the mews a tad. She was saying – that's Ethel I mean – "Of course. Anyway it's mine!" Right sharp she spoke. "It was my mother's."

"'But won't Clara and the family need it?" Then he says, "Look 'ere the door's locked."

"'What if the door's locked, get out of my way man." And she pulls a key out of 'er purse.

"'Where'd you get that, Ethel?" he asks.

"'Where'd yer think?" she says, "took it from Dad's trousers pocket, didn't I."

"'What! When 'e was on 'is deathbed, woman? It's not your 'ouse."

"'It's not 'ers either. My father paid the rent."

"'You make sure that key gets back to Clara or she'll be in trouble with the rent collector come Monday!"

"'Bert, this is my business. Now let's get that table out of here."

'Well I let 'em see me watching as they rolled that beautiful golden table top out along a blanket an' up into the van. Ah, you 'ad a lovely shine on that wood, Clara. 'Er 'usband 'ad a fair old struggle with the heavy pedestal, then I 'eard 'im shout, "Where yer think yer goin' now, woman?" She was in there a bit of a long time, then she comes out in a hurry, leavin' the door unlatched an' carrying your two cushions off the easy chairs under her arm.

"'S'pose those were yer mother's too?" 'e said, an' she said, "No. We gave these to Dad when they got married. We're 'avin 'em back!"

"'Good God, woman they've got to be seventeen years old." Ooh Albert sounded exasperated

440

'e did.

'I've bin keepin' an eye open for yer, dear. She left the key on the dresser. Didn't want anybody in there pinchin' it 'cos you'd 'ave ter pay for a replacement.'

The Willows

'S'pose you saw all of that then?' commented Ol' Po to the candle stick and snuffer, 'You bein' on the dresser 'n all.'

'Well, no I didn't,' Tubby replied. 'Ethel, she shoves me outta the way and plonks the new oil lamp off the table down in front o' me.'

'I could see though,' chipped in the snuffer. 'When Ethel took those cushions from the fireside chairs she stopped an' she lifted a postcard down off the mantle shelf and read it.'

'Ah so that's what made Albert wonder what kept her so long just picking up those two cushions.'

'Yes, that was it. A card from Frankie.'

'Yes of course, he'd not been able to get to the funeral because he'd just started his new job at the Trocadero in Piccadilly.'

Clara

Time had travelled on sixteen years or so since Tom and Clara had come to St George's Mews. Clara would miss her family of neighbours. Alfred Moffat, gentle rock of ages, and all the workmen in the mews, they were a community of good honest working men. Clara had never felt un-comfortable or threatened by any of them. The printer's shop on the corner had kept the walls colourful and lively with their regular supply of newly printed sample posters. But it was Jenny Starr, Clara would miss most of all. Jenny with her halo of orange frizz, it stayed that way morning, noon and night. 'Can't do a blasted thing with this hair,' she'd half groaned and laughed the first time she and Clara met. Jenny worked for her family, and all who needed her help, worked herself to the bone. Small she might be, but never bent by work, never put down by unfriendly folks. No she wasn't tall, she just stood tall. She was respected by all. Clara didn't know what she would have done without her at times of need over those sixteen years.

And nor would their neighbour Maudie. Maudie had worn badly, slouching back and forth in a pair of ragged old slippers, her body heavy from constant childbearing by a boozy husband. That man knew more about the inside of the many public houses between the railway station and the Steine than he did his own house.

'Ha! Don't know which is worse,' Jenny would exclaim, 'the boozer or the bugger knocking eight bells outta that poor wife of 'is every Friday night.' Jenny only had six young 'uns herself be-cause, as she said, 'she knew 'ow to stop 'em reaching the touch line'.

One thing about the women at the four houses in St George's Mews, they all got on well together when Clara lived there. The yard along the back of the houses where the washing was done was the women's domain; their territory. When the sheets were pulled and twisted out and the cobbles brushed clear of rinsing water, the four could sit having a cuppa and a laugh. Or more likely putting the world to rights. Clemmie said it was the best part of her life, that time they had their gossip. The years when the children were little and playing on the dirt over in the corner. Well now, that was the only peaceful time she knew. Yes. Clara would miss her neighbours.

She turned back at the front door, taking a last look into the empty living room. The walls Tom had painted were now dull and grey. The brick floors she had scrubbed clean that first time were still clean. Light pierced through from the scullery window where Trilby used to keep watch for mice. The door to the staircase stood ajar as she had left it every night, to allow the warm air from the kitchen range to creep up into the bedrooms. When they first came they only had Freddy. As she stood thinking, the sound of her children's happy voices echoed through this small room, filling the house with her brothers' and sisters' laughter. Tom's family, friends and neighbours, she could picture them all. This room had seen and heard sadness too.

A small hand slid inside hers; Dolly joining her mother's moments of thought.

'Well, come on love. Bye bye Trilby.'

Dolly couldn't say goodbye. She wished her mother had not said it. But then Clara had said it for them both.

The publishers hope that this book has given you enjoyable reading. Large Print Books are especially designed to be as easy to see and hold as possible. If you wish a complete list of our books please ask at your local library or write directly to:

Magna Large Print Books
Magna House, Long Preston,
Skipton, North Yorkshire.
BD23 4ND

This Large Print Book for the partially sighted, who cannot read normal print, is published under the auspices of

THE ULVERSCROFT FOUNDATION

APL		CCS	
Cen		Ear	
Mob		Cou	
ALL		Jub	
WH		CHE	
Aid		Bel	
Fin		Fol	
Car		STO	
m		HCL	